The
Midwife
of
St. Petersburg

A Novel

The Midwife

of

St. Petersburg

LINDA LEE CHAIKIN

WATERBROOK
PRESS

THE MIDWIFE OF ST. PETERSBURG
PUBLISHED BY WATERBROOK PRESS
12265 Oracle Boulevard, Suite 200
Colorado Springs, Colorado 80921
A division of Random House Inc.

ISBN: 978-1-4000-7083-1

Copyright ©2007 by Linda Lee Chaikin

Published in association with the literary agency of Janet Kobobel Grant, Books & Such, 4788 Carissa Avenue, Santa Rosa, CA 95405.

Library of Congress Cataloging-in-Publication Data
Chaikin, L. L., 1943–
    The midwife of St. Petersburg : a novel / Linda Lee Chaikin. — 1st ed.
      p. cm.
    ISBN 978-1-4000-7083-1
  1. Midwives—Fiction. 2. Soviet Union—History—Revolution, 1917–1921—Fiction.
I. Title.
    PS3553.H2427M53 2007
    813'.54—dc22

                         2007000454

Printed in the United States of America
2007—First Edition

10 9 8 7 6 5 4 3 2 1

In memory of my husband's grandparents,
Julius and Sarah Chaikin,
who came to New York's Ellis Island from Russia
at the turn of the century

Part One

"For I know the plans I have for you…"

JEREMIAH 29:11, NIV

ONE

The Challenge

June 1914, Kazan

N ewly promoted Colonel Aleksandr Kronstadt stood on the terrace of the Roskov summerhouse holding his crystal glass and watching yellow, blue, and purple painted boats ply up and down the waterway of Kazan. The sight offended his disciplined nature. Whoever heard of a purple boat? Who would want one? He supposed the same citizens of Kazan who painted their houses red with green roofs.

Alex smiled to himself and looked toward the slopes of the high western bank and saw the twilight veil of indigo shadow. All in all, his holiday in Kazan with the Roskovs was pleasant enough, but if the truth were known, he'd much rather be in St. Petersburg with his regiment. He'd captained one of the most elite Imperial Cavalry groups in the czar's special military forces. And now...

He frowned and drummed his fingers on the terrace rail.

The summer night was clear, the stars like diamonds, as bright and glittering as the diamonds in Tatiana's blue-black hair—diamonds he could not afford, even if he was the adopted son of the renowned Countess Olga

Shashenka, who had married his father. He looked across the terrace toward Tatiana, General Roskov's daughter. He and many others considered her a beautiful woman, and tonight, seeing her with her hair pinned up, diamonds glimmering, and gowned in cream satin tulle for the grand musical to be presented later, he should be content. In all likelihood, she would become his wife. He refused a frown that tested his brow. He raised his glass and tasted the drink. Like everything in the Roskov household, it was exceptional. He ought to be content. He watched Tatiana. She stood across from him, chatting and smiling with several of her guests, yet one more thing in his life that contradicted who he really was.

His restless gaze swept the river. Everything about Kazan, including his two-week stay with the Roskovs, seemed a gaudy display that threatened to overwhelm him as surely as the mist would soon engulf the misfit boats when it settled over the waterway.

Alex was not especially troubled about Tatiana, although it seemed to him that she had changed recently. Or had he? The change in Tatiana that irritated him most happened to be a religious one—but he wouldn't think about that now. He did not care to grow angry.

Issues other than the general's daughter hounded him. He had received a letter that morning from his Kronstadt cousin in New York. Mikhail, or rather *Michael,* since his cousin had chosen the American spelling, had left the Russian Orthodox Church to enroll in an independent Bible seminary. *Independent—an interesting word.* Alex repeated it to himself. The letters Michael wrote to him—more like journals, Alex thought—discussed Christ and biblical doctrines and declared how pleased Michael was to be an *independent* American, free to study the Bible as never before.

Alex was surprised to find himself somewhat envious of his cousin's confidence in his relationship with God, as well as his new citizenship. Michael had tried to talk him into leaving Russia with him three years ago, but Alex had refused, feeling responsible for his twin Sokolov cousins and the countess, to whom he owed much. She had asked him to remain loyal to Imperial Russia, and he had. Even so, there were times, such as tonight, when he felt smothered by expectations not his own and wished he could transport himself into Michael's New York flat.

Independent. Yes, a very intriguing word.

Just an hour ago, he'd learned from his future father-in-law, General Viktor Roskov, that he had been promoted, forced from his prized elite command in order to serve in a special unit of the czar's secret police, the *Okhrana.* All against his will.

He blamed Tatiana and her mother, Madame Zofia, for meddling to further his career. Instead of joining his regiment at the front, he would be stationed in St. Petersburg at the Winter Palace. With war certain to erupt any day, leaving his cavalry regiment for dull police activity felt like a betrayal. Despite his feelings on the matter, there seemed little he could do to change the general's mind, unless he could convince the countess to exert her influence. The countess, however, remained at her summer retreat in the Crimea. He planned to see her later in the year at her winter residence in St. Petersburg, but by then, his regiment would already have ridden into Poland with a new commander.

"Well, *Colonel* Kronstadt, congratulations."

Alex turned from his view of the misty, moonlit river to find Captain Karl Yevgenyev standing a few feet away. He wore a dress uniform much like Alex's, the white uniform coat ablaze with shiny buttons, the trousers black with a thin white stripe down each leg.

Yevgenyev was tall, slim, and dangerous. His blond hair was wavy, closely clipped on the sides, and he carried himself with strict military bearing. Tonight, Yevgenyev looked as if he was on a hunt for trouble and smelled blood.

This is all I need. Alex's irritation made him tense. He disliked the ambitious officer, the spoiled son of an Okhrana official, and the feeling was mutual. They had been competitors since cadet school. Unfortunately,

Yevgenyev's father commanded Major-General Durnov, to whom Alex would now report.

Yevgenyev's gaze burned. He was undoubtedly jealous of Alex's promotion, as well as the news of his impending engagement to Tatiana.

Alex felt Tatiana appear at his side, looping her arm through his. She, too, must have recognized Yevgenyev's bitter mood.

The sight of Tatiana holding possessively to Alex's arm only heightened Yevgenyev's anger. Alex could easily read the cold rage in his light eyes.

"A mere landowner's son is unworthy of the honor given you, Kronstadt." Yevgenyev's voice was thick with his favorite drink, vodka.

Tatiana gasped.

Alex smiled and challenged his gaze. "You use the term 'landowner's son' as if you consider it an insult. I consider it an honor, for it is the middle-class merchant growers of Russia who feed the czar's soldiers while the titled feed their egos by dueling and having their fathers safeguard them from justified courts-martial."

Yevgenyev flushed. He had fought many duels in St. Petersburg and been protected from reprimand by his father. He took a step toward Alex, arm raised, and Alex swiftly grabbed his wrist.

"You've been drinking, Karl. And your foolish behavior in front of Miss Roskova is quite boring. If you were as smart as you think you are, you'd go home to bed."

Yevgenyev jerked his arm free, his eyes coldly furious as he confronted Tatiana. "What you see in this merchant-planter's son is beyond understanding. My father will speak to yours, and you will come to see that Kronstadt does not deserve you."

"You are making a spectacle of us both, Karl," she hissed. "Do as Alex says and go home."

"I demand a duel, Kronstadt. We shall see which of us is man enough for military honors."

"Don't be a fool, Karl," Alex said.

"You're a coward. You see, Tatiana? He fears me. He will not duel as a gentleman must when insulted."

General Viktor Roskov's bulk appeared in the ballroom entryway. "What is the difficulty?" he called.

"I think this man is an imposter," Captain Yevgenyev replied distinctly, his eyes on Alex. "He is not a military man of courage and honor, for he will not duel me. He is a coward."

General Roskov turned sharply. "Captain Yevgenyev, this is despicable and outrageous behavior—"

A servant passed with a tray of wine glasses. Yevgenyev snatched a glass of purple wine and threw it in Alex's face.

Liquid ran down the collar of Alex's uniform. He heard Tatiana's cry and the general's shocked intake of breath. A murmur of voices gained volume as guests came out on the terrace to see what was happening. Alex's pristine white jacket was stained as though from a sword thrust.

Remain calm, he told himself. His fist itched to connect with Karl's front teeth. *Remember whose house you're in. A man can bear an insult to safeguard others.* He saw Madame Zofia take her daughter's arm and pull her behind General Roskov as though fearing a brawl.

Alex calmly removed a white linen napkin from the nearby refreshment table and wiped his face. He folded it neatly and placed it back on the table, aware that all eyes were upon him. Beneath his calm reserve, he could have killed Karl at that moment.

"You see?" Captain Yevgenyev said in a firm voice. "The new *Colonel* Kronstadt is a coward."

"This is contemptible, Captain Yevgenyev. You're drunk," the general said angrily. "Leave my premises at once. You can be assured I will speak to your father first thing in the morning."

Yevgenyev appeared not to hear the general. "Well, Colonel?"

"I accept your challenge to a duel," Alex said, "but not here and now. General Roskov speaks well; you are drunk. I will not have your father accuse me before court of taking advantage of an intoxicated man."

Yevgenyev gritted his teeth. "Name the day and hour."

"One month from this day at twelve noon in St. Petersburg."

Yevgenyev's hard mouth turned into a cruel smile. He picked up another glass of wine from the tray of the astounded servant, toasted Alex with mockery, then tossed it down in a gulp. He set the glass aside, clicked his heels in a short bow, and strode from the terrace.

A murmur of voices followed.

Alex smothered his frustration in silence.

General Roskov walked up to him, his face grave. "Count Yevgenyev is the one at fault. His temperament has been fully passed on to his son. I'm sorry it's come to this. Karl is an expert dueler. I'll speak to his father. Maybe we can stop it."

Alex knew nothing could stop it. "I'd better go up to my room and change."

General Roskov shook his head with disgust, then went into the ballroom.

As Alex was about to leave the terrace, Tatiana came to his side and put her hand on his arm.

"Oh, Alex, I'm so sorry. I shouldn't have invited him. I almost didn't, but he and his family are in a high social stratum, and both Mother and I agreed we couldn't ignore him. Oh, good—Mother's gone to the orchestra leader and asked him to start the music early. A waltz should get everyone's mind off what happened, at least for a short time.

"Oh, that's a splendid waltz, isn't it?" Tatiana continued. "So beautiful. It comes from London. I forget the name of it." She looked at the stain on Alex's jacket. "Oh dear, I really can't expect you to accompany me now, can I? That jacket looks as if you're wounded—" Her hand went to her mouth, and her dark eyes widened. "Oh, that sounded awful."

They were alone on the terrace. The night had deepened, and the moon gleamed above the river. Boat lights shone in colors of blue, green, and red all along the waterway.

Alex heard the music, the symphonic sounds meant for love, for grand themes, and for virtue. He looked at Tatiana and considered his emotions. She was beautiful, but her inability to appreciate the shame and depth of what had just occurred turned his heart as cold as the steel pistols he and Karl would aim at each other in St. Petersburg.

Alex lifted Tatiana's hand from his arm and held it. "I'll be back down as soon as I've changed. Then we can waltz."

Tatiana smiled, squeezed his hand, and disappeared into the glittering ballroom.

Alex climbed the staircase to his room, his steps heavy with his thoughts.

As the steamer moved up the Volga River, Karena Peshkova decided that Kazan was as exotic as Cousin Tatiana had written. In Karena's vivid imagination, the river ran like a silvery ribbon, stretching between their big steamer and the western banks. She gazed at rows of colorfully painted ships and houseboats with black hulls and yellow roofs.

With the promise of many entertainments ringing in her ears, Karena and her sister Natalia had left Kiev for a two-week holiday at the Roskov family summer residence in the prosperous port town of Kazan. Tatiana had written that her mother planned a lavish "water ball" aboard a large ship, boasting a thousand colored lanterns and an orchestra. Karena and Natalia had brought their best gowns, dancing slippers, and jewelry, though they feared they would appear simple and plain in comparison to Aunt Zofia and Tatiana, who were accustomed to entertaining nobility. Aunt Zofia even knew the Czarina Alexandra Romanova.

Natalia joined Karena on deck as the steamer neared port. Karena noticed with satisfaction that her sister's mood had improved since their departure from Kiev.

Natalia was worried about Boris, her young man in Kiev. She had expected to marry him in the coming spring, but the growing certainty of war with Germany had put an end to their dreams. The Peshkov and Gusinsky families would not hear of their daughter and son marrying before Boris went off to the front.

"This will be a delightful interlude," Karena had told her sister. "For two weeks, we're going to put aside our personal worries and enjoy ourselves." For Karena, it was not worries over the coming war, but whether she would again be denied entry to the Imperial College of Medicine and Midwifery at St. Petersburg this September. This was her third try. If she was turned down, it could mean the end of the dream she'd nourished since she was a small girl.

Karena was already over twenty, well past the usual age of marriage, and it would be impossible to hold off the wishes of her family any longer, should she be turned down again.

"The coming war hasn't dampened Tatiana's love affair," Natalia said, obviously comparing their cousin's situation to her own. "She wishes to become engaged to the dashing Captain Aleksandr Kronstadt before the war begins."

"That doesn't mean Aunt Zofia and Uncle Viktor will allow it," Karena said. She remembered a photograph Tatiana had sent of herself and her beau at a winter's skating party in St. Petersburg. Kronstadt was one of those rugged Imperial officers who looked dashing in either dress uniform or war-stained battle gear. He was in Kazan, visiting the Roskovs, so Karena and Natalia would be able to meet him.

"Tatiana seems to think her father approves." Natalia sighed. "Tatiana is always the lucky one. She wears diamonds, owns wardrobes created in

Paris, and no doubt will have her love match with Captain Kronstadt, and his mother will give them a honeymoon in the Crimea."

Karena wondered if Countess Shashenka would also be in Kazan. She was a friend of Madame Zofia and known as a world traveler. Since Tatiana hadn't mentioned the countess as a guest, it was likely she was spending the summer and fall at her residence in the Crimea until she returned to St. Petersburg for the Christmas and New Year's celebrations.

I, too, will be in St. Petersburg to attend Aunt Zofia and Tatiana's winter entertainments, Karena thought, *if I'm accepted into the medical college. I should like to attend a skating party and afterward return to Tatiana's house for refreshments by the fire.*

Natalia shaded her brown eyes with a cupped hand, squinting at the colorful houses that came into view as they neared the dock. June breezes, still chilly, tossed her light brown hair.

She laughed. "Oh look! A chocolate brown house with yellow window shutters and a green roof! I'll tell Boris those are the colors I want on the guest bungalow in the wheat fields. We'll live there when we marry, until Papa builds us a bigger house."

"Uncle Matvey's coming to stay the summer. If he hears the bungalow's been painted brown, yellow, and green, he'll disappoint us and remain in St. Petersburg," Karena said with a laugh.

"Dear Uncle Matvey. It must be his dull research books that have sobered his mood. He used to be such fun, telling us stories about his childhood in Poland. He seems worried lately. Perhaps it's the looming war."

The looming war. Everything from poor crops to poor health was blamed on the rising war clouds over Europe. Karena's brother Sergei joked about the tired phrase. When Aunt Marta had a crick in her joints or Papa Josef had to stay up late grading school papers, Sergei would blame on the *looming war.*

As for Uncle Matvey's dull research books, Karena didn't agree.

"We ought to know history, Natalia. I've volunteered to help Uncle Matvey this summer with his new book."

"Oh? What's it about this time?"

"The Jewish Messiah."

Natalia's eyes widened. "Does Uncle actually believe a future Messiah is coming?"

"I don't know. He has a dozen books that he ordered from London and America. He had to go into Finland to pick them up from an associate's house because he was uneasy about having them sent to his apartment. I'm going to find my research intriguing, if nothing else."

"He'll have arrived by the time we get back to Kiev," Natalia said. "Sergei's traveling back with him on the train from St. Petersburg."

"At least Papa will be there to greet them both."

Karena felt a gust of cool wind, but the sun was bright and hot on her fair skin. That morning, she'd wound her golden hair into braids and coiled them at the back of her neck. Now, as the steamer came into port, she put on her red sun hat, hoping it looked fashionably perky against her common blue traveling skirt and white blouse. She held her hat in place with one hand, irritated with herself for failing to sew on new ribbon ties as she'd intended.

A tugboat chugged down the river, towing a string of black barges, followed by a massive timber raft that looked to be at least five hundred feet long. It carried a cargo of ready-made wooden bungalows with fancy carved gables to be sold in the regions along the lower Volga, which had no forest.

Another massive barge floated by, carrying people—a floating settlement of peasants. The men all wore cherry-red shirts and the women, long blue skirts and dark tuniclike blouses with colorful embroidery. As the steamer slipped past, Karena saw the peasants gathered around a large campfire built near one end of the raft, drinking hot tea or perhaps coffee.

The steamship was slowly secured to the dock at Kazan. An hour inched by while Karena and Natalia waited on the crowded deck, until at last they were permitted to depart. Karena arranged to have their trunks sent to the Roskov residence, and with only their portmanteaus to carry, she and Natalia descended the gangway. Her footsteps echoed on weathered wooden planks, and Karena heard the ringing of bells, a shrill ship's whistle, and a cacophony of voices in strange dialects and languages. She smelled stale fish and oil mingled with the scent of the river.

Beyond the riverbank sat a row of wooden shops and loading-houses, all painted bright colors like the houses Natalia had seen earlier. There was a lavender house with a gleaming tin roof, a crimson one with an emerald roof, one sky blue and red, and even an orange house with an olive green roof. One very large building seemed to display every color available on its three stories.

They made their way through the crowded dock toward the horse-drawn taxis and carriages lining the street, awaiting passengers.

"Aunt Zofia and Tatiana should be waiting for us by now," Natalia said. "I wonder if the ball is tonight or tomorrow?"

"I hope tomorrow. Our gowns will be terribly wrinkled."

"You forget we have maids here," Natalia said cheerfully. "They'll wait on us hand and foot. Even steam the creases out of our clothes. You heard Mother. She'll never be able to live with us again, we'll be so spoiled."

Karena smiled. "Just like Tatiana."

"Hah! No one could be as spoiled as she."

"Don't be an old cat," Karena scolded lightly. She scanned the carriages. "I don't see the Roskov coach. Suppose they forgot we were arriving?"

"Tatiana might forget, but not Aunt Zofia. Ah! Here comes the coach now."

Karena followed her sister's gaze. Two soldiers on horseback rode ahead of a large, black coach, an *R* on the red- and gold-fringed flag, being pulled by two white horses.

Karena let her gaze slide past the coach to one of the soldiers, who wore the uniform of an officer in the elite Imperial Cavalry. She admired the effortless and disciplined way in which he sat on the horse and guided its movements, her interest sparked by his masculine manner. As he rode nearer, she realized who he was.

Natalia, too, recognized him from the photograph Tatiana had sent last New Year's. "Isn't that Captain Aleksandr Kronstadt?" she asked.

"I couldn't say…" Karena kept her voice indifferent. "Yes, perhaps he's the one in the skating photograph. We know he's staying with her family."

"I'm surprised she'd have us here now."

Karena glanced at her sister. "Why do you say that?"

Natalia pursed her lips. "She seems self-absorbed."

"Don't be unfair. She and Aunt Zofia both have asked us here, and they are expending themselves for our benefit. We should show gratitude. She's beautiful, and she'd be naive not to realize it. And she has nothing to fear from us."

"Not from me anyway. I love Boris and always will." She looked at Karena.

Karena fussed with her hat and looked away from her sister's sympathetic gaze. She was not in love with Ilya Jilinsky, the young man her family hoped she would marry. Natalia understood that she did not wish to marry for some years in order to pursue medicine.

"Tatiana mentioned another officer she's been entertaining in St. Petersburg," Natalia said, changing the subject. "I believe his name is Captain Yevgenyev."

"Well, it looks as though Captain Kronstadt has won. Do you wonder that he did?" Karena tucked the corners of her mouth into a smile.

"No, but I wonder if that other soldier is Yevgenyev. He looks rather put out about things, don't you think?"

"Well, if it is Captain Yevgenyev," Karena said wryly, "Tatiana is either very brave in having them here together, or most unwise. I wouldn't think there'd be a moment of peace in such a triangle."

"Why would she have them both here unless she enjoys perpetual competition? It may be exciting, but it's also dangerous."

"It all seems rather silly." Karena took hold of her sister's arm, pulling her forward. "Come along, there she is now. Do be *nice.*"

"Karena! Natalia! Over here!" Tatiana called as she opened the coach door. She was smiling and waving her white-gloved hand. Beneath the glove there would be diamonds; Tatiana was fixated on the glittering gems from South Africa.

Karena smiled and returned her wave, hurrying forward. The wind played with the hem of her skirt, and she had to hold her hat in place.

Captain Kronstadt lifted Tatiana down from the coach step onto the planks lining the street, and for a moment she looked up at him, laughing. Karena thought it an endearing scene. The only thing missing was snow or perhaps the statue of Peter the Great on his horse in the background.

"Cousin Karena, Natalia," Tatiana said with a laugh, hugging first one, then the other. "How delightful to see you both again."

"It's been much too long," Karena said. She held Tatiana's hands in hers and looked her over, still smiling. "And how lovely you are."

"And *you*! I can hardly believe you've not been snatched up by some country gent in Kiev."

Some country gent. "You know me, Cousin. My first love waits in St. Petersburg," Karena teased, referring to her well-known passion for the medical college. She became aware of Captain Kronstadt standing nearby, but she didn't look at him. "Where's Aunt Zofia?"

"Mother stayed at the house. She's in turmoil. We just learned an hour ago that we've a very special but very unexpected guest coming tonight. Mother is trying to rearrange the seating order for dinner from thirteen to fourteen."

A gust of wind whipped Karena's red hat off her head. It skipped along the wooden planks, rolling as if bent on escape. She could imagine the wind laughing mischievously in her ears.

Tatiana gave a feminine squeak and held to her own fashionable, periwinkle blue hat, though it was firmly tied beneath her chin and could not have come off. "I'd better hold on to mine. It's from Paris, designed by Macquinet-Dushane-Hudson and well worth its fashion in gold."

Natalia turned to Karena. "I'll see if I can find it."

"I think it's too late. It may have gone off the edge into the water."

"It is just as well it did." Tatiana laughed and tugged at Karena's coil of golden braids. "How quaintly stylish. I must have my maid do mine like that sometime. You do so well, and without a maid too. Now don't frown over your lost hat. I've the perfect one for you. A black one that will be stunning with your fair hair and blue eyes. Oh, I envy you…just like your mother. How you and Madame Yeva can be so fair when she's Jewish—"

Tatiana's voice trailed away. She stared at something behind Karena. Her expression made Karena strangely uneasy. She turned to see Captain Aleksandr Kronstadt approaching with her red hat.

"Your hat, Miss Peshkova." He smiled and bowed lightly.

There was no way to avoid eye contact with him.

The photograph did not do him justice. She fought against her reaction to his handsome features—the strong jaw line, the nicely shaped mouth, the dark wavy hair, the intense green-gray eyes under straight brows. She sensed powerful shoulders beneath his uniform. He affected her in a far different way than Ilya Jilinsky.

From his extended hand, she took her hat. "Yes…thank you very much, Captain."

Captain Kronstadt studied her face with no apparent embarrassment and smiled. "My pleasure," he assured her.

Karena blushed. She saw him look at Tatiana but could read nothing in his eyes. Perhaps they were deliberately incomprehensible.

Karena turned toward her cousin, relieved to break the heated gaze, only to meet the calculating eyes of Tatiana, which moved from her to Captain Kronstadt. Then the moment passed; Tatiana smiled, and she slipped an arm around Karena's waist.

"This is Alex," she said. "*Colonel* Aleksandr Kronstadt. He's on my father's private staff. Alex, meet my cousins from Kiev, Karena and Natalia Peshkova. My mother, Zofia, is their aunt."

He bowed. "Ladies."

"My apologies for calling you a captain," Karena said, chagrined.

"Officially, I remain a captain until the end of June. Then much agonizing pomp and ceremony await me in St. Petersburg."

Karena smiled. "Then perhaps I should offer my sympathies."

"That might be more in keeping with my feelings just now."

Whatever his feelings, they did not appear to coincide with Tatiana's as she looped her arm through his.

"I'm relieved you'll be in St. Petersburg where I'll see you often," Tatiana said to Kronstadt. "The countess will be pleased too. She must come back to St. Petersburg for the Christmas and New Year's holidays when we announce our engagement." She released his arm and turned to Karena and Natalia. "The wind is dreadful today. Let's get inside the coach before we're blown into the Volga."

With another small bow, Kronstadt walked back to his waiting horse. Karena's eyes followed him.

Tatiana grabbed her hand. "Come along, Karena, Natalia. Alex has business elsewhere for the day. We won't see him until the ball tonight. I wonder if you and Natalia have everything you need in your wardrobe…"

As Tatiana and Natalia discussed what they would wear to the ball, Karena wondered if she had imagined tension between her cousin and Kronstadt. *Why did Kronstadt's face harden when Tatiana mentioned how delighted she was that he would be stationed in St. Petersburg?*

When they reached the coach, Natalia noticed a flower cart down the street and impulsively dug into her coin case. "Gardenias! Aren't they wonderful? I shall buy some for Aunt Zofia. Maybe they'll soothe her spirits. I won't be long."

Natalia hurried off as the Roskov driver settled their portmanteaus in the back of the coach. Karena was left alone for a moment with Tatiana.

"You'll be elated to know who else will be here tonight," Tatiana said. "Arranged by the good fortune of fate, of course."

Karena looked at her animated face.

"Dr. Dmitri Zinnovy," Tatiana announced.

"Dr. Zinnovy!" Karena was unable to keep the excitement from her voice. She stared at her cousin. Dr. Zinnovy had been one of the chief physicians at the Imperial Medical College and held a great deal of sway over the admissions department. Karena had written to him on several occasions, seeking his assistance on her quest to enter the school, but she had received not so much as an impersonal response from his secretarial assistants.

"I knew you'd be thrilled when I told you of my accomplishment," Tatiana said. "Tonight you shall meet him!"

Karena laughed. "To think I've spent months writing letters to no avail, and you, within my very reach, knew him all along."

Tatiana smiled. "There's hardly anything I can't get for you, Cousin."

Then her eyes hardened, or perhaps it was a shadow as they walked nearer the coach that made them seem to darken. Karena followed the direction of her gaze to Colonel Aleksandr Kronstadt mounting his horse.

"Alex, however, is forbidden," Tatiana warned. "He belongs to me. Remember that."

Karena felt as though she'd been slapped. "That's preposterous, Tatiana," she said. "You're beautiful and socially powerful. What man wouldn't choose you above all others?"

Tatiana continued to smile. "That's exactly what I intend, so we must not want the same thing. I'm afraid if we did, we would become enemies."

"Enemies? Why, we're family."

"Yes, and families must not undermine one another. We must keep it that way."

Karena's clasped hands tightened. "Of course."

"Good. Now let's forget that. Are you wondering how I arranged for fate to bring Dr. Zinnovy here this evening?"

Karena nodded, shaken by the confrontation. Tatiana's ability to jump emotionally into a new mood and topic of conversation was disturbing. This was a facet of her cousin that she'd not seen until now. She listened in strained silence as Tatiana explained how she'd wrangled Dr. Zinnovy's son Fyodor into bringing his father to the ball and all she'd had to go through to flatter Fyodor and gain his help.

"Fyodor still doesn't know why I wanted his father to come tonight," she said. "I never mentioned your name, so don't worry about that. When Fyodor and Dr. Zinnovy meet you, they will only think of your family relationship to me. Then I shall arrange for you to waltz with Dr. Zinnovy, and the rest will be in your hands."

Karena made the correct response of gratitude and surprise over how it had all come about, but the excitement she'd felt earlier was dampened. She was all the more troubled as her beautiful cousin, whom she'd often admired, continued talking and smiling at her. If anyone had been watching them, they might appear to be discussing nothing more serious than what gown they'd wear to the ball.

Everything appeared normal, but things were not as they seemed.

TWO

The Promised Guest

As the driver maneuvered the Roskov coach through the busy streets, Karena noticed many Byzantine-style churches. "Kazan once flourished as the capital of the Islamic kingdom of the Tartars until Ivan the Terrible sacked the city in 1552 and made it a part of Russia," Karena mentioned to Tatiana and Natalia.

The two young women looked at each other and laughed.

Karena smiled at them. "Ha, ha," she said dryly.

"Don't allow my ignorance to trouble you, Karena," Tatiana said. "I failed history in school."

"You probably failed more than history," Natalia goaded with a wicked grin.

Tatiana made a face at her.

"Now, if you'd care to discuss history with Alex, you might find a willing audience," Tatiana continued to Karena. "He loves to debate theology, as well. He has this awful seminary cousin in America who bombards him with letters full of theological discussions. I told Alex he ought to discuss Christianity with Rasputin, but he only gave me a look. Alex is absolutely wonderful and maddening, all at the same time."

Alex again. *Is she baiting me?* Karena wondered. From the corner of her eye, she saw Natalia's warning glance. Karena needed no additional warning.

"I should know more about the Bible by the end of summer," Karena said.

"The end of summer? Why is that?" Tatiana looked genuinely interested.

"Uncle Matvey's come from St. Petersburg," Natalia piped up. "Karena's doing research for him on a new book about the Messiah."

Tatiana narrowed her eyes at Karena. "The *what*?"

"Messiah," Karena said pleasantly. "The promised Deliverer spoken of in the Jewish Torah, the Old Testament."

"Oh. A Jewish problem."

"No, it's not that way at all—" began Karena, but Tatiana interrupted her.

"If anyone wishes to become truly spiritual," she said, "Rasputin the starets is the one who can disciple them. He is so gifted by God. Even the czarina depends on him."

A starets, from what Karena had heard, was a spiritual guide who gathered followers. Many of these men, usually self-proclaimed, were not officially recognized by the Russian Orthodox Church because they were outside the monastic hierarchy, living at times like hermits or traveling monks.

While Tatiana chattered on about Rasputin and mysticism, Karena turned her attention out the coach window. Several ethnic groups of Russians seemed to be represented in Kazan, their street clothing bearing witness from each district. Chinese, Bukharese, and black Africans, all mingled with Russian merchants, peasants, landed gentry, and aristocrats. *What an interesting city. It's going to be a delightful holiday!*

The Roskov summer home artfully bespoke aristocracy. Kazan rugs covered the wide floors; golden, hand-carved wood shone with a warm gloss; and eastern tapestries hung on the high cream walls. Silver and crystal glittered from carefully placed lamp stands.

The servants carried Karena's and Natalia's portmanteaus up the graceful, winding staircase, and the housekeeper, flanked by two maids, stood at rapt attention as Madame Zofia imparted last-minute orders for the dinner and dancing this evening.

Zofia's black hair was sleeked and rolled elegantly at the back of her swan neck and studded with a silk net of tiny seed pearls. One large milky pearl was mounted on gold near her lace collar. Her dove gray gown gave the onlooker the sensation that she might have been *Princess* Zofia Peshkova-Roskova.

Karena's eye drifted to a painting on the wall of her aunt and uncle. Beside Zofia, Viktor, in uniform with his honey red mustache and deep-set eyes, looked as noble and unsmiling as a Romanov. Karena suspected that was why the great painting was prominently placed. Nearby, in a painting all her own, was Tatiana.

Her instructions complete, Madame Zofia joined the girls at the staircase to walk them to their rooms.

"Two balls in two nights," Natalia said, awed.

"My dear niece," Zofia replied as they mounted the stairs, "in St. Petersburg, there are balls *every* night. One grows accustomed to such demands. If I did not give frequent balls and entertainments while summering here in Kazan, I would be rejected socially and left out when we return to our winter residence." She smiled. "One looks forward to a quiet holiday in the Crimea."

Tatiana laughed at Natalia's expression. Karena only smiled.

"At certain seasons of the year," Tatiana said, "we dance our way from ball to ball, six days a week, for months. If it isn't a ball somewhere, it's the opera or dinners or sleigh rides."

"One must have very good shoes," Natalia said.

They laughed, and Madame Zofia put an arm around her waist.

"On the wheat farm, we have *none*," Karena said. "Balls, that is. Kiev, of course, is very different, though we do attend the opera as a family. So you see, we are very excited about the dancing. And grateful, Aunt Zofia."

"My dears, we are delighted to have you with us for two weeks. I wish you could extend your stay until September. I was telling Tatiana only last week that we so seldom see you."

"They can't stay until September," Tatiana said. "Karena is helping her uncle research a new book."

"Oh, is Matvey writing another book? Splendid. Then you and Natalia should come to St. Petersburg this Christmas season. I'll badger Josef about coming, too," she said of her brother. "And he simply must force Yeva to come with him. The last time your papa visited me, he came alone."

Karena's mother, because she was Jewish and had married Josef after his first wife died, was uncomfortable with the Roskov family. She felt they had never accepted her. Karena did not know if that were true. She, herself, had always been treated well by Papa Josef's two older sisters, Aunt Marta and Aunt Zofia.

"Mother's an old stick-in-the-mud," Natalia said as they went down the long upstairs hall, their footsteps softened by a golden carpet. The wall sconces burned cheerfully, and not a corner of the hallway held a shadow of gloom.

"She won't leave the manor for anything except to treat cases of illness among the peasants or deliver a baby," Natalia continued.

"So dedicated. And our dear Karena is following in her footsteps, all the way to medical college in St. Petersburg," Tatiana said, smiling.

"I hope I shall be accepted this time," Karena answered.

They came to an adjoining bedroom. The upstairs maid opened the door from the inside and stepped aside. "Everything is ready, Madame Zofia."

"Tell Gawrie to have my nieces' trunks brought up as soon as they arrive from the dock. And tell Katerina to send up tea." Zofia turned to Karena and Natalia. "We won't keep you talking long. You must have some quiet and rest before the ball tonight."

The two bedrooms were done in light pink and ivory tulle and joined together by a large vanity room with mirrors. It contrasted sharply with what Karena and her sister had at the manor.

"Tonight will be so exciting," Tatiana said. "Karena will meet Dr. Zinnovy, and my other surprise guest will stun everyone."

Madame Zofia sighed heavily. "After last night's tragedy, I would gladly annul this ball tonight if I could. Unfortunately—"

"Annul it? Mother, impossible! I won't hear of it."

"I know we can't postpone it. Viktor, too, tells me he has an important official coming tonight. Besides, I know exactly what would happen. If I postponed the event, the scandal of last night would spread even faster."

Scandal? wondered Karena. The lines around Madame Zofia's mouth tightened, and a glance toward Tatiana showed an unsmiling face. She began to massage her forehead in a poor attempt at theatrics, and Natalia caught Karena's gaze and tried not to smile.

"Already there are rumors," Madame Zofia said. "For Tatania's sake, I must proceed tonight as planned."

"What scandal? Or should we not inquire?" Karena asked in a sympathetic voice. She had a strong affection for her aunt and felt sorry for her. Tatiana pushed ahead with her plans with little consideration for her mother. As for Viktor, he probably didn't care what his daughter did, as long as she married an excellent soldier. Karena suspected Uncle Viktor adored Colonel Kronstadt.

"Perhaps it's better not to discuss it now," Madame Zofia said with a concerned glance at Tatiana, who had turned her back toward them and dramatically pressed a perfumed handkerchief to her mouth.

"No no, my cousins should know the truth," Tatiana said. "Tell them, Mother."

Madame Zofia fingered the lace on her collar. "We had a monumental tragedy last night." She lowered her voice. "One of the many young men in love with my daughter insulted Colonel Kronstadt in front of her and the guests. It was dreadful." She placed a slender hand to her forehead and shook her head, eyes closed, but this time Karena read genuine dismay.

"I can see it still—that red wine all over the front of his white dress uniform and face—to force a duel, you see." She crumpled her lace handkerchief in her palm. "It was the only way Captain Yevgenyev could break Alex's composure. Alex, of course, had to accept the challenge or be branded a coward."

Karena stared.

Madame Zofia heaved a sigh. "So…the duel will take place next month in St. Petersburg." She paced rapidly. "Oh! Awful! Poor Alex. And the scandal stains Tatiana as well."

Tatiana, who'd been standing with her back toward them, head bent in a waxen pose, now whirled, full of vigor. "Stains me! I don't see that. Why should it?"

"Your reputation, darling—"

"My reputation is stained because two very excellent men care enough about me to duel for me? Hah! I like that! See how my mother underappreciates me?" She looked at Karena, then back to Madame Zofia, who wore a pained expression.

"Darling—"

"A good many women can't even get a man to defend them in a brawl, let alone have honorable soldiers fight a duel over them. A duel is customary when a soldier is insulted. I see no reason to believe either Alex or I have had our reputations 'stained' in the slightest."

Tatiana stopped for breath, her handkerchief hanging limp from her jeweled hand.

Karena looked at her in silence. Natalia slowly sat down on the edge of a green velveteen chair.

Madame Zofia went to her daughter, trying to get her to sit down. "Tatiana, darling, you're all upset. I'm sorry I brought it up, but you must see that while I'm not suggesting you're at fault—"

"At fault! Of course I'm not, Mother."

"Even so, your friends—and mine—will talk about this for weeks. And if Alex or Karl is wounded in this absurd duel—"

"It won't go that far," Tatiana insisted. "I won't allow it. Sometimes Rasputin can foretell what will happen. I'll ask him."

Karena turned away to conceal her emotions. Her cousin hadn't always been this way, had she?

"If we go forward, we have not an hour to lose." Madame Zofia turned to Karena and Natalia. "My dears, do you have proper gowns to wear? silk stockings? slippers?"

Natalia sighed wistfully and looked at Karena.

Karena laughed. "Well, not exactly, but we each brought a dinner dress."

"Really, Mother," Tatiana said, "they're not likely to be hauling French gowns from Uncle Josef's farm. However, I've silk stockings to spare. I was going to give them each a pair as a gift anyway."

Madame Zofia smiled. "Well, I'm sure you'll be fine." She glanced at the clock on the table by the window and threw her palm to her forehead, her gold bracelet shining. "It's already noon. I wonder if Svetlana was able to order the extra piglet. I must go check. That girl is so forgetful. Ah, here is your tea."

A maid entered with a tray, and Tatiana moved toward the door. "I must begin getting my hair ready," she called over her shoulder. "If you need anything, come to my room at the end of the hall."

"Yes, do," Madame Zofia said warmly. "I shall see you girls later."

Karena called her thanks as her aunt moved with stately purpose through the door, muttering to herself. "I've simply a horrid notion that Svetlana forgot the extra piglet. Well then, I'll need to settle on lamb, that's all there is to it. Everyone enjoys lamb."

The bedroom grew silent except for the sound of tea being poured into china cups by the round-cheeked maid. Her stiff satin skirts made a scratching sound as she moved. She left quietly, shutting the door.

Karena turned slowly and looked at her sister. Natalia's face was tired and tense. She groaned, massaging her temples. "I wish I'd stayed home."

Karena drew in a breath and tucked a strand of loose hair back into the braided coil. "Let's have tea. We'll feel better. A nice bath and a brief nap, and we'll be ready to whirl about the fancy ballroom. At least Dr. Zinnovy will be here. I'm still shocked by that."

Natalia lifted her head. "I'm surprised Tatiana would trouble herself to arrange the meeting for you. I may be cynical, but my first guess is there's something in it for her."

"I hardly think so. She seemed quite genuine about having arranged it." Karena smiled. "And she did promise us each a pair of silk stockings. I'm going to take complete and selfish advantage of her offer. Imagine, *silk*." She pulled up the hem of her traveling skirt, exposing her cotton hose, and made a face.

Natalia laughed. "Come on," she said. "It will take us all afternoon to get ready."

Alex returned to the Roskov residence that afternoon and entered his bedroom with a scowl. He had laid out his future with the care of an architect, and now, while the structure was just being raised, he felt the tremors of an earthquake.

He threw his jacket on the bed. "If not an earthquake, then a blizzard!"

"Is something wrong, sir?" Konni, the tall valet who had long been in the service of Alex's stepmother, came from the next room at the sound of the door snapping shut. Konni had cared for Alex in childhood until he went to cadet school. Even now, Konni usually traveled with him when Alex was not staying in officers' quarters. Alex had requested his assistance on the journey to Kazan mostly because he was fond of the old gentleman.

"What could possibly go wrong?" Alex asked dryly.

Konni's face was expressionless as he picked up Alex's coat and hung it properly until he could take it out to brush it.

"My plans were made," Alex said, "and now, suddenly, something occurs that threatens to send them crashing down in ruin—if I allow it, which, of course, I will not."

"Just so, sir."

Alex sighed and rubbed his face. "The aroma of coffee tempts me."

"The coffee is here, sir, waiting as usual." Konni went into the adjoining room and returned with a silver serving tray

"This ruinous occurrence, sir... Do you speak of a woman?"

Alex scowled in his direction, undoing the buttons on his shirt. "Now why would you ever think that? Since when does a woman, even a charming young woman, ever ruin a man's sensible plans?"

"Just so, sir," Konni said, not fooled at all. "I saw her alight from the coach. Most charming in her red hat."

"That red hat! And now I can't get her out of my mind. Miss Karena Peshkova has supplanted Tatiana. How could I have allowed it?" Alex tossed his shirt onto the bed and groaned. "Her eyes, Konni, blue as a periwinkle. And a mouth that needs to be kissed."

Konni made a clucking sound of sympathy as he poured Alex's coffee. "And completely the opposite of Miss Tatiana, I should say. While one is dark, the other is fair. While Miss Tatiana is strong-willed and assertive, Miss Peshkova shows sweet discernment and proper sense—"

"That will be enough. If I hear any more of your wisdom, I shall break down and weep in my coffee." He took the cup from the tray. "How do you know she's sweet? She might, beneath that aura of fairness, be a pickle."

"A guess, sir. A girl with a red hat is always sweet."

"A brilliant deduction."

Konni lifted a note from the table and carried it to him on a small salver. "From Miss Tatiana, sir."

Alex opened it and read the brief note. "Rasputin," he muttered.

"I beg your pardon, sir."

"The magnanimous Crow sisters are bringing Rasputin to meet the guests tonight, and I am blessed to be among the chosen few. From what I've heard, Konni, he's a boor. It bothers me that Tatiana is so taken by him."

"Yes sir, I quite understand. And all the more distressing when your military advancement is based upon marrying her."

Alex glared at him. "You make it sound like I'm about to take on a liability."

"Oh, no sir! Miss Tatiana is very beautiful." Konni looked as innocent and saintly as ever.

"This marriage arrangement is deceiving no one." Alex tossed the note onto the table. "Tatiana has her reasons, as I have mine."

"And now, sir, there's the duel to be fought. A very worrisome matter." Konni frowned slightly.

"That couldn't be helped," Alex said. "Yevgenyev's malice goes beyond

Miss Roskova. This is a personal grievance." He sank into a chair and propped his feet up. Konni refilled his cup.

"I must say, Konni, I was a little surprised to discover Miss Peshkova and her sister were Tatiana's cousins. She's not mentioned them before."

"With good reason, perhaps, sir."

Alex put a hand behind his head and leaned back. He'd been on business for General Roskov all afternoon, and he was not looking forward to the evening.

Weariness, however, was not his only reason for contemplating how he might quietly escape the ball. The next two weeks could, if he allowed it, develop into a situation he wished to avoid. Alex finished his coffee and scowled at the cup. He pondered the moment of awareness that had occurred when he spoke with Karena Peshkova and marveled at how easily his plans could to be put in jeopardy by the arrival of a lovely girl with a red hat.

"The question, Konni, is what do I do about it, if anything?"

"You have my sympathy, sir. Ambition is a harsh taskmaster. Pardon me for saying so, but you are not the only one who wrestles with it. Miss Tatiana also seems an ambitious woman."

"If I were smart," Alex told Konni, "I'd pack my bag now and make some excuse to rejoin the Sokolov twins in St. Petersburg."

Konni looked at him soberly from across the room, then went to the wardrobe and took out the travel bags. "I could always claim you came down with the Russian grippe, sir."

"English grippe."

"As you say."

Alex drummed his fingers on the arm of the leather chair. He looked up at the ceiling and considered his options.

"I have never been a coward when it comes to women," he said, "and I won't start now. Who knows? By the time the clock strikes midnight, this attraction may have disintegrated. I'll come home from the ball with a clear mind, amused to think I even considered her."

"It often happens, sir. Then again, it might turn out the other way. In which case, you won't come home amused, sir, but smitten to the core by a poisoned arrow—straight to the heart. Then, sir, there's no hope."

Alex narrowed his gaze. "You're most graphic, Konni. Yes…it could happen as you say, but I won't allow it to happen to me. She's just a girl. A little girl with braids."

"Just so, sir." Konni replaced the travel bags and closed the wardrobe doors.

Alex was sure he'd seen old Konni's lip twitch with secret amusement.

Konni disappeared into the other room, and Alex leaned his head back against the chair and shut his eyes, hoping to sleep for an hour before going downstairs.

His plans for the future were too important to let slip from his grasp. If he must change them at all, he would do so only if he knew the military would not reward him with the future he wanted. In that situation, he might consider joining Michael in New York.

He stretched like a lazy lynx. What was another beautiful young woman? Brunettes, blondes, redheads—what did it matter? There were many such women. Karena Peshkova was simply one more. Tatiana was enough for any man. After two weeks, the girl with the golden braids and red hat would be a vanishing memory. She would return to Kiev, he to St. Petersburg. The war would come, and this brief episode would fade, carried along with the winds of time.

Alex drifted off sleep.

The afternoon was filled with last-minute preparations. Karena enjoyed her soak in the tub, then arranged her long, fair hair into the latest fashion with assistance from the able hands of Madame Zofia's personal maid. Having accomplished that intricate task, and well satisfied with the effect, Karena put on her modest peach and ivory dress with lace trim. This was her best evening dress, the one she wore to the opera in Kiev when Papa Josef took the family once a year to see Tchaikovsky's *Swan Lake*.

As Karena stood for Natalia to button the clasp at the back of her neck, the bedroom door opened and Tatiana breezed in, smiling.

"Silk stockings, darlings!" She dropped two new pairs on the large, satin-covered bed.

"Ooh, delightful," said Natalia, picking up a pair.

Karena admired Tatiana's gown. It was a splendid creation of wine and black velvet. Tatiana appeared aglow with satisfaction, convincing Karena that she had news.

"*He* will be here tonight, after all. This was quite a feat on my part, I can tell you. I can hardly wait to introduce you to him."

Karena was so excited she hugged her cousin. "Tatiana, this is wonderful! I've talked briefly with him before, but I'm sure he'll not remember me. I usually see him from afar."

"You've met him before? But when?" Tatiana asked, pulling away to stare at her.

"In Kiev, when I've gone on medical errands."

"Oh, I see. Well, I suppose I should not be too surprised. By now, his reputation would have grown." Tatiana glanced in the mirror and straightened the diamond brooch worn just below her shoulder. "The czarina adores him. The czar, too, for that matter. Everyone will hear how he's come to my ball. They'll be so envious. The news will burst like a firecracker all over St. Petersburg."

Karena looked up from smoothing a final wrinkle from her dress, confused. *Is Dr. Zinnovy truly that influential?*

"It was the Crow sisters who introduced us. He's the talk of society in

St. Petersburg. Many there would die to have him at their parties, but I won out."

Karena realized her mistake. "Then you are not discussing Dr. Zinnovy."

"Zinnovy? Oh, you thought I meant the doctor." Tatiana smiled. "No, of course not. I was speaking of the starets."

Karena's enthusiasm melted, but she forced herself to look interested for the sake of her cousin.

"Everyone in St. Petersburg is discussing Rasputin. It couldn't be otherwise with the czarina relying on him. He's graced of God."

Graced of God. The words caught Karena's attention.

"Not that I am his disciple yet, but Mother is beginning to take him seriously, thanks to the czarina's good friend, Anna Vyrubova. Anna introduced the czarina to Rasputin. The Crow sisters are bringing him. They know everything there is about holy men. They are going to arrange a table talk tonight."

Karena wrinkled her nose. "Whatever is a table talk? A religious study of some sort?"

"I don't know exactly. As I say, I'm just learning. But the Crow sisters are experts at this sort of thing. They've been traveling with Rasputin on some of his pilgrimages. You know—cooking, washing him—"

"Washing him?"

Tatiana shrugged and smoothed her hair before the gilded mirror. "I don't know what that means, but it's all holy, you can be sure. Anna Vyrubova can tell us everything we want to know. Anna is Rasputin's main disciple. She saw Rasputin heal the czarina's son. Think of it." She turned to Karena, a spark of shrewdness in her dark eyes. "The little czarevitch, Alexei, has a blood disease, you know. A *bleeder,* they say."

"A hemophiliac, you mean," Karena said. She'd spent many hours studying her mother's medical textbooks. Madame Yeva had attended the

Imperial College of Medicine and Midwifery in St. Petersburg. Karena had already decided that once she'd gained her legal certificate in midwifery, she would seek as much information as she could on various diseases and their cures. If little else, she could keep a journal of all she learned and use it among the peasants in her village.

"Imagine," Tatiana said, "actually healing poor little Alexei. Yet Rasputin already has enemies at court. There are some in the *Duma* trying to convince Czar Nicholas to send him back to his village of Pokrovskoe. The czarina will never allow that to happen. If anyone wishes to be included in her inner circle, they'd best embrace Rasputin or expect to make themselves enemies of the Romanovs. I, for one, will embrace him."

So that was their motive for arranging Rasputin's reception tonight. News of the Roskov family receiving him as their honored guest would find its way into the private chambers of the czarina. But what did Madame Zofia and Tatiana expect to gain from the czarina's favor?

"Who would have ever thought Siberia would give the Romanov family and holy Russia such a gift from God as Rasputin?" Tatiana asked, her eyes meeting Karena's in the mirror.

Karena looked at her, troubled and uncertain. "Do you really believe that?"

"Of course. Why not? Anna is a witness. She was there in the czarevitch's bedroom when Rasputin healed him."

Karena wished to avoid controversy as much as possible—after all, she was here as a guest. She was also aware that she didn't know enough about the Bible to be able to refute such a belief. "If it's true, then it would be most thought provoking," she finally said. "However, Sergei says—"

"Sergei says, Sergei says." Tatiana's eyes flashed with quick temper. "Your brother is a cynic. A Bolshevik, as well. Oh yes, he is—don't protest. You're always defending him. He'll end up in the Siberian mines someday soon if he doesn't keep a civil tongue about the czarina. That street disturbance in St. Petersburg would've brought about his arrest if my parents hadn't intervened with the czar. There Sergei was, shouting on the street with the revolutionaries supporting the factory workers' walkout."

"But he's not a Bolshevik," Karena said firmly. "He became involved by accident."

"He *is* a revolutionary. He was expelled from the university and sent home last month."

Karena was surprised. "How did you know? Papa Josef tried to keep it quiet."

"You forget my father is a general in the Okhrana. The czar's secret police know everything. With all the assassination attempts on Czar Nicholas, they must stay vigilant."

While Tatiana's father was in the Okhrana, she had no right to private information. Karena only knew about Sergei because he had confided in her about the trouble he was in with Papa Josef. How had Tatiana heard? Surely Uncle Viktor would not discuss his highly secretive work at the dinner table with two women as talkative as his wife and daughter.

Tatiana's mouth turned. "No, I didn't snoop in my father's records, though that would be easy. He brings home files. Especially anything to do with friends and family. He wishes to protect us all, you see. No, it was Alex who asked me about Sergei. He was riding with the Cossacks at the time. They'd been sent in to break up the demonstration. He saw Sergei there and mentioned it to me just this afternoon."

Karena remembered Kronstadt was now in the Okhrana. "Why is he inquiring about Sergei?" she asked cautiously. Sergei's part in the factory demonstration posed no threat to anyone. He'd even been permitted reentry into the university this September.

Tatiana gave her a once-over. "He wanted to know if you shared your brother's interest in the Bolshevik Party."

"Sergei is highly opinionated about everything, and the gathering lured him. He was punished, and it's over now. And you know very well I have no interest in either Marx or Lenin."

Tatiana smiled. "Of course I do. Let's not discuss it anymore. Come. It's time we went down. Where's Natalia?"

"Coming," Natalia called from her bedroom. She hurried out a moment later holding a pendant on her palm, her face flushed pink with exasperation and excitement.

"I can't close the clasp."

"Here, let me." Tatiana reached for the pendant. There was a flash of red and white, and Tatiana's breath caught. Karena stared at the glimmering jewels, an unusual ruby and diamond pendant in the form of a tulip, an emerald at the stem.

"It's stunning...," Tatiana breathed, transfixed.

Karena looked sharply at her sister. "Natalia! That belongs to Mother. It was her aunt's from Finland. She didn't allow you to take it, did she? Why, I've only been permitted to see it once."

Natalia lowered her eyes, her cheeks crimson. "It's kept in the safe. I borrowed it. Don't worry so, I'll return it. Stop looking at me like that, Karena."

Karena couldn't help herself. "Mother doesn't know you borrowed it?"

"No. She wouldn't have let me take it, and you know it."

"Natalia," Karena began, then lapsed into silence. She didn't want to embarrass her sister before Tatiana any more than she already had.

"I wanted to wear something grand tonight," Natalia said defensively. "Just look at Tatiana. Do you wonder why I borrowed it?"

Tatiana fingered her diamonds. "Mine are nothing compared to that pendant. It must be worth a fortune. How shocking that Aunt Yeva would have such a pendant all these years and never mention it. Why, if I owned that, I'd show it to everyone just to see their eyes pop."

Karena opened her mouth to defend her mother but hesitated. The pendant would have paid for a dozen years in the best medical school in Europe and then some.

"I had completely forgotten about the pendant," she admitted instead. "How did you get it from the safe?"

Natalia sank onto the edge of the bed. "I've seen where she and Papa keep the key. I knew neither of them would miss it. They so seldom take it out and look at it."

Tatiana still held the pendant. Karena frowned and reached to take it from her palm, but Tatiana danced away, laughing.

"Natalia can't wear it tonight," Karena said. "It would turn into a scandal."

"Scandal?" Tatiana's dark brows rose.

"You know what I mean. Everyone will notice, and Aunt Zofia will write Mother and want to know all about it."

Natalia jumped to her feet. "Nonsense! Mother won't be half as indignant as you are. I want to wear it."

Tatiana held the pendant against her throat, her eyes glowing.

Karena gave Natalia a meaningful stare. Natalia glanced uneasily at Tatiana admiring herself in the mirror, bit her lip, and silently mouthed, *I'm sorry.*

Too late, Karena mouthed back.

Natalia winced and walked to where Tatiana stood before the full-length mirror. "I'd better put it back. I shouldn't have brought it in the first place." She held out her hand.

"Oh, don't be a goose," Tatiana said. "No one will suspect you stole it from your parents' safe. But it doesn't go with your green gown. In fact, it would look hideous. Here, take my diamonds, and I'll wear the pendant."

"Tatiana, I can't allow—"

But Tatiana had already removed her diamonds and dropped them in Natalia's palm. She placed the pendant around her own neck, and with practiced skill, she snapped the clasp. She laughed and danced about the room, avoiding Natalia, who begged for the pendant back.

"Of course, I'll return it," she said in response to Natalia's pleas. "After the ball. Odd, though…I'm certain I've seen it before. No, it was a pair of earrings and a matching bracelet of the same design. They belonged to Countess Katya Zinnovy—oh!"

She turned, hands clasped at her heart, and looked at Karena. Karena knew her anger at Tatiana's outrageous behavior must be visible, but Tatiana seemed oblivious.

"I forgot to tell you the sad news. Dr. Zinnovy was called away tonight on urgent business. His wife, Katya, is ill again. He's rushed back to St. Petersburg to be with her. Oh, Karena, I'm so sorry. But his son is here. You can meet Fyodor Zinnovy."

Natalia marched up to Tatiana, throwing her shoulders back. "Here are your diamonds. Return the pendant, please, or I shall never hear the end of it."

"You won't let me wear it?"

"I'd better not, Tatiana."

"Oh, very well. Here—" She unclasped the chain and handed Natalia the pendant, then took her own diamonds to the mirror.

While Natalia returned the pendant to its box, Karena's thoughts focused on her disappointment over Dr. Zinnovy's cancellation. Fate seemed determined to thwart her. Would she ever achieve her dream?

THREE

Stolen Hearts

Karena and Natalia followed Tatiana down the hallway until they came to the lighted stairway. Tatiana paused on the brightly lit landing until many eyes were turned her way, then descended slowly for effect.

Karena and Natalia followed two steps behind.

"I feel like the princess's bridesmaid," Natalia whispered. Karena tried not to laugh.

The crystal chandelier above them sparkled, pouring forth light. The polished floor gleamed, leading to an archway that opened into the ballroom. The orchestra began to play prelude music for dinner. Karena scanned the hallway.

A group of gentlemen gathered at the bottom of the stairs. Karena recognized the figure in military uniform at once as Colonel Aleksandr Kronstadt. Two men were with him, presumably to escort her and Natalia to dinner. She thought one of them was Dr. Zinnovy's son Fyodor. Despite her interest in the Zinnovys, Karena glanced at Colonel Kronstadt. His intense, green-gray gaze met hers.

She immediately looked away. Tatiana must surely have noticed.

Tatiana made the introductions. "Karena, this is Dr. Zinnovy's son,

Fyodor. And Natalia, this is Count Philipov's son, Misha. Gentlemen, may I present my cousins, Karena and Natalia Peshkova."

Karena turned her attention to the young man bowing to her, his soft chin pulled into his wide neck. His soft blue eyes looked sleepy. He seemed nothing like his father. *Perhaps he takes after his mother,* she thought, though she'd never seen her.

"I am sorry to hear of Countess Zinnovy's illness," Karena said. "I hope it isn't serious."

"The countess is often ailing. It's one of the reasons I'm studying medicine."

Her interest was snagged immediately. "I've admired your father's work from afar. I can see why you wish to follow in his steps."

A momentary silence followed. Fyodor's cheeks turned a ruddy color, and Karena realized she'd made a blunder. His mouth tightened, reminding her of King Henry VIII in a painting she'd seen of the English monarch.

"Everyone," Fyodor said stiffly, "admires my father."

Karena was at a loss over how to respond. She glanced at Tatiana for help, but her cousin remained silent.

"And how are your studies in St. Petersburg progressing?" Alex asked him, his tone nonchalant.

Karena breathed easier, attention having shifted away from her.

"If the staff knew what they were doing, my studies would be going exceptionally well. But there is bickering, jealousy, and pride among the doctors on the teaching faculty."

"Oh? How unfortunate."

Karena glanced at Kronstadt and was sure he was merely pretending interest with Fyodor who continued to explain that his struggle with grades was due to problems with the professors.

"If my father was not director, I'd transfer immediately to the Imperial College of Medicine and Midwifery in Moscow."

Natalia spoke up. "Midwifery is my sister Karena's specialty."

Fyodor looked at her with forgiven interest. Karena sensed Alex was watching her as well.

"Is that so, Miss Peshkova?" Fyodor asked politely. "Well, Moscow and St. Petersburg both have the finest training in Russia. Which school will you be attending?"

"I'm hoping to enter St. Petersburg's in September. This is my third attempt. The quota for new students was full last year and the year before. I'd hoped Dr. Zinnovy would be here tonight. I was going to ask about prospects. Not that he'd know my personal status, of course—but he'd know how crowded the new term looked."

"Why, I'd hardly expect enrollment to be overcrowded," Fyodor said. "I'm sure you'll be accepted."

"Well, it's not so simple, I'm afraid. There's only a two percent opportunity allotted to openings for—for certain people."

An awkward silence followed. Karena wished she hadn't been so open.

"Oh, I see," Fyodor said. "Yes, yes, there is that law, isn't there."

"You're Jewish, Miss Peshkova?"

The question came from Colonel Kronstadt. She turned toward him, wondering what she'd see in his gaze.

"My mother is Jewish," she explained, perhaps a little too defensively, feeling embarrassed with all eyes turned upon her.

She could read little in his gaze except a thoughtful consideration that told her nothing of his feelings.

"Poland?" he asked.

"Finland. But I've an uncle from Poland. He once taught history at Warsaw University until—" She caught herself before explaining further. It would be an error to mention Uncle Matvey had once been arrested for his politics.

Tatiana laid a hand across her forehead. She looked up at the ceiling in her usual manner of frustrated agony. "This conversation is becoming distasteful. It's little wonder you've been treated with small interest at the Imperial Medical College, Karena. One doesn't go about blaring trumpets and telling everyone you've an uncle who isn't loyal to Czar Nicholas."

Karena felt her flush deepen. "Professor Menkin is absolutely loyal to the Romanovs—"

Ignoring her, Tatiana moved between Alex and Fyodor, looping her arms through theirs. She looked first at one young man and then the other, her small white teeth showing in a dimpled smile.

"Alex…Fyodor, have you heard my exciting news? We're having a surprise guest coming tonight after dinner. Before the dancing begins, some of us are going into the great-parlor where he'll speak to us."

Karena shook with anger and embarrassment. Tatiana might just as well have called her a silly little fool in front of the men. *Oh! Sometimes I could squeeze that neck of hers!* She was tempted to turn away and go up to her room, but she didn't want Tatiana to think she could be defeated so easily. Why had Tatiana reacted that way? Why had she even invited her to Kazan if all she saw in her was someone with whom she must compete whenever they were with guests?

Why shouldn't I be honest with Fyodor? I am not ashamed that Mother is Jewish. And Uncle Matvey is one of the most intelligent men I know.

Karena refused to slink away. She glanced about for Natalia and vaguely recalled that she'd wandered into the next room with the talkative son of the count. Karena lifted her chin and stood her ground, pretending interest in Tatiana's conversation with Alex and Zinnovy that deliberately excluded her. Karena noticed the pathetic smile on Fyodor's face each time Tatiana turned to smile at him, including him in her attentions, her fingers holding onto his arm.

He looks like a lovesick calf, Karena thought. She could have laughed but found her heart felt sorry for him. She sensed that he wanted to be liked for himself instead of his father's renowned name in medicine. Tatiana was merely using him for some reason of her own that wasn't clear. *He doesn't see that she has no more genuine interest in him than in a dandelion.* Karena didn't know what Alex's response was because she steadfastly refused to look at him, nor could he say anything with Tatiana talking and laughing constantly.

"I think," Colonel Kronstadt said with affected gravity, apparently relieved, "that was the dinner announcement we just heard."

"Yes, shall we go in?" Tatiana said. "You must prove yourself cheerful company tonight for the general's sake, Alex. My poor father is in a worse mood than you are. You too, Fyodor," she added with a quick smile thrown his way.

As though he were a big-eyed spaniel in need of a pat on the head, Karena thought.

Tatiana, dividing herself unselfishly between Alex and Fyodor, her arms still looped through theirs, was beginning to lead them away captive when Alex turned back toward Karena.

He wore a faint smile. "We must not forget Miss Peshkova," he said smoothly, releasing Tatiana's hold and extending a hand to Karena with a light bow. "She might be sorry she left Kiev and board the first steamer to the train station."

Karena smiled and took his hand, ignoring the glimmer of displeasure in Tatiana's eyes. His warm hand closed about hers and placed it on his arm, and his reassuring touch made her heart beat faster.

"I shall hardly run away, Colonel."

He looked into her eyes. "No, on second thought, I don't think you would."

FOUR

The Starets

Light cascaded from a mass of white tapers in golden chandeliers. The large dining table, covered with ecru lace, sparkled with silver and crystal.

Alex noticed a change in Tatiana. It was unlike her to be silent. Perhaps she was agitated because he had escorted Karena into the dining room. Following her gaze, he realized Tatiana was watching not the Peshkova girl but the medical student seated beside her. Now why would the moody Fyodor occupy her thoughts?

Alex leaned toward her. "Not feeling well, darling?"

"Oh. Oh, yes, quite well." She smiled at him sweetly. "Why do you ask?"

He lifted a brow. "You're too quiet."

"Am I?" she laughed. "I'm saving all my energy for the dance." She paused. "I hope you won't mind if I dance with others tonight? Fyodor, for instance…I would like to lead off with him. Do you mind?"

Alex stifled a grin. "Dance to your heart's content. Just watch your wee toes. He may be good with a scalpel, but don't trust him to do the light fandango gracefully."

She laughed again. A moment later she sobered and murmured, "Alex, do you think Fyodor is as handsome as his father?"

"I've not given the matter much thought," he teased, "but—"

"Oh, bother!" she grabbed her napkin from her lap and touched it to her velvet skirt. "I've spilled a dash of wine. I need to go up and get my lady to clean it."

Alex stood, pulling back her chair. "I'll escort you."

"There's no need, Alex. Do stay and enjoy your meal. I won't be long."

Alex looked down at her chair before reseating himself and noticed her linen napkin. He picked it up. It was unsoiled—there'd been no wine spilled.

Karena was conversing with Fyodor, and her sister with the count. The entire table of guests appeared occupied with those seated near them. A minute later, Alex left the dining room.

In the foyer, a few serving people were moving quickly about. The butler hovered nearby, keeping a watchful eye on the dinner party. Alex looked over at the grand staircase. "Did Miss Roskova go up?"

"She did, sir, just a moment ago."

"Where is her room?"

"Down the corridor to your right, sir. The end of the hall."

Alex went up the stairs. He found the second floor quiet except for the faint murmur of voices and music that drifted up from below. Tatiana's bedroom door was shut. He tapped. There was no response. From down the corridor he heard movement in one of the rooms. He walked there and found the door ajar. He saw enough to know that this was the room assigned to Karena or her sister. Tatiana stared into the open box in her hands, so entranced that she didn't hear him enter as she removed its contents.

"Not very hospitable of you, darling."

Her breath caught, and she whirled. "Alex!"

"Yes, and you should be grateful it isn't one of your cousins."

"I wasn't stealing it!"

"I didn't say you were." He came up beside her, carefully removing the pendant from her hand.

"Alex—oh, you can't think I'd take it from them!"

"No, I don't." He lifted her chin gently and studied her eyes.

She shook her head. "They have so little. I'd never take from them. I—I was just looking at it." She placed her trembling palm against his hand. "I want you to believe me," she whispered.

"I do, Tatiana." It was a deliberate act of his will to believe.

She let out a sigh of relief. Tension fled from her face. "Thank you, Alex."

He caught sight of a red hat by the wardrobe. *Karena...* He frowned. *Why can't I get her out of my mind?*

Tatiana stepped back, oblivious to his moment of frustration, and brought her handkerchief to her eyes.

He looked down at the pendant and examined it. "Exceptional."

"Yes. Very." She sank onto the edge of the chair. "That's what made me so curious. Jewelry of this value would be hard for the Menkins to come by."

"Then the pendant isn't your cousin's?"

"Oh no. Karena has very little. The Peshkovs are not wealthy. Uncle Josef—Mother's younger brother—is a wheat farmer. You saw Karena's gown tonight. Quite dull, actually. I had to give her and Natalia silk stockings. They're country gentry. But I love them dearly, of course." She stood, making jerky movements with her hands. "That's why the pendant is so curious to me."

"If it isn't your cousin's, whose would it be?"

"Well, they say it belongs to their mother, Madame Yeva, from the

Menkin side of the family—the Jewish side. Natalia says she borrowed it from a safe and brought it here to wear to the ball. Karena was very upset about that."

"Then Madame Peshkova doesn't know Natalia *borrowed* it?"

"No, and Karena made a terrible fuss and refused to allow her to wear it tonight."

"Undoubtedly wise. Other than its value, why are you so taken with it?"

A flash of resentment showed in her eyes, then diminished. "I've seen two other pieces like it, and I can't understand how Madame Yeva would have come by it."

Alex kept silent. He thought he could see down the path Tatiana was taking. He knew almost nothing about the Peshkov family of Kiev and even less of Madame Yeva and her Jewish roots.

"Why didn't you go to your cousins and ask to see it again?"

"Karena made such a fuss over Natalia having it here, as I've said."

He looked at her. "So what were you planning to do?"

"To *borrow* it for just an hour to show it to Fyodor and see if he agreed it's part of the countess's set."

Alex's temper flared. "A grave mistake. It is none of your affair."

"And if it is part of Countess Zinnovy's set?" she asked defensively.

"Regardless, you would embarrass your cousins and cause a furor. Just imagine if you rouse Fyodor's suspicions. Once he gets riled, he's like a hound. Do you want Karena and Natalia to be questioned and persecuted by someone as powerful as he? It would lead to trouble all around."

She lowered her eyes. "I see what you mean… I hadn't realized the consequences. I was merely curious and thought he could explain."

He studied her for an uncomfortable moment. "Let me handle this, will you? Say nothing whatsoever to Fyodor, or anyone else."

"Yes, Alex, of course I will."

He placed the pendant back into the box. "Is there a key to the box?"

"Natalia keeps it in the crystal container. Earlier, I watched to see where she put it. It's over there—on the vanity table."

He locked the box and had Tatiana carefully place it where she found it. After returning the key to the cut-glass container, he glanced at Tatiana. She looked uneasy with herself, and he was encouraged by it.

"You'll not mention this pendant to Fyodor?" he asked.

"I'll say nothing."

"We'd better return before we're missed," he said. "All we need is to be caught by your cousins, after hovering over their mother's pendant."

Tatiana had returned to good temper and seemed normal again. She smothered a silly giggle. Alex playfully pinched her dimpled chin.

"Out, my girl. And make it quick, or one of these days, I will stop flying to your aid."

"Do so, and I shall mourn and waste away."

He gave no response. She reached up suddenly, threw her arms around him, and kissed him.

Alex propelled her from the room into the corridor. He could just imagine bumping into Karena as he was exiting her room, Tatiana's lip rouge on his mouth. He rubbed it off with his kerchief.

After dinner, Alex reluctantly joined the dozen or so special guests in the great-parlor. Rasputin was to arrive soon with the Crow sisters, and Tatiana had gone out to greet them.

The great-parlor with connecting terrace, which overlooked the river full of twinkling houseboats and barges, was a pleasant area with comfortable damasked furnishings and fine paintings. Across the room, Alex noticed Karena beside Fyodor. The medical student's sullen mood was gone, and he seemed more animated than before. Karena listened and smiled.

A patient young woman, Alex thought. *And modest.* She and her sister were the only women wearing gowns that concealed beauty instead of displaying it. The other women showed no restraint in donning low-cut dresses and weighty jewels. Accustomed to seeing more than he should, Alex found himself intrigued by Karena. Was she religious? Jewish, she had said, but if she, her mother, and her sister practiced Judaism, they would need to live "within the pale" in Odessa, where the czar insisted all practicing Jews must live. Since they were wheat producers from Kiev, he assumed she had adapted to worshiping in the Russian Orthodox Church.

Alex joined Karena and Fyodor by the terrace. They stood with Natalia and the count's son beside the grand piano. "Are you prepared to meet Grigori Rasputin, Colonel Kronstadt?" Fyodor asked, turning toward him.

He smiled. "With breathless anticipation."

Karena was listening to the casual exchange and turned toward him, as if to judge his seriousness.

"He was in Kiev, visiting our famous monasteries, before his recent pilgrimage," she said.

Alex looked at her directly to interpret her remark. He recognized a subdued flicker of pleasure in her eyes over his presence. He was irritated that he could find more stimulation in her small response than in Tatiana's overly amorous attention.

"Do you follow your cousin's enthusiasm for Rasputin's spiritual guidance?" he asked her.

"At the risk of being misunderstood, I'm not impressed with the starets, Colonel Kronstadt. I told Tatiana so earlier this evening, and I'm afraid her feelings were nettled."

"Oh?" He studied her face, hoping she would reveal her thoughts.

"My uncle knows about him, and I trust his judgment," she said in a low voice that even Fyodor might not hear. "He happens to know the trends in society and says the starets's pilgrimage was to make amends for stealing a neighbor's horse a few years ago in his village of Pokrovskoe."

Alex knew this as well. Rasputin had lived a wild life as a peasant. Many said he still did.

"His supporters aren't apt to give much credence to that," he said, "even if it's true. It merely emboldens them to rally against his *persecutors*."

"I suppose you're right, Colonel."

"This individual in St. Petersburg you mention, perhaps he's an acquaintance of mine?" he asked, wondering if she referenced her beau. He could hardly imagine a young woman with her qualities not having a suitor.

"Professor Matvey Menkin, my uncle on my mother's side. Have you heard of him? He's written several articles in educators' journals and is now doing research for a book on a matter of Jewish interest."

This was the second time she'd mentioned her Jewish connections, as though placing a bulwark between them. Her face was a lovely mask, her eyes veiled. What were her motives?

Before he could respond, his attention shifted across the room. Madame Zofia appeared with a gracious smile, escorted by General Viktor.

A moment later, Tatiana swept in, followed by the elderly Crow sisters. Their eyes were bright with apparent excitement over introducing their newest find in the world of mysticism. Between the sisters stood Grigori Rasputin.

This, thought Alex, with a sense of grief, *is what our Russian nobility embraces as their spiritual shepherd.*

He glanced at Karena, encouraged by a look of dismay as she bit her lip and lowered her eyes. Fyodor's soft face was blank; he stared, took out his monocle, cleaned it with his kerchief, and placed it in his eye.

Around the room, guests fidgeted and chattered like nervous birds. Alex knew they all hoped to witness a miracle from this supposed man of God.

Alex marveled that Rasputin could find a following in the parlors of well-educated men and women. Deception, he decided, was not limited to the peasants. Something that Michael had written him in a recent letter jumped to his mind: *"When men do not receive the love of the truth, they are vulnerable to strong delusion."*

Alex glanced at Tatiana. Her cheeks wore a pink flush. *She's awed by his presence!* Alex made up his mind that he must confront her over this.

Rasputin wore a dark, soiled tunic over peasant trousers bloused into scuffed boots. His long hair was drawn back and looked as unkempt as his beard. Women said his eyes were mesmerizing, that he had an ability to exert a bizarre force of will with them. Alex found them shrewd.

"Curious," Alex murmured to Fyodor. "Could he have learned the art of hypnotism? maybe on one of his pilgrimages?"

"Perhaps," he replied quietly. "I don't trust him, but in St. Petersburg, one risks his career by saying so. My father is now one of several physicians to the Romanov family, so I must watch what I say."

"Oh! Then Dr. Zinnovy's no longer head of admissions at the medical college?" Karena asked.

"I believe he remains in charge until the end of the year. I've no notion who'll take his place. Some say it will be a woman—Dr. Lenski," Fyodor said stiffly. "She is his colleague and a friend of the countess."

"Dr. Lenski?"

Alex looked at Karena, whose voice had revealed sudden excitement.

"You sound as if you know her," he said.

"My mother knew her well. They were roommates during their studies. They've not seen each other in years, but I'm sure Dr. Lenski would remember."

"Then Madame Peshkova is a doctor?" Alex inquired.

"I'm afraid not. She left the college to marry my father. She remains the village midwife and medical practitioner. I've been going with her on her calls since I was eight." She smiled. "Do you wonder that I desire to enter medicine?"

"A worthy ambition. So Madame Peshkova must have many old friends from St. Petersburg," Alex said.

"Oh yes, letters are frequently exchanged, though she has no time for visits. When Natalia and I were younger, we would go to the Roskov residence for Christmas festivities, but our parents remained in Kiev."

"Then Dr. Zinnovy must be a medical school friend of your mother, as well."

"He was one of her instructors."

"I see."

She looked at him, a flicker of alertness in her eyes as she seemed to wonder what motivated his interest.

He smiling disarmingly. "Why not write Dr. Lenski about your difficulty in gaining entry? She may be influential. And you, Fyodor, might speak to your father. With help from two esteemed doctors, perhaps Miss Peshkova could be admitted." He looked at her. A faint gleam of suspicion shone in her eyes. "It would become Russia's loss if one so dedicated should be denied the opportunity to pursue further studies."

"Quite, quite," Fyodor agreed. "I could deliver a letter from Miss Peshkova to my father when I return to St. Petersburg."

"You're leaving in the morning, Fyodor?" Alex asked.

"Yes, immediately after breakfast." He glanced toward Rasputin. "Well, Colonel, it looks as if Miss Tatiana is one of Rasputin's chief admirers."

Rasputin was seated in a chair with guests gathered around. Tatiana collected the group's written questions and handed them to one of the Crow sisters, who read them to Rasputin.

Rasputin was mumbling about dreams and about how the future could be known…sometimes. He put questions under his pillow for the czarina when he went to sleep at night, and in the morning, he said, the answer was usually clear.

Rasputin glanced around the room at the hearers. His gaze stopped on one of the women whose name Alex had forgotten.

"You will know the answer to your question soon."

There followed a thrilled murmur of wondering voices. The middle-aged woman looked shocked, then gave a quavering smile, her eyes tearing.

"Oh, but, Teacher, I didn't even write out my question. The perplexity is so heavy for me to bear. How did you know I even have a question facing my future just now?"

Rasputin mumbled something Alex couldn't hear, and then his voice trailed off, as though he'd forgotten what he was saying. He reached for another dessert cake, and three people vied for the privilege of handing it to him.

General Viktor eased up beside Alex. "Russia is in a pretty mess," he said in a low voice.

Alex followed the general's sober gaze. Rasputin was dropping crumbs on the Persian rug. He poured his tea onto the chinaware saucer and slurped it up.

"If I did that," the general growled, "Zofia would send me to the kitchen."

Alex smiled. The contradiction was obvious. If Rasputin were a middle-class shopkeeper rather than a peasant boasting mystic powers from heaven, the finely bred ladies would have revolted at his lack of etiquette. Such was not the case. They watched with thrilled gazes. Rasputin's un-polished behavior was thought childlike and innocent, accentuating his availability to God. Alex had heard that this characteristic was one that especially appealed to the czar and czarina.

General Roskov finished his refreshment and set the glass down with a rap of impatience. "Look at my daughter. Something must be done about this, Alex. I'll not have her joining a group of silly women who've become this charlatan's disciples."

"Agreed, sir, but as long as the czarina acclaims him, it will be difficult to convince Tatiana that he is unworthy."

"Yes, I realize that. He claims he's been called to St. Petersburg to serve as the czarina's personal starets."

"Just so, General. It's bound to bring more division at a time when we need to speak with one voice to the enemy."

"Some in the Duma worry over the czarina's dependence on him. You heard him say he answers her questions by putting them under his pillow? What if those questions begin to involve choosing men for cabinet posts or the direction of battles? It will lead to disaster. Questions on paper under his pillow," the general snorted. "Isn't that a pile of poppycock? Can you imagine the confusion?"

"Surely Czar Nicholas won't permit him that kind of power, sir."

"Czar Nicholas is a courageous man, but the czarina holds great sway over his heart. He's a devout family man. He'll not deny her. The young Prince Alexei's disease puts much stress on both of them, and she is convinced their son will live only as long as Rasputin is there to keep him alive. The czar will not send the man away."

"An incredible tragedy, sir."

Alex watched Rasputin take Tatiana's hand in his. Her docile compliance angered Alex. She was looking at Rasputin as though he were the great apostle Paul.

"Are you going to permit that, General?"

"Look at my wife, and then tell me to stop it."

Madame Zofia stood beside her daughter, one hand on her shoulder, a look of humored kindness on her face as she watched Rasputin.

"When I stated that something must be done, I meant it," General Roskov murmured. "The question is what? I'll tell you this—there will be a secret meeting in September. We must convince Czar Nicholas to send Rasputin back to Siberia. Now that you're in the Okhrana, Alex, you may be called upon to play a part. In the meantime, try to talk sense to Tatiana."

"I'll do what I can, sir. Your daughter has ambitions to please the czarina that are not easily turned aside."

"Yes, it's the same with her mother. Sometimes I envy my brother-in-law, Josef Peshkov. He lives a quiet life, growing wheat for the czar and teaching history at a local college. And look at his daughters. Both have sound heads on their shoulders. Do you see them over there gaping at Rasputin?"

"No sir." Alex looked over at Karena. She was talking to her sister. A moment later, they both slipped away.

"Perhaps I could also have your niece speak to Tatiana about Rasputin."

"Yes, a good idea." He clapped Alex on the shoulder and then left the room.

Alex scowled to himself. He went out onto the cool terrace to think. The general's words returned: *"Now that you're in the Okhrana, Alex, you may be called upon to play a part."*

FIVE

Disenchantment

Flowers lined the flagstone walkway to the Roskov summerhouse where colored-glass lamps glowed, dangling over the porch. Inside, the candles gleamed in golden sconces. As the orchestra played, dancers moved gracefully across the polished floor of the ballroom, the rainbow of gowns complementing the black-and-white finery of the men.

Alex was late in attending. He'd returned to his room in a hopeless mood. He must end the growing attraction between Karena and himself. It could not be allowed to drag on, not if he was to please General Roskov and move on to the life he had chosen for himself.

"This is absurd!"

"What is, sir?" Konni asked.

"How a woman—a complete stranger—breaks suddenly upon the scene like a storm and leaves a man's plans in ruin!"

"Just so."

"Well, it's not going to be that way, Konni. Reason is going to conquer emotion. I've made up my mind. My plans are settled. I'm going through with them. Besides, the general has informed me of how much protection Miss Tatiana needs. If I abandon her now, it would be worse than going through with the engagement. She needs someone to look after her."

"If you say so, sir. But it seems to me, you should select the best situation for your own life. It's not all that fair for General Roskov to hand his daughter over to your care if you're not in love with her. He's taking advantage of your honor, sir, and your sense of duty. Duty to Miss Tatiana isn't the same thing as true love. If you've got a heart for Miss Red Hat, then she might be the right one for you."

"Life doesn't work so easily, Konni. Duty and honor play integral roles in one's decisions. I can't just turn my back and walk away because a pretty face comes along."

"No sir, and if I may take the liberty, that's not what this is about. You've seen many pretty faces recently besides Miss Peshkova's. I hate to see you walk away before you understand why this one seems different."

"I can't play with fire. It's time to end it. I have my work to do…" He gestured to the pristine uniform laid out on his bed. "How did you get the wine out?"

"I wasn't able to wash it out, sir. Your jacket is hanging in the wardrobe, a testimony to the arrogance of Captain Yevgenyev. This one was delivered this afternoon by Madame Zofia."

"Does it fit?" Alex frowned at the dress jacket. If there was anything he despised, it was a jacket too tight across the shoulders.

"It is precise, sir. I measured twice. How she came up with this one, Madame did not explain."

"As long as it fits," Alex repeated firmly.

"Try it on, sir. You had best make speed. You've two women waiting for you."

Alex gave him a scowl as Konni's mouth twitched with restrained humor.

Alex fastened the brass buttons on the white dress military jacket and reluctantly departed for the ball.

At the bottom landing, he looked across the entranceway to the ballroom, where the glittering chandelier cast its radiance upon the dance floor awhirl with color.

He stood near the wide arch leading into the ballroom and saw Tatiana, who had added a net of pearls to her blue-black hair. The orchestra was playing a composition by the great Tchaikovsky. Tatiana was waltzing with Fyodor and smiling with enough charm to tantalize the calf-eyed medical student into revisiting his dreams of conquest. Alex remembered her wish to lead off the dancing with him.

If she breaks her word to me and asks him about his mother's jewelry…

He turned away and scanned the floor for Karena. She was dancing with the count's son.

Karena noticed Alex's arrival. She'd been covertly glancing about for the last twenty minutes. Now that he'd entered and was looking in her direction, she tried to calm her beating heart.

"I think I shall sit this waltz out, Count Philipov…"

"Some refreshment perhaps, Miss Peshkova?"

She raised her fan and, lowering her lashes, was able to steal a glance to the side of the room. *Alex is coming.* He'd entered the palmed arch and was edging his way around the perimeter of the floor toward her.

"Um…yes, a lemon water will do wonderfully, thank you."

Count Philipov left, and Karena swished her fan as Alex bowed, straightened, and smiled. "This is my dance, Miss Peshkova, I believe."

She accepted his hand, and he led her onto the floor. As his arm went around her waist and his hand closed about hers, her heart beat rapidly. For a few minutes, he was hers. If Tatiana were watching with a hard look of jealousy, it did not matter while the music played and they danced in perfect harmony.

"The moment I laid eyes on you, I knew it would mean trouble," he whispered.

It would be wise not to let him know she understood their attraction. Instead, she asked, "Because of Sergei?"

He lifted a brow. "Sergei?"

"My brother. Sergei Peshkov. You asked my cousin about my possible interest in the strike for the factory workers in St. Petersburg in May. Tatiana said you rode with the czar's Cossacks and broke up the demonstration."

"I knew you weren't with your brother. I'd have remembered you. You are, Miss Peshkova, very memorable."

She could have swooned. Instead, she lifted her brow. She was amazed at her own composure. "I know nothing of the sort, Colonel. And I hope you don't think we're Bolsheviks."

"Are you?"

"I'm loyal to my czar and the Romanov family."

"And your brother?"

She hesitated. Sergei was a dedicated socialist.

"I don't speak for Sergei. If you knew him, you'd realize why. He doesn't need any help articulating his beliefs."

"Most Bolsheviks don't. You can hardly get two of them together without a brawl."

She narrowed her gaze. "Are you trying to provoke me, Colonel? You work for the secret police, and you ask me to incriminate my brother?"

"When I said you meant trouble, Miss Peshkova, I was not thinking of my commitment to the secret police."

She tore her gaze from his. She wasn't about to take the bait and inquire what he *did* mean.

"My cousin Tatiana, your fiancée, is exceedingly jealous of you," she stated. "I'm afraid even this one waltz will upset her."

"I am not officially engaged to her. Nor have I vowed my love and commitment. She's assumed as much because she wants it that way."

"And you do not?"

"I have my reasons for going with the tide. I admit the engagement is expected—by her and, more importantly, by General Roskov. Still, I'm not a prisoner unless I decide it's what I want."

"Is it his expectations, then, that mean more to you than Tatiana's?"

"I've cooperated this past year with all of their expectations for reasons of my own. No one twisted my arm about Tatiana. Nor am I easily pressed into a marriage I don't think will benefit my plans. Perhaps I am shocking you? I'm sorry, but I'm speaking the facts—hard, cold, and true. Would you care to hear the rest of my confession, Miss Peshkova?"

No, I would not. She was dazed by his blunt assessment. Her emotions were in brutal conflict. In one heartbeat she had hoped he did not love Tatiana, and in the next, she was offended that he would consider marriage when he did not.

"No, it does not concern me, Colonel."

"Oh, but it does, and I'm sure you realize it."

She kept silent but felt herself blushing.

"I shall confess, regardless," he said. "I've considered marriage to the general's daughter because she *is* the general's daughter. He can further my career in the military in the years to come."

She looked at him, trying to meet his warm, brittle gaze with a steadiness that matched his own. "I didn't take you for such a callous man, Colonel Kronstadt."

"Callous?"

"Well, I can only think that a man who'd marry a woman he wasn't in love with for military advancement must be wretchedly cold-hearted."

"And terribly unfair to your sensitive cousin."

"Yes, that too."

A crooked smile lifted his mouth. "Anything else?"

"Need I say more? The music is ending, and I think we'd best conclude our conversation."

"Without knowing why your poor cousin is willing to marry such a wretchedly cold man?"

"Well, it's all quite obvious, isn't it? You've deceived her. She's in love with you, and you've taken advantage of her. She has my sympathy."

His mouth tipped at one corner. "She is not the one who is beguiled. I think you should know why your cousin so wishes to marry me."

"It's none of my concern," she said loftily.

"Nevertheless, I've begun an explanation and would like to finish it, please."

She looked at him mutely. This was her first meeting with him that had romantic potential, and it had turned into a battleground. Idealistic thoughts had come crashing down upon her. The dashing Colonel Kronstadt was a cool, arrogant cad.

And yet—despite this realization, she was surprised with herself for continuing to talk with him. *Have I gone mad since I stepped off the steamer?*

"General Viktor wishes our marriage. He's told his daughter that if she doesn't agree to marry me, the Roskov wealth—which, as you probably know, is considerable—will not be left to her discretion. It will be dribbled out in small annual amounts that she considers the wages of the poor. So you see, the marriage is an arranged affair for both of us. She's no more in love with me than I am with her."

"Tatiana *is* in love with you. She's green with jealousy whenever you look at another woman."

"It's jealousy over a fortune she fears could slip through her fingers."

"I think all of this is dreadful—"

"You know as well as I that arranged marriages are as old as the Bible."

"Arranged marriages are common, but it's not something I wish for *my* future—" She stopped abruptly as Ilya came to mind. Ilya Jilinsky, the young man her father wished her to marry. He'd already mentioned a possible arrangement before Ilya might join the army, should war come.

His brow arched. "You were saying?"

"I do not wish to speak of it. And I don't know why you are saying all this to me."

"Fibbing, Miss Peshkova, doesn't become one so idealistic. Perhaps I wanted to confess in order to shock you. To make you turn your back on me and walk away."

The music stopped. She stood looking at him, angry, hurt, and yes, disenchanted. From the glimmer of something aching in his own gaze, she believed he spoke the truth. He was deliberately driving a wedge between them.

"If you walk away now, I won't need to reconsider my plans… If you decide not to, then you would make it difficult for me."

Of all the temerity! "Colonel, there is no need for you to worry. I think you're the most awful and arrogant officer I've ever met."

He bowed gravely.

She turned on her heel and walked away, looking straight ahead. She blinked hard.

He didn't love Tatiana, yet he would marry her if the union furthered the one thing he cared about: his military career.

And I had thought him so dashing, so honorable. The most handsome man I've ever met. This ends all my silly notions about romance. I hope I never see him again. Two weeks I shall be here. I must find ways to avoid the scoundrel.

Alex watched as she walked away with shoulders back and head high. Understanding the loss he'd just sustained in exchange for his career, he clenched his jaw. He'd made a deliberate choice tonight. He'd gotten what he wanted—at least, he told himself he had.

Forget her. Your path is laid out in the direction you need to go.

True, finding himself in the Okhrana was a setback, but the general had assured him the change would be temporary. In a year or so, he would be promoted again, to the czar's personal bodyguard.

She thinks you're a man who mocks love and honors the steel of sword and gun. Now she won't tempt you to throw it all away.

Alex was turning to leave the ball when he spotted the ensign who served as his messenger in St. Petersburg. The young man stood in the archway, holding an envelope.

Alex left the ballroom and joined him in the hall.

"For General Roskov from Major-General Durnov, sir."

Alex looked at the envelope. Durnov was not in St. Petersburg but in Kiev. Why would that be?

He released the ensign to sample the food and drink. "Don't stray far. I may need to send a reply to Durnov."

"Just so, Colonel. Thank you, sir.

Alex located General Roskov in the library, enjoying the reprieve of his leather-bound books.

"From Major-General Durnov, sir," Alex said, handing him the envelope.

The general took the letter to his desk, opened it, and read.

Now what? Alex thought. He had a premonition that his status at Kazan would be affected.

The general stroked his honey red mustache. He frowned. A few moments later, he looked at Alex.

"This is unpleasant and rather personal, Alex. Durnov informs me of an arrest at the local college near Kiev where my wife's brother Josef Peshkov teaches history. His colleague, Professor Chertkov, was arrested for spreading revolutionary ideas to his students. Chertkov claims he's innocent. The local gendarmes found books by Hegel, Kant, Marx, and Engels in his desk. Also a dozen of Lenin's Bolshevik newspapers."

"So many books stashed in his desk strikes me as overdone, sir."

"Yes…I don't like this. Sergei highly regarded Professor Chertkov. And both my nieces took his classes at the college. They'll be upset over the news." He rubbed his forehead. "This arrest will not go over well with the students and instructors. The local chief of the gendarmes, a man named Grinevich, expects the worst. It seems a Bolshevik meeting turned ugly a year ago, and the group moved to St. Andrew's Church. When Grinevich arrived, shooting erupted. The Bolshies broke windows and set a room ablaze. Grinevich falsely blamed the Bolshevik Jews. He ordered a brutal retaliation, and by the time the truth came out, a woman and child had been killed and a rabbi beaten."

"Was Grinevich ever called to answer for his rash action, sir?"

General Roskov looked at him, surprised. "Of course not. It was a mistake. The point is, he's afraid the same violence might break out again and wants soldiers to back up his police."

The general pushed Durnov's letter aside and sat down on the edge of the desk. He removed a cigarette from a silver box and stared at it thoughtfully.

Alex took a box of matches from his shirt pocket and dutifully lit the general's cigarette.

"Durnov has requested that I send you to aid his investigation. You will be reporting to him. Unfortunately, Alex"—he inhaled deeply and then scowled—"Count Yevgenyev is over Durnov."

"I'm fully aware, sir."

"I haven't written Count Yevgenyev about the reckless behavior of his son. I think it best I speak with the count directly, after I return to St. Petersburg. Don't expect much from Durnov with the count overseeing his work. He'll be looking out for his own neck."

"I understand, General."

"As soon as I can, I'll get you transferred back to the Okhrana."

"I was hoping for a return to the Imperial Cavalry, sir."

"You'll be needed here. In the meantime, Durnov expects Captain Gusinsky and his half dozen to arrive with you. You are to collect information on Chertkov and go to St. Petersburg. This matter in Kiev won't supersede the Duma's concerns about Rasputin. The secret police will have their plans in place by September or October. After watching Rasputin tonight," he said, displeasure hardening his face, "it's clear his influence must end."

He stood and clasped Alex's shoulder affectionately. "I'll be joining you in St. Petersburg in the fall. Zofia and Tatiana will be anxious to return since your time with us has come to an end."

"Tatiana will be disappointed, but I'll see that she understands."

Alex left the general's study, troubled. He found himself becoming more entrenched in work he neither wanted nor approved of. The cords that he'd first visualized as a means to advancement and freedom were threatening to become chains of iron.

He went upstairs to his room to inform Konni he would be leaving at dawn.

Part Two

❦

The harvest is past,
The summer is ended,
And we are not saved!

Jeremiah 8:20

Six

The Secret Meeting

August 1914, Kiev

The August moon ascended above the vast Peshkov fields of ripened wheat like a mammoth globe of shimmering gold. Across the sky, trails of fiery red, deepening into copper, drifted over the distant steppes. Karena, flanked by Sergei and Ilya Jilinsky, walked along the dusty wagon road between the fields awarded to the family more than two generations earlier by the grandfather of Czar Nicholas II.

The warm, scented winds stirred, bringing the fragrance of rich vegetation, baked earth, and a copious harvest. Dust stirred up around Karena's high-button shoes, and she worried about soiling her lace-hemmed, red and white skirt. She wanted to look intelligent and professional when she met Dr. Lenski's son Petrov and his sister Ivanna at the Bolshevik meeting that evening.

"You worry too much, Ilya," Sergei continued. "Nothing will go wrong. The meeting will be safe. No one even knows Lenski's here."

Ilya's brows, made fair by the long, hot summer in the fields, formed a straight furrow above the bridge of his nose. He shoved his sun-browned hands deeper into his trouser pockets, a behavior Karena knew indicated he was not convinced.

Sergei, with dark hair and eyes, was, on the other hand, typically smiling, though his demeanor was often hard and joyless.

"The Okhrana knows everything," Ilya said a moment later, his quiet voice loud with insinuation. "The secret police have been prowling about ever since Professor Chertkov was arrested two months ago."

"Of course they know," Sergei snapped. "The czar's secret police have infiltrated all the socialist groups. But Lenski's smart. Smart enough not to trust anyone outside his immediate friends, which includes me," he boasted, striking his thumb against his chest.

When Sergei returned home this summer after his second year at St. Petersburg University, he'd made new friends who venerated Lenin, Trotsky, and Stalin. She knew Papa Josef was worried about his increasing zeal, but Sergei made light of his father's fears, throwing his strong arms around him and laughing, telling him not to worry. Karena set her mouth grimly, her thoughts straying to Colonel Kronstadt and his interest in Sergei's activities. She'd not seen him since he suddenly departed the Roskov summerhouse the night of the ball. Afterward, Tatiana had explained his absence had something to do with a mission near Kiev. When Karena and Natalia returned home after their two-week visit, Alex had already left for his new position in St. Petersburg at the Winter Palace.

"I've heard the czar's soldiers are passing through on their way to Poland," Ilya said. "If there's any trouble with Lenski, they'll be on us like hawks. Karena, it's too much of a risk. Don't go."

"Ivanna Lenski will be there. I simply must meet her," she insisted. Ilya's protective spirit was beginning to trouble her. She didn't want him to care so much. She had plans for the future, and they did not yet include marriage, although Grandmother Jilinsky hoped they would marry soon, as did Papa Josef.

On the issue of medical school, there'd been no correspondence from Fyodor about delivering her letter to his father. She was beginning to think he'd forgotten. She was, however, anticipating an answer to the letter she'd sent Dr. Lenski. Perhaps it would come tonight through Ivanna. Oddly, Madame Yeva had, in the past, tried to dissuade Karena from contacting her old friend.

Karena frowned as she walked, her thoughts straying from their discussion to her mother's behavior. Perhaps it could be attributed to the shock she'd received when Natalia tearfully confessed that she had taken the jeweled pendant. Mother had nearly become ill over it.

I can't let her know I've already written Dr. Lenski. And what of Sergei's relationship with her daughter?

Sergei was romancing Ivanna, whom he'd met while attending the university, but he was keeping her a secret.

So much is wrong in this family, Karena thought unhappily. *So many secrets.*

Sergei cast Ilya a glower of impatience. "Do you think I'd bring my own sister if I thought there was danger? I tell you, Ilya, not even the secret police know Lenski's returned to Russia. They think he's in Geneva with Lenin. He disguises himself. How do you think Lenin and Trotsky pass in and out of the country?"

Sergei was apt to be right. He had told her earlier that Lenski had served two years in the mines in the Ural Mountains. The revolutionary groups that formed the various socialist and communist movements in Imperial Russia had caused havoc throughout the summer, and Karena had heard of several assassination attempts on czarist officials. Lenski had to know his presence would not be well received.

"There are risks and dangers, but is nothing worth taking a stand for?" Sergei continued. "Be tolerant and do not feel strongly about any cause, lest you get criticism from an opponent. Right, Ilya?"

"No, that's not right. Some things are worth standing up for," Ilya said, stopping on the dusty wagon road, facing Sergei. "And others only divert our energy and waste us. In my opinion, the meeting tonight is not worth the risk of facing the Okhrana, and I don't think you should allow Karena to go. I have but one life. I want to make sure it is spent on a worthy cause."

Sergei's sun-bronzed face turned thoughtful, and he clasped Ilya's shoulder. "You're right. You must not become involved. Grandmother Jilinsky needs you; so does my father. We all need you in the family." He grinned now. "If you don't manage the peasants, then I must. You must take over as manager of the wheat lands, so I can go to New York and train to be a journalist."

Ilya smiled. "I doubt if I'll live to see the day when your father lets you become a journalist, least of all in New York. You'd better be content to become the lawyer he wants in the family."

"I'll join the army before I take up the boredom of being a lawyer in Russia." Sergei turned to Karena, spreading his hands. "Well, Sister, the choice is yours. Will you come to the meeting or walk back to the manor with Ilya? If you go home, perhaps I can arrange for you to meet Ivanna and Lenski some other time."

Karena turned to Ilya. Her eyes pleaded with his to avoid a struggle.

"I asked Sergei to let me come with him tonight," she admitted, attempting to strengthen her earlier explanation. "Ivanna attends the Imperial College of Medicine in St. Petersburg. I want very much to talk with her."

At the mention of the medical school, Ilya seemed to understand. After a moment of silence, he shrugged his shoulders.

"It is not for me to tell you." He glanced from her to Sergei, then turned and began walking away.

Her gaze followed him, a solitary figure taking a shortcut through the gently rippling wheat, soon becoming a distant silhouette. He was on his way to the bungalow where he lived with Grandmother Jilinsky and, more recently, Uncle Matvey.

Karena was aware that if she chose to do so, she could follow Ilya to the bungalow where a wholesome supper cooked by Grandmother Jilinsky waited. Afterward, she could enjoy an evening on the front porch with Uncle Matvey. She could even now make the decision to forget the college of medicine and settle into a married life of raising children, growing wheat, and overseeing the peasants. It would be a good life, and though Ilya did not stir the passion that Alex had during their brief encounter, she had a quiet affection for him. But she could not make that decision now. Another love was wooing her heart—medicine, midwifery, and spending her years serving others. *Perhaps I shall never marry.*

Sergei, noticing her contemplation, flipped her golden braid. "Stop worrying, Sister. He will get over his feelings. He is more reasonable than most. He's upset because you did not do as he wanted." He sobered, and his dark eyes took on a thoughtful glint as he looked toward the horizon.

"Besides, Sister," he continued in a quiet voice, "Ilya's right about the war coming. Did you hear about the assassination?"

"Oh no, not the czar—"

"No, Archduke Franz Ferdinand of Austria, a few weeks ago. There will be war now for certain. Already, thousands of German soldiers are massed along the borders of Poland. It could be days or hours, but soon, someone will fire the first shot, and the war will begin. You know what that means for us?" She knew, and the thought ravaged her soul. Young men full of bright ideas, hopes, and dreams would be blown to pieces.

"Ilya will find himself conscripted. Most of the young peasants will be called up. Ilya was right about the czar's soldiers riding this way en route to Poland. And you can be sure they will take many peasants with them. I, being gentry, will not be conscripted, but eventually, I will be called to uniform too." He looked at her, troubled. "This is not the time to think of marriage with Ilya—or anyone else."

Sergei understood her heart well; he always had.

"Come, or we may be late," he said. "Ivanna should be there by now." Lenski's talk would be held on the grassy square at the college from which Sergei and Karena had graduated several years earlier and where Natalia was in her final year—the college where Professor Chertkov had taught before his arrest. The professor and five other revolutionaries had been brought to the Peter and Paul prison fortress in St. Petersburg for trial. The verdict—a death sentence—was handed down weeks ago, but the dark news had arrived in Kiev yesterday with Lenski. News of tonight's meeting to protest Professor Chertkov's death sentence had gone out by way of the Bolshevik underground.

"There are many of us," Sergei admitted. "I don't believe in their use of violence, assassination, and murder, but I see no other hope to end autocratic rule over the Russian people than to organize in opposition to the Romanovs."

"But you could go to the gallows. You must keep talking to Uncle Matvey. He supports more authority for the Duma to enact laws."

"A parliament, yes, but what happens?" he scoffed. "When the Duma meets, their criticism of Rasputin enrages the czarina. She becomes hysterical over the threat to her 'darling Rasputin' and insists the czar disband the Duma and send them home—as though they were children."

Karena kept silent and followed Sergei to the familiar stand of chestnut trees, planted as a windbreak beside the dusty road to town. He'd hidden one of the horses here so that Papa Josef wouldn't hear him riding away from the manor house after dinner. She had waited for him to leave by the kitchen door as planned, and she followed a short time later, undetected by the other members of the family.

As they came to the stand of trees, Sergei untied the horse, mounted, and helped Karena up behind him, her arms around his waist.

"Professor Chertkov was arrested on lies," Sergei told her as they rode off in the moonlight. "Even the Bolshevik leaders say Chertkov wasn't one of them. It was a false charge, all because the professor openly stated support for a few human rights for the factory workers on strike in St. Petersburg. It seems incriminating books were planted in his desk, and copies of Lenin's little newspaper *Iskra* were found in a box. It was all a blatant trap. I think it was the rat, Grinevich."

Karena knew how Sergei detested the chief gendarme. He insisted Grinevich had personally hounded him since youth because of his refusal to quietly accept the man's corrupt authority.

"You weren't here when Professor Chertkov was arrested," Sergei continued. "There was a riot on the green. Grinevich ordered his police to beat several students as well as a hapless old man named Pavel who wandered into the demonstration and had nothing to do with the trouble. Pavel died from a concussion. Did the czar send someone to look into it? No. Pavel was only an uneducated peasant.

"There was no justice for Professor Chertkov; he's dead. Lenski says he was taken out of Peter and Paul with five other revolutionaries and hanged."

He looked at her over his shoulder, his face hard. In the moonlight, his eyes radiated frustration. The intensity of his emotions worried her. He'd always been volatile and impulsive. Where could his indignation lead but to trouble?

Yet she understood his anger. Professor Chertkov was a gentle man, one of her favorite instructors. His death was nothing less than murder, she decided. From the philosophy of his teaching, she was certain he had not been a Bolshevik.

They reached the college grounds, and Sergei concealed the horse by a shallow creek under a stand of trees. He hurried toward the college square and across the grass to the meeting. Karena followed, her thoughts now on Ivanna. Would there be a letter tonight from Dr. Lenski?

Sergei paused on the grass until she caught up.

"What if someone notices we've gathered tonight? They might alert the police."

He shook his head with impatience. "We have a man watching Grinevich's house. Should he leave and start in this direction, we will be notified. Students gather on the green for picnics all the time. Stop worrying. We must not show ourselves cowards in the face of tyranny."

When they arrived, the meeting was under way on the far side of the campus. The late summer's night air was warm. The leaves on the linden trees lining one section of the green shuddered, as if tired from the long, demanding heat wave. Two torches burned, but Sergei insisted that the firelight and the gathering were not cause for alarm. Even so, Karena remained uneasy. He wouldn't hesitate to err on the side of recklessness.

Petrov Lenski looked to be in his late twenties, a medium-sized man with a square build, and when he turned toward the crowd, his face glowed from the torches. He stood on a makeshift platform of stacked harvest crates, and his voice carried venom as he cursed the autocracy for the unfair arrest and death sentence carried out against Chertkov. While Karena was familiar with the views of revolutionary groups, hearing the arguments for revolution in public caused her to shudder. *Must he speak so loudly?* It seemed the entire town could hear.

"Where is Ivanna?" Her voice broke with low urgency.

Sergei glanced about the group on the green. He shoved his hands in his pockets. Karena read a shadow of disappointment that flicked across his face. "I don't see her yet."

"Sergei! You are certain she is coming?"

"How can I be certain of anything?" he hissed.

"You usually are." She smiled wryly.

"She was supposed to be here. I've no reason to trick you."

Karena, however, knew he was always trying to talk her into joining his revolutionary friends.

"In his letter, Lenski said Ivanna was coming with him from St. Petersburg. Maybe she's just late—you know women. She may have decided to remain at the house where they're staying, with a headache or something. We'll just need to wait and ask Lenski after his talk."

Karena swallowed a lump of disappointment. She was not interested in Lenski's harangue against the czar. Perhaps Ivanna had not come to Kiev after all. Her plans might have changed.

Despite her deflated mood, Karena surveyed the crowd hoping to see a woman whom Sergei earlier described as having auburn hair and a sophisticated demeanor. If Ivanna were here, though, she should have noticed Sergei and joined him.

Karena looked at her brother. His broad, handsome face, tanned by long days in the family wheat fields, glistened with perspiration. His gaze was fixed on Lenski, whose rhetoric boiled with volcanic intensity.

Worried, she began looking about to see who was here and whether they posed any danger. She discovered the usual people she'd gone to school with, plus a few strangers, probably from the more populous districts of Kiev. The throng contained mostly men, though at least a dozen women were scattered among them, many Karena's age. Many of these women would soon be leaving the farming village to work in the large factories of Moscow and St. Petersburg.

The young men stood with their arms folded across sweat-stained *bushka* shirts, nodding in agreement with Lenski. Several older men from the Odessa region were scowling; one formed a calloused fist and smashed it against his other palm. Sometimes they looked at one another in agreement as a babble of voices broke out in anger.

"That's right," Sergei called out.

"Yes, yes," another shouted.

Karena grew more uncomfortable, though no one appeared to notice her, their attention riveted on the speaker. She tried to think of something else and noticed the young woman, Anna.

Anna lived with her brother and his wife in a peasant bungalow on Peshkov land and worked with the other women in the fields. Did her brother know she was here alone at the protest? It was a well-known secret that Sergei had been seeing Anna all summer, despite his more serious interest in Ivanna. Anna did not appear to notice Karena, or was it that she had eyes only for Sergei?

Karena did not recall Anna ever displaying interest in revolutionary ideas, but perhaps she came tonight with the hope of impressing Sergei with her new show of intellectualism.

Karena worried about Anna. She was well into her pregnancy, and though Sergei denied he was the father, Karena was not convinced. Papa Josef did not know, but Madame Yeva did, though no decision as yet had been made concerning Anna's future or the child's.

As she looked back toward Lenski, Karena's gaze tumbled upon a man standing in the shadows on the outer edge of the crowd. Had he been watching her? She did not recognize him; the hat tipped low on his forehead obscured his face.

He turned away, reaching inside his battered bushka. He took out a cigarette, turned his shoulder toward her, and struck a match, cupping it in his hand.

Karena looked around. Lenski's verbal blows grew muffled and distant as her mind took shelter from the raw and harsh and focused on the awe-inspiring expanse of night sky. For a curious moment, the full moon appeared to be suspended above the cross on the Russian Orthodox Church of St. Andrew across the street. It captured her emotions and, for a reason she could not explain, suggested rest and peace, yet both were out of her reach. Sadness drenched her soul as she recalled holy days spent with her family at that church. She'd found little there that revealed God.

Karena checked to see if the stranger was still there. He was. She noticed something vaguely curious about the way he stood. It seemed he might be a soldier, but that could hardly be—unless he dared to show up at a meeting such as this. Of course, he could not show up here in uniform. He'd be placed before a firing squad. Unless he was supposed to be here—but that was silly. Her imagination was running away with her. Sergei had sworn the authorities knew nothing of this meeting, so there could not be any soldiers here.

He turned his head in her direction again; she looked away.

Is he one of the friends who came with Lenski from St. Petersburg?

Just then, another latecomer walked up from the street. He looked older, sober faced, with a mustache and short beard—

Dr. Dmitri Zinnovy. What was he doing *here*?

He was the last person she would have suspected of collaboration with the Bolsheviks. Why would someone of his prominence risk an appearance here tonight when his medical reputation had come to the favorable attention of the czarina?

He was known to take long evening walks. Perhaps he'd merely wandered here out of curiosity after noticing the torches and gathered group. That he was in Kiev was not unusual, for he came each year on a work of medical charity, but she'd never seen him before in the village. Through the years, he'd developed a special program with medical practitioners who lacked a full medical degree and worked among the peasants. He held lectures and arranged for medical supplies to be brought to the wilderness regions of Siberia.

Once a year, Madame Yeva sent Karena on the half-day trip to Kiev to the Zinnovy warehouse for supplies, granted because of her past studies at the Imperial College of Medicine and her work in the village.

On one of those visits, Karena had seen the renowned doctor with several practitioners from the frozen regions of Siberia. Dr. Zinnovy was a handsome man, always wearing a black frock coat, a white shirt, and round, rimless spectacles. He would watch the supplies being loaded onto the wagons of those eligible, but he did not speak. She remembered he had an excellent memory, for he knew who she was.

Had he seen her now? Would he recognize her? If he did, what would it mean, if anything?

Lenski's voice cracked like thunder—"Ten years at a work camp in the Urals was not enough to satisfy the czar! Professor Chertkov was hanged, yes, *hanged*!"

A murmur rippled through the crowd. "*Our* Professor Chertkov, *hanged*?"

"Yes," Lenski shouted, "that gentle and decent elderly intellectual was *murdered* by the czar and his henchmen. And during the professor's agony, no doubt the czarina—that foreigner, that *German*—entertained Rasputin, a debauched drinker of spirits and adulterer, in her gold and satin parlor, eating dainties. She cares nothing for the ordinary Russian people! And what was the professor's crime? He called for justice for the factory workers in St. Petersburg. Men and women just like you labor eighteen hours a day for mere coins! While she hand-feeds Rasputin with sweets, the workers can barely afford to buy a loaf of bread for their children. But the czarina entertains her lapdog Rasputin with *German* chocolates."

The crowd's murmur swelled like a wave of the sea.

Those trying to get closer to Lenski jostled Karena. For one of the few times in their lives, they were hearing someone voice their frustrations—their growing anger with the Imperial autocracy.

Karena shot a glance at her brother. Sergei's face revealed his intense concentration. His eyes sparked and alarmed her. Karena could see how this flood of enraged speech shared by hundreds of thousands of Russians could become a tidal wave, drowning the land in violence.

Sergei unbuttoned his shirt collar, tossed his bushka over his shoulder, and raised a fist of support to Lenski.

The wind rushed through the trees on the college square and whipped her long red and white skirt about her ankles.

"Down with Policeman Grinevich!" snarled a voice from the throng. "He's the one to blame for the professor's arrest."

"Grinevich is a murderer!" another voice shouted.

"Yes! A murderer who hides behind a gendarme's uniform!"

"Down with Grinevich! Down with the czar!"

Sergei pushed forward toward the platform, and Karena caught his sleeve to stop him, but it slipped through her desperate fingers.

"No, Sergei," she cried.

Sergei leaped up onto the wooden harvest boxes beside his friend. Lenski laughed, slapped him on the back, and beckoned him to speak.

Karena's nails dug into her palms.

"It is Grinevich who has terrorized us in this town," Sergei called. "How many of your friends have been beaten senseless by his thugs? How many accused of crimes they did not commit?"

"Too many!"

Karena saw angry, flushed faces all about her now. Rage was like an epidemic, and it did not take many words to spread the hatred until all were infected.

She looked across the lawn to see how the stranger was reacting. He was gone. She skimmed her gaze along the perimeter and saw that Dr. Zinnovy had also slipped away.

"What of old Pavel?" someone called. "Did not Grinevich accuse him of stealing horses? Where is Pavel now, after the beating?"

"Dead," the voices called back. "Pavel is dead."

"There are too many dead Pavels. Too many dead Professor Chertkovs," Sergei called back. "Dead because of Grinevich the bribe-taker, Grinevich the thief, Grinevich the murderer!"

"Down with the swine!"

Karena pushed her way closer toward the wooden box platform. "Sergei!—"

But as the throng surged forward, she was squeezed out and pushed back toward the outer edge of the crowd.

"Lower your voices!" someone called out.

"Oy!" someone shouted. "Police! Run!"

Confusion spread quickly, and Karena was overwhelmed by the retreating crowd. "Sergei!"

"Look! It's the murderer. Get him! Get him!"

"Karena! Run!" Sergei's shout came to her from somewhere ahead.

People fled into the night, swallowed by inky shadows. Others held their ground and then surged forward, straight for Policeman Grinevich. In the darkness and confusion, it looked to Karena as though Grinevich's own police had abandoned him to the attackers.

Karena sought for Sergei but could not see him. Had he escaped?

Then she saw a group of men surround Grinevich. Though a big man, he was wrestled down to the grass. Fists smashed into him with vengeance. Booted feet kicked. The night breezes carried the sounds of grunts and thuds.

Karena turned her head, sickened at the sounds. She reacted blindly to the horror, starting toward those who were beating Grinevich, but strong fingers caught hold of her arm and pulled her back across the lawn toward the shadows. She whirled to confront her captor.

Small, round spectacles gleamed in the moonlight.

"Dr. Zinnovy!" she gasped.

"Run into the trees at once, hurry," he commanded and then disappeared.

SEVEN

The Black Carriage

Dazed, Karena fled into the darkness as police whistles shrieked in the night.

I should have listened to Ilya. The police would know she'd been present at the gathering tonight. Sergei would not escape detection this time, as he had in St. Petersburg. They could both be detained in Peter and Paul prison.

She dashed back to the trees where Sergei had tied the horse—

It *was gone.* She whirled, scanning the area. Had Sergei escaped and left her?

No, not Sergei. Her brother was reckless at times, but he'd not leave her in danger.

She made a quick search in case the horse had wandered, but she knew Sergei would have tied the reins securely.

She ran back to the road and looked in both directions. Except for the crackling of dry leaves in the little bursts of wind, there was nothing.

Then, farther down the road came the sound of approaching hoof-beats and the rush of carriage wheels. She stepped back in caution. A moment later, a black carriage stormed into view, the driver in a red cap with a short, dark cloak floating behind. The passenger thrust his head out the window, peering along the road. As the carriage came closer, she saw with a burst of relief that it was Dr. Zinnovy. She stepped to the roadside and lifted her hand. He told the driver to stop and swung open the carriage door. "Quickly, inside."

Karena put her foot on the carriage step prepared to climb to safety when policemen burst from the darkened trees.

"Halt! In the name of the czar!"

Karena turned her head. Her spirits crashed to the dust. Men she recognized from the local gendarmes bolted toward the carriage.

She stood still. The horses snorted, and her heart thumped in her ears.

Leonovich, Policeman Grinevich's second in command, strode up. His lecherous gaze betrayed his thoughts. "Eh? Well now. So it's *you*, Miss Peshkova?"

"Yes, it's me. Is there any trouble? If you'll excuse me, sir, I'm in a hurry—"

"Hold on there, miss. I thought I was chasing down that girlfriend of your troublemaking brother."

"Anna? I haven't seen her since she was working our fields this morning, just as she always does. I'm most certain she's home with her brother and his wife, eating supper."

Dr. Zinnovy leaned out with great bluster. "What is the meaning of this delay, Constable?"

"Uh, good evening, Dr. Zinnovy, sir. I didn't know it was you. Mind telling me where you've come from?"

"Certainly not. From my hotel. What's all this about? A robbery?"

"There's been another Bolshie meeting on the college square. Gendarme Grinevich was attacked and beaten. We must question everyone in the vicinity."

"Surely I am excluded as a revolutionary," came the warning voice.

"Recently I've been called to Tsarskoe Selo to take up residence as a physician to the royal Romanov family."

There came a startled hesitancy. "Just so, sir, just so. I plead your pardon. But this young woman was at the meeting. She was seen by one of our policemen."

"Surely there's an error. Miss Peshkova's been with me, reporting on the medical supervision of the peasants on the Peshkov lands. She left to walk home not more than fifteen minutes ago, but hearing police whistles I rushed here to make sure she was safe. I intend to bring her home to her parents without further delay."

"She was with you, Dr. Zinnovy?"

"She was indeed. Do get in, Miss Peshkova. Schoolmaster Josef will be expecting you." He leaned out the door and held his hand toward her.

Karena stepped into the coach, aware the policeman was unable to resist Dr. Zinnovy's relationship with the Romanovs, at least for the present.

"Good night, gentlemen. I wish you good fortune in your hunt for the disorderly Bolsheviks."

"Yes—Dr. Zinnovy, sir. A good night to you, sir. And to you, Miss Peshkova."

"Thank you," she said, surprised by her own calm.

The coach door closed after she was securely inside, the horses pulled forward, and in a few minutes, she had left the nightmare behind on the dusty road.

Karena looked across the seat at Dr. Zinnovy's grave expression. She heard a breath pass through his lips as he sank back into the coach seat. He removed his spectacles and wiped them with a handkerchief.

"Unwise, very unwise, Miss Peshkova."

"I don't understand why you helped me, Dr. Zinnovy, but if not for you, I would have been arrested. I am in your debt. "

He shook his head. "You owe me nothing."

She looked at him more astutely. His eyes were blue beneath graying black brows. Twenty years ago, he would have been a very handsome man. He placed his spectacles back on the bridge of his nose.

"You were foolish to go there tonight."

"Yes," she admitted, too polite to mention he'd been there as well.

"Mr. Lenski is wanted by the secret police. Any connection with him will place you and your family under the highest suspicion."

"Yes, I—realize that. However, sir, I am not a Bolshevik."

"You would have a most difficult time convincing them. Your brother is reckless. It was most foolish of him to mount the box as he did and begin verbally attacking Policeman Grinevich. What if there'd been a spy in the crowd? Your brother could be arrested and sent to a labor camp."

"Which is his argument, Dr. Zinnovy—men should be respected for freedom of speech."

"I do not disagree. I mean only to warn you that the Okhrana is aware of him. If you were noticed tonight, despite my bluff with the policeman just now, they will be aware of you also."

Has Sergei escaped or is he even now under arrest? And what of Lenski?

The doctor straightened his glasses. "I do not mean to sound as if I'm intruding, but will you tell me why you were at the assembly tonight?"

Dr. Zinnovy was a strong, fatherly figure, and she liked him at once. This was her opportunity—if not to ask for his intervention with the Imperial College of Medicine, then at least to show him how much she desired to attend.

"I went to meet Dr. Lenski's daughter, Ivanna, a student at your medical college. I believe Dr. Lenski is a friendly colleague of yours. My brother knows Ivanna quite well, having met her in St. Petersburg. I'd written Dr. Lenski asking for her help in gaining admittance to the medical program and thought Ivanna might be bringing me a letter tonight from her mother. Ivanna did not show up. For her sake, I'm relieved she did not."

THE MIDWIFE OF ST. PETERSBURG

He appeared thoughtful behind his light blue eyes. "Yes, Dr. Lenski and her daughter Ivanna, of course. I know Dr. Lenski well. She was one of my students."

Karena smiled. "My mother was as well. In fact, she and Dr. Lenski shared a room at the college. Do you remember my mother, sir? Her name then was Yeva Menkin."

He frowned, removing his spectacles and staring at them. Again, he polished them. "Menkin, Menkin... Perhaps... Yes, she was an excellent student. So you wish to follow in her steps, do you?"

Karena leaned forward. "It's been my ambition all my life. I've applied for the medical program, but my mother is Jewish, which means the quota allowed each year is very small. I've been turned down each time."

He said after a moment, "Well, Miss Peshkova, your determination is to be commended. I'll speak to Dr. Lenski when I return to St. Petersburg. Perhaps something can be done."

Excitement and joy flooded her heart. All traces of weariness and fear fled away.

"Dr. Zinnovy, if I'm accepted into the program, I shall be the happiest woman in Kiev!"

She became confused for a moment at the sad, almost apologetic flicker in his smile.

"Then we must see to your happiness, Miss Peshkova. Rest assured, if your parents agree, I shall do what I can to assist your acceptance."

Karena could have thrown her arms around his neck and kissed his cheek, but she did not. She sat primly, her hands clasped so tightly they tingled.

She laughed. "And I thought tonight was going to be the most harrowing of my life! Amidst darkness, there is light. Who would have believed it?"

Dr. Zinnovy made no comment but smiled with pleasure. Her

happiness appeared to affect him deeply. *What a kind and generous man! I shall become one of his best students.*

"I saw you there on the edge of the crowd," she said.

"Yes. I was out walking. I stopped for a few minutes to see what was happening. I recognized Petrov on the soapbox. Dr. Lenski would be grieved to have heard him. She's an ardent supporter of the Romanovs, and she's disowned her son for turning to the Bolsheviks. I'm certain she didn't know Ivanna accompanied him to Kiev."

Despite the tragic situation of the Lenskis, Karena could hardly keep her excitement from brimming over. Only when she remembered Sergei were her emotions dampened. Had he gotten away? If he'd not taken the horse, then who did?

"Anna," she breathed suddenly.

"Anna?"

She looked at Dr. Zinnovy. "A peasant. She works our land." Karena hesitated, wondering how much she should reveal. Since he was a doctor, she didn't feel it necessary to keep Anna's plight hidden.

"Anna's just a girl, but she's in love with Sergei. Sadly, they've made a serious mistake. She's going to have a child. The horse Sergei and I came on is missing. If Anna rode the horse, it could bring on early labor."

"Yes, if she was frightened, she might not consider the consequences."

"She came to the meeting tonight. If she was arrested—"

"Yes?"

"I think she would talk, despite her loyalty to Sergei."

He frowned. "I shall look into the matter. You will want to know your brother escaped with Petrov before the police could encircle them."

Relieved, she lapsed into silence while the carriage approached the manor.

Dr. Zinnovy was peering out the window. "This peasant girl, Anna. I think it wise that I discover how she's faring. Is her family's bungalow nearby?"

"It's not far at all. Shall I inform Madame Yeva to come and assist you, Doctor?"

He looked toward the manor, his face solemn. "No. I think it best not to disturb her. Anna may not have taken your horse. Even if she did, it doesn't necessarily mean she will go into early labor. It depends on her health and how she rode."

"I could go with you and assist," she offered.

"I gather you have had training?"

She smiled. "From the time I was a small child, I followed my mother in her medical mercies whenever she ministered to family, friends, and peasants in the fields, although I've not delivered a child on my own yet."

"If you could carry the lamp for me, my dear, and calm her down when we arrive, that will be of great help to me."

"It will be an honor, sir."

"She may not want her family to know she's been out tonight. We shall use appropriate discretion. We had best waste no time."

I'm actually going to assist the great Dr. Dmitri Zinnovy. Mother will be amazed.

He hadn't wanted Madame Yeva to come with him, although she was by far the more appropriate assistant…

Maybe he simply wants to give me the experience and privilege of going with him.

But why? Then again, why had he helped her at all?

EIGHT

Doctor's Assistant

The oil lamps cast shadows on the walls of the peasant bungalow with a gently sloping roof and thickly dressed logs. The small room, the *gornitsa,* held a bed and an undersized stove. It was usually reserved for guests, but Elena Lavrushsky used it for her sister-in-law, sixteen-year-old Anna.

Both Elena and Yuri, Anna's brother, wore grim faces when Karena was ushered inside. Did they know about the meeting and the police raid? Karena believed they did and that Anna had alarmed them, coming home in such a hurry. Elena was pale and tense. Yuri kept rubbing his palms against his trousers and looking out the window.

"How is Anna?" Karena asked in a low voice.

"She is well. Why do you ask?"

"You need not fear, Elena. You know she was out tonight, don't you?"

She sighed. "Yes, I tried to stop her from going, but she left anyway. She came back in tears, saying there'd been a police raid at the college green. Something about revolutionaries."

Karena explained that Dr. Zinnovy was waiting in the carriage and why they had come. Elena's eyes widened with alarm at the mention of the horse ride. She brought Karena immediately to Anna's bed. The girl was awake, and Karena sensed her tension and fear.

"It's all right, Anna, I'm here to help you. Did you borrow Sergei's horse tonight?"

"Yes…I was so afraid. I didn't think until I was halfway back to the bungalow. The horse is in your stable. The boy Stesha brought him back for me. Are the police coming here?" She grabbed Karena's wrist.

"No, I don't think so. Dr. Zinnovy, a very important man and friend of the czar, will see no harm comes to us. He's outside now in his carriage. We are worried about you. Are you feeling any sickness? Any sudden pains or bleeding?"

Anna's teeth chattered nervously, her brown eyes wide and frightened. She shook her head no. Karena smiled and held her hand, stroking the back of it as her mother had taught her to do to calm a patient.

"Good, then. You are a strong, healthy girl. Maybe we don't need to ask questions. But Dr. Zinnovy is the best doctor in St. Petersburg. He wants to see you and make sure everything is normal."

Anna looked from Karena to Elena. Elena nodded. "It is best, Anna. You will never again have a better doctor."

"Yes, I will see him."

Karena went out and returned a few minutes later with Dr. Zinnovy. He smiled benignly at the shivering girl.

"So this is Anna. Everything is going to be all right. Have you been examined before by a doctor?"

She shook her head no. "Madame Yeva helps me. She's very kind."

Karena looked proudly toward Dr. Zinnovy to see his reaction and was bewildered by a look of pain on his face.

Yuri stepped outside to smoke, and Karena remained with Dr. Zinnovy during Anna's examination. He used special soap he carried inside his bag and asked Elena for hot water from her stove. Only afterward did he place his hands upon Anna's bulging abdomen. With precise movements, he felt the position of the baby. Karena watched his face, but he showed no emotion in the presence of his patient, and Karena had no way of knowing whether all seemed well.

"Anna," he said, his voice grave but confident, "I will not examine you internally. I am concerned your baby is in a delicate condition right now. I do not have all the right medicines and instruments with me. I want you to stay in bed and rest for a few days. Meanwhile, I want Madame Peshkova to send for a doctor from Kiev. I'm going to write down his name and give it to Miss Peshkova. She will give it to her mother in the morning."

Karena looked on, trying not to reveal her concern. If Dr. Zinnovy was afraid that an examination would disturb the baby, then he must be concerned about a miscarriage.

"I'm going to leave some medications with your sister. She can discuss them with Madame Peshkova tomorrow. Right now, I'm going to give you something to help you sleep. It's the best action we can take for your baby and yourself."

He measured certain elixirs, turned them over to a worried Elena, and explained the dosages to her. Karena felt Anna's hand tug at her sleeve. Her eyes searched Karena's. "Is Sergei safe?"

Karena nodded, putting a finger to her lips. They exchanged smiles. Anna looked easier and settled down in her narrow bed.

A short time later, Karena departed the bungalow with Dr. Zinnovy. As the carriage brought them to the gate of the manor house, she turned to him.

"Is Anna in danger of a miscarriage, Dr. Zinnovy?"

"I fear she is. But if she follows my orders, I think it will lessen the possibility." He leaned over and opened the carriage door.

Karena climbed down and turned to face him. "Will you come in, sir?

Schoolmaster Josef and Madame Yeva will wish to thank you for coming to my aid on the road."

"Ah? Do you truly wish for me to inform them that you were at a Bolshevik meeting and that I helped you escape the Okhrana?"

Her face warmed as she considered. "No, Doctor. Neither I, nor Sergei, would want them to know."

"It's wise for me to return to the hotel. I shall be leaving for St. Petersburg early in the morning, and I am confident the Okhrana will call on me tonight with many questions. I shall do my best to keep you out of this trouble, though I cannot promise they will be satisfied. They are most insistent," he said with a touch of acidity. "They will, no doubt, come here, looking for Sergei."

His eyes were cool and firm. "I want you to deny that you were there. My witness that you were with me will hold more sway than anything said to the contrary."

"I don't know how to thank you, Dr. Zinnovy."

"Do not try. Go inside now. I would advise you to go straight to your room and avoid talking to anyone tonight. Give my recommendation for Dr. Novikov to Madame Peshkova in the morning."

She thanked him again and watched the coach pull away until its silhouette faded from view in the moonlight.

Karena stood on the road, looking toward the manor, cheered by the lights glowing in the windows. She listened for Ilya's approach on the gravel path that led from the manor to the bungalow where he lived with Grandmother Jilinsky and Uncle Matvey. She half expected Ilya to be waiting on the porch for her. She heard little except insects humming in the hot night and the rushing sound of the wheat in the breeze. The fragrance of harvest grains filled the air. She refused to dwell on the despicable beating of Grinevich or its inevitable consequences for Sergei, should his presence become known.

If Lenski expected to avoid another prison term in the Urals, he had better escape to neutral Geneva while he could. Soon, news of what had happened tonight would sweep through the telegraph wires, and soldiers and police would check every departing train.

A thought made her heart catch. What if Sergei believed he must flee with Lenski to save himself? She thought of her father. If Sergei disappeared, it would be a heavy blow to Papa Josef.

She hurried toward the manor, the sounds of the night chasing her heels. Sergei's words earlier that evening repeated mockingly in her mind: *"Nothing will go wrong. The meeting will be safe."*

The sound of the wind moving through the miles of wheat was not unlike rushing water. At times she found it the loneliest sound in the world.

An owl swept silently overhead, its wings visible in the moonlight. The moon was nearing the end of its journey for the night, sinking toward the horizon. Karena neared the Peshkov manor and made her way along the vegetable garden path that smelled of onions and chives, blooming oregano, and leafy basil. She came up the wood steps to the back porch, just as she and Sergei had planned.

On the porch, she retrieved the key she had placed there. If her luck held, Aunt Marta would not be busy in her beloved kitchen. It was past supper hour, but the family thought she had walked over to the bungalow with Ilya to sup with Grandmother Jilinsky and Uncle Matvey.

The click of the key in the lock might as well have been the crash of tin pans. She envisioned stepping inside and blinking as Aunt Marta and Madame Yeva came to meet her.

She closed the kitchen door, leaving it unlocked for Sergei. If he'd escaped with Lenski, would he even come home? How quickly life could change!

I wish I could talk to Uncle Matvey. She felt comfortable confiding in him, for he was imperturbable.

The comforting fragrance of Aunt Marta's fresh bread hung enticingly about the kitchen. The bread would be there on the back of the big black stove, covered with a white cloth and waiting for the family gathering at the breakfast table.

A gleaming copper match-holder hung on a hook on the wall behind the stove. The floor was recently scrubbed, and the sideboard was in perfect order. This was Aunt Marta's cherished domain, and the family honored her strict rule.

Karena replaced the key on its hook, hoping Marta hadn't noticed.

There were no sounds coming from the other rooms. Her father would be reading in his favorite chair and her mother most likely going over the expenses of running the manor or the medical needs of the peasants and families. Her younger sister Natalia would be in her bedroom, probably writing letters. And Aunt Marta would be at her needlework.

She removed her shoes. She went like a ghost across the floor and through the door into the hall with narrow stairs to rooms on the second floor. The wood floor creaked beneath Aunt Marta's small, multicolored rag rugs. Karena crept up the stairs. Reaching the top, she sped the last few steps to her tiny room with one window facing the front yard.

Once inside, she closed the door and collapsed onto her bed. Was she safe? Tomorrow the sun would rise and unveil everything that had happened in the darkness. What then?

Troubling News

The next morning, Karena awoke late, with the hot sun blaring through her window. She rushed to dress for family breakfast, the scattered crocheted rag rugs sliding beneath her thin-soled black slippers on the hardwood floor, her heart already racing over what the day might hold.

After returning to her room last night, she had lain awake for what seemed like hours, hoping to hear Sergei coming home. But finally she had drifted off sometime after one o'clock.

She poured water from a white enamel pitcher into a bowl and washed, then chose a pale blue blouse with puffed sleeves and ribbons at the wrists and a gathered full peasant skirt of the same blue with added weavings of red and black.

Her long, thick, naturally wavy hair was the color of pale gold. She pinned her braids around another section of her hair that she had brushed back into a fashionable, swirled knot at the back of her neck. She had learned the intricate design from Tatiana. Thinking of her cousin caused her mind to travel the well-worn path back to Kazan…and Colonel Kronstadt—Alex. For so brief a time in his company, she recalled him too well. Tatiana had hardly mentioned him in her last letter. Instead, she wrote of her spiritual growth—due, of course, to Rasputin.

Karena rebuked herself. How could she be thinking of Kazan when she was not even certain whether Sergei came home last night?

She came down the steps and entered the dining room. Its heavy wooden furniture was bright in the morning sun pouring through the pastel green curtains. Her family members sat around the large square table with a white cotton tablecloth that had been meticulously ironed by Aunt Marta. Relief flowed through her when she saw Sergei in his chair at the left hand of Papa Josef. As her gaze met Sergei's, his brown eyes confirmed that no one suspected. They were safe.

Even so, neither he nor Papa Josef wore a pleasant expression. There must have been yet another dispute over Sergei's return to the university.

It is enough for Papa that he is a schoolmaster at the college and a respected Russian who swears allegiance to the Romanov family, Karena thought. She was sure it grieved him that Sergei flirted openly with the Bolsheviks. If Papa learned about last night, it would surely make him ill. He adored Sergei more than any of his children and wanted the best education for him. Even so, Sergei did not appear to appreciate his father's dedication to his success.

"Karena, you are late to take your chair this morning," Madame Yeva stated, as precise as ever. Karena could hardly think of a time when she had seen her mother otherwise.

"Everyone is seated, as you can see," Yeva continued. "You must not keep your papa waiting. You know what a busy man he is at the college."

"Sorry, Papa. I slept so soundly this morning." She took her seat.

Josef Peshkov was not muscled and tanned like his son but rather was of medium height with slightly hunched shoulders and a worried disposition. When troubled, he tended to pace and smoke cigarettes, to the dismay of his elder sister Marta. Surprisingly, Madame Yeva rarely complained of anything her husband did.

Even though her usual appetite was lacking, Karena accepted a heavy slice of brown bread. She didn't want to draw a comment from Aunt

Marta, who derived satisfaction based on the amount of food consumed by her family. Karena wondered how she and her mother could remain so slim when she could outeat her sister Natalia, who tended to be heavy.

Karena spooned eggs and cheese on her plate, along with fried red cabbage and onions. She remembered the time that Tatiana had put a hand to her stomach and turned pale when Natalia asked for fried red cabbage and onions for breakfast. This morning, Karena sympathized with her cousin.

Sergei wore a dark scowl and ate too fast, his fork scraping loudly against his plate.

"Sergei, please," Madame Yeva said gently.

"Lenski visited London this summer," Sergei told her, then looked at his father.

Why is he bringing up Lenski? Karena tried to catch his eye with a glower. *Lenski is the last person he should be discussing now.*

"England is not backward politically like Russia," Sergei grumbled.

"Russia is not backward." Josef held his cup toward his sister Marta to refill with coffee.

"Not backward?" Sergei leaned forward in his chair laughing. "Come, Papa! In England, the poor are no longer bound to the landowners. The people who used to be serfs now *own* land. Did you hear me, Papa? They can buy and *own* land. Peasants are free. They have rights. They are no longer chattel."

"Peasants can own land in Russia ever since Czar Alexander gave them the right in 1860," Josef countered.

"In America, they call that sort of ownership nothing but *sharecropping*. The peasants can't do anything more than grow their food on the land. In America, there is liberty to buy, sell, and travel. And you know what? Lenski says that Jews do not have to carry cards to show to policemen. Jews are free in New York. Lenski says they can ride the train, and they need not walk off the sidewalk in the gutter."

Karena looked over at him, her fork in midair. "Jews can live in the finest areas of St. Petersburg if they bribe the right officials. And if someone important throws his mantle around you, you're safe enough."

Madame Yeva looked across the table at her.

"Who told you about bribing them?" Papa Josef asked Karena uneasily.

"Uncle Matvey. Tatiana says the same. Her letter tells of life in St. Petersburg. She even wrote that the czar will change the official name of the city to Petrograd."

"She ought to know," Sergei said wryly, "about bribing people, I mean. Uncle Viktor bribes everyone. A wise general is he."

Josef lifted a hand in his direction to stop the family slander. "America," he went on, "is another world, Sergei. Forget America. Forget England. You are Russian. Once you become a lawyer, you can buy land in St. Petersburg. General Viktor knows a man who will sell to you. I wish you were marrying the man's daughter, Sonja. She will be very rich one day."

"As for Jews in Russia," Sergei persisted, ignoring his father's words, "the czar may deny it to the British government, but he has a deliberate policy of persecution. When his chief man, Stolypin, was assassinated, did not the czar silently approve the pogrom against the Jews, even though the hysterical cry that Jews were to blame proved a lie?"

Karena remembered because the assassination had taken place at the opera house in Kiev with the czar and his daughters in attendance.

Sergei frowned. "Come, Papa, you know what I am saying. Czar Nicholas treats Jews and peasants worse than animals. At least his horses eat oats, and a veterinarian treats their ills." Sergei pointed his hunk of bread toward Karena. "Karena knows this as well. The czar's horses are treated with better medicine than the Russian peasants on the streets of St. Petersburg."

"Sergei, you forget your manners," groaned Aunt Marta. "Your bread drips butter on my tablecloth. One would think we had never taught your son how to behave, Josef."

No one paid Aunt Marta any attention, and Sergei took a big bite of his bread.

Karena, indignant, carried on. "In Moscow, they'll bring a peasant woman to have her baby at the medical school, then discharge both mother and baby in the dead of winter. Their grave is the snow."

Sergei waved his bread in Madame Yeva's direction. "Mother could tell us what the czar thinks of peasant women—especially *Jewish* peasant women."

Karena looked across the table at her mother. Yeva had told her these facts and many more, but again, Josef held up his hand.

"Do you think I am a schoolmaster for nothing, my son? I know of such matters. And your mother knew these things before I met her—" Josef stopped, color coming to his protruding cheekbones. He smiled gently. "Ah, those were the days, Yeva, when we were young, were they not?"

Karena looked at her mother. Yeva's eyes were on her cup of tea. She stirred slowly, deliberately. Her mouth was tight. "Yes, so long ago, Josef. One hardly remembers."

Josef cleared his throat. "Marta, is there more tea?"

"Of course, Josef, a full pot. Here, Natalia, pass this to your papa."

Karena nibbled her bread and considered Sergei's words. Karena had seen Jews and peasants treated like scavenging dogs by soldiers and the gendarmes. In certain instances, Jews were forced to ride in a train's baggage car, along with the unwashed peasants and wanderers. She'd heard people were packed so tightly they sometimes suffocated. And when the train pulled into a station at short stops, they were forbidden to get out to buy food or relieve themselves. Sergei had told her the Jews could not get off in any of the towns because "the good gentry did not wish for their offensive presence."

"Enough of this talk," Josef said. "Things are not so bad as you say."

"Not on our land," Sergei countered. "But many landowners flog the peasants just as the Imperial Navy flogs their sailors."

"That was years ago."

"They still do it, Papa. Little has changed since Czar Alexander's reforms. You are one of the few landowners who treat your peasants as humans. What Mama does with her medical skills here in the village is unheard of elsewhere in Russia. Lenski says anyone can murder a Jew and it is called an accident!"

Yeva spilled her tea. Josef frowned. "You are upsetting your mother, Sergei."

"I am sorry, Mother. But you know these things."

"Yes, I know them, Sergei. But such talk does not make for a pleasant breakfast," Madame Yeva said quietly.

"Murder is never a pleasant topic, whatever the time of day. And it doesn't matter who commits it, either. Murder was committed by Policeman Grinevich. They hanged Professor Chertkov just three weeks ago."

Karena tightened her fingers on her napkin. If Papa Josef asked him how he knew… To her relief, he merely scowled and shook his head.

"Professor Chertkov was a decent man."

Aunt Marta winced. Karena looked at Natalia. She sat very still, her brown eyes large and watchful as she ate. She'd hardly spoken this morning. *She's most likely worried about her own Jewish roots and the persecution that might yet come.*

Karena looked at her plate, setting her fork down. She would choke if she ate another bite.

"If you wish to keep speaking this way, you will bring us all down to the grave," Josef stated.

Sergei leaned toward him, an affectionate hand on his shoulder. "Ah, come, Papa. You are a member of the local zemstvo. We have a right to discuss political matters with you. It is your duty to bring our complaints before Czar Nicholas." He grinned.

As a land manager, Josef had been chosen by his community to deal with problems of local or provincial administration. Once a year, such men appeared in St. Petersburg, where the Duma was held, and they would send their complaints to the czar. "Our complaints might just as well have been ferried off on the wings of pigeons to who knows where," members of the zemstvos bemoaned.

Czar Nicholas was an autocrat and refused to acknowledge complaints. Indeed, a complaint could be considered outright rebellion, deserving of imprisonment. Although the czar had in a time of revolution permitted a Duma to form, he'd done so with great reluctance and then ignored the body. The Duma could not make laws or change an injustice, and it became merely a platform to protest the czar and czarina. When members became too critical of the autocracy or of Rasputin, Czar Nicholas often closed it down and sent the delegates home, infuriating the Duma members even more.

"Seriously, Papa, I don't agree with the Bolsheviks on many issues, and I don't accept their tactics, but what are we to do when the czar is deaf and dumb to making reasonable changes in Russia? Who has answers to our problems, except the revolutionary leaders?"

"Uncle Matvey says the socialists have no real answers," Karena spoke up. "Their changes are all merely external. It's men's hearts that need a revolution. Uncle Matvey's beginning to think there really is a Messiah who will be born and save Israel."

Sergei groaned. "He doesn't believe that. I've talked with him. It's all that study he's doing on the 'Zionist movement' of Theodor Herzl. Uncle Matvey discusses the idea of a savior out of intellectual curiosity, that's all. If we are to be saved, we must have a revolution."

Josef's fist came down on the table and rattled the glasses and plates. "Silence!"

There was silence.

A minute later, when Josef was calm again he said, "I will remind you, my son, that there is little I can do about all your complaints. While the czar has permitted the Duma and the zemstvo to exist, he has granted us no authority and will not meet with us."

"You see?" Sergei crowed. "My very point, Papa. We're nothing but his puppets."

Karena watched her father with sympathy. Sergei constantly argued politics, but Papa Josef remained a stalwart defender of the royal family. She admired her father for having tried early on to make social changes. He'd joined with the other zemstvo members outside the Winter Palace when Nicholas Romanov became czar after the end of the repressive regime of his father. The zemstvo representatives were mostly from cultivated families, members of the nobility, landlords, and those who had made money as speculators and entrepreneurs.

The zemstvos had carried a petition asking Czar Nicholas to grant Russia a constitution. Nicholas utterly refused. But while disappointed, the zemstvos, unlike the Bolsheviks and other radical parties, did not desire to end the House of Romanov, nor did they want war with the autocracy. They preferred a peaceful path to freedom, in stages.

Papa Josef sighed and looked at his son. "You lack patience, Sergei. Eventually the zemstvo will tackle more general problems, like taxation, the infrastructure, and so on, and will engage in politics. Now it is not possible. Czar Nicholas considers such reforms detrimental to the cause he believes has been entrusted to him."

"Yes, Papa, *safeguarding the supreme right of autocratic rule,*" Sergei said sarcastically. "To preserve sovereignty for his son. Patience, you say. Patience for what? to await the autocratic reign of his young son!"

Debate didn't flourish just in the Peshkov home, it was everywhere and growing, though reserved for the inner rooms of Russian homes. It was plain to see the nation was divided. Perhaps they were already in civil war—a war of ideas, a cultural war that was as real as any battle, yet without bullets.

"Already my head is aching, and the day, how long and hot it will be," Aunt Marta said. "Can we not eat in peace at least?"

"Peace, peace," Sergei teased, "when there is no peace." He looked at Karena. "Another verse from Uncle Matvey. He's becoming quite a reader of the Scriptures. There can be no such peace, my sweet aunt. Not as long as the despot keeps us in chains." He looked at Josef. "Papa, you think that ignoring Russia's condition will make it better?" He shook his head slowly, with marked determination. "Remember when we were children, Karena? Natalia?" He looked at his sisters. "Both of you would cover your heads with a blanket when you were afraid a ghost might come into the room at night."

Karena smiled at Natalia.

"You thought you were safe under the blanket. A true ghost would rip the blanket from your hiding place and get you." He cracked his knuckles. Natalia jumped, Sergei grinned, and she picked up a piece of bread as if to throw it at him. A warning look from Madame Yeva stayed her hand.

Aunt Marta moaned, shaking her head. "There are no manners in this house, none. Tatiana puts you all to shame."

Sergei began to mock Tatiana, picking up a glass with his little finger extended, dabbing his napkin against his pursed lips, and twittering.

Natalia laughed at her brother. "Ah, but what beautiful gowns she wears to the opera," she said with a sigh. "And what a dashing colonel is committed to her in Aleksandr Kronstadt."

"Colonel Kronstadt is not committed to her," Karena said flatly. "He's becoming engaged to her to please Uncle Viktor."

"Oh, don't even suggest such a thing, dear," Aunt Marta said.

"Yes, Karena," Madame Yeva said quietly. "You don't want to start a chain of gossip. Words can sometimes do more evil than an outright attack."

"Gowns," Sergei said loftily, hand at heart, "will turn to ashes, my charming ladies, but politics is the mother's milk of change! We may think we can go on living our lives without becoming involved, without making a decision about whose side we are on for Russia's future, but we are wrong. More bloodshed will come."

"I forbid you to keep company with Lenski," Josef said.

Karena knew that Josef had forbidden this many times over.

"Papa, be logical. Whether you want a revolution or not, it will come. Even if I never see Lenski again, it must come. The time is ripe. The autocratic rule of the czar is coming to an end. His actions against the people of Russia must face the sword of ideas."

"Talk of peace, Sergei, dear," Aunt Marta said. "The more we speak words of peace, the more we reinforce the good that is all around us until, eventually, good will prevail."

"Pardon my saying so, and I love you dearly, Aunt Marta, but I have never heard such rot. Try speaking good words to the stinkweeds in your herb garden and see if they're choked out by your sage and peppermint. The stinkweeds will take over if you don't attack them—tear them out by the roots."

Aunt Marta shrugged in surrender and turned to Natalia to discuss her day at the college. When no one responded to Sergei's words, he smiled triumphantly and returned to his food.

Karena caught her father's gaze upon her. He leaned toward her across the table. It was his way to come close when he wished to speak seriously, as though by leaning forward he could hold her attention.

"Daughter Karena, you must be very strong this morning."

The table became silent. She gripped her fork.

"I seem to disappoint Sergei with my lack of boldness. Now I must also deliver news that will disappoint you."

Karena felt the gaze of those at the table. Papa Josef took an envelope from his black frock coat pocket and held it for a moment before setting it on the table with a tap of his finger.

She caught several of the words on the envelope: "St. Petersburg…
Medicine and Midwifery…" Her heart turned to mush.

He cleared his throat. "Daughter, you will not be attending the Imperial College of Medicine this year. I know you have been hoping all summer to do so."

Silence tightened around the table. Sergei stopped eating and looked quickly in her direction. Aunt Marta plucked at her collar. Natalia took an oversized bite of cheese, and Madame Yeva looked down at her plate.

Karena did not move. None of them yet knew that Dr. Zinnovy had agreed to come to her aid. She managed a smile.

"Something wonderful has happened, however," she said. "I met Dr. Dmitri Zinnovy yesterday in town, and he's assured me that he'll work with Dr. Lenski to make my enrollment possible."

Madame Yeva dropped her spoon with a clatter and stared at her. "What is this, Karena?"

She began describing Dr. Zinnovy's visit to check on Anna's condition, avoiding mention of the fact that Karena had ridden home in his carriage, as well as the reason Anna had ridden a horse. "…and when he finished with Anna, he wrote about a doctor he recommends for her." She reached into her skirt pocket for the folded paper and passed it to her mother.

Madame Yeva was tense and silent. Karena took her alertness for concern for her patient Anna.

Sergei stared into his coffee cup.

Papa Josef cleared his throat. He smoothed his mustache with one finger, looking troubled. "That is all very fine, Karena. If Dr. Zinnovy can use his influence to help your admission to the medical school, that is good news. However," he said and glanced at Madame Yeva who sat stiff and silent, "I'm afraid there are serious things happening now. War is breaking out between Russia and Germany, and Czar Nicholas has promised military help to France. These are dangerous days, and we cannot have you in St. Petersburg."

Sergei started to argue, but Josef laid a hand on his arm for silence.

"But, Papa," Karena protested, "St. Petersburg will be safe. And I shall be staying part of the time with Uncle Matvey. Cousin Tatiana also wrote last month that Aunt Zofia and General Viktor will spend the coming year in St. Petersburg. I can visit them and shall have all the care I need. If anything, I shall have too much care and not enough independence."

"Independence?" Madame Yeva raised her golden brows, concern in her eyes.

"Mama, you know what I mean," Karena hastened. "War or no war, I shall fare well enough."

"War with Germany—a stupid mistake," Sergei said, anger in his voice.

"Papa, I am not afraid of war," Karena interrupted her brother.

"Not afraid of war! Then you have much to learn, Daughter."

"I mean, it does not make me afraid to go to St. Petersburg."

Professor Josef held up a palm and looked at her sternly. Karena knew that look and stilled her tongue. Even Sergei's fork stopped, and Natalia held her glass of milk midway to her lips, looking at Karena with sympathy.

"There is always next year, Karena," Josef said.

Next year. If I hear "next year" one more time, I think I shall scream. For three years now, I have been told next year, next year—

"And there are, well, other reasons." Josef cleared his throat. "Our financial situation has not been the best this year. What money we can spare now for higher learning must go to Sergei, as firstborn son. He will be returning for his third year at the university."

"Do not place the blame on me, Papa," Sergei argued, lowering his fork. He shook his head. "I do not want to be a lawyer. I have said so many times."

"Too many times," Josef stated. "You talk so convincingly, my son, that you are well fitted to be the best of lawyers."

Natalia gave a short laugh, then ceased as both Josef and Sergei fixed their gazes upon her.

"Let Karena go to the medical school if Zinnovy can arrange it—" Sergei began.

"Do not contradict your papa."

Josef turned calmly again to Karena. She sat rigid in the hard-backed chair, sickened by disappointment.

Professor Josef removed his spectacles from his pocket. He breathed moisture on each round lens and polished them thoughtfully with a napkin, before pressing them in place. "Perhaps next year." Then more confidently, "Next year, there will be money enough. Dr. Zinnovy may be able to reserve a place for you." He smiled, but as he glanced about the table at the fallen faces, the smile faded. "We shall see…we shall see." He picked up his cup of coffee and finished it.

Karena looked at her mother. Madame Yeva had been unusually silent all morning. She kept her eyes on her breakfast plate. Karena understood now why she had been so quiet. She must have known about the letter. Her mother, better than anyone else, understood and shared her crushing disappointment. And now! She'd come so close, with even Dr. Zinnovy on her side.

Next September, she was sure she would hear similar arguments once more. There seemed no options except to settle down and marry Ilya.

She felt a lump lodged in her throat. She reached for her glass of goat's milk. Her stomach churned with nausea. She stood up, pushing her chair back, feeling her face grow warm. She exited the room quickly.

Karena rushed out the front door. Madame Yeva turned toward her husband. She reached over and laid her hand upon his black coat sleeve.

"Josef," she urged, "is there nothing to be done?"

"There is nothing, my dear."

Sergei pushed back his chair noisily and stood to his feet. "War or no war, I have to work in the fields today with Ilya." He looked down at his father as if to say something more, but turned and left. A moment later, the back kitchen door gave a decided bang.

Josef sat in aggrieved silence. Yeva sighed.

Natalia stared at her fork as though she wondered what it was. Aunt Marta was looking at her brother Josef with sympathy. Yeva lifted her cup of tea and drank; it was now lukewarm. She would talk to Karena later. Her daughter already knew much about birthing, and she could teach her still more. There was no reason why Karena could not take over the medical work here on the land. There was certainly enough sickness to keep anyone busy these dreadful days!

Natalia slid from her chair. "I must go into town, Papa. I am to help Madame Olga with her shopping before classes. She wants to get it all done and be back home before it gets too hot. She's promised to pay me today."

Josef nodded. Natalia came over to him and bent to kiss his bearded face.

"You be a good girl today," he said.

"Papa, Boris will be conscripted soon. If we can't marry, at least let us seal our engagement!"

He patted her hand. "We'll see, Daughter, we'll discuss it with your mother later."

Aunt Marta began to clear the table. "Don't forget to bring Madame Olga the loaf of bread I baked for her," she told Natalia. "It's wrapped and sitting on the table by the door. She owes me for the other loaves too. Be sure you collect my kopecks. I want to order new yarn."

"Yes, Aunt Marta."

Madame Yeva spoke up. "And tell her I will call on her tomorrow morning if her new supply of cough medicine arrives by post. On second thought, tell her I will call on her regardless."

"Yes, Mama, because if you don't, she will complain you are neglecting her aches and pains. She is always complaining of something."

"That is not for you to say. She is old and needs your sympathy. Go now, so you will not be late."

Natalia kissed her cheek and hurried off. Madame Yeva remained at the table, troubled. She tried to concentrate on her own difficulties to mask the pain she felt for Karena's.

Czar Nicholas II was soon expected to declare war with Germany and her allies, including Turkey, which bordered Russia. For now, life went on normally in the Peshkov household, but already she was concerned about her medical supplies. With war coming, would she still receive shipments? The breeze coming through the open window stirred the curtains. "It will be most warm today," Yeva commented.

"The cabbage must be picked before it begins flowering," Aunt Marta told Josef. "I will need to do preserving all week. Tell Sergei to help me clear out the storage room."

"Sergei is busy in the fields, Marta. He's also preparing for his return to the university. And, Sister, Sergei does not like to do women's work. Ask one of the young peasant boys to help you."

"Women's work," Marta snorted. "If you saw how I break my back from dawn to dusk, cooking and slaving for the family, you would have more respect for my work."

"A job of great importance," Yeva spoke up in a soothing voice. Sometimes her husband infuriated her. She looked at him. "Is that not so, Josef?"

"Yes, yes, by all means, Marta. The food this morning was most wholesome." He pushed back his chair. "I must go, or I will be late to teach the summer class."

After Josef left, Marta went off to her domain, the awesome kitchen and the great Peshkov vegetable garden. Yeva went her own way to organize her medical duties for the day. She would need to call on Anna this morning to see how she was feeling. She must write the recommended doctor in Kiev, though who would pay for his services? Anna Lavrushsky had little money.

Yeva frowned. *Sergei must be the father, even though he denies it.* Josef refused to believe it and would not hear of giving money to the family. *I must do something.* She walked to her medical supply closet. She would also need to stop by her brother Matvey's bungalow to bring him his needed medication.

She located her last clean, ironed apron. The starched, striped linen felt good between her fingers. The very smell brought back memories of her youth in training at the medical college. She enjoyed wearing the professional-looking student apron. Odd how long these aprons lasted—twenty years—but she had treated them as precious relics, like her mother's wedding dress, now two generations old and still functional, though out of fashion. She remembered packing this apron when she'd fled the Imperial College of Medicine and Midwifery in 1893...

Oy, so be it. Disappointment dogged one's footsteps from childhood to the grave. There was nothing to be done about it but to keep struggling and moving onward, hoping tomorrow would be better.

Vaguely, Yeva thought of Dr. Zinnovy...*Dmitri.* She had not kept up with his glowing career.

Perhaps it was an error to have allowed Karena to entertain plans to attend the same medical school. Becoming involved with her old friend Lenski, and now Zinnovy, invited trouble.

Josef wanted Karena to marry Ilya. He'd spoken to her just recently about such a marriage.

"Karena is now well past the age, Yeva."

Yeva ran her fingers across her forehead, thinking. Yes, she must think. She must make no rash decisions. She would think long and hard about consequences; there were always consequences. She was glad her brother was here until next month. She would discuss the matter with him.

TEN

Trouble, to Be Sure

A summer of national and personal discontent was ending. Harvest was in earnest in the wheat fields, and the grass in the wide front yard was now shriveling beneath the Russian sun.

Karena walked along the wagon road, wrestling with her emotions. She wanted a long walk this morning with nothing more than the song of the field larks and the bright sun on her back. She neared the cutoff to the wide public road to the village. The harvest winds that blew against her were bidding farewell to so many things, reminding her that both earth and man were fatigued. The approaching winter would arrive with brutal indifference, smothering all in a vast, icy shroud.

The wind caught away her red hat, and she rushed after it. Horse hooves thundered against the road, and she saw Imperial soldiers riding toward her. She stepped back from the road, her hand holding to a rustic fence post where wildflowers persisted in defiant bloom. She waited.

Trouble, to be sure.

The dozen Russian soldiers rode down the road, slowing as they neared where she stood. Sergei had described them as czarist demons on horseback; it did them injustice. These were no ordinary peasant foot soldiers. All rode smart-looking horses and were led by a crack Imperial officer—

Colonel Aleksandr Kronstadt looked her way.

Karena drew in a breath and lifted her chin. He dismounted, tossed the reins to the rider beside him, and walked toward her, removing his gloves. Looking toward the bushes, he paused to retrieve her red hat.

She saw the same handsome features, the interesting green-gray eyes.

"Miss Peshkova." He bowed lightly and with exaggerated fanfare presented her red hat.

Karena snatched it.

He leveled a look toward her that caused her flesh to prickle.

"You haven't changed," he said. "You're exactly as I remember."

"Indeed, Colonel Kronstadt? I'm sure I don't know what that may mean."

"A compliment, of course." He glanced toward the wood-and-brick manor house, perhaps a hundred yards back, and then toward the golden wheat fields bending in the wind.

"Pleasant," he said. "I like the swaying of the wheat in the wind…" His gaze returned to hers.

Karena stared back as coolly as she could manage. "Are you looking for someone, Colonel?"

His eyes narrowed. He flipped the back of a glove against his other palm. "Yes, I am, Miss Peshkova, but it will wait until this afternoon. I'm on my way into the village to report to Major-General Durnov, who's arrived from Kiev. There was trouble last night with the revolutionaries. Your chief gendarme was attacked. I don't suppose you'd know anything about it?"

She did her best to keep her gaze from wavering under his. So the higher authorities already knew. Policeman Leonovich must have sent a wire to Kiev to the Imperial officer in command, named Durnov.

Alex hadn't expected her to know about the violence, for he went on, his voice casual. "I have several hundred foot soldiers and their captains about three miles down the road." He gestured his dark head in the direction he'd come from. "They're on their way to Warsaw to join up with the Russian army. I suppose you know Russia is at war? Our men and horses need to bed down for the night. We'd like to use Peshkov land across the road, behind those trees over there, where nothing is planted."

Who would dare refuse the soldiers of Czar Nicholas II? That Alex even asked was unusual.

"Yes, by all means, Colonel. The unused and harvested areas are at the soldiers' disposal. I'll make mention of the need of food to my mother."

"The soldiers are obliged. I suppose you understand why the commander in charge is here?"

Karena's heart went heavy. She saw his alert gaze watching her response, but she remained silent.

"The army needs more soldiers," he said without emotion. "I'm afraid your village will be missing most of its young men within a week." He looked off toward the ripening wheat fields. "This isn't going to help your father's grain harvest. Calling up men now seems unfortunate, but the orders came from Petrograd."

So then, now it is Petrograd... To her it would always be St. Petersburg.

Karena thought sadly of Ilya, Boris, and the rest of the young men she knew and nodded. She wondered if Alex was on his way to Warsaw, but she dared not show interest enough to ask. She had thought, from Tatiana's last letter, that he was stationed at the Winter Palace, working with Major-General Durnov in the Okhrana.

His jaw flexed as he watched her. "Then I'll be on my way to the village. I'll be here a few days with Durnov to look into last night's violence." He nodded good-bye, turned, and walked to his horse, mounting with the ease of an experienced cavalry officer.

Karena, anxious at the turn of events, remained by the fence post, watching. He sent some men back to the main column with news of where they would make camp, then rode with two soldiers toward the village.

Troubled, she hurried back toward the manor house. Her mind was now on Sergei and Lenski and the ordeal that must surely be ahead. What Alex had communicated was telling beyond his carefully chosen words: the secret police were here to learn the details of Grinevich's beating, and although he had not mentioned Sergei, she believed Alex suspected his involvement.

Karena hurried up to her bedroom to be alone for a few minutes in order to think through her dilemma. She was not there long before Madame Yeva's stout voice dispersed her musings.

"Karena?"

Karena massaged her neck and face, trying to relax into her usual smile before she appeared before her mother.

She stepped out onto the wooden landing and leaned over the rail to look below. There must be no sign of dismay. She did not wish her mother to worry over the disappointment she'd received earlier that morning at breakfast—*or to guess that she was with Sergei at last night's meeting.*

Madame Yeva stood between the kitchen and the front hall. Neighbors said they looked much alike, mother and daughter—golden haired, fair skinned, blue eyed—though her mother was a few inches shorter. Karena was also fairer, due to her gentile father. Madame Yeva attributed her fair appearance to maternal grandparents from Finland, which was now under the Imperial boot of the Russian czar.

"Come down, Karena. I need you to make a medical call."

Karena hurried down the plain, scrubbed, wooden steps.

"Is it Anna?"

"No, not Anna."

Madame Yeva waited with her shoulders held as straight as a Russian officer's. Her expression did not reveal any concerns simmering in her heart, for all emotion was washed away with practiced indifference. Karena wondered at times if some incident in her past had hurt her.

Madame Yeva's fingers were intertwined, hands resting against her striped medical apron. She wore a white cotton blouse with puffed sleeves, tight at the wrist, and a straight, ankle-length dark blue skirt. Her high-buttoned shoes were polished, though the heels showed signs of wear. The once all-golden hair had a liberal amount of gray in the braid wrapped around her finely shaped head. Karena could see lines of worry drawn, as though by an artist's brushstroke, here and there on her face. She was forty-five now. *She would have made an excellent doctor,* Karena thought proudly, *if only she'd been allowed to complete her training.*

Madame Yeva made a brave attempt at a smile, but her faded blue eyes showed internal worry. *I understand your disappointment,* they seemed to convey.

Karena managed to return the smile. Yes, mother and daughter were alike. *I am enduring my disappointment,* her smile suggested, *but please do not ask me to speak of it now.*

Afternoon sunlight trickled through the wooden window slats. Karena watched her mother move briskly across the room to the walk-in closet where the medications and birthing supplies were stored. She unlocked the door and lit the small lantern she kept inside on a trestle table. The light revealed floor-to-ceiling shelves that in earlier times had been neatly filled with apothecary supplies in bottles, tins, and vials. Karena followed her inside and surveyed the precious, dwindling supply.

"Your Uncle Matvey's gout is troubling him again. I'd like you to walk over and see him. Bring his medication. Let us hope it helps him this time. Tell Grandmother Jilinsky to stop feeding him the rich mutton pan drippings. Here is the dosage. It will be enough for three or four days. See that he takes the first dose while you are there, will you, dear?"

"You know how he hates to swallow these big tablets. He says they get caught in his throat."

"Smear a bit of butter on the pills the way I showed you. They'll go down much easier. Tell him I shall be over to see him in the morning on my way to Madame Olga's. There's something I want to talk over with him."

Karena glanced at her. Talk over? Was it about her? She nodded and watched as her mother took an opaque bottle from the shelf, shook some pills onto her palm, counted them, and then placed them in a small white cloth. Her mother was obsessed with cleanliness, insisting the English nurse, Madame Florence Nightingale, had been right about the spread of disease in the hospitals. She recalled Dr. Zinnovy using his own soap and boiled water.

Yeva gathered the cloth at the top then tied it with a length of narrow ribbon from a roll that she kept on a wall peg. She wrote a note to herself on the ledger hanging there and then surveyed the shelves once more, shaking her head with apparent concern.

"I do not know what we shall do."

Karena had grown up seeing her mother guard the medicine closet as though it housed the crown jewels of Czarina Alexandra Fyodorovna Romanova. Each year at the end of the summer it was always the same; her mother began the tedious process of making a resupply list before the long twilight of Russian winter.

"This may prove to be one of our worst years," Madame Yeva was saying. "Everything will be needed for the war. I would not deny our brave soldiers anything." She closed and locked the door, dropping the key into her pocket. "Even now, the simplest things are becoming scarce. The supplies you brought in from the warehouse two weeks ago were lacking quinine and bitterroot. I sent off to Moscow for more. I wonder if we will get them."

Karena slipped the tablets for Uncle Matvey into her skirt pocket and turned to her errand when the sound of running footsteps came up the front porch and hesitated outside the door.

Karena's nerves clenched. The large manor house grew still and strained with expectation.

The front door opened, and Natalia stood in the doorway.

She widened her eyes expressively and looked from Karena to their mother.

"We are having company tonight, Mama. Soldiers—Imperial soldiers."

Karena bit her lip. She was sure she knew who they would be.

Natalia leaned in the archway of the open door, placing a palm on her heart, drawing in a deep breath, as though saving the worst news—where she was concerned—for last.

"And Boris has been conscripted into the army—just as we expected. The soldier knocked on his door just a short while ago with orders. He leaves tomorrow with the company of soldiers that just arrived. He's going to Warsaw. The captain told Boris they need a veterinarian at the front. The officers are coming home with Papa to supper!" She entered the house and slammed the door, causing Madame Peshkova to raise a palm to her forehead.

Natalia continued excitedly. "The younger officer is Colonel Kronstadt, he's at the school now—asking questions of Papa."

Asking questions! Karena glanced at her mother to see her reaction.

Madame Yeva looked calm, as usual, refusing to be caught up in Natalia's emotions. "That is no way to enter a room, Natalia," she chastened.

Natalia looked abashed and disappointed that her stunning announcement failed to have a greater impact. "Sorry, Mama, I have been running."

Madame Yeva continued mildly, "Do remember that you are a lady now, Natalia. You will soon be married."

"Yes, Mama."

Karena suppressed the grin that tugged at her mouth.

"What is this about guests for supper?" Madame Yeva asked. "Sit down and explain yourself." Their mother's emphasis on guests, rather than on Imperial officers who were there to ask questions, was typically hospitable.

Natalia lowered herself into the faded brown chair, then folded her hands and repeated her news like a child for her teacher.

"I was on my way home with Madame Olga when we happened to see Boris across the market square. He had brought in bins of corn to barter and sell."

Karena could see that Natalia had not deceived their mother about a chance meeting with Boris. What Karena wondered was how Natalia had managed to slip away from the widow to talk to Boris. Madame Olga was of the gentry class, and Boris's father was a peasant who had done well. Because of this, he had been able to afford having Boris attend the Russian Orthodox Virgin of Kazan school. Boris, unlike most peasants, could read and write and had excelled in his studies to become a veterinarian.

"And suddenly I saw Papa across the street at the college. He was with an Imperial officer who looked familiar. And whom should he turn out to be but Tatiana's fiancé, the colonel! Papa noticed me and called me over. He hastily wrote this." She produced a folded piece of paper and handed it to Madame Yeva. "He told me to bring it to you at once. He also said to tell Aunt Marta about feeding two, possibly three, officers who are coming for supper."

Alex was asking Papa questions! Karena's heart raced with fear. *Why would he single out my father? Alex and Durnov must be suspicious about last night.*

Madame Yeva took the paper and walked to the window, where the light was brighter.

Karena exchanged urgent glances with her sister and whispered, "Did you see Sergei?" *Is our brother in trouble with the secret police?* her gaze inquired.

Natalia shrugged and crossed herself as she looked anxiously in the direction of one of the Orthodox icons displayed in the red room.

Karena did not follow Natalia's lead and cross herself. The tradition used so often by Natalia and Aunt Marta had lost meaning. Karena wasn't sure what she truly believed. Was she a Jew? Was she a Russian Orthodox Christian? Was she both? Rituals were many and varied, but they did nothing to change her heart. *Knowledge is what I need, knowledge of the true God and not merely religious traditions.*

Unlike Papa Josef and Aunt Marta, her mother held no sincere interest in the Orthodox Church of Holy Russia. Yeva had been raised in Jewish orthodoxy, but she had given up her Torah and her "Jewishness," as she put it, to marry Josef Peshkov. She attended the Russian Orthodox Church with the family and was considered a Christian by her friends in the village. Aunt Marta, however, complained that Yeva did not cross herself enough.

"No wonder we are born unto afflictions," she often said. "The Virgin notices, Yeva."

"If I hadn't consented to baptism," Yeva had once told Karena, "I could not live outside the pale, and during pogroms, the mobs would think nothing of burning down your father's home and fields."

Karena remembered the time she had first understood what it meant to be a Jew in Russia and Poland. She was frightened and angry to learn that there were only certain areas in Russia where Jews could live, go to school, and attend synagogues. Even then, there was risk of sudden Cossack raids. The soldiers or armed citizens would come bursting into the Jewish areas to beat, loot, and rape. The pogroms occurred frequently, with almost any excuse. Sergei, with sarcasm in his voice, had once said, "They have their pogroms like they have their special religious holidays. It is a wonder the Russian Orthodox Church doesn't have Persecute-a-Jew Day."

Recently, with assassination attempts on members of the czar's government, the hatred against Jews had increased once again. The autocrats blamed the factory strikes and violence of the Bolsheviks on the Jews, who were all Bolsheviks, according to the propaganda. "The Jews control all the money in Russia and Europe. They are plotting to take over the world and run all the banks."

It infuriated Karena. For every rich Jew, there were ten gentiles who were just as greedy and godless.

Their mother didn't share Natalia's excitement about dinner guests. She lifted her fingers to massage her forehead. The sight brought a surge of sympathy to Karena. She watched as Yeva read the message, wondering what her father had said.

Madame Yeva sat down slowly in the nearby chair. The color faded from her face, leaving a sickly pallor. Karena went to her side.

"What is it, Mama?"

Madame Yeva shook her head and quickly folded the paper, stuffing it into her apron pocket. She drew back her shoulders.

"Is it the soldiers?" Karena asked, daring to persist, noting her voice was tense. "I saw them this morning. They arrived early on the road. They requested land on which to camp and food for their soldiers."

Yeva looked up at her. "You said nothing about it at breakfast. You should have mentioned this to your father and Sergei." She stood.

Karena tried to sound casual. "It was after I left the table, Mama. After Papa told me about the letter from St. Petersburg—Petrograd. I went out for a walk…"

Yeva caressed her daughter's arm and moved over to the window again. She tapped her pince-nez against her wrist and stared out thoughtfully. Again, Karena exchanged worried glances with Natalia. Natalia didn't know about last night, though she did know Sergei secretly attended Bolshevik meetings.

Natalia had sobered, but excitement remained in her eyes. "Do you think the officers coming here with Papa have anything to do with Policeman Grinevich being attacked last night by revolutionaries?"

Madame Yeva turned sharply toward Natalia. "Who told you about Policeman Grinevich?"

Then her mother knew as well. Josef must have mentioned the ugly matter in his message.

"Boris told me. The news is all over town."

Madame Yeva turned toward Karena. "Did Colonel Kronstadt speak of Policeman Grinevich to you?"

"He was on his way to the village to meet a Major-General Durnov of the Okhrana," she admitted quietly.

"Colonel Aleksandr Kronstadt will soon become engaged to your cousin," Madame Yeva said in passing. "We will have to wait and see. His presence may be to our benefit. Let us hope so."

Aunt Marta came into the room from the kitchen. She had little of her younger sister Zofia's outward beauty. Marta was tall, with the same blue-black hair. "Did I hear you mention guests, Yeva?"

"Colonel Kronstadt is coming," Natalia told her.

"The chief gendarme Grinevich was attacked last night by outside revolutionaries," Madame Yeva said. "Imperial officers will be here for dinner."

"Oh my," Aunt Marta cried.

Outside revolutionaries? Karena glanced at her mother. Calling those involved last night *outsiders* was deliberate, Karena thought. Did her mother guess the truth?

Yeva paced. "Sergei will get us all into trouble. 'Whoever guards his mouth and tongue keeps his soul from troubles.'"

Karena recognized the words from the book of Proverbs.

"We will receive the officers with honor and feed the foot soldiers, as requested. We have no choice." Madame Yeva looked at each of them, confirming her instruction.

Natalia cast Karena a smile, apparently far less concerned over the purpose behind the visit than the meeting itself. "It could be entertaining," Natalia suggested. "Wait until we write Tatiana about how we had Alex to ourselves for an evening."

Karena was aware of more serious implications. This would not be a social call, as her sister wished, but an interrogation into their whereabouts last night and any connections they may have with the Bolsheviks. She and Sergei would need to watch every word if they were to keep their lives. One slip, and they would be arrested and hauled to Peter and Paul prison for further questioning. Fear hovered like a hungry hawk, menacing her every move. *God of Abraham, help us,* she prayed. Then, uncertain which faith was appropriate, she added, *Jesus, have mercy, amen.*

"So. Now I am a miracle worker?" Aunt Marta complained. "Am I Rasputin the starets that I am able to feed them? How many? Three? Four? A dozen?"

"Three," Yeva said. "But there will be foot soldiers as well. Mush will be good enough for them, and maybe some cabbage soup."

"They *say* there are three officers. Who can believe it until they walk in? The hens, they are barren, I tell you. The hens, they do not lay eggs enough to feed so many. For breakfast, I had hardly enough for Josef and

Sergei. And now am I also to feed at least three Imperial officers?" Aunt Marta crossed herself. "They will be starving. They always are. What am I to do?"

"Let them eat cake," Natalia quipped.

Aunt Marta cast her a scolding glance.

"Natalia, do be serious," Madame Yeva said.

"Don't mind her," Karena said lightly. "She has been studying the French Revolution."

"Revolution? What about hens? I will need eggs, Yeva," Marta insisted.

Karena wondered why this summer had opened the door for pessimism and discontent in so many hearts. Even the hens had become a subject of hopelessness for Marta.

"Then we will make cabbage soup," Yeva suggested absently, still pacing and rubbing her forehead.

"Oh, Mama," Natalia groaned. "Peasant food! Where is our social pride? And with Tatiana's handsome Colonel Kronstadt here? I will blush when next I see her if we serve him cabbage and onions."

"I am most sure this will not be the social call you imagine, Natalia. And you have grown spoiled. Cabbage soup on the table of the hungry would bring praise to the saints."

"But *peasant* food, Mama! And for the czar's Imperial officers? Colonel Kronstadt is the son of Countess Shashenka."

"Imperial officers or peasants—who cares?" Aunt Marta said. "They are all trampling beasts, but one thing I know," she said and tapped the side of her head. "Russian officers of His Imperial Majesty expect many eggs and much bread. *And* vodka. I expect they will want butter these days too. Who can please such men? I do not feel these Imperial servants of the czar will appreciate my special cabbage soup, though I admit my onions add a special zest. Ah well. I shall do my best," Aunt Marta said, turning her shoulder toward them. "It is all the czar can expect of me, some eggs. But"—she shook her finger toward Natalia, who smiled fondly at her—"there will be no cake."

Natalia jumped to her feet. "Oh, but we must have little cakes. For Boris, if not for the czar's officers." She looked pleadingly from Marta to her mother. "I will not see him for a long time!" she pleaded.

"Then you persuade the hens to lay me six more eggs," Aunt Marta told her. "I cannot make cakes without eggs."

Madame Yeva held up her hand to show the discussion must end. "Do what you can, Marta."

"We can borrow eggs from Uncle Matvey and Grandmother Jilinsky," Karena suggested. "They usually have more than they need. I am on my way to deliver his medicine. I shall ask."

"Yes, why did I not think of it?" Aunt Marta said as she headed back toward her kitchen. "I lack adequate time to prepare this meal, so hurry, Karena," she called over her shoulder. Soon pots and pans rattled, and the prized family glassware tinkled precariously. Karena and Natalia exchanged glances and held their breath. Thankfully, the glassware that was to be shared between them when they married remained unbroken.

"Natalia! I need your help," Aunt Marta called, and Natalia went to the kitchen.

When they were alone again, Madame Yeva hurried to Karena. The pallor on her high cheekbones was a warning.

"Your brother—"

Her mother tried to make her voice sound normal, but the attempt was unsuccessful.

Your brother. It was always Sergei. Sergei, who had once again managed to bring heightened concerns to the family.

"Sergei is with Ilya in the fields. Go to him. Tell him to come home at once. It is his father's command. It is most important."

The dismay in her mother's eyes confirmed Karena's worst fears.

"And Policeman Grinevich?" Karena asked in a low voice.

Madame Yeva closed her eyes and shook her head slightly. "He has broken ribs and a concussion."

Karena shuddered, remembering.

"The attack last night was most bitter," Madame Yeva whispered. "I'm desperately afraid Sergei will be blamed. Grinevich may identify Sergei. This is your father's chief fear."

Karena's mouth went dry. Her heart beat faster, and her stomach felt sick. *He was there. And so was I.*

"Let's hope the men involved wore masks," Madame Yeva murmured to herself. "They do when they beat someone—if it is planned. It's all horrible. They must have planned to get Policeman Grinevich."

She looked at Karena a long moment. "There was a full moon last night," she said thoughtfully. "Let us hope Sergei was not there, but I have no such confidence, Karena. We both know him."

Karena bit her lip. *I am merely keeping back what will bring her more pain. Dr. Zinnovy warned me to keep silent.* If anyone understood the risks, it was Dr. Zinnovy. In this situation she would follow his advice.

"Mama," she whispered, "tell me, please, what was in the message Natalia brought from Papa? What did he say?"

"Policeman Leonovich telegraphed the authorities in Kiev last night after the attack on Grinevich. There was already a company of soldiers riding this direction on their way to Warsaw. Your father expects more arrests."

More arrests. Fear jumped to Karena's throat. If they questioned Sergei, what would he say? Could he convince them he was not there? Would he even try? And what about herself?

"And now some of these very soldiers will billet here on Peshkov land," Madame Yeva said. "Matters are turning severe. Your papa is very worried."

"Then the officers are coming here to interrogate us?"

"Most assuredly, they will ask questions. Your father wants Sergei prepared to deny he was at the meeting last night. At any and all costs."

"Have they arrested anyone else? anyone who may have seen who was at the meeting?"

Madame Peshkova's lips tightened. "It is too soon to know, but we must take precautions. Josef has a plan to try to protect Sergei. I can tell you no more now. But all this is very serious, and your father may pay a heavy price."

Karena looked at her for a horrified moment. She nodded in silence, then hurried into the front hall, anxious and uncertain. She caught up her blue headscarf from the hall table, intent on finding Sergei. Afterward she would go to the bungalow to tell Uncle Matvey the dark news.

A plan to protect Sergei… What could it be?

ELEVEN

Winds of Change

K arena left the manor house and hurried down the porch steps and across the front yard toward Uncle Matvey's bungalow. The wind kicked up, and she felt the warmth embrace her. Straight ahead, she could see the bungalow with peasants hard at work in the surrounding fields and, in the distance, silos and barns silhouetted against a clear August sky.

She did not see Uncle Matvey sitting out on the porch as he often did when writing, nor was Ilya about; perhaps he was still with Sergei in the fields overseeing the peasant workers. In a few days, most of them would be conscripts in the army and be replaced by their fathers. The older women worked alongside the young girls; they lived in thatch huts on the other side of the field where a small river flowed. The women worked a communal plot of land where they grew their food and shared it according to the mouths to feed in a particular family.

Individual ownership and thought were not prevalent. The concept of the rugged individualist was not part of their culture. They worked alongside their men, bent over for hours, uncomplaining, their blue head scarves reminding Karena of faded cornflowers.

Karena was used to the sight of the peasants working long and hard days and thought little about it, though Grandmother Jilinsky wondered with a shake of her head how they could endure. "If I bent over for more than five minutes at a time, I would not be able to straighten again."

Karena reached the field nearest the bungalow and saw Sergei, who looked her way and waved. She beckoned him to come. He walked toward her carrying a sickle over his shoulder.

She waited, breathing the fragrance of earth and ripened wheat.

He came up, taking out a kerchief to wipe his face and neck, soiled with harvest dust and sweat. He slapped at an insect.

"Sergei the farmer," she teased, knowing he balked at the notion. "You should take over the lands after Papa. You could marry Anna and have many children."

He laughed, showing white teeth. He always seemed to know when she was teasing him. "Papa wants me to become a lawyer, remember?" he goaded back. "The only thing I like about farming is eating the harvest. It is *you* who will stay here and marry Ilya and have many children. But I am full of rebellion. 'Sergei the radical!'" His brown eyes were humorously challenging.

"After last night, do you make light of such a matter?"

His grin faded, and a furrow appeared between his brows as he glanced toward the road.

"Yes…last night. Not good, Sister. Not good at all."

"What happened to Lenski? And did Ivanna come?"

"She's here and safe. She had nothing to do with what happened last night. They are both in hiding. For my safety as well as theirs, I wasn't told where they are. Nor do I care to know right now. The secret police have their ways of making most any man tell all."

"If Ivanna's in hiding with Lenski, his reputation with the Okhrana will place her in danger too. You haven't told me whether she's also a revolutionary."

He looked away and shrugged, pulling the stopper from his canteen of water. "They would question her most severely if they thought she had information." He scowled. "If they associate you with me and Lenski, they could do the same to you. Ilya was right. I was a fool to bring you there." He drank thirstily.

Karena glanced toward the road uneasily. "Mama sent me to call you back to the house. There may be serious trouble. Officers in the secret police are in town asking questions. One of them is Tatiana's fiancé, Colonel Kronstadt." She explained the message from their father. Sergei listened, shifting his sickle as he looked toward the village.

"Yes, I saw the soldiers ride in early this morning. As for trouble, there's always a cauldron brewing somewhere. If it's not terror from the autocrats, then it's terror from the corrupt police, or war with Germany, or famine and death." He looked toward the horizon, as if he could see German and Austrian troops. "There is no hope for this life, Sister."

"I've never heard you so pessimistic. If you believe there's no hope, why risk so much for a revolution?"

"Sometimes I wonder why I bother. If it weren't for Papa, I'd leave Russia tonight. I mean it. I'd go to London and try to emigrate to New York. Freedom is already planted there."

"Uncle Matvey believes in hope for this life, and even afterward. I'm finding the research he's doing most interesting. God has a plan to reveal himself to mankind, a Messiah who will be a Redeemer. He hasn't wound up his universe like a clock and gone off and left us. Maybe you should talk more seriously to Uncle about what he's discovering."

One corner of his mouth tipped. "I'll read his book when it comes out—if it doesn't bore me to death."

She folded her arms. "You sound just like Tatiana. Sometimes you see nothing but what's before your eyes. Uncle says God's dealt with every generation of the past, and we've many lessons to learn from them. We're not the smartest generation that ever lived."

He smiled affectionately. "Lectures, lectures. My sister the preacher."

"Well, we must have hope, Sergei. People cannot live without hope—a cause to live for and even to die for, if need be. But the sacrifice must be worthy of the cause."

"You are whistling in the dark, as the Americans say." He popped the stopper back into his canteen. "Think about it, Karena. There is little hope for us. Russia's army is not ready for war. We will be defeated. Then what?"

"To say such a thing borders on treason."

"You remember what Uncle Viktor said? It was months ago when he came to visit, but it still holds true. Did he not say what I'm saying now? His words were softer, more palatable, but the truth comes out the same."

"Boris received papers this morning to report for military duty," she said dully. "Natalia is most unhappy. You are likely to be called too. If not today, tomorrow."

He shook his head. "Uncle Viktor will see that I am not conscripted. Papa told me so this morning."

She wondered how Papa could be so confident. Were they not all depending too much on the position and authority of General Viktor Roskov?

"I am to be pressed back into the university to become the family lawyer. The bourgeois!" he scorned. "And I ask you, Sister, this war with Germany and Austria, why should Russians fight for France? Tell me that! Napoleon hurled his might against us, did he not? Had it not been for Russia's glorious winter—"

"France is now Russia's friend. You know that. What will you do about last night?"

"Do not speak of the matter. You were not there, remember?"

"The officers will ask questions," she warned. "You must be ready. Papa has a plan to protect you."

His eyes narrowed. "A plan?"

"Mama did not explain. She's worried. You'd best go home quickly."

He frowned. "Papa is not a Bolshevik. He should not get involved."

"He is already involved, as am I. Nothing could go wrong, you told Ilya, remember? And now look. You see what happens when we associate with rebels?"

"Right now, I'm only wondering why the person watching Grinevich failed to warn Lenski in time. Perhaps he turned traitor. Am I to blame because that jackal Grinevich hurls himself into the meeting? A goat among starving lions will be pounced on every time. Still, I had nothing to do with Grinevich's black eye."

"He has more than a black eye. His ribs are broken. He has a concussion."

His mouth hardened. "I'll lose no sleep over him. He's a spy for the czar."

"For the czar! Grinevich? How do you know that?"

"I know. That's all."

"He doesn't seem wise enough for that."

"Spies watch us all the time. 'Shadow people,' Lenski calls them. They set traps. They join our ranks. The czar's police are all alike, sworn to our demise, to our silence. And that includes Tatiana's man, Kronstadt. The autocrats have nothing on me. Even so, I'll go back to the house. I want to know what Papa wrote in that message."

Sergei flicked her braid, grinned bravely, and left her on the harvest path holding his sickle. She watched him walk briskly across the field toward the manor.

Heaviness weighed upon her. She didn't share his confidence.

She took in the bountiful scene of harvest, and a sadness descended upon her. It was carried on the wind that rushed through the sea of grain, in the leaves turning from green to sienna, and in the call of a solitary bird escaping the approaching winter.

She remembered a verse Uncle Matvey had underlined in his Bible, and the words struck her now with their sudden, personal meaning.

"The harvest is past, the summer is ended, and we are not saved," she murmured.

※

Karena neared her uncle's bungalow and saw that the window curtains were down. *Most likely being washed again.* Grandmother Jilinsky complained the blowing dust made them impossible to care for properly.

Nostalgia stirred as her gaze stopped on the apple tree growing close to the side of the bungalow. In summer it cast a pleasant shade over the porch, and in winter it stood strong in a world of limitless white. When the snow arrived this year, only Grandmother Jilinsky would be living there. Uncle Matvey would be gone, and Ilya would be on the front lines in Poland. There'd be no time on the battlefield for his favorite pastime of reading Tolstoy and Dostoevsky and writing poetry.

"Karena?"

She turned. Ilya walked toward her, the wind flapping his sweat-stained shirt. She was disturbed, for as much as she'd tried in the last few years to think of him as her love, somehow the feelings were not there. She'd known him since they were children, and he was more like a brother. She sighed, trying to shut out the image of Alex on the road that morning. She'd deliberately kept him out of her mind all summer, but it seemed he could walk in anytime he wished and unsettle her heart for days.

She waited for Ilya, another reluctant farmer. She forced a smile, seeing the dust rise from under his heels. His hair glinted with reds and golds, and his eyes made her think of pools of water—silent, still. He was tall and lean, strong from his years of working the land.

Ilya, too, had met disappointment this summer. He'd finally given up pursuing poetry and writing at Warsaw University, where once Uncle Matvey had held his professorship. He had resigned himself to the family's expectation of managing the land and said he was grateful to Josef for the opportunity.

Her heart sympathized with him; he would fit better into the world of literature and opera than a life of growing wheat for the government. She imagined him as he wished himself to be, an aristocrat, discussing the works of Russian and Polish writers while the classical music of the Russian grand master Tchaikovsky was playing in the background. But ethnicity, social class, money, and war brought the inevitable defeat of dreams. Ilya's parents had both been Jewish.

As he walked up, a thoughtful frown on his face, she assumed he did not know about last night.

"Where is Sergei going in such a hurry? To keep the noon meal with Anna?"

"Have you seen her this morning?" she asked.

"Yes, I saw her about. Is anything the matter?"

Relieved, she shook her head. "Not if you saw her this morning. But I need to tell you about Sergei. He's in trouble. For that matter, we all are. Something happened last night."

He took her hands between his calloused ones. They looked at each other, any pretense of happy times ahead shed like autumn's leaves.

His voice dropped. "Grinevich, last night?"

She nodded. "You know what happened?"

"Sergei mentioned it when he arrived this morning." His fingers tightened around hers. "I warned you to not go. Why did you not listen to me, Karena?"

"I told you. I expected assistance from Lenski's sister at the medical college. Now that no longer matters. I was told this morning I will not be going to St. Petersburg with Uncle Matvey next month. There are no finances to spare for this year."

"I am sorry. You would make a good doctor, Karena. But do not despair, you will also make the best of midwives." He smiled wistfully. "Even now, with Anna, you feel more compassion than scorn. I know about her and Sergei. That is what I find so beautiful about you. You wish to help her."

"Ilya, you make me feel worthy. I wish—" She stopped. What good was wishing to love someone romantically?

"Then listen to me. Even if you don't graduate from the Imperial College, Madame Yeva has taught you what she knows. What you bring to the peasants is a gift of mercy. It's more than most will ever receive."

They heard horses coming and looked toward the road, squinting against the noon glare.

"Soldiers," he warned. "Many of them."

So soon! Their horses could be seen farther down the road. Had Sergei had time to reach the manor?

Ilya released her hand. "Go inside and warn Uncle. I'll talk to them."

Heart racing, Karena rushed to the porch steps. Was Alex with the soldiers? She paused, her hand on the rail. She heard the horses on the wagon road and smelled the rise of dust.

The front door opened, and Uncle Matvey Menkin stepped out onto the porch—tall, of comfortable weight, with sharp, clear eyes that held a glimmer of good humor just below the surface. His face was pleasant, and smiles came more easily in the last year. The wind blew his jaw-length gray hair and stirred the hem on his embroidered, tan peasant tunic with loose sleeves gathered at the wrists in a wide hem of blue. He wore a calf-length brown boot, but his right foot was wrapped in a woolen sock, swollen from the painful effects of gout. He used a cane today as he came down the porch steps.

It struck her unexpectedly that her uncle was the only one who hadn't experienced a summer of discontent. He had sought escape from the noise of the city and striking factory workers, to bask in the sound of the wind rushing through the grain fields and the sight of clear nights with gleaming stars. "A perfect environment to study the Torah," he'd said.

Karena waited below, holding the rail as she looked up at him, knowing alarm must show on her face. He came down the steps slowly but made not a grumble for better days.

Karena met him, and he took hold of her arm. He patted her hand, as if to assure her he was not afraid, and so neither should she be. "This is a time for dignity," he often told them. "If the Torah is accurate, we are made in the image of Elohim. We will keep our dignity in the face of injustice."

Those words now resounded in her soul. Perhaps she ought to tell him that she was there at the meeting last night, but it might obligate him to his own harm, for he would not betray her.

"The czar's soldiers are asking for Sergei, are they?" he inquired.

She moistened her lips and nodded.

"Where is he now?"

"At the manor." She quickly explained the details of Josef's message.

He nodded. "I will hear what they have to say for myself. Go inside, Karena. Grandmother Jilinsky is most upset. See if you can calm her."

He left her on the steps and worked his way slowly toward the wagon road and the group of approaching soldiers.

Karena went up on the porch and watched until he came up and stood beside Ilya. There remained an Old World charm about Uncle Matvey that lent a dignity to his posture. She was proud of the Jewish side of her family in Warsaw that he represented, despite their being hated in Poland and throughout Russia. Was it the same in other countries? Some bishops called them "Christ killers," providing propaganda for persecution, also saying that God was through with Israel. Uncle Matvey, however, had told her, "Though Israel has been set aside for not recognizing their Messiah, if we believe the Scriptures, we must believe the many wonderful unconditional promises God made specifically to Israel that are still to be fulfilled."

Does Uncle Matvey believe Jesus is the Messiah? Perhaps that was why, even now, he had more peace and enthusiasm for life than ever.

TWELVE

Okhrana's Arrival

Colonel Aleksandr Kronstadt drew his horse alongside Major-General Durnov. Farther ahead, the road split off toward the land managed by the local zemstvo representative, Josef Peshkov.

The large manor house of wood and brick came into view. In front of the manor, the wide lawn suffered from summer's end, and beneath a willow tree, a man-made pond beside a small creek offered white and brown ducks a refuge from the sun.

Off to the side of the wagon road stood a medium-sized bungalow with a large roofed porch with chairs and a table. Several shade trees loomed over the bungalow, which gave Alex the impression of an island in the middle of the sea. If his research over the past few days since arriving in Kiev was accurate, Professor Matvey Menkin's bungalow was indeed an island, an isolated oasis of ideas in a sea of political and religious struggles. How long before the bungalow would be swallowed by the waves? Alex and Durnov drew up beneath the freckled shade of a linden tree while the contingent of conscripts moved farther to select an area to set up their gear. In the morning, Captain Suslov's soldiers would travel on toward Warsaw to join up with Russia's main forces.

Alex lowered his hat against the sun's glare and peered toward distant plains. He took a moment to watch the shadow play of clouds upon the steppes. The sight evoked a vague longing in his heart. The waves of wheat, swaying in the breeze, hypnotized him. The rushing sound filled his ears, drowning out his soul's troubled thoughts.

Land—magnificent *land.* He could congratulate the Bolsheviks on one thing: they knew how to bait the heart-longings of the peasant.

"Bread, peace with Germany, and land!"

The revolutionaries' rallying call appealed to restless masses. To the common Russian, the arguments for war between various thrones were merely disagreements over which autocrat was awarded desirable lands and peasants to enlarge their rule. Royal cousins maneuvered within their grand palaces, deciding how many of their peasant-pawns they could afford to lose on the battlefield to achieve their gains.

But the peasant-pawns were stirring, wondering why they should spill their blood for the czar, the kaiser, the president of France, or the king of England. The peasant masses were hungry, weary, and angry.

All around him, he saw an uneducated mass without rights, who moved in lockstep.

Major-General Durnov removed his military headgear and wiped a hand over his bald head, his tufted gray brows lowering as he replaced his cap. He sighed, sounding like a disgruntled bear.

"How does the chief of secret police expect us to arrest the nephew of the wife of General Roskov?"

"I also wonder, sir. After what happened to Grinevich last night, he'll demand his head."

Durnov spat in the dust. "Grinevich will demand nothing."

Alex looked at him for explanation.

"Grinevich will not be reaping his pound of flesh," Durnov said. "He's dead."

The silence that followed was filled with the rush of the wind. Alex hid his groan. The charge of beating Grinevich would be changed to murder.

Durnov hunched his shoulders as he slouched forward, resting his forearm on the horn of his saddle. "My back will be the death of me yet... Well, Kronstadt, it is going to be worse for these Bolsheviks than I had first thought. I am most certain one of them will be made to talk. The Okhrana is adept at that."

Alex tightened his jaw and remained silent. Not even Durnov knew that he had gone to the meeting last night disguised as one of the peasants.

"Peshkov's son should cast dust on his head," Durnov went on.

"There were several involved in the beating. Grinevich was hated by many in this village. More than one landed a good kick."

"He had a bull head. I warned him in his younger years he was the sort of bully to die by a mob. I was right! But I tell you, the revolutionary leaders will hang for his murder. That will be Lenski and young Peshkov."

"Why Sergei Peshkov? I have found nothing yet to prove he was behind the organized demonstration. It was Lenski who arranged to speak in the college square last night and Lenski's rhetoric against the czar that fired up the peasants. And, sir, it is Lenski who is in hiding. Sergei Peshkov hasn't made a run for it. He must feel he has nothing to hide."

Durnov gave a heavy shrug. "Do not get me wrong, Kronstadt. Personally, I do not care that Grinevich is dead. He was not a pleasant fellow. But we have our orders from Petrograd. The Bolsheviks must be arrested. Do not forget Sergei is on file with us for distributing *Iskra*."

"I interviewed many in the village. Lenin's newspaper is not to be found."

Durnov reached into his military jacket and pulled out a cigarette. He held it between his blunt yellow teeth, searching for a match. He struck it, protecting its feeble flame from the hot wind.

"Never mind the Bolshies for now. Begin with Menkin. What did you discover about this old Polish Jew?"

He kept his voice unemotional, acting the perfect military officer newly pressed into the secret police. *How can I gain a transfer back to my regiment in the Imperial Cavalry? I would rather face Germans!*

Alex pulled his notepad from inside his jacket and flipped it open.

"Professor Menkin arrived in Kiev two months ago from his apartment in Petrograd to work on a religious manuscript—"

"Possibly a front. What kind of religious manuscript? Rasputin again?"

Alex flicked an insect off his notepad. "No, quite the contrary. Its title is *Messiah, Religious Philosophy or a King?* Menkin arrived here in June and went straight to work on his research. His niece, Miss Karena Peshkova, has been working with him as his secretary, also aiding with the research. There's no evidence of Menkin's involvement with Bolshevik propaganda. He did not know Professor Chertkov, nor is his name on a list of Chertkov's defenders. He was born—"

"What of Miss Peshkova? Did she know Chertkov?"

Alex leafed through his notebook, as though searching to renew his memory. "She took several of Chertkov's history classes before she graduated the college. That was over three years ago. No trouble where she is concerned," he added smoothly. "She has an ambition to become a doctor. She is trying to get admittance into the Imperial College of Medicine and Midwifery. She was refused for the third time just recently."

"A woman doctor? What is Russia coming to?"

"She appears to be most intelligent, sir. I checked her college grades, and she received excellent marks."

Alex tapped the end of his pencil on the notepad. He found it frustrating to have his mind fixated on Karena. He'd thought of her many times since Kazan but had fully intended to keep away from her. That is, until events had forced him to collect information on her family. He knew, for instance, or he should say *suspected,* a past relationship between Madame Peshkova and Dr. Zinnovy. The jeweled pendant Tatiana made so much about in Kazan must have been given by Zinnovy to Madame Yeva when she was a student at the college.

He also discovered Ilya Jilinsky was expected to marry Karena. Would her family see her married to the Polish peasant before he marched off into the upcoming war? Alex did not think so, as Ilya would be leaving with the other conscripts camped across the road.

"So Miss Peshkova shows a tendency against the standard role of women in Russia, and she also took a class from Chertkov," Durnov said thoughtfully.

"She does not seem the type to involve herself with the rowdy Bolsheviks. Her mother attended the Medical College in Petrograd. It is natural for the elder daughter to carry on the tradition."

Durnov turned his head and looked at him searchingly, smoking his cigarette. Alex tried to become unreadable.

"And the Polish Professor Menkin?" Durnov asked.

"He was born in Krakow of the Jewish Menkin family. He's the older brother of Madame Peshkova. A few of the Menkins, including their grandparents, were gentiles from Finland. They were all loyal to the czar." Alex flipped through his notebook.

"Ilya Jilinsky and his grandmother also live here. Both are from Warsaw—"

"Jews?"

"Yes. They occupy the bungalow year round. They're related to Madame Peshkova through marriage, not blood."

"Why are they outside the Jewish Pale of Settlement?"

Alex leafed the pages again, irritated. "They have renounced Judaism. They were baptized into the Russian Orthodox Church over a dozen years ago and attend St. Andrew's with Josef Peshkov."

As he and Durnov both knew, baptism into the Russian Orthodox Church allowed Professor Menkin and Madame Peshkova to escape state persecution and have more freedom to live as they wished, although Jews were still watched, whatever religion they claimed.

"Menkin is acquainted with the writings of the revolutionaries Lenin and Trotsky," Alex went on. "However, I do not think he is a Bolshevik. He is known to dine with Miliukov when in Petrograd."

Miliukov was one of the founders of the cadets, a group that favored a constitutional monarchy, such as Great Britain. Their name *cadets* was taken from the Russian initials of the Constitutional Democrats.

If Alex agreed in part with any movement to end the autocratic system in Russia, it would be the cadets. Another side of Professor Menkin he appreciated.

Durnov squinted off toward the bungalow. He drew on his cigarette. "What of his revolutionary work in Poland?"

So Durnov knows. Alex had toyed with leaving out that information but saw the danger of it now.

"Menkin's politics in Poland were radical and nationalistic. He supported an independent Poland, free of Russia and Germany, which was the cause of his dismissal from Warsaw University. He attended a meeting held by a revolutionary-backed students' group, and the government moved in and ordered the university to remove him."

Durnov crushed his cigarette on the bottom of his boot. "That does not look good for him. One so intellectual should have been more cautious in his associations."

"It does not seem likely either Menkin or Josef Peshkov would be involved in organizing a Bolshevik rally with Lenski," Alex said.

Durnov pursed his lips.

"They would seek to influence Duma members and military officers," Alex persisted.

"Anything more on Menkin?"

Alex went on in a monotone, convinced he was digging the unfortunate professor's grave. "Menkin spent two years in a Siberian work camp for his seditious writings while at Warsaw University. He then went to Petrograd, where he now resides. He writes for various publications in and out of the country. He has friends and connections in New York, and his essays are seen on a regular basis in a Jewish intellectual quarterly. None of his writings deal with Poland or the czar."

Durnov's saddle squeaked. "That will be Menkin now coming down the road. The young peasant must be Jilinsky."

Alex surveyed the fair-haired Ilya Jilinsky who had paused to wait for Professor Menkin to join him before walking to meet them. Ilya appeared rather boyish, slender, and browned by the sun. The professor had straight shoulders and walked from the bungalow using a cane.

Alex would have liked to ride forward to meet Professor Menkin, but Durnov remained seated on his horse in the shade. It was a way to show superiority, to make *them* come to him.

Alex turned his full attention upon Professor Menkin, who stopped a short distance ahead and stood leaning on a cane, his loose-fitting peasant tunic flapping in the wind. He was far from being in his dotage. The deep-set eyes were intelligent and piercing beneath a swath of silver gray hair that fell across his tanned forehead. His jaw was square, his stance resolute.

"You are Professor Matvey Menkin, the uncle of Sergei Peshkov?" Durnov demanded.

"I am Professor Menkin, yes. Sergei is my nephew by marriage. What do you want with me?"

"Your business here in Kiev—what is it?"

Alex edged his horse forward. He saw Menkin measure him with a steady eye, and Alex liked the flicker of courage.

"I am a writer and a historian. I came for the summer to work on my manuscript, to be published in New York. If you have come to the Peshkov manor for supper, then this young lad here"—he nodded to Ilya Jilinsky—"will take you there. I believe the family will soon be prepared to spread a festive table before you, though I cannot vouch for the Madeira."

Alex found a smile tugging his mouth as he glanced at Durnov. Durnov was blunt and businesslike, but he had never been a cruel man. There was little Durnov liked better than a good supper—though he had a reputation for preferring to wash it down with vodka.

Durnov sighed his regret.

"That is good, Professor Menkin, that is good." His tough tone eased. "My soldiers will eat, and Colonel Kronstadt and I will wait for your brother-in-law, Josef. Unfortunately this is not a time for good food and social talk." Durnov paused, and Alex shifted slightly in his saddle. "Chief Gendarme Grinevich is dead. Murdered by the stinking Bolsheviks from your village. I am under orders from the Okhrana to arrest Sergei Peshkov for beating and kicking Grinevich to death last night."

The thunderous silence was sickening.

THIRTEEN

HaMashiach

Karena entered Uncle Matvey's bungalow thinking of Alex. He was likely to arrive soon with his commanding officer, and then interrogations would begin. She thought of her brief meeting with him earlier on the road. For a moment, his eyes had looked directly into hers, and once again, as on that fateful day on the wharf at Kazan, she had sensed his awareness of her, not as a possible revolutionary under suspicion, but as a woman.

Then again, maybe it was her own feelings she was interpreting. She was reading too much into his look. Perhaps he was merely noting the differences between wealthy aristocrats like the Roskovs and the gentry. The difference was a chasm. While most of Karena's wardrobe was for life in the countryside of Kiev, Tatiana had jewels and Parisian gowns.

The bungalow was not typical, although it once had been, before Ilya and Grandmother Leah Jilinsky came here and settled after a pogrom in Warsaw had left them destitute and alone. Papa Josef had added two tiny bedrooms, so that when Uncle Matvey came from St. Petersburg, he could have the larger room connected to a cubbyhole for use as an office.

The original bungalow was built of thick, dressed logs with a hall and two rooms. One of these was used as the kitchen, containing the stove, which reached nearly to the ceiling. Close to the stove and just under the roof was a platform wide enough for the family to use as the warmer sleeping area when the snowy Russian winter came. Karena and Natalia had used it growing up, when they had come here to spend a night and visit Uncle Matvey. Karena could still remember waking those early mornings to the delightful aroma of Grandmother Jilinsky's sweet breads, fresh and warm, waiting on the back of the stove.

On some evenings, Uncle Matvey and Ilya would have dinner at the manor house, and after supper, they would gather with Papa Josef and Sergei around the large kitchen table, drinking coffee and smoking their pipes, and discuss everything from the future of Russia to emigrating to America through Ellis Island in New York—something her father would not even consider.

The peasant's bungalow was normally lined with wooden benches along the walls, but Grandmother Jilinsky had furnished her kitchen with a large dining table and six comfortable chairs. One corner of the room displayed an icon hanging in a niche, though neither the Jilinskys nor Uncle Matvey paid it any attention. It was there to assure any outsiders and watchful officials of their loyalty to the state church.

Orthodox Jews considered such icons in their home tantamount to gentile idolatry, but Grandmother Jilinsky boasted her eyesight was getting so poor she could hardly trouble herself to see it in her "good Polish kitchen," and Ilya, having lost his parents in a pogrom, was not inclined to think much about religious traditions.

By the side of the house, an enclosed yard had stabling for two horses. There was also a bathhouse and a small cellar. In the latter, Grandmother Jilinsky stored her root vegetables for the winter, along with preserved foods and salted meat.

Karena caught a waft of cabbage and beef cooking and went to the kitchen through the open doorway. She found the big pot simmering on the stove and lowered the flame. The water in the coffeepot was boiling, unattended.

Grandmother Leah Jilinsky stood in front of the small window, staring out toward the road and the soldiers. Her eyes, when she turned toward Karena, were brimming with fear and hatred. She had spent a half century enduring the pogroms in Nalewski, the Jewish quarter in Warsaw, and her past cast long shadows on the present. Her aged face and sunken cheeks told of a lifetime of insecurity. Her home, usually a place of refuge from the uncaring world, had always been a knock away from the invaders.

Russia had its own pogroms, as Karena knew well enough. She'd been a child when she heard about the dreaded Kishinev pogrom of 1903 and the devastation to Russian Jewry. Jewish families were grabbed from their very beds, their eyes gouged out, and their babies and children tossed from windows onto the pavement below. Many even had nails pounded into their flesh and were left to die in their sufferings. The rampage had gone on for three days in autocratic Russia, where a person could hardly breathe without the czar's approval, yet the czar had done nothing.

That was also the time she had first heard the name Theodor Herzl, the founder of the World Zionist Organization, and his call for a Jewish homeland. Herzl had since died, but the Zionist movement lived on under its new president, Chaim Weizmann. Karena had learned much of the movement to return Jews to Palestine through working with Uncle Matvey on his manuscript, for as he said, "You cannot adequately discuss the Messiah without also understanding the land and the people to whom the land was promised."

After Karena returned home from Kazan, she'd spent the rest of the summer, at her uncle's request, writing letters to Chaim Weizmann, who was born in Russia and emigrated to England, asking questions that would be dealt with in Uncle Matvey's book.

Grandmother Jilinsky wrung her thin, wrinkled hands. "The soldiers have come for Sergei," she said as she left the window. "There is no place of refuge, my child, not for any of us. They will take him away. They always take them away somewhere, somewhere."

Karena looked for faith to comfort the older woman and found she had little to offer.

"We will pray to the icon," Karena murmured from custom. "St. Nicholas will help. We will light a candle."

Grandmother's eyes smoldered. "St. Nicholas! *Oy vey!* Why not the God of Abraham, I ask? Are you afraid to answer, my child? Then I shall speak! It is because neither St. Nicholas nor the God of Abraham can help us! They have not helped me in the past. Why should I still believe?"

Karena went to the side of the kitchen chair and put an arm around her, patting her in wordless comfort and feeling her bony structure through the worn peasant blouse of bright colors. "Oh, Grandmother, you are so distressed. Why, look what Uncle Matvey says. He's convinced God has not given up the seed of Abraham. That's why he's writing Chaim Weizmann."

"What can Weizmann do for the Jews?"

"God may be using his movement to bring Israel back to the land to become a nation again. Uncle says some Jews think that Jesus was the promised Messiah. And many Christians say the Scriptures teach that Israel will be a nation again, and when it happens, the Messiah's second coming may be drawing near. Mr. Weizmann is negotiating with the British parliament. He has something important that could be used in the war. In return, the British government may work for a Jewish homeland. Just think! A nation all our own. No more pogroms!"

Grandmother Jilinsky looked doubtful. "Matvey, he is turning into a goy. I do not know what to make of him when he says that crucified one was the Messiah. My rabbi in Warsaw, when I was a girl your age, would groan in his grave if he heard that. How could the Messiah have come?

Where is the kingdom promised to King David and his people? We are not even in the land."

"Grandmother Jilinsky, you just heard me explain about the new Zionist movement and what it may mean."

"We are scattered all over the world, forgotten, despised. Our bones are dried up; who can make these bones live again? Not Chaim Weizmann."

"No, not Mr. Weizmann. The Zionist movement is secular, but Matvey has researched another group of Jews, called Messianic, who are looking for Messiah to come to the nation Israel, to rebuild the Jewish temple in Jerusalem and establish peace."

Karena remembered Matvey's references to the prophet Ezekiel. "You just quoted from Ezekiel 37: 'Can these bones live?' The bones are the whole house of Israel. And Matvey says many Bible scholars believe Israel will become a nation again. That isn't all. God told Ezekiel that *after* we become a nation again, a time will come when God will breathe new spiritual life into Israel. So you see? There's hope. Grandmother Jilinsky, what if Jesus truly *is* the promised Messiah?"

The older woman stared at her. Karena hadn't realized it, but in putting forth what Uncle Matvey was writing, she'd grown to embrace the ideas with unexpected enthusiasm.

"Oh!" Grandmother Jilinsky exclaimed and rushed past her toward the black stove. Karena heard something sizzling in the fire. She turned and saw the water for coffee was boiling over.

Karena laughed, and even Grandmother smiled as she added the right amount of coarse grounds to the pot, stirring it with a big spoon.

Karena's laughter faded into thoughtfulness. Talking about Jesus had brought a special mood to the little kitchen. *Maybe I will do what Uncle Matvey suggests—read the book called Matthew.*

Through the window, Karena and Grandmother Jilinsky watched the czar's conscripts make camp for the night in a distant section of the field where the wheat had already been harvested. Karena remembered that food needed to be scrounged up from somewhere—enough to feed a large group. She needed no reminder that Colonel Kronstadt and his superiors would dine at the manor house.

And Sergei... What would happen? Surely there was no proof of his attending last night's meeting. Maybe after questioning everyone, they would ride on in search of Lenski.

"They intend to camp out on the land as the colonel requested this morning," Karena told Grandmother Jilinsky. "They will want food."

"Poot—colonel requested!"

"Actually, yes. He did ask to camp his men for the night. They are on their way to Warsaw," Karena said dully, "to join the general there. The war has begun."

"I was up early this morning baking. And now will Sergei's enemies take my bread?"

"Grandmother Jilinsky, please, do not upset yourself. You know what Mother said about your heart."

"My heart beats well enough. They will not take my bread."

"Is there any choice? If they wished, they could take over the manor and bungalow both. They could bed the soldiers down, and there would be nothing we could do. So far he has requested only necessities and been polite. Colonel Kronstadt is a friend of Uncle Viktor Roskov and Aunt Zofia. He is likely to become engaged to Cousin Tatiana."

Grandmother Jilinsky looked at her sharply. "The colonel who is here to arrest Sergei?"

"He may not arrest him. Maybe Uncle Viktor sent him... Maybe it will bode well for Sergei after all, for all of us," she added, thinking about her own presence at the college square last night.

Karena looked out the window and watched the older man in uniform with the slouching jacket and cap ride away from the other three toward the manor house. Alex dismounted and remained talking with Ilya and Uncle Matvey for a few minutes. She did not think the older man could be an Imperial officer, but some other specialized bureaucrat in the military section of the Okhrana, whereas she knew from Tatiana that Alex had gone to the elite officer school. Karena took note of his precise military manner and how authoritative he looked as he spoke to Ilya.

Alex finished speaking to Ilya, remounted, and rode toward the path that led to the manor house. Ilya turned to Uncle Matvey for a moment and then followed Alex.

"Uncle Matvey is returning alone," Karena said. "The other men have gone up to the manor." She considered going, but remembered Uncle Matvey wanted her to remain here.

Grandmother Jilinsky pushed herself up from the wicker chair.

"He will want coffee."

The kitchen door opened, and Uncle Matvey entered. Even in his ailing health, his presence brought a feeling of security into the room. Karena stood expectantly, waiting for news. Grandmother Jilinsky hovered at the stove with the coffee.

He reached for his pipe on the shelf. He filled it with tobacco, pressing it in with his thumb.

"There is distressing news. You know this, both of you." He struck a match. "They will be asking Sergei some questions." He puffed the pipe. "Sergei told me he wasn't at the meeting last night."

Karena shifted her gaze to look at him. Did Uncle Matvey really believe that?

"When did you see him last?" Karena asked quietly.

"This morning, helping Ilya with the harvest." He took the coffee from Grandmother Jilinsky. "Leah, the soldiers will camp in the field tonight. Major-General Durnov will need some food for the men. I told him you would gather what provisions you could from the storehouse. The rest will be provided by Marta. One of the soldiers will come by the back door to receive it. Could you please get it ready for him?"

Grandmother Jilinsky grumbled her displeasure and left by way of the back door.

❧

Leah restrained the words that simmered in her heart as hotly as her cabbage on the stove. Having gone without food many times in her life, she found it painful to give up what she had been storing away for herself and Ilya.

If I had arsenic, I would put it in the soldiers' mush and feel no shame. Are they not murderers? Yes, all of them. Russian soldiers, bah! What did the czar do to stop the murder of my people under the heels of his officials? What did he do to stop the Jew haters? He did nothing. Nothing, except to blame the Jews. "The revolutionaries snarling at my ankles are either Jews or backed by Jews." A lie! There were no more Jews involved than Russians!

Now she was to take her food stores and feed how many? Maybe fifty hungry soldiers. It would take a firm bite from her hard work of canning and preserving.

She entered the storage pantry. In the dimness, she paused, her thoughts spinning back to Warsaw and the robbery done to her son, Ilya's father, and to the other shopkeepers. The raw memories marched across her soul. The clatter of cavalry on the old cobble streets echoed in her ears again. The shattering glass, the smoke, the heat burning her cheeks as she searched in a frenzy for Ilya—Ilya, in the back of the store while his father fought to stop the Polish soldiers and students. Houses, shops, whole buildings burned to the ground, and the watermen would not come to put out the fires. The synagogues were broken into, objects smashed, rabbis kicked and beaten, men and boys killed, women and girls violated.

Leah's sob shook her back to the reality of the moment. She was not in Warsaw but in Russia, and the nightmare was now a memory—it was over.

Her wrinkled hands trembled as she pushed her silver hair back from her damp face.

She set her mouth grimly. She respected Matvey's articles and books written when he had taught at Warsaw. His last book, too, was worthy of him, the one on Russia's last war with Japan. But the book he was working on now! Why was he wasting his latter years on empty research? The Messiah! The Deliverer.

She snatched containers and cloth bags and grudgingly began taking potatoes, onions, flour, and dried strips of beef from the storage bins. How painful this was to her.

She straightened her shoulders. So be it. Karena had spoken the truth: there was no choice.

"The Messiah," she said aloud, and then again in Hebrew, *"HaMashiach."* It tasted pleasant on her tongue. Not at all bitter, as she had thought it might.

She looked up at the cracked roofing, but it did not come crashing down in wrath. "HaMashiach," she said louder.

FOURTEEN

Papa Josef's Plan

As soon as Grandmother Jilinsky left for the storage room, Uncle Matvey moved swiftly toward Karena.

"I need to speak to you alone."

Karena peered at him closely. "You have news you don't want her to hear."

"She's overburdened in spirit. It will do us no good and harm her. Now, quickly." He took hold of her arm, his voice becoming grim as he talked. "We don't have much time, Karena. Is there anything I should know about last night?"

She looked away, shaking her head, and moved toward the window. "No, nothing." She loathed involving him after his past arrest in Warsaw. Once a report of sedition against the Imperial power was written up against anyone, the mark never left the files of the secret police, even if later proven false. She guessed this was on his mind as well.

"They'll interrogate us all before they depart tomorrow morning," he said. "Colonel Kronstadt will question us here at the bungalow. It's important I'm told the truth beforehand."

She turned to face him. "But why question you? You had nothing to do with the meeting last night. You don't even know Policeman Grinevich."

"They will question each one of us as normal procedure."

His deep-set eyes fixed on her intently. Normally, she would have told him everything, except she recalled Dr. Zinnovy's orders. She looked down at her hands as though she had never seen them before.

"Come, come, Karena. Do you not trust your old uncle?"

Her anxiety melted, and she went to him quickly and hugged him. "More than anyone."

He patted her head. "Good. It would give me great ease if I understood the risks we face, especially for you. Were you there last night, Karena?"

She brushed back the hair from her damp forehead. She lowered her voice. "Yes. I went for personal reasons. I wanted to see Ivanna, Dr. Lenski's daughter. She attends the medical school. Sergei's been seeing her in St. Petersburg. He and I both thought she might be able to put in a favorable word for me." She turned away. "It was all useless anyway. Ivanna didn't even come to hear her brother's speech."

Matvey's eyes were grave. "Who saw you there?"

"No one saw me, except a few peasants. Everyone was listening to Lenski. Oh yes, and Anna."

Alarm showed in his face. "Anna was there?"

"I don't know if she looked my way. She must have come to please Sergei, even though he didn't appear to notice her. It makes me think he didn't invite her. Suddenly, someone shouted, 'Police!' I ran, but the horse was missing—"

"The horse?"

"Sergei and I rode a horse to the meeting. The police were out searching."

His worry was such that she could not hold back and hastened in a whisper, "Dr. Zinnovy came by in his coach and stopped, threw open his door, and ordered me inside. I recognized him. I had just reached his coach door when police came running up, ordering me to halt. Dr. Zinnovy told them I had been with him that evening, doing some work for him, and that he could swear to my whereabouts. They acted as though they believed him and apologized—though Policeman Leonovich looked suspicious. They let us go, however. Dr. Zinnovy brought me to the front of the manor house. Then we called on Anna to make sure she was all right. Later, I entered through the back door unseen and went straight up to my room."

The startled expression on Uncle Matvey's face when she mentioned Dr. Zinnovy now turned wary. "Dr. *Dmitri* Zinnovy, or do you mean his son Fyodor?"

"The *renowned* Dr. Zinnovy—" She stopped. She would not mention that Zinnovy, by chance on his evening walk, had shown up at the meeting, even to Uncle Matvey.

"Well now, that is what I call good fortune. Dr. Zinnovy's reputation as a Romanov family physician could not be better where you are concerned. I am most surprised he remains in Kiev, though. I'd heard he was returning to St. Petersburg three weeks ago."

"It was astounding, Uncle. He even promised to make a way for my entry into the medical school, but—" She stopped again. "Papa said the finances aren't available this year."

He walked to the stove and refilled his cup.

"I'm still in shock that he'd help me as he did," she said, "but I'm not about to argue with providence."

"You appear to be in a firm position with Dr. Zinnovy's backing. I suppose he told you not to mention the facts to anyone, even though Yeva and Josef must know you were not working for Dr. Zinnovy. Undoubtedly, he assumes the alibi he gave you will be sufficient to quiet further questioning. Well, hopefully, that should satisfy Durnov and Kronstadt." He rubbed his chin and then looked at his watch. "Zinnovy's help brings me great relief. I only wish he could have vouched for Sergei, but one cannot have everything." He walked over to the door and unlocked it.

"Unless I'm mistaken, Kronstadt will be here any minute now. Keep to your story at all costs, Karena. You have a friend in Dr. Zinnovy." He looked at her, and then a tiny frown stole over his face.

Karena wondered what it was about Dr. Zinnovy's favor that worried him. She spoke up. "Colonel Kronstadt's likely to discover your secret dinners with Miliukov in St. Petersburg."

He turned his head. "How did you find out? Sergei, I suppose."

She thought about the intellectual group her uncle met with whenever he was in St. Petersburg. She hoped they were not considered revolutionaries.

"We must not be afraid of ideas, Karena, as long as we have a foundation of truth to judge right from wrong. It's when a people no longer hold on to the foundation that all ideas are judged to be equal. Then a nation, however great, is in grave danger of the greatest deceptions."

She looked at him. "You've changed."

He raised his white brows. "How so?"

"I grew up hearing you tell me how all truths are relative."

He bit the end of his pipe and watched the smoke rings. "Perhaps I am only now discovering how wrong I was. We are all mortal, with feet of clay."

The kitchen door opened suddenly. Ilya came in. He was out of breath from running and looked over at Uncle Matvey. Some wordless message passed between them.

Karena stood, her gaze darting suspiciously from one to the other. "What is it?" she asked.

Ilya was still looking at Matvey. "Sergei is waiting at the back of the bungalow, Uncle. He wants to talk to you."

Karena started for the door, but Ilya stopped her.

"Wait, Karena, please. Sergei needs to see Matvey alone," he said quietly.

She watched as Matvey went out the back kitchen door and around the window to the side porch.

She turned to Ilya. "How did Sergei slip away from the officers?"

"So far, he's managed to avoid them." His voice was low and tight. He walked over to the stove, lifted the lid on the large kettle of stew and sniffed. She handed him a bowl and a spoon. He scooped out a hearty portion and leaned against the wall, ignoring the chair and table.

"Is my father at the manor?"

He nodded without speaking.

A horrid suspicion rose in her chest. She began to pace the kitchen floor, occasionally glancing out the window. Ilya ate his stew in silence. She looked over at him. What was he keeping from her?

"Kronstadt will come here to talk to you," he said a minute later. "If you even hint you were there last night with Sergei, they'll take you to St. Petersburg. You should have listened to me. I knew he'd lead you into trouble."

"Sergei didn't drag me there. I went of my own will."

"If he says anything—or if Anna talks—"

"I will not be arrested." She paced. "I have an alibi."

"What good is an alibi? They will break it in two."

"Not this one."

Ilya looked at her curiously, no doubt wondering what gave her such confidence.

"If you think Kronstadt will deal gently with you, you're wrong. Just because your Uncle Viktor favors him doesn't mean Kronstadt can be trusted to do anything for the family. He will do what furthers his own reputation. I don't like him. Why isn't he going off to war like the rest of us? Instead he goes to the safety of St. Petersburg."

She nearly rushed to Alex's defense, wanting to explain how he wished to join his troops in Warsaw but could not. Instead, she cut a slice of apple pie and served it to him. He ate, but his gray eyes were despondent. He put his plate down as he chewed the last bite.

"I was talking to several of the conscripts in the field," he said finally. "There are stories about Kronstadt. He's the spoiled son of a wealthy countess."

"There are always stories. I'm surprised you would listen to them. You know how some men are when they're being pulled away from their families and forced into the army. I understand, but—"

"Kronstadt's been in trouble at the officer's school. He cares about nothing but riches, women, and entertainments. He likes to shoot and ride, and there's a scandal about a duel, and worse, the military cadets he was with were involved in a pogrom."

She sat down, her fingers tightening on the arm of the chair. "Those are some despicable charges, Ilya, even if they're not true."

He shrugged. "I didn't make them. They are common talk. And most times, common talk is based on some fact."

"Some fact," she said wryly. "Have you met him before?"

"You know I haven't. Just be careful with him, will you? Such a man is dangerous."

Uncle Matvey came through the kitchen door. Sergei was not with him.

"He went back to the manor," Uncle Matvey said when she looked at him for explanation. "Ilya, when you have finished, please find your grandmother, will you? I saw her leave the storage pantry and walk to the chicken coop for eggs. If you can walk her over to the manor, it will be best for her. The colonel will be here soon."

Ilya looked at Karena and seemed about to say something more, but instead, he went out.

Uncle Matvey watched him leave. "I detect trouble of another kind with Ilya."

"He doesn't like Colonel Kronstadt."

He walked over to her. She expected him to reassure her that matters were not as grim as they appeared. He did not.

"You need to be strong," he said with a level look. "Grinevich is dead."

She sucked in her breath.

"He died a few hours ago. You know what that means?"

She did not move.

He nodded. "Yes, naturally, you do." He appeared to have difficulty finding words. "Your father is at the manor. You must prepare yourself, Karena."

She dampened her dry lips. "What do you mean? What has Papa Josef to do with this? I mean, I know they will interrogate him, but he has done nothing."

There was muted pain in his eyes. He laid a hand on her shoulder. "There may be more than one arrest."

More than one?

"Your father will be going to St. Petersburg with Major-General Durnov to answer more questions."

The surprise came like a fist.

"But—why Papa? He wasn't there last night. I can swear to that—"

He grabbed her arm, his eyes warning her. "You will say nothing, Karena. Nothing."

She closed her eyes for a moment to steady her emotions. "Didn't Sergei explain to the officers that his father wasn't there? And Mother is a witness. They were home together all evening. Natalia knows that as well."

"We all know as much. It is Josef himself who states otherwise."

"Papa? That makes no sense."

"Karena," he said, "you must find courage. Josef is confessing that he is a leader of the Bolsheviks here in the village."

She gasped. "Absurd! He said that? How could he? It isn't true. Papa would never be so foolish!" She stared at him and saw the answer in his gaze. She groaned. "Oh no. He's doing it for Sergei. Did Mother agree to this?"

He nodded. "It was Josef's idea. It would be, naturally. In return, Sergei has promised him he will leave the Bolshevik Party and become a lawyer."

She closed her eyes, as if the momentary darkness would make everything unpleasant fade away.

"Yes, I know, my dear child, this is a sickening shock to us all," he said. "But when we stop to think about it, it's not so surprising. Not when we remember what Sergei means to Josef. It would hurt Josef far more to see his son arrested than to make this confession in his place."

Her mind fought its way back from the whirlwind of anguish and grief.

"Such love on Papa's part," she said. "He's willingly going to take Sergei's punishment."

Uncle Matvey looked down at her so sharply that for a moment she wondered what she might have said to upset him. Then she saw he was not angry with her, but thinking of something that had suddenly arrested his mind. His distant gaze was directed out the window again, as he absently fingered his pipe.

She stood, curling her fingers along the back of the chair. She shook her head slowly, doubtfully. "But Papa's arrest may not be enough to satisfy them. Sergei could still be arrested. If Grinevich saw him there last night—if he named Sergei before he died—they could hang both Papa and Sergei, and Papa will have done this for nothing."

He shook his head. "No, Josef arranged to place the guilt of evidence on himself alone this morning when Policeman Leonovich called on him. By the time Kronstadt talked to him, Josef had already settled his plan. Leonovich agrees with Josef that he was there last night, that he was the one who arranged for Lenski to speak. Leonovich satisfied Major-General Durnov, at least. Josef has made some kind of bargain. I do not know what it is. Neither does Sergei, but it's enough to safeguard your brother."

Karena was horrified. Bargain? What bargain could he make with the Okhrana?

"What of Colonel Kronstadt?" she asked. "Is he privy to it also?" Anger churned in her heart.

"No, I am quite sure he is not, though Ilya thinks differently."

"Papa Josef, as a zemstvo member, dismissed the extreme notions of Lenin," she said. "It is most absurd to think he would be the head of the party in the village. Who would believe it? Every Sunday he is at the church. The Bolsheviks are mostly atheists."

"Josef took Sergei's incriminating evidence from his room and planted it in his own so they would find it."

He had planned everything. Sergei must keep silent; he must promise to go to the university and become a lawyer, so that his father would be proud. How this ironic turn of events must be stabbing Sergei's heart! If he spoke the truth, he would be arrested, and his father would be devastated. And yet, to allow his father to take his place—

Karena's gaze met her uncle's. Matvey nodded as he read her question.

"Yes, that was why Yeva wanted Sergei to come back to the house. She knew of Josef's plan. She wanted to tell Sergei that she had reluctantly agreed to let Josef do this, because he meant so much to his father." Uncle Matvey added quietly, thoughtfully, "Yeva realizes Josef is more devoted to Sergei than to anyone or anything else in this life. At present, very little matters to him, except that Sergei lives."

What will we do without Papa Josef? What of the farm? How will we manage?

Karena's heart might as well have been sawn in two, so divided were her loyalties. Young, reckless Sergei and her sober, quiet papa. How could this be? Was there no way to escape this crushing destiny?

They must lose either Papa or Sergei, and Papa had all but decided the outcome on his own. He had chosen to become the scapegoat.

She turned toward the kitchen door, but Matvey intervened.

"I understand your feelings in this, but it is not for you to decide."

"Not mine?" she questioned.

"No, it is between Josef and Yeva." His face was grim, his eyes sympathetic. "You must respect your father's decision. It's his alone to make."

The long moments ticked by. Slowly, she turned away from the door and sat down.

Uncle Matvey watched her with sad approval. "Some things must be borne," he said. "We must be brave. Yes, be brave. You see? There is no choice. Josef has made up his heart. Yes, I stated it correctly, his heart, not his mind."

He put his hand on her head as though she were a little girl again. "And if Yeva can let her husband go for his son's sake, then you and I must release him."

She slowly lowered her head as her eyes dimmed with warm tears.

"I see you understand," he said quietly. "These bitterest of decisions leave no pleasant consequences."

After a moment she blotted her cheeks dry.

"But Sergei!" she said. "Surely he won't agree. I know him well enough. He argues with Papa Josef. He makes light of his stolid support of the autocracy, but he loves him dearly."

"Josef left Sergei no choice. We may not agree. We may see the cliff's edge and desire to rush in to stop one from going over, but ofttimes we are helpless. I suppose there is no pain quite as bad as that. All we can do is share in the heartbreak. Let us hope that Sergei will invest his life at the university. For now, he lives for two men. No," he said thoughtfully, "Sergei's life touches all of us. This is not easy for Sergei, believe me. It has cut him to the quick. Perhaps God will use this tragedy to mold him. Sergei finds himself in the Potter's hand."

Karena's throat pinched with pain. She swallowed hard, pushing her hair away from her forehead. Uncle Matvey's strange words created new footprints across her soul.

"In such situations as these, Karena, we see that God alone is able to move in our lives and reach us. Without knowledge of God, there is no faith, and without faith in a sovereign God who is both Creator and Savior, there is no ground for hope."

She jerked her head up. She had never seen him more serious, nor his eyes more intense. *Does he believe what he is saying?*

"You sound like you've changed your mind about the God of the Bible."

"I am only learning, Karena. I've been reading many books, as you know, including the New Testament. I thought it wise to understand about Jesus if I'm to write honestly about Messiah. I can now say the gospel of Matthew, with its many clear references to fulfillment of Old Testament prophecies, has all but convinced me there is to be a personal Deliverer, a Savior, through the royal line of David. Isaiah 53 tells me this person, the greater son of David, will suffer. I cannot read that chapter without the Crucifixion coming before me. I have read it dozens of times, and each time I am more convinced that it is not speaking of Israel's sufferings, as the rabbis claim, but of Messiah himself. Questions remain, but if the answers keep coming as they have so far, I will see no obstacle to Jesus being the Messiah, or as the Greek language has it in the New Testament writings, the Christ."

A hundred different thoughts came to her mind, and each one led off to a question of its own. These were things she could not think on now.

She turned to the window and stared helplessly at the manor house.

FIFTEEN

Questions

It was nearing four o'clock in the afternoon, and Colonel Aleksandr Kronstadt had not arrived at the bungalow to question them. Karena was emotionally spent and felt that she must take her mind off the situation or go mad.

"Uncle, if you're not going to use your office now, I've some work to do on your manuscript."

Matvey reached for a book of poetry on the shelf, took out his pipe, and crossed his long legs, wincing. He settled back with his coffee. "My office is yours."

"Oh! Poor Uncle. I forgot!" She reached into her skirt pocket and brought out the medication Madame Yeva had sent her over with earlier in the day.

"Another horse pill?"

"If we coat it first with butter, it will slide down very nicely." She smiled and went to the kitchen. She returned with a small dab of butter in a spoon. When she left him, he was looking dubiously at the large tablet he held between thumb and forefinger, while holding the spoon in his other hand.

Karena entered the small room connected to his bedroom and faced the cluttered desk and two chairs, one of them beside his overcrowded bookcase. Several thick research books lay open on the table. His typewriter sat amid a confusion of manuscript papers and other books, several of which Karena knew to be of rabbinical origin: writings on messianic hopes or the refutation of such hopes. The Old Testament, the *Tanach*, was there, along with the Talmud, which was Jewish history and commentaries written by ancient rabbis. Uncle Matvey had noticed that, for some reason, all the Jewish commentaries referred only vaguely to the coming of a personal Messiah.

Why? she wondered, drumming her fingers. She bowed her head in a short prayer:

God of Abraham, open my eyes, for I want to see. I do not want to be deceived. If Jesus is the promised Messiah, I want to know, and if he is not, I want to know. Amen.

Beside the Scriptures was a stack of letters from Jewish organizations. A Russian New Testament was there as well, and she saw that Matvey was deeply involved in a study of the gospel of Matthew. She saw a verse underlined: "Behold, the virgin shall be with child, and bear a Son, and they shall call His name Immanuel...God with us."

The letters from the rabbis were in response to Uncle Matvey's question, "If the Messiah were to come in 1915, how would you recognize him?" Karena had typed the dozen or so letters that she had then mailed to Basel, London, and New York. Each rabbi had answered, but she was disappointed to see their lukewarm responses. "Do not stir up more trouble for the Jews," one of them wrote back. And another, "Do you intend to reinforce the teaching that we are 'Christ killers'?"

Karena shivered with dread.

Out of a dozen or so letters, only one rabbi, an Orthodox Jew, believed in a personal Messiah. And while the rabbi gave his opinion on the matter, he did not refer to even one passage of Scripture.

Karena frowned, glancing up toward the window. Perhaps she shouldn't be surprised. Even the World Zionist Organization, begun under Theodor Herzl, was secular.

If there was no personal Messiah, then where had the idea come from?

Karena gathered a stack of Uncle Matvey's handwritten manuscript pages and sorted through them. Her interest was snagged at once. He had painstakingly written out reference after reference of promises and teachings about the coming of the Messiah from the Old Testament, beginning with Genesis, and added his own notes in parentheses:

"Messiah is first mentioned in Genesis 3:15 as the seed of the woman. Notice that it is not the seed of the man, but of the woman. Here is the first suggestion of the virgin birth. God said, 'I will put enmity between you and the woman, and between your seed and her Seed; He shall bruise your head—*(judgment of Satan)*—and you shall bruise His heel." Then Matvey had scribbled: *"(This is our Messiah wounded for Adam's fallen offspring)."*

He had found a New Testament verse describing the fulfillment. She typed the reference, Galatians 4:4–5, then struggled to find Galatians. At last she compared it to Uncle Matvey's notes: "But when the fullness of the time had come, God sent forth His Son, born of a woman *(the seed of the woman)*, born under the law *(He came when Israel was under the Law given to Moses)*, to redeem those who were under the law"—and here Matvey had underlined—"that we might receive the adoption as sons."

Amazing, Karena mused. She typed the next reference to the Messiah. *"The promised Messiah is also of the Seed of Father Abraham in Genesis 22:18, and its fulfillment is mentioned in Galatians 3:16:* 'To your Seed' *(Abraham's),* who is Christ."

"Another very early reference to the Messiah in His redemptive work," Uncle Matvey wrote, *"was in the offering of Abel in Genesis, in the bringing of a lamb from the flock. Redemption was always accomplished by a substitutionary blood sacrifice, and around seven hundred years before Messiah was born of the virgin Mary, Isaiah the prophet wrote,* 'the LORD has laid on

Him the iniquity of us all' *and that Messiah would be* 'led as a lamb to the slaughter.' "

Karena mused over the verses. Her heart was warmed. She sat thinking; then she looked over to the open window. She heard hoofbeats. Her heart began to race. That must be Colonel Kronstadt.

A few minutes later, she heard the expected knock on the door and from the kitchen the voice of Grandmother Jilinsky, who'd returned from the manor. Her footsteps hurried to answer.

Karena nervously smoothed her fair hair into place and straightened her pale blue peasant blouse and skirt. She picked up one of the rabbinical books, some manuscript pages, and a pencil so she would have a pretense for searching out her uncle, and then walked to the doorway of the study.

Colonel Kronstadt was already being shown inside.

Grandmother Jilinsky displayed her raw nerves by waving her hands about uselessly and talking too fast. She spoke not in Russian but in a mixture of Yiddish and Polish. Karena was surprised to hear Kronstadt reply in excellent Polish. Karena, who could speak Polish as easily as Russian, heard his voice, calm but firm, telling Grandmother that he was sorry to be late and to disturb her at this hour, but that he had his orders, and as any good Polish woman such as herself knew, orders must be followed. He would speak to Professor Menkin and to Miss Peshkova.

"And to Miss Peshkova."

Stay calm. You have your firm alibi.

"It's all right, Leah," Uncle Matvey interjected, coming from the kitchen. "I am expecting the colonel. Why don't you go to your room and rest awhile? If the colonel wishes to ask you a few questions, he'll call for you."

"I shall make the coffee first and leave it to stay hot on the stove, and a platter of sweet breads to go with it." She turned to Kronstadt. "Colonel," she said stiffly, bowed her silver head, and left them. At the doorway, she glanced over her shoulder.

Karena stood in the doorway to Uncle Matvey's office, her arms full of research. She was deliberately looking at her uncle rather than at Alex, even though she sensed that Kronstadt was looking at her.

"My niece, Miss Karena Peshkova," Uncle Matvey was saying, and Karena was obliged to turn and acknowledge him.

"Colonel Aleksandr Kronstadt," Matvey told her. "He is well received by your Uncle Viktor and Aunt Zofia."

Karena realized Matvey didn't know they had met in Kazan.

Alex, however, walked forward and bowed smartly, expressionless and self-contained. He was well built in his precise-fitting officer's uniform.

"Miss Peshkova," he stated.

Their eyes met. His were interesting, not merely because of their unusual green color, but because they were so confident. His dark, chocolate brown hair, the flinty jaw, the flawless Imperial-officer manner—all served him well and could easily be intimidating.

She was sure he was watching the heightening color in her cheeks.

"I had the privilege of meeting your niece in Kazan in June," he told Matvey, "and again briefly on the road this morning."

"Yes, we've met." She found her voice and was proud of herself for sounding as collected as he. "We met this morning before I knew you were here in our village to arrest my father as a Bolshevik. Something, sir, I can assure you that he is not. My father is loyal to Czar Nicholas, as are we all."

Uncle Matvey cleared his throat and took a step forward as if to redirect Kronstadt's attention to himself, but the colonel's calm scrutiny of Karena continued.

"I am under orders, Miss Peshkova. My duty is to the czar. My personal opinions of what may have occurred last night do not enter into the matter. I haven't said your father is a Bolshevik; he has called himself one."

With Josef confessing he was a revolutionary to protect Sergei, how could she protest to the colonel that her father was loyal to the czar?

Uncle Matvey's voice came between them, assuring the colonel he would see him *alone* in his office.

Colonel Kronstadt bowed toward Karena. He was turning to follow Uncle Matvey into the next room when the heavy rabbinical volume that she was holding slipped from the stack of papers to the floor with a thud.

She was about to stoop and pick it up, but he did so for her, looking at its title without a hint of qualm.

"Research on your book, Professor?" He turned to look at Matvey.

"I'm up to my ears in books, Colonel, but enjoying myself immensely with the topic. I fear I've made a mess of things, however. Karena's been assisting me since I arrived in June by putting the manuscript into order. I'll miss her when I return to Petrograd."

Alex smiled as he returned the book. The smile seemed to change his entire personality.

"You heard his plea, Miss Peshkova. Perhaps you should return with him to save your uncle from drowning in his sea of books and papers. I'd like to hear your interpretation of his work sometime."

Karena hardly knew what to say to the veiled challenge and remained silent.

She took the book he held toward her, meeting his direct look and finding it far from lukewarm. "Thank you," she murmured meekly.

"Colonel, you must come by my apartment, and we can discuss my findings," Uncle Matvey said, handling the challenge for her. "Karena is likely to be there as well, since she hopes to enter the medical school."

"I'll remember that," Kronstadt said.

Karena could have reminded Uncle Matvey that she would not be going to medical college this year, but if there was any chance she could get to Petrograd, she wasn't about to throw snow on the kindling.

"It should be a most interesting discussion," Alex told him. "My cousin Michael is attending a Bible seminary in America, somewhere around New York. He is determined to carry on a theological debate with me. He's hoping I'll join him there."

"I'll plan on an interesting discussion, then, Colonel."

Alex turned to Karena. She made no comment.

"I'll speak with Professor Menkin alone first. Please remain here, Miss Peshkova. I must question you before I return to the manor house where Major-General Durnov waits."

That was that. The mask of Imperial military professionalism came down again, and his face told her nothing more. He bowed and followed Matvey into the little office, closing the door.

She sank into the nearest chair and waited.

Alex proved the epitome of politeness, but underneath she sensed a man who was committed to Imperial Russia. That put her and her family at dangerous odds. She could not imagine Kronstadt compromising his military duty, whatever it might be, in order to lessen the consequences for anyone who had presumed freedoms that were not theirs to enjoy. His strength could certainly prove an asset, but she was also wary of his inflexible commitment to duty. He knew what he wanted in life and would allow nothing to interfere.

Even so, she was relieved it was Kronstadt, and not Durnov, who asked the questions.

Perhaps twenty minutes plodded by. She heard their low voices, but not well enough to distinguish which man was talking. Just when she believed that it was going well for Uncle Matvey, his voice rose in denial, followed by the calm voice of Colonel Kronstadt.

Soft footsteps sounded behind her. She whirled. A wiry-looking man in plain clothes, but carrying a gun, stood watching her. *Policeman Leonovich.*

Leonovich had a wide mustache and unruly brown hair that dipped in a wave across his narrow forehead. His eyes were oddly pale—she had always thought so when she had seen him in the village. He carried a cup of coffee in one hand and a sweet cake in the other. He must have entered the kitchen by the back door. It disturbed her that he had entered without her noticing. Something in the way he watched her always made her uncomfortable. He was oblivious to the crumbs dropping on Grandmother's clean floor.

"You might use a plate, Mr. Leonovich," she said coolly. "Grandmother does not appreciate sticky crumbs trampled about."

He might have been deaf for all the attention he gave to her words. Those strange eyes took her in from toe to head as they had at other times. Her skin reacted unpleasantly.

"Are you alone?" he asked, licking the crumbs from his fingers and wiping them on his trousers.

"No. But what concern would that be to you? I did not hear you knock on my uncle's door."

"It was open. I hear your father has been arrested, and that arrogant brother of yours is leaving for St. Petersburg—or it's Petrograd now, or soon will be. The name change is all about hatred for Germans and loyalty to Russia."

She kept silent.

"Three women alone in the manor house will mean more labor for you now. Maybe I can get one or two of the fellows together, and we can cast in our time to help you fair ladies now and then."

"We won't need any help. We can take care of ourselves and the land. Besides," she said a little too hurriedly, "Ilya will be here to manage the fields and workers."

He smiled. "Ilya is being conscripted. Just about everybody is. And your uncle is going back."

Leonovich slurped his coffee and looked around as though deciding on a new home. His presence sparked her anger, but also a looming fear.

"What do you want?" she asked bluntly.

"Where's the fellow from the secret police?"

"Colonel Kronstadt is in the next room, questioning my uncle."

He seemed to reconsider whatever was in his mind and patted his jacket pocket, then brought out a rumpled package of ready-made cigarettes. He reached in his other pocket for a match and lit a cigarette.

"I think you better come with me down to the station, Miss Peshkova. I must interrogate you."

"Colonel Kronstadt ordered me to remain here. He, too, wishes to ask me questions." For once she was relieved to face questions from Alex.

A sardonic smile touched Leonovich's lips. "It is not for me to interfere with the Okhrana. But the local police are very interested in this case, Miss Peshkova. We all worked for Grinevich, you see, and we too have questions that must be answered to our full satisfaction." He gestured his head toward the kitchen. "In there, then. At the table."

It would be unwise to deliberately anger him, but she wondered who it was in the local gendarmes that had authorized him to come here now. With Grinevich dead as of only this morning, would there have been time enough to select his replacement? Major-General Durnov would likely be the one to do so.

She didn't think Leonovich had first tried to see Sergei or anyone else at the manor house. For that matter, how had he known she was in the bungalow? It was chilling to think he might have been watching her.

She affected indifference, as though she had no reason not to trust him, and walked past him into the now-stuffy kitchen. The afternoon sun was intense and streamed through the window near the table. She wanted to open the window and let some air in, but Leonovich had decided to stand in front of the table with his back next to it. She pulled out a chair and sat down. He placed his cigarette between his lips to let it dangle while using both hands to remove a scarred leather folder from under his jacket. He flipped through soiled pages, preparing to take notes, and came up with a stubby pencil.

"Now then, Miss Karena, let us get down to the bony facts."

"Mr. Leonovich, I wish to be called Miss Peshkova, thank you."

His lip jutted out. "I beg your pardon. Miss Peshkova. Miss Karena Josipovna Peshkova." He leered. "Any other names, Miss?"

"Simply Miss Peshkova will do sufficiently well, Mr. Leonovich."

"What do you know about what happened last night?"

"Last night?"

"Miss Peshkova, I don't like to play fencing games. You know exactly what I mean."

"I know only what I have heard reported by the authorities."

"Which is?"

She shrugged. "There was a disturbance last night?"

"A riot."

"In which poor Mr. Grinevich was injured."

"His head was kicked in. He died this morning of brain injuries."

"I am very sorry, but I don't know anything about such horrible cruelty."

"You can be thankful you were not there, Miss Peshkova." His lower lip curled again in a sardonic smile. "After all, you've got Zinnovy to swear you were with him, right? At least, that's what you're saying, that you weren't there."

She remained silent. Could Leonovich possibly have seen her there?

"Sergei Peshkov was there, though, right?"

"Was he?"

"You know he was there."

"There's no proof he was there, according to Major-General Durnov. And your questioning of me is useless. The Okhrana has already arrested my father for arranging last night's Bolshevik meeting. You're the policeman who first spoke to my father about Grinevich, so you see, it no longer matters about Sergei. Major-General Durnov is satisfied that he has arrested the revolutionary."

His hard smile appeared to be frozen in place. He altered his course. "Has Sergei talked to you before about politics?"

"No."

"Never?"

"Seldom, if ever."

"Seldom. You are lying to me. It is very serious to lie to me."

"He may have said a few things in passing about the coming war, but hardly anything that interested me."

"Your brother is interested in this war, is he? What did he say about the war?"

"That Russia would win against any and all of her enemies. That the good Russian people must send the soldiers off with songs and pray for them to have victory over the Germans. That our great czar will lead us to victory."

The curl of his bottom lip deepened. "How patriotic! And your father? He is leader of the *patriotic* Bolsheviks in town, is he? You support your father, do you?"

"My father is not a Bolshevik."

"He has admitted that he is. He knows Lenin, Trotsky, the other revolutionaries. He has books and pamphlets by Karl Marx in his office at the college. He had secret meetings with Chertkov. You know who Chertkov was, Miss Peshkova?"

Yes, she knew exactly who Chertkov was.

"Yes. I see you do. Is there any reason why your father should not join his professor colleague, Chertkov, Miss Peshkova?" he asked with a leer.

"My father is not a Bolshevik." Her temper flared. "I am not a Bolshevik."

He leaned toward her and banged his fist on the table. "Lies! Now we are back where we started."

She heard footsteps behind her halt just inside the kitchen, but her eyes were fastened on Leonovich.

He raised his eyes and looked past her shoulder. She saw his face change, and he straightened from the table.

"Who gave you authority to question Miss Peshkova?"

Karena turned her head. Alex stood in the doorway with an unpleasant countenance.

Leonovich looked uneasy. "I am from the local gendarmes. Grinevich was murdered last night."

"We are fully aware. Any and all revolutionaries are under our jurisdiction."

"What about Menkin? Where's he?"

"He waits in the other room. The interrogation has been handled as fully as possible at this stage. I just received this message from Major-General Durnov." He held a piece of paper on which something brief had been written. "You are to report to him at the manor house. At once."

Leonovich eyed him. "What about Miss Peshkova?"

"You need not concern yourself with Miss Peshkova."

Leonovich narrowed his eyes but appeared to step back.

He looked at Karena, then at Kronstadt. "Why is she here at all? She should be returning to the house."

Karena wanted to go to the manor house, but only in the company of Matvey.

"She's been ordered to remain here, Leonovich. I'll see that she's brought to the manor. I'll need to give my initial report on Professor Menkin to the general anyway. I'll take Miss Peshkova with me. I think I can quickly verify certain necessary points in her statement. I shall let you know the Okhrana's findings, of course, so that our files on this case may supplement those of the local police."

Alex walked up behind her and firmly grasped her arm.

"This way, Miss Peshkova. We'll talk in your uncle's office."

He helped her to her feet. Her eyes met his, but she saw nothing in the hard green that offered conciliatory reasons for his action in removing her from the clutches of Leonovich.

She was being led determinedly from the kitchen through the hall and into her uncle's office. In his other hand, Alex had an equally determined grip on the written notes from his interview with Uncle Matvey, to be later delivered to Durnov.

She walked to the desk, her back toward him. He shut the door against intruders.

Uncle Matvey was gone.

SIXTEEN

Cat and Mouse

Heartsore and weary of mind, Karena faced Colonel Aleksandr Kronstadt in the small, crowded office.

"What have you done with Professor Menkin?" she accused.

He opened the one small window as wide as he could and pushed aside the curtains, looking out. He loosened the collar of his shirt and unbuttoned his jacket, watching her with that intense, thoughtful look that made his gray-green eyes as warm as the room.

"Where is my uncle now?"

"You need have no worry about Professor Menkin. He will not be held. He's on the porch under guard, waiting for Leonovich."

"If he will not be held, why is he still under guard?"

"Merely a matter of procedure. Major-General Durnov will have questions. Then Professor Menkin will sign a document and be released. However, I cannot say the same for your father. He's chosen his path. I'm sorry, but he will be brought to Petrograd for further questioning."

He pulled out a chair. "Please take a seat."

How could she persuade the colonel of her father's innocence without betraying his love for Sergei?

"I tell you, my father is innocent of the attack on Policeman Grinevich. He's not a revolutionary. He's a local representative of the zemstvo."

"I am aware of his position." He picked up a thick leather notebook. "It's recorded here that your father's grandfather was awarded governance of these lands by Czar Alexander I for loyal service. Is that so?"

"Yes." Why was he bringing this up now?

"Do he and Madame Peshkova realize his confessing that he is a revolutionary leader in the Bolshevik Party means these lands will be taken from his immediate family and heirs?"

Stunned, she sat still.

His jaw hardened. "No? That's what I thought. His decision today to throw himself on the altar for his son means he's surrendered the inheritance of his wife and children."

Karena, shocked, could not speak. She put her hand to her forehead.

"I'm sorry." His voice softened. "I tried to tell him this, but he seemed fixated on his decision. I don't think he's thought this through. Believe me, I find no pleasure in telling you this. But it's wiser for you to know now. You will need to make plans." He pushed aside the clutter on the desk and sat on the edge. "I told Professor Menkin. He'll do what he can. Your best hope is with General Roskov and your aunt in Petrograd. He may be able to appeal to Czar Nicholas."

Leave the manor house? Leave the land on which she had been born and raised?

"As for your stepfather, being a local representative while also claiming to be a Bolshevik may only reap a harsher judgment. Those who hold Bolshevik political beliefs have as their goal to assassinate our czar."

Her head jerked up. "Never. My father is a gentle man, most loyal. No one in my family would ever hope to do Czar Nicholas harm. And he's not my stepfather."

"Do you know how many attempts there have been through the

years? An attempt was made not long ago here in Kiev at the opera house."
He tilted his head, his gaze combining thoughtfulness with decision. "Do
you wonder that we must be careful?"

"No. But my father would never attempt such evil."

He studied her, considering her frank declaration, taking in her face.
Her blush did not seem to trouble him.

"I would know by my father's political beliefs whether he nurtured
revolutionary ambitions."

"I don't doubt that, but as an astute teacher, he's fluent enough to present his politics in whatever form is expedient. You have heard of the Bolshevik underground? I see by your face you have. Most have heard of the
writings and newspapers and books smuggled in from men like Lenin. A
collection of Lenin's works was found in your father's office. Personally? It
looks too contrived to me, and I have my doubts about his guilt. Nevertheless, your father swears loyalties to Karl Marx and Lenin."

He gathered up Uncle Matvey's manuscript and set it aside. She
watched him, alert. "Then—you don't really believe he's telling the truth?"

"For myself, no," he said bluntly. "He's protecting your brother."

She looked down at her hands, straightening a ring on her right hand.
Did this mean he and the other officer, Durnov, might not arrest him?
Would they change their minds?

She looked up. "What about Sergei? Are you taking him to St.
Petersburg?"

He leafed through some other scattered papers on the desk.

"Your brother is free to go," he said mildly.

Her breath caught. "What about Policeman Grinevich's testimony? Did
he by any chance mention anything about my father or Sergei?" *Or me?*

Even though he apparently saw through Josef's false confession, Alex
remained silent a moment too long, which heightened her tension.

"I didn't speak with Grinevich," he said at last. "Policeman Leonovich and Major-General Durnov were the last ones to see him alive. Durnov is satisfied your brother was not there, and it is his report that will be delivered to Petrograd. Are you suggesting that if I'd heard Grinevich's testimony, it would contradict the report as it stands now?"

His bland voice coupled with an even stare unnerved her. *He knows… or does he?* If he did know for certain, wouldn't he include this in his own report?

"No, I'm not suggesting that," she said, avoiding his gaze. "I have no reason to think he would be involved in that sort of violent rioting. Absolutely not."

"Absolutely not," he said softly.

Karena stood abruptly but made as though she did not see his momentary, sardonic smirk. She looked deliberately at Uncle Matvey's manuscript in his control.

"The manuscript is far from finished." She found herself snapping the words. "He has worked for a year on the research alone. He's just begun the writing this summer. What do you intend to do with it?"

His brow shot up. "Read it for any hint of disloyalty to Czar Nicholas," he admitted frankly. "Don't worry, Miss Peshkova. I will see that it is returned in perfect order to your uncle, should it prove, as he says, a work of harmless religion."

"Thank you, Colonel Kronstadt," she said formally. She touched her hair and drew in a breath. "Am I permitted to go about my work now?"

He smiled. "Not yet. Please be seated again." He picked up his black leather notebook and walked over to the window where the breeze blew in. He looked quite handsome in his uniform of mostly gray and black, his boots just below the knee. There was also some gold braid and red ribbon on the jacket, which identified a special officers' corps, but she was not familiar enough with the markings. She noted a gold ring on his finger. It looked familiar. Had Tatiana given it to him? He glanced at her when she remained silent, and she was sure he had caught her gaze on the ring.

"Did you attend the Bolshevik meeting last night?"

She glanced at him, but he was looking at his notebook. She turned away, straightening some papers.

"No," she said, and bit her lip

A moment of silence trapped her.

"You did not hear Lenski last night?" he repeated.

"I said no, Colonel."

"So you did, Miss Peshkova. Did Sergei attend?"

"No." She folded her arms.

"Is he a friend of Lenski?"

Her heart was thudding. "No."

A gust of wind came through the window and stirred the papers on Matvey's desk. Karena moved to anchor them.

"He's seeing Ivanna in Petrograd, is he not? They have a favorite nightclub they attend frequently."

She closed her eyes. So he knew about Ivanna. Of course he would. *The Okhrana knows everything,* as Ilya had put it.

"Do they? Then why ask me? I know nothing of bright lights and dance clubs in Petrograd," she said.

"I'll ask the questions. Ivanna attends the Imperial Medical College. You did not go to the meeting last night to meet her, to try to gain her support to help you get into the program?"

She clasped her fingers tightly behind her back. "Did you locate Ivanna? Is that what she told you?"

"Did you go to meet her last night?"

She turned away to straighten the books on the shelf, unable to face him. "No."

"Did Ilya Jilinsky or anyone in your family attend the meeting?"

"No."

"Did you hear about any friends or neighbors who attended?"

She thought of Anna. "No."

"Are you aware of any persons in your family or among friends who wish to overthrow the Romanovs?"

"No," she said, straightening her back.

She was afraid and infuriated at the same moment. He had her lined up against the wall, and all the time she had a growing feeling he knew she was not speaking truthfully, yet he was going along with what she said, accepting her answers. Where was this leading?

"Where were you last night between six o'clock and ten?"

She whirled to face him. He watched her with affected indifference. She knew she must be showing emotions of misery and defiance all at once. She lifted her chin and folded her arms. Now she had him.

"Why, I was with Dr. Dmitri Zinnovy. He's returned to St. Petersburg, but he can testify to my whereabouts and will do so when you ask him. He brought me home around nine o'clock in his coach. There are witnesses." She turned her mouth into a little smile. "The gendarmes themselves stopped us on the road but then permitted us to go on. Policeman Leonovich was in charge. In fact, Colonel, you could ask Leonovich now, if he's still in the kitchen, dropping sugary crumbs all over the floor."

The silence was painful. He watched her. She felt the flush warm her cheeks. Her gaze slid aside, and she stood, angrily walked over to the desk, and stacked Uncle Matvey's books neatly together.

"Very nice, yes. Very well done, Miss Peshkova," he said smoothly. "So then, Dr. Zinnovy, the czar's family physician, is your alibi. Congratulations. I admit I'm relieved. You had me in quandary, for the last thing I wish is your arrest."

She looked at him.

"I should say you will be quite safe now, for a time," he said. "Unless you permit yourself to foolishly attend such an unlawful meeting again."

Again? She met his gaze.

"Then you are sure you don't recall the names or faces of any peasants who were also at that meeting?" he asked silkily.

"No—" She stopped. She stared at him. Peasants... *Peasant!* One particular peasant, a very comely one, with dark hair—

She narrowed her lashes and looked him over with keen observation. Alex was the peasant who'd been watching her at the meeting! The man with the hat pulled low, who had lit the cigarette—who had stood right next to Dr. Zinnovy...and who had seen her there! It was Aleksandr Kronstadt!

"You—," she whispered.

Karena's knees almost went out from under her. The trap he had set for her seemed perfect. He could prove she had lied to most everything he had asked her. And he could even prove Dr. Zinnovy had been at the meeting.

He straightened and snapped his leather notebook closed. The sound all but convinced her that she was doomed.

He seemed about to say something when there came a terrible pounding on the front door. Karena tensed and moved toward the hall.

She heard Grandmother Jilinsky hurrying to answer, followed by the voice of Ilya in the kitchen.

Karena sank to a chair. It was over for her. Alex was witness to her and Sergei's presence at the rally when Grinevich was assaulted. What would Durnov do if Alex informed him? He would need to release Papa Josef and arrest her and Sergei instead. Kronstadt had expertly baited his trap. Her feelings toward him were a poisonous mixture of attraction and aversion.

She heard an anxious voice from the porch asking for her by name. It was a woman's voice. Natalia? She listened, trying to make out who was there.

"Oh, Madame Jilinsky, where is Karena? I must find her now! It is most urgent. Oh please, is she here?"

Karena then recognized the frightened voice of Elena Lavrushsky, Anna's sister-in-law. Forcing aside all other worries, Karena went to the doorway that faced the little hall.

Elena stood on the porch, looking past Grandmother Jilinsky who held open the front door. Ilya came from the kitchen, concern on his face.

"Elena, what's wrong?" Karena asked.

The young woman crossed herself. "It's Anna. She's gone into early labor. I fear for her life! I went straight to the manor house, but Madame Yeva was not there, and no one knew where I could find her. Your sister told me I'd find you here. Please, come and do what you can!"

Karena caught her scarf from the hook in the hall and turned toward Alex, who was leaning in the doorway. Their gazes locked. For a moment she did not move; then, not knowing whether he'd reach out and stop her or not, she turned from him and hurried out the open front door after Elena.

Anna needed her. That was all that mattered at the moment. Seven months! Could the baby live? She'd read about a baby who'd survived a six-month pregnancy. The child was a little slow mentally but lived a normal, happy life.

Would Alex send a soldier to guard the Lavrushsky bungalow and bring her back? He'd known all along she'd been at the meeting. He'd been toying with her like a cat with a mouse. Who knew what would befall them now? Papa Josef's self-sacrifice for Sergei might prove to be in vain. Sergei could yet be imprisoned.

The sun was setting on the horizon, spilling a golden pink over the distant wheat fields.

Karena sent Elena rushing to the manor house to retrieve Madame Yeva's medical bag and to see if she was there.

If not, I shall deliver this baby—entirely on my own.

SEVENTEEN

New Life

The oil lamps cast shadows on the walls of the peasant bungalow. As Karena entered the room to see Anna, she tried to show the same confidence that Madame Yeva displayed with her patients. Her mother had told her, *"The woman about to give birth looks to the midwife for courage and confidence. If you are timid and nervous, the woman will also become so. Show confidence and calmness."*

One look at Anna, however, and Karena felt her insides tense. The girl looked to be in anguish. Her large brown eyes were apprehensive, and sweat dotted her face. She clutched at the bedcover with both hands, plucking it nervously.

"Karena," she whimpered, trying to sit up, "are the secret police coming? Where is Sergei? I must see Sergei! It's his baby. I swear it is! There was no other—"

Karena soothed her with gentle hushing sounds, smiling kindly, and picked up the towel to blot her young face. How tragic when a young girl like this stumbled so soon in life. What would become of her? Karena doubted that Sergei was in love with her but rather had been playing around selfishly with no thought of anyone except himself. Anna was a pretty girl, willing to be deceived by his false attention.

"Sergei is well," Karena told her. "There is nothing to fear. He is going back to the university to become a lawyer. And the police have decided to leave also. We are all safe," she said untruthfully. *But if I tell her the truth, she will panic,* Karena excused herself, talking to her conscience rather than to God.

Karena noticed that after reading about the Messiah from Uncle Matvey's work, the pinprick of conviction felt sharper.

Anna's head fell back against the pillow. "Sergei will not be arrested?"

"No, of course not. Josef made him promise to finish his schooling. Forget Sergei now. We must think of you and your baby. When did the pains start?"

"Hours ago. I—was frightened, in a hurry, I tripped."

Karena masked her dismay. "Any spotting of blood?"

"Yes—yes!"

Karena struggled to keep her calm face. *Mother, where are you?*

"I will need to examine you," Karena told her. "Elena will return in a few minutes with Madame Yeva's birthing kit. My mother isn't here right now, but she will be back soon. Meanwhile, I know what to do. Try to relax, breathe calmly, relax your muscles…that's fine."

Anna reached out and grasped her hand. "Please, Karena. I must see Sergei, if only for a minute. I must!"

Karena tightened her mouth. Sergei. Where was he? That scoundrel. She was furious. He was to blame for everything. Where had he gone after he'd left Uncle Matvey? Could he still be somewhere on the farm?

Wagon wheels creaked slowly outside the bungalow. Karena went to the window. It was Elena driving the oxcart, but Madame Yeva was not with her. In the back of the wagon were several boxes that she knew contained birthing equipment, medicines, sheets, the clean apron Karena was to wear, and a special soap that Madame Yeva had bought from a Jewish herbalist in Warsaw years earlier. She always used the soap on her hands and arms, to supposedly reduce birthing sicknesses. Yeva had emphasized this for the health of her patients when she read about Florence Nightingale, who had campaigned diligently for cleanliness in the hospitals of London and on the battlefields of the Crimean War.

Karena left Anna and went outside to help Elena with the boxes and to set up the birthing station.

"Where is Yuri?" she asked Elena.

"He was working in the field with Sergei earlier." She plucked at her sleeve. "What is it?" she asked.

"Elena, I'm sorry to keep you running about, but could you see if you can find Sergei or Ilya? If we could have Sergei here, it would help Anna. He should know the child he's responsible for is about to be born. Anna wishes to see him before he leaves for St. Petersburg."

Elena pushed her windblown hair from her forehead and nodded, scowling. "She's been very upset. I know it would help if Sergei would come and talk to her, even for a few minutes. Yuri was going to talk to him, but…" She shrugged helplessly. "He is so angry about his little sister."

"He has just cause," Karena said with weariness.

"Then I will look. It will take me time to find Yuri. He may be on the far side of the field."

"Try. Or if you see Ilya, he will do. You will need to hurry, Elena. Oh— did you ask Natalia where Madame Yeva went?"

"Natalia said she went with Master Josef and the policeman into town to the gendarme station. She will be back tonight."

Then Papa Josef was already arrested. He would likely be held in the town jail until the Okhrana officers left in the morning for St. Petersburg.

Karena's anger simmered on coals of indignation. Could they not even leave him to sleep in his own bed for the night? What did they think? That he might flee Kiev? If he'd wanted to flee from them, he would never have confessed so openly.

Karena suspected that Sergei had already slipped away to Kazan to travel to St. Petersburg to the Roskovs. Most likely, Sergei was bringing Uncle Viktor a letter from Josef explaining what he was facing and asking for his help in protecting Sergei and in reinstating him in the St. Petersburg University.

Elena left to search the fields, and Karena returned to Anna's side. The sweltering afternoon inched by. The wind always came up in the late afternoon and blew incessantly here near the fields. The gusts would strike the bungalow with a force that convinced Karena the wall could come down.

Another wave of contractions hit Anna, and Karena placed a cloth between her teeth. Anna gripped the cloth tightly, biting into it as Karena spoke words of courage and confidence that she hardly felt within herself.

She washed the sweat from Anna's face and neck between contractions. The girl's delicate white skin had taken on a puffiness that worried her, and the dark circles beneath her eyes showed how her suffering had dragged on since the night after returning from the meeting.

The afternoon wore on until evening approached. Karena sat on the low stool below the bed, and despite the heat of the day, water boiled on the stove. Beside her on the table there were yards of boiled, white cloth.

Anna arched as another powerful birthing pang caused her to scream. The process was not going normally. Anna had been dilating for almost two hours, and Karena was convinced that the baby was in the wrong position to enter the birthing canal. Fear such as she had never known assailed her. Now what? A breech baby! *Oh, God, what shall I do? Bring Mother! Oh, where is she?*

For a time she froze. Anna was weeping and in agony, but also crying out in fear.

Karena tried to soothe her, all the while searching her mind for what Yeva had told her about the delivery of a breech baby.

"You must try to turn the baby. It is the only way."

Elena had not yet returned. She must be searching everywhere for the men. The only way was to tell Anna the truth.

"Anna, you must be brave and help me. I must work to turn the baby, to direct the head into the birth canal. This is not going to be easy, but we can do it if we work together."

"Yes…yes," she murmured weakly.

Karena ran to the front door and stepped out onto the porch; a gust of wind shoved her backward. The moon was up, big and yellow, and she could see some distance down the wagon road, but there was no sign of Elena coming in the wagon with Madame Yeva or the men bringing Sergei. She hurried back inside.

Karena tried to recall everything her mother had said about moving a baby in the womb. *"It's most important to discover the baby's position in the womb as early as possible." Why did I not see this earlier?* she chided herself.

Karena gravely remembered that the prognosis for such cases was not good. Success depended on whether or not the baby could be righted.

She must attempt external manipulation to turn the baby into the right position, and if that failed, there was only the drastic internal manipulation, which would be exceedingly painful for Anna.

"Any sign…Sergei?" Anna rasped.

"Not yet. Anna, it is crucial that we gently turn your baby's head down. I want you to take a deep breath and try to relax."

With a prayer on her lips, Karena laid her left palm over the right part of Anna's abdomen and felt the baby's head. She used her other hand to clasp the mound that would be the infant's bottom. Then, slowly, between Anna's agonizing contractions and gasps, Karena pushed and stroked and manipulated the baby's small head downward. Anna's birth pangs were now coming less than a minute apart, and growing more agonizing. With each small victory of manipulation, Karena kept the baby in position during the contractions and was almost certain she could feel the baby's head moving down into the pelvis.

"The baby's coming. It's going to be all right, Anna! You are being brave. Keep trying."

Karena had Madame Yeva's forceps, but her mother lectured against their use when at all possible. Babies died from head injuries, and mothers were often cut or torn and suffered from infection or excessive blood loss.

Karena was sweating as profusely as Anna, who was drenched and panting.

"Ah!" Karena cried. "The baby's moving! Soon now, Anna," she said with the first genuine confidence she had felt in hours.

Sweat mingled with Anna's tears, and anguish furrowed her brow.

"Karena…," Anna's ragged whisper came. "Not good…I…"

"Soon, Anna, soon." But something new frightened her, and she wondered if she had the right to reassure her. There was too much blood.

Anna's body tensed in another push to free the tiny baby.

Karena could see the infant's head and then its bloody face looking downward while emerging. The little one's eyes were sealed with creamy vernix.

"Poor baby," Karena whispered. "Poor little sweetheart. Welcome to the dreadful world." She used her two fingers to tenderly wipe the mucus from its button nose and cleaned inside its tiny mouth to start clearing and draining the air passages.

"Almost here," Karena cried to Anna.

Karena eased out one shoulder and then the other one to victory, and then, with gentle pulling and one last push, the new child was free of its womb.

"A daughter, Anna," she said happily.

She gave a quick wipe to the baby and held her over some clean towels, letting the lungs drain, the umbilical cord remaining uncut for the moment.

Anna watched, crying, unable to speak.

Karena wiped the baby's eyes, face, and nose again, and the baby sucked in its very first breath, followed by a cry. Karena was jubilant. She held the baby high enough for Anna to see.

"May God bless you and guide you on the long, difficult pathway of life," Karena whispered.

Karena worked quickly now with brown cord, a boiled knife, and an odd assortment of ointments. The main work for this third-stage delivery was almost done, though aftercare was to follow.

As she worked, she hardly heard the sounds outside the bungalow give way to wagon wheels, horses, and voices.

A moment later, Madame Yeva rushed into the gornitsa and looked around, gave a nod of apparent satisfaction, and caressed Karena's shoulder in a display of pride over her success. Their gazes met, and smiles were exchanged.

"Good, Karena, very good." She lowered her voice to a whisper. "But only seven and a half months..." She frowned.

"The infant looks perfectly healthy, Mother. I can see nothing wrong."

"We will hope. I will also examine her—and Anna." Yeva went to the bedside and spoke to Anna, laying a palm on her forehead. She frowned. "Do you have a fever?"

Anna gave a quiet, exhausted sound.

"First, let me have a look at your new baby." Yeva took the infant over to a table.

A minute later, Karena could not silence her own gasp. "Mother!"

Karena stared at Anna, shocked. What had happened? A moment ago, Anna had managed a weary little smile when she saw the baby. Now—

Anna was turning a pasty color with purplish splotches beneath her eyes. The weak wails of the newborn filled the bungalow as the gusty wind shook the walls. Anna's lips formed words, but her voice was so weak that Karena could hardly hear. "Sergei. Serg..."

"Take the baby," Madame Yeva told Karena.

Karena laid the infant beside Anna and then wrung a wet cloth and applied it to Anna's face and throat.

Madame Yeva hurried to examine Anna.

Karena joined her. "Did I do something wrong?" she kept whispering, but her mother was too intent to answer.

Fear clamped around Karena's insides like iron fingers. Her eyes went to the cloths beneath Anna, staring at the area of bright crimson.

Yeva kept massaging and kneading Anna's womb, her face tense with perspiration.

Karena could not move. The exhilaration she felt only minutes ago drained away, and horror now rushed in to take its place. Guilt shouted down upon her conscience. *I must have done something wrong. I should have waited for Madame Yeva or gone for the other midwife, Marina.*

Elena came in and, seeing what was happening to her young sister-in-law, let out a muffled sob.

"Karena!" Madame Yeva snapped. "Hand me more cloths."

Karena could hardly move; her hands felt heavy and clumsy.

What did I do wrong? Unless the hemorrhaging could be halted... She fumbled in her attempts to help her mother with the blood-soaked cloths.

Elena knelt before the icon displayed on its shelf, a replica of the special icon called the Black Virgin of Kazan. She struck a match and lit the candle below the image. She brought her palms together and lifted her face. "Saints of Holy Mother Russia, come now to our aid and save Anna, my dear sister."

Karena watched, knowing that Anna was going to die and that there was nothing she could do. She had failed her. She had come with confidence, assured that she could deliver the baby on her own. There were times in the process when she'd been almost pleased that Madame Yeva had not been here. And now...

Karena took Anna's hand. How cold and clammy she felt. She held it between her own, as though by holding tightly, she could hold on to the girl's life.

"Sergei…tell him…tell…Sergei…take care of…our baby."

"I will tell him," Karena whispered as tears flooded her eyes at last. "Yeva."

Madame Yeva laid a hand on Anna's brow. "I am here, Anna."

"Promise…baby…Sergei's baby."

"Yes, I promise, Anna. We will not forget it is Sergei's child."

Karena bent over Anna, took her limp hand, and placed it on her newborn for the last time. Anna's fingers tried to pet the tiny body nestled beside her.

There was a banging on the front door—or was it the wind? A moment later, the door flew open, and footsteps sounded. Ilya stood in the doorway but did not enter. He turned to look back over his shoulder and gestured. Sergei came forward, tense. He looked frightened. He stared at the scene, the blood, and Anna.

Karena rushed to him, snatching his arm, urging him forward. "Quick, Sergei, she's dying. Go to her. Tell her you love her. Promise you'll be a good father to your daughter. Allow her a brief moment of your of love. You owe her that."

Sergei looked grief stricken. He dropped his head against his palm and shook it in desperation.

Karena pushed him. "Go." He seemed to rally and went to Anna's bedside.

Karena and Madame Yeva moved back to allow them a final moment together, alone.

"Anna, Anna, I'm sorry—forgive me—I love you, Anna."

Karena stood, devastated. Sergei was kneeling beside the bed, his dark head bent, his arms around Anna, his face on her neck. Anna's hand came to life again and managed to reach his dark head, where she patted him.

Against the lone whine of the wind came the wail of the baby girl—a girl, so soon without a mama and with a papa who must ride away into the dark night.

❧

Karena sat on the porch step, her head resting on the post, the wind pushing and tugging at her with brief gusts.

"I failed her," she said in a low, dull voice.

Madame Yeva stood on the porch above her, looking down. Karena saw pain in her faded blue eyes, in the pale, damp face, as the wind mussed her golden hair touched with gray. Yeva's lip quivered. Karena felt her mother's hand on her head, smoothing her hair.

"You did not fail, Karena. What happened was beyond your control. It would have happened whoever delivered this baby. I could not have stopped it—not even Dr. Zinnovy."

Karena saw a distant thought reflected in her eyes as she gazed off toward the fields.

"Such tragedy as this happens all too often in the Louisa and the Catherine wards," she said.

Anna's sheet-draped body was carried silently out of the bungalow. The most pathetic sound for Karena was the cry of the motherless baby.

"What did Sergei name her?" Karena asked quietly.

"Anna, of course. He could hardly do less."

"What will become of her? Sergei must go to St. Petersburg."

"I've asked Elena and her husband to care for her. After all, Yuri is her uncle. I've promised to pay them. Elena is not unhappy to have the baby here. They have none of their own, and she has desired a baby girl. Sergei agrees that, for the present, it seems the best solution. Elena has a cousin who recently birthed, and she will have mother's milk enough for baby Anna."

"If only she hadn't gone to that meeting last night. If only Sergei had taken the matter of Anna seriously. Maybe none of this would have happened."

"Do not speak of last night, Karena," Madame Yeva said in a tense, hushed voice. "The decisions are made, and we must leave them and move on."

Karena could not help thinking about it. Poor Anna, sixteen, and her life was over with a whimper. Since a very young age she had worked in some capacity in the fields with her family, and then to have fallen for a reckless young man like Sergei, who selfishly took advantage of her. *If I had known sooner about what was going on, could I have stopped it from ending in this bitter harvest? I could have talked to Anna—tried to make her see that her recklessness would lead to a path of thorns and briars.*

And Sergei. In one day, he had lost both his father and Anna. And the baby, if she lived, would be greatly affected by her parents' sin.

Karena would remember baby Anna and do all she could for her as she grew up.

Ilya Jilinsky walked up from the carriage waiting on the road. His fair head shone in the moonlight.

"Sergei's safely away now, Madame Peshkova. Shall I bring you and Karena back to the manor house? Or do you want to wait longer to see how the baby does?"

Madame Yeva lifted her scarf over her head and came down the steps. "There is nothing more we can do tonight, Ilya. The child is in capable hands with Elena's nursing cousin. Come along, Karena, before you fall asleep leaning on the post. Thank you, Ilya, you have been a great help this night in finding Sergei for us. Where is Uncle Matvey?"

"I saw him when I was looking for Sergei. That must have been two hours ago. At that time, he was talking to Colonel Kronstadt. By now, Uncle's probably retired to our bungalow."

Then Aleksandr Kronstadt had not departed when the Okhrana officer Durnov brought Papa into town under arrest. Was he staying the night, prepared to ride out in the morning? Karena had, for a short time, forgotten her own dilemma, and now it all came thundering back. What awaited her with Kronstadt?

Separation

T he next morning, on the first day of September, Karena awoke late. When she came down, the house was quiet and shrouded with a sense of gloom.

Natalia met her with a sad face.

"Any news?" Karena asked.

"Mother has ridden over to see how the newborn is today. Ilya was here earlier. He said Major-General Durnov has not shown up this morning. And Colonel Kronstadt rode out early for St. Petersburg."

Karena looked at her sharply. "Kronstadt—has left for St. Petersburg?" *What? Without me?* she almost said, but caught herself. Natalia knew nothing of her visit to the political meeting, and Karena wanted to keep her younger sister uninvolved.

"Yes, he left. Are you surprised?"

Karena shrugged. "I expected the Okhrana to hang around longer and make our lives miserable," she said quietly.

Natalia's face changed, showing her true horrors. "Poor Papa." The tears were about to start, and Karena went to her quickly and gave her shoulders a little shake.

"Stop, it will only weaken us. We must be strong, Sister. It is not over yet. Remember, Uncle Viktor has the ear of the czar. He may be able to do something for Papa. In the meantime, we must carry on. If we allow ourselves to weaken, we will fall like a house of cards."

Natalia wiped her eyes and nodded. "Boris left with the conscripts." She swallowed hard, and Karena made a soothing sound.

"He will come back."

"If he doesn't—"

"Don't think that. The more you think such things, the more despondent you'll become." She looked down at Natalia's left hand and acted shocked. "What is this, I ask?"

Natalia smiled through her tears and held out her hand, showing a glimmering ring with a small pearl. "My engagement ring. Isn't it absolutely beautiful? It's wished on, so I can't take it off. Boris got it from his grandmother yesterday to give me before he left for Warsaw. Mama is pleased too."

"And no wonder. Boris is a fine young man. I'm sure you'll have ten children like Job and his wife—seven sons and three daughters."

Natalia smiled. "Ten children! Five maybe."

Karena had steered her away from her fears, and now Natalia was all chatter and large plans. They would stay on the land, and if Karena married Ilya, they could all be one large, happy family raising children and wheat.

Karena kept smiling at the words "stay on the land," but her throat tightened. Natalia did not yet know, and Karena could not bear to tell her. Madame Yeva be must the one to speak of the prospect of losing the farmland and manor house. It would not only mean leaving everything that was home but also their friends among the peasants, people they knew and cared about, like Elena and Yuri.

Karena turned her mind back to Aleksandr Kronstadt while Natalia lost herself in discussing her dreams. Why had Kronstadt left without arresting her? Or had he left? Maybe he would come back to take her to St. Petersburg.

"Oh, I almost forgot… Colonel Kronstadt left you a message. It's over there on the sideboard by the coffee and pancakes."

Karena went at once and found the sealed envelope leaning against the vase of flowers placed by Aunt Marta. She opened it quickly. The firm black writing read simply:

Miss Peshkova, I must report for duty at Petrograd. I am unable to continue our discussion of yesterday. I am sure this brings you much regret.

Karena smiled faintly and read on:

I have spoken to your uncle, Professor Menkin, about the upcoming order to abandon the land now occupied by your family. Unfortunately, I don't have the authority to rescind such an order. I will send a report to General Roskov with the suggestion that the Peshkova women find lodging with the Roskov family. Accordingly, we are likely to meet again in Petrograd. I look forward to resuming our discourse.

Col. Alex Kronstadt

Alex…not merely Colonel Kronstadt, not even Aleksandr, but *Alex*.

She felt the first renewal of something akin to excitement. Was this his casual way of saying her secret would remain with him?

She was aware of Natalia's watching her.

"You look pleased about whatever he said," Natalia commented with mock seriousness. "What could it be, I wonder?"

Karena smiled ruefully and proceeded to take a plate and serve herself breakfast. The strange exhilaration continued.

When Madame Yeva came down to the dining room, her mouth drooped and she looked pale. "I'm sorry to say I feel I'm coming down with the grippe."

"Sit down, Mama, and rest. I'll get your coffee and cakes," Karena said.

Aunt Marta emerged from the kitchen, her eyes red-rimmed from crying. Yeva, who never showed herself without her hair neatly braided and pinned, looked as though she'd merely repinned yesterday's braids into a roll at the back of her head. Karena suspected she'd been awake most of the night. This was a crucial time for her, as well as for her daughters, for she was only as secure as her gentile husband.

Colonel Kronstadt had been right when he upbraided Papa Josef for blindly throwing himself in the fire for Sergei and leaving Yeva and the rest of his family unprotected. Poor Papa! He must not have thought through all the consequences of his actions in his harried effort to save Sergei.

"Matvey, Grandmother, and Ilya are coming over from the bungalow," Yeva said. "We are to have a serious meeting this morning about our future here in Kiev."

Natalia exchanged glances with Karena. Aunt Marta sat down, dabbing her eyes with her white handkerchief, her black dress hinting of her funereal mood.

"It's not possible," Aunt Marta murmured. "How could this have happened?"

Uncle Matvey arrived first, while Ilya assisted his grandmother down from the carriage. With Papa Josef gone, Matvey was now head of the family, though it might be argued that it should pass to General Viktor Roskov. For Karena, it would always be Uncle Matvey.

When the others joined them in the sunny dining room, Madame Yeva, sitting very straight in her chair with her hands in her lap, looked at her daughters and then the others.

"I've been informed by the authorities that the Peshkov family is no longer in charge of the land. We must leave the manor house."

Aunt Marta dropped her forehead against her kerchief and shed tears. Grandmother Jilinsky clasped her hands together and murmured in Yiddish. Natalia gasped. Ilya looked at his shoes in sober silence.

Uncle Matvey had been watching the response of the others. "I am leaving for St. Petersburg tomorrow to petition the czar and speak to General Roskov."

"Of what hope is that?" complained Aunt Marta through her tears. "Will the czar even hear your petition?"

"I hardly have faith in that, my dear Marta, but that is where your brother-in-law Viktor is our ally. He will bring our petition before Czar Nicholas."

"Mother, where will we go if we must leave the house?" Natalia asked.

"There is only one thing we can do, and that is perhaps the saddest part of this tragedy. I fear that, for a time, we must separate."

There was an intake of breath, followed by Grandmother Jilinsky's and Aunt Marta's quiet tears. Karena sat without moving, trying to take it all in. Separation…

"We cannot all impose on Uncle Matvey with his little apartment in St. Petersburg, nor on Aunt Zofia, but Uncle Matvey has agreed to take me and Karena."

"Mother!" Natalia cried, as though betrayed. "What about me?"

"Natalia, dear, you will be much better off with your Aunt Marta in St. Petersburg, to stay awhile with Aunt Zofia and Tatiana."

"But so would Karena! She's closer to Tatiana than I am."

Karena's heart beat faster. She was going to St. Petersburg. They would stay with Uncle Matvey, which she had desired ever since his arrival in early June, and she'd been asked to help him with his manuscript.

"I'm going to St. Petersburg, dear, to seek work as a nurse," Madame Yeva told Natalia, "and Karena is needed to help your uncle complete his manuscript."

And Dr. Zinnovy is nearby, Karena thought.

Natalia appeared to accept the logic of this, but she looked depressed. "What about Grandmother Jilinsky and Ilya?"

Ilya walked over from where he'd been standing by the window and laid a tanned hand on his grandmother's shoulder. She looked up at him and covered his hand with her own.

"Ilya's leaving us," Grandmother said.

Karena looked at him quickly. He explained, meeting Karena's gaze. "Like Boris, I've been conscripted into the army. Word has come over the telegraph that war is declared."

"Oh, Ilya, no."

"I haven't much time," he said. "Another wave of conscripts is moving out today. The army's been hauling men in for duty all summer."

Karena stood, and he walked slowly across the floor, his hands outstretched. She clasped them, and in the silence, Grandmother Jilinsky could be heard sobbing quietly.

Karena and Ilya left the dining room, and the family meeting went on without them. Together they walked slowly out the front door and onto the porch. Karena held on to the post, gazing off toward the fields, thinking how they now took on a lonely, forlorn appearance.

"Strange," she said after a moment, "how things change so drastically when one least expects it."

"Yes. I've looked at those wheat fields all summer and never thought much about them. Then something happens that threatens to take them away, and now they look more precious than ever."

She turned and looked at him. So many of her loved ones had slipped through her fingers: Papa Josef, her brother, Anna. The family was separating, and while they anticipated the separation would not last for long, who could be certain?

And now Ilya.

He joined her in watching the wheat bending in the wind. His lean, tanned face looked grim and haggard for such a young man.

She tried to ease at least one of his burdens. "Do not worry about Grandmother. I'll not let anything happen to her if I can possibly prevent it. We'll make room for her somewhere, somehow, even if she has to sleep in my bed."

"Thank you," he said in a tight voice. "It will be all right." But they knew, in reality, it would not be all right. Nothing would ever be right again.

"Let's walk," he said.

They set out along the wagon road between the wheat fields. The morning sky was clear toward the steppes, as though stretching outward without limit. The steppes brought images of Cossacks, of brilliant horses and horsemen, soldiers, and thousands of the czar's Imperial Cavalry. Kronstadt—Colonel Alex Kronstadt. She glanced at Ilya, feeling guilty for dwelling upon him now.

"What do you think of him?" he asked.

Ilya's question surprised her. He walked along, trying not to raise dust, and Karena hurried to keep up. So much had happened in the last few hours, her feelings seemed unable to recover.

"Colonel Kronstadt?" she asked, curious.

"Yes. What do you think of him?" he repeated, a thoughtful tone to his voice.

She looked straight ahead. The last thing she wanted to do was to hurt Ilya.

"He knows the Roskovs—Aunt Zofia approves of him."

"Your father's sister?" he sounded surprised by that, so she guessed he had not known about Alex knowing the family.

"Yes, evidently it was the general who arranged for Kronstadt's transfer from the cavalry to the Okhrana." She added, "Tatiana claims they will soon become engaged."

He was silent for a minute. "His relationship with the Roskovs could benefit your family."

Ilya paused on the dusty road and looked at her, lines of worry tightening around his mouth.

"I fear this war will do Russia more harm than Germany," he said. "We are not prepared for a long war, and though many say we will be home for Christmas, I see the clouds gathering for a long and dreary storm."

Karena could sense the bleak winds of war and shuddered.

"The czarina is of German blood," Ilya continued. "Some say she surrounds Czar Nicholas with Germans…spying for her and the starets."

"You don't think she is for Germany?" she asked, incredulous.

He shook his head. "Who knows? I am only a country peasant."

She smiled at him. "You are teasing me, Ilya. You have so many long conversations with Uncle Matvey. You should have an idea what the war will bring to Russia."

His self-abasement vanished. "Trouble, so Uncle Matvey also believes. The Bolsheviks are not patriotic. They would just as soon see us worn out on the battlefield so that the czar is weakened. Anything to end his rule."

"That the czarina is German should not sway the czar from his alliance with France, should it?" she questioned.

"The czar and Kaiser Wilhelm of Germany are cousins, but Russia will fight for her ally France. Great Britain, too, may join us, making an entente."

Sadness filled her mind. Russia shuddered under its national load. Was the trumpet sound of war the beginning of victory, or did it herald worse tidings to come? The summer of discontent was coming to its end, but what would take its place?

War, loneliness, and fear rode on the winds of August.

The next few days passed quietly, but Karena could sense the ominous tension hovering over her.

Uncle Matvey had already left for St. Petersburg to petition the czar, and by now, Sergei should have reached Kazan. Sergei would tell the Roskovs, no doubt through tears, all that had happened and his unwise part in this bitter outcome.

Ilya and Boris had said their sad good-byes, then marched out with the conscripts toward Warsaw. Little remained of the army's encampment along the creek except vacant, smoothed areas and dead campfires.

The peasants were quiet and watchful and remained at work in the wheat fields, but they knew of the arrest of Schoolmaster Josef and were grieving for the Peshkov family. They worried about who was going to manage their work now that Ilya had marched off to war.

The unhappy word had made it to the fire circles of the families as they gathered to eat their supper, how the Peshkov family had been ordered to leave the manor house. Such callousness was cause for mourning. The wheat lands had been reclaimed by the Imperial government, and a new bourgeois family, outspokenly loyal to the czar, would be coming to Kiev within the month.

As August came toward a close, Aunt Marta recovered sufficiently from her trauma over her cherished brother Josef. She came to the dinner table with a wan smile, holding a letter.

"It's from Zofia. Sergei is safe and keeping out of the public eye for a time."

As expected, Aunt Zofia, always generous with her older sister's requests, invited them all to come for an extended stay until the matter of Josef was known and the fate of the land decided. Whatever happened, Zofia and Viktor would keep a roof over her relatives' heads during the bleak winter of 1914–15 that lay ahead.

Aunt Zofia, referring to her amity with the czarina through Rasputin, would also make an appeal for Josef.

"Zofia is most confident," Aunt Marta said. "The rainbow crowns our vale of tears. Rasputin, she says, has held out a glimmer of hope that all will be satisfactory in the end. Zofia finds comfort through him. The czarina, too, is absolutely enthralled with his special spiritual gifts."

"So unwise," Madame Yeva said.

"She claims Rasputin is able to bring wellness to the little czarevitch, Alexei."

"Uncle Matvey suggests we change Rasputin's name to Balaam and bring him a donkey," Natalia said.

Madame Yeva smiled ruefully, but Aunt Marta blinked.

"Balaam?" she repeated. "And a donkey?"

Natalia looked at Karena, and they laughed.

"It's in the Bible, Aunt Marta."

"Well, Zofia says we will have much opportunity to see and hear the starets for ourselves," Aunt Marta said. Her brown eyes narrowed, as she seemed to suspect Karena and Natalia of teasing her. "And you, Natalia, can tell Rasputin yourself that you think he should change his name to Balaam."

The shadowy mood that they had brought with them to the table passed into one of shared optimism. Whether based on fact or mere hope, their last meal together for some time turned into one of cheer.

The next day, Aunt Marta and Natalia, with two trunks packed and a third, larger trunk filled to overflowing with precious family objects from their years in the manor, departed for St. Petersburg.

NINETEEN

Danger!

T oward the end of September, the night wind took on a chill that told Karena the harvest season was well over and winter was on its heels. The manor house was too quiet, with many invading memories carrying their baggage of joys and regrets.

Karena was anxious to depart Kiev for St. Petersburg, but Madame Yeva appeared reluctant. She was waiting, she explained, for a letter from Uncle Matvey, informing them that a different apartment in the same building, which had one extra room, had indeed become available. The occupant, an American journalist who was covering the revolutionary riots of the factory workers, was soon to leave for Warsaw and had offered it to Uncle Matvey while he was away. The only trouble was, the American had not yet left, due to difficulties with his official papers. There was some mention of changing apartments, but Uncle Matvey had so many research books and boxes of writing materials that a temporary change would be too burdensome.

"If we cannot take young Hadley's apartment, then it may be wiser to take up residence in Moscow," he had written, "though I understand the reason for your wish to be in St. Petersburg."

Reason, indeed, with the medical college not far away. The days slipped by, and they waited for Uncle Matvey's letter. Travel plans remained undecided.

One evening, Karena was in her room, struggling to decide what clothes to take. She had an unpleasant notion that new clothes would be hard to come by on her wage, and she was reluctant to leave anything behind. She was allotted only one trunk, and choosing garments was inevitable. What remained behind would be given to the peasants, unless Uncle Viktor came with wagons and helped with clothes, glassware, and indeed, all of the furnishings from the Peshkov household. Karena could see Madame Yeva's internal agony. Her life was bound up in the manor and all it had held for the last two decades. Karena felt great loss at leaving behind favorite clothes, books, mementos, and shoes. The list was endless.

"Now I know what Mrs. Noah must have gone through," Madame Yeva commented as she stared at two exquisite lace tablecloths. "She had to look at all the family's belongings and decide what to bring into the ark and what she must leave to be taken away in the great flood."

Karena glanced at her. "I'd never thought of that. But Mrs. Noah had a very large ark. Lot's family had to flee with nothing."

"Well, Lot's wife didn't want to leave. I suppose there are great spiritual lessons in these struggles."

"Did you know Uncle Matvey thinks Jesus was the promised Messiah?"

Yeva paused thoughtfully, handling the lace tablecloths as though remembering something fond and far away. "No, I didn't know. He's not discussed his book with me in weeks. If he *was* the Messiah, then he still *is*. Christians believe Jesus rose from the dead." She went on, changing the subject, "Everything left behind will remain in place. Just leave it as is, Karena. There's still a chance this horrible situation might be overturned by Czar Nicholas. And if not, Viktor may be able to move the furniture and draperies to Kazan. Someday," Yeva said firmly, "we will have our own house again."

Karena wondered where the finances for a house would come from. What if Papa Josef were sentenced to years in a slave-labor camp in Siberia? Would his health even hold up under such torturous conditions? Every winter for as far back as she could remember, they worried about his becoming ill with pneumonia.

"One of my deepest regrets is leaving baby Anna," Madame Yeva said. "She's come down with a slight chill, and I would feel so much better if I knew it wasn't going to choke up her bronchial tubes. A fever can be devastating for a newborn."

"At least Elena loves her dearly and worries about her as much as you do," Karena said, trying to cheer her. She knew that it was a grief for her mother to leave her grandchild behind, even if the baby was not a blood relation. She and Aunt Marta both had raised Sergei, and Sergei's baby would be tremendously important to Papa Josef when he learned of her birth.

"We promised Anna we would watch over her baby. It troubles me to leave her. And now she's not fully well." Madame Yeva stared down at the pile of linens with distress clearly drawn across her tired face.

"Yes, but I don't know what we'd do if Elena didn't want her. At least baby Anna is with her aunt and uncle until Sergei can claim his daughter."

"I suppose you're choosing to be practical," Madame Yeva said, "but I hate leaving her. Especially now that the wage I promised for her upkeep cannot come as frequently as I had intended."

"If we brought her with us, who would care for her while we're both working?"

"I almost wish Grandmother Jilinsky had not gone to the Roskovs," Madame Yeva said. "She is wonderful with children. Money will be scarce too. Even so, leaving little Anna behind troubles me when I've no idea whether we'll ever be permitted to return here. Elena is not in such good health herself after two miscarriages in three years. And Yuri may soon be conscripted, maimed hand or not. If the war goes badly for Russia, the czar will need every available man."

Karena frowned. What would they do with baby Anna? "There's only one thing we could do if the worst happens. We'll need to come back for her. Or by then Sergei will come himself."

Yeva gave a brief nod but did not look entirely convinced. She went on folding the linens to be stored away, and Karena continued her own packing. For years, she had longed for the day when she would pack her trunk and journey to St. Petersburg. Now that the day approached, she found the experience sad and unsatisfying.

Outside, the wind had risen, and there were creaks and groans in the manor house that had been unnoticed when the family was all at home. The various sounds put Karena on edge. She went to shut the window where the wind had pulled the curtains out. The front yard was alive with swaying silhouettes as the wind shook and bent the bushes in an uncanny dance. She drew the curtains in, closed the window, and locked it.

"Elena doesn't want to give up baby Anna, does she?" Karena asked. "I can hardly believe it of her and Yuri."

"Neither of them do," Yeva answered. "Elena is sure she'll never carry one of her own to full term. If they wished to relinquish her, I wouldn't hesitate to take her with us, though I have no notion where we could place her. Certainly not in Matvey's apartment. But the lack of money burdens them. I should leave them with something. It will be some time before I get a job and can send them anything."

Karena thought of her savings earned from jobs done in the village. Uncle Matvey, too, had insisted on paying her this summer, knowing she had been saving in the hope of entering the medical college.

She went to her bureau and removed the box of money she had expected to use in St. Petersburg.

"Then we'll share what I have with them and baby Anna. I think it will help us all sleep better."

Madame Yeva at first refused, but when Karena kept urging her mother, she relented, cupped her face between her cool palms as though Karena were again a small girl, and kissed both of her cheeks.

"You are a good girl, Karena. You make me very proud."

Karena, embarrassed, was nonetheless blessed by her mother's sincere praise. "I have an interest in baby Anna too," she said with a smile. "She's my first delivery."

"Ah, but she won't be your last. You have the gift of loving babies and the poor women who carry them into this heartless world."

Madame Yeva put the money in her pocket and picked up her scarf from the bureau.

"I feel vexed over the child's cold. I'm going over to the bungalow to check on her. Yuri will be there. I want to put the money in his hands. And I think it wise to leave Elena some medications."

While her mother went off to select the medicines, Karena went back to her packing, kneeling before her trunk, trying to choose. A few minutes crept by. She folded a blouse and then paused, lifting her head at the sound of the creaking stairs. Why was Madame Yeva so hesitant in going down the stairs? Karena turned her head toward the bedroom door, listening. Or was she coming up?

She placed the blouse in her trunk and stood, facing the bedroom door. There it was again, that creaking stair, heard plainly this time in the momentary lull of the blowing wind. A creaking stair under a heavy footstep, quite unlike her mother's.

She went to her door, glanced in both directions, and then looked down the flight of stairs to the front hall. The front door stood open. The lamps on the table below the window facing the front porch cast a golden glow of warmth.

Karena went down the stairs and across the hall to shut it.

"All alone?"

She whirled. Policeman Leonovich stood on the bottom stair, slouching against the rail with a leer on his broad face, his arms folded across his chest. He laughed silently, his shoulders shaking.

"Where have all the heroes gone, I wonder? Big heroes, eh? They went to fight the Germans. Do you miss Ilya, eh? Well, we'll do something to cheer you up. Yes, we will. You can pretend I'm pretty boy Ilya."

He straightened from the rail and walked toward her, his coarse smile disappearing.

Fear clutched Karena's heart. She could see the effect of vodka in his movements as he came toward her, hands clenching. "I've been thinking about you for a long time."

His eyes were bright and lustful, his hard mouth determined. She sensed at once he could not be reasoned with.

Karena, already at the front door, turned to flee. His heavy hand latched hold of her hair like a claw. He jerked it with such force that her head snapped back and she lost her footing.

"You'll cooperate or I'll break every bone in your body."

Like a hungry vulture, he pounced, knocking her down to the rug. She screamed, clawing at him, her nails scraping his face, drawing blood. His foul breath met her face as his mouth smothered her. She bit hard.

God, help me! Help me! Please! She struggled, and gaining one free hand, she grabbed a hank of his bushy hair and yanked, taking out a clump. He cursed, and she felt a fist smash her face. Her eyes saw flashes of light, and she was spiraling down into a pit. Then there was a crack of thunder, and she smelled acrid smoke and heard his shocked intake of breath. She felt his body jerk as if struck, then he was off her and on his knees.

Karena dizzily sat up, trying to crawl away. Her sight was blurred, but she could see him on his knees, looking toward the stairs.

Madame Yeva stood there with Papa Josef's gun in her hand. Karena could see her now, her face cold and hard, her eyes blazing.

"There is no justice," she said, her voice frighteningly soft. "No justice for Jews or anyone else, not with swine like you calling themselves policemen. How dare you put your filthy hands on my daughter!"

There was an expression of sudden sobriety on Leonovich's sweating face. Karena saw the scarlet patch on the back of his shirt grow larger. His voice rasped.

"I'll—kill—you—" He got to his feet, staggering toward Yeva.

"Get out of here, or I'll shoot again." She backed up onto the bottom steps as he lunged toward her, wrenched the gun from her grip, and tossed it upstairs.

Karena struggled to her feet, grabbing hold of the table to steady herself. She reached for the marble bookend. If she could get behind him…

Like a wounded bear fierce with rage, Leonovich grabbed at Madame Yeva's neck. Karena watched, trying to focus, feeling as though she were paralyzed and everything was happening too quickly. She heard horrible choking sounds from her mother. He was squeezing the life from her. Karena moved toward them, hearing the struggle, the panting. Her mother fell to her knees on the stairs, and Leonovich bent over her, his hands around her throat.

Karena moved in desperation, the marble bookend clutched in both hands. She made it up to the bottom stairs until she was just behind him, and then brought it down with all her force.

He slumped and fell backward, and she stepped aside. He tumbled past her and came to a stop below the bottom stair, his bloodied head on the rug.

Gasping, she dropped the bookend and struggled to reach her mother.

Yeva's face was still purple, but she was breathing. Her eyes opened, and her hand felt her throat, where Karena saw red bruises.

Madame Yeva sat choking and sputtering, and then slowly, painfully, caught her breath. She grasped hold of the banister and raised herself awkwardly to her feet. Karena leaned back against the railing, her brain still dizzy, and she felt an eyelid growing puffy and beginning to swell. She touched her lip with her tongue and felt a cut and the stale taste of blood. Her heart thudded steadily like a drum.

After a minute of recovery, Madame Yeva moved down the steps to Leonovich, passing him cautiously with her skirt pressed back. She nudged him with no response.

Karena, looking down from where she leaned against the banister, saw the bloody mat of his hair.

Turning his head back, Madame Yeva looked into his contorted face, raising his eyelids and peering at his pupils. She snatched one of his heavy hands, feeling for a pulse.

After a moment, she let his wrist drop. She looked at Karena and nodded at her questioning gaze. The silence became an announcement of death.

Karena brought a trembling hand to her eyes. *I've killed him.*

The wind groaned, and the door flung open. Karena nearly screamed, expecting more police. It was only a gust of wind.

Madame Yeva moved across the hall to shut and bolt the door, then the window, and drew the drapes across.

"If anyone heard that gunshot…," Karena whispered.

Madame Yeva snuffed out the oil lamps. Finding a candle from under the hall table, she lit the wick, her hands shaking.

"If anyone should come, we won't answer," her voice rasped. "They may think we're asleep. They'll check elsewhere." She walked back to the stairs and held the candle high over the body. "We haven't much time,

Karena. If the gendarmes discover he was shot here, we will both be arrested."

"And hanged!"

"Hush. We'll get away from here."

"But we can't leave him in the house." The steadiness of her own voice surprised Karena. "They'll hunt for us. We'll need to get rid of his body."

And there's blood on the floor where he fell.

Madame Yeva put a hand to her forehead. "Yes, then we'll put the body in the wagon and leave it somewhere off the road near town, as far from here as we can. We'll wrap it in this rug—it's already stained."

"But someone may recognize the rug."

"We'll bring the rug with us and dispose of it once we're out of town."

Madame Yeva set the candle down on the table beside the stairs and took hold of the body by its arms. Karena helped her drag the body to the rug and roll it up inside. Her throat ached with emotion. *Dear God, what are we going to do? We've killed a man—not a man, a beast.* Would the authorities see it as self-defense—or murder?

As she pulled and dragged the body, she realized her fingers were stiff and her head throbbed. She wanted to sit down and weep. Her life was all but over.

"All right, leave it for now," Madame Yeva said of the rolled carpet. "We'll need to pack a few things to take with us."

In Karena's bedroom, her mother set the candle down and extinguished the oil lamp.

"We've never been in such peril, Karena. The gendarmes will take the side of Leonovich's innocence. I don't think we can involve Matvey in this either, for his sake. He is already under suspicion because of Warsaw."

"Maybe we should go directly to the gendarmes and explain. Leonovich threatened to kill us both. Perhaps they will listen."

"Ah, Daughter, you are yet trusting. I lived through the pogrom of

1903, even as Leah lived through pogroms in Warsaw. There is no hope for us now with Josef arrested. Perhaps there are a few police who would try to be fair, but here? With Grinevich's gendarmes?"

"But they could see our bruises. They could not deny that."

"They could, and would. They will say that I had you deliberately lure Leonovich to the manor house tonight. They will charge that we planned to kill him before we were forced off the land. They are angry about Grinevich. Because we are Jewish, it will be most easy for them to hold us responsible, claiming Leonovich's murder is in revenge for the arrest of my husband. Oh, I know how these matters work. Of course, they know it isn't true. But I have seen it all before…oh, so many times. And after Josef has confessed his involvement with the Bolsheviks? Ah! If they can say Leonovich was murdered here by Josef's wife and daughter…we will receive their form of justice, which will start with our immediate arrest."

Karena felt a wave of desperation. Her mother was right. Unless they had the right kind of help, they were in danger. They could not bring Leonovich's body to the police station and report what had taken place. Who knew what these men, friends of Grinevich and Leonovich, would do?

"Quickly, now. Grab a satchel and take some warm clothes. Bring every ruble you can find. Do not forget your fur coat."

Her mother went off to her room. Karena urged herself to hurry, but her movements seemed laboriously slow. She fumbled with swollen fingers to change into traveling clothes and refused to look in the mirror. What would people think when they saw her looking like this on the train?

When she finished dressing, she went to the doorway of her mother's bedroom. Madame Yeva was relocking the door to the safe. She had a small box in hand that Karena recognized: the box Natalia had brought to Kazan. She saw her mother hide it at the bottom of her satchel.

Yeva turned and, seeing Karena standing in the doorway, went over to the table and picked up a bottle of ointment. "Clean your abrasions with this." She handed her the bottle and a clean cloth. Then she moved toward the door. "I must bring the medical supplies from downstairs with us, or else we will never be able to work."

Karena winced from the sting of the ointment. Then, with as much haste as she could muster, she went back to her room, packed some warm clothes, and stuffed her winter shoes into a leather satchel. She looked at the trunk, too tired to feel the loss. She turned her back on her possessions and, with candle in hand, went down the stairs.

Wait! Food and water. Her brain must be functioning after all. She set her bag down and went to the kitchen. Hastily, she grabbed a hunk of cheese, a loaf of bread, and an assortment of dried fruits and nuts, put them in a cloth bag, then filled a water flask from the jug on the counter.

Madame Yeva waited in the hall, looking cautiously out the window. The shadowy environment with Leonovich's corpse lying in the rug beside the door made Karena's skin tingle.

How was it possible to escape the dark, pervasive consequences of this appalling night? Where would they go? What would they do if they did not go to Uncle Matvey?

Madame Yeva's skin was pale, and yet her cheeks were flushed. Karena went to her. "Mother, you're ill."

Madame Yeva shook her head in protest. "I'll be all right. Hurry, we've no time to loiter."

Karena's own dizziness had not yet abandoned her, yet she could not burden her mother with more worry at this time. Their best chance of escape was to move quickly. But even then—would they live a life of being hunted by the authorities? hiding somewhere in Moscow or St. Petersburg?

Madame Yeva unlocked the front door. The wind grabbed at them like snatching fingers trying to thwart their escape. Karena saw the horse-drawn wagon her mother had intended to drive to see baby Anna. Now, even the baby must wait. They could not involve Elena and Yuri by going there for even a few minutes. They would have to send the money once they were safe.

Karena firmly grasped one end of the rolled-up rug. She could hardly lift it. They struggled, mostly dragging the rug over the polished wood floor and out onto the porch.

"Wait here. I'll bring the wagon close to the porch," Madame Yeva said.

The clouds had covered the moon, and the feel of rain was in the wind. Karena's head was thudding with pain, and she was sure her eyelid was swelling shut. How could this horrible situation have occurred? By tomorrow, there would be discoloration on her face. She had brought her hat and a scarf, and if she kept her head low, perhaps she could avoid too much attention while on the train. She assumed they would travel by train, unless they journeyed by a hired droshky, but to travel apart from the train at this time of the year could be risky. September and October were terrible months in St. Petersburg, with rain and mud and dampness until the snow arrived in November.

Whatever her mother's plans were, they were hers as well, and they had best make wise choices.

Once the wagon was in position, they resumed their gasping struggle with the rolled-up body. Karena climbed into the back and pulled while Madame Yeva lifted and pushed.

Fear nagged Karena with every breath she sucked in, with every rustle of branch and leaf. With every stomp of the horse's hooves, she cast glances over her shoulder. If someone were watching them, or came upon them unexpectedly…

At last, they prevailed. The body was in the back of the wagon, their satchels stored beside it, plus one other satchel with medical supplies. They were on their way, but to where?

Karena looked back at the manor house. Would she ever come back? Would there be a family reunion one day with Papa Josef? with baby Anna? with Ilya?

Madame Yeva guided the horse onto the road, and Karena faced forward. She could not bear to watch her home disappear into the darkness.

After a time, they came upon a thick line of chestnut trees growing alongside a deserted, windswept road that appeared to traverse a gully. Madame Yeva pulled over to the side and stopped. The tree branches and leaves shuddered their disapproval.

Madame Yeva climbed down from the driving seat, wind whipping her dark scarf, and hurried around to the back. Karena forced her hurting body to follow. If only Ilya were here, or Sergei, to lend their strength and help, though into her mind walked another man who had no right to be there. She saw the face of Colonel Kronstadt and wondered, for he offered her no safe harbor; indeed, he held a damaging secret that could entangle her more deeply with the prison system in St. Petersburg. She ought to be thankful he was not here, that he'd departed weeks ago for his new post at one of the Imperial military compounds near the Winter Palace.

"Keep a lookout," Madame Yeva said, climbing into the rear of the wagon. "I'll need to unroll the rug."

Karena's heart thumped wildly, and her throat was dry with fear.

All was quiet and dark as the wind raged.

Karena watched her mother struggling to loosen the body and winced at the unpleasant sight. *This must be a nightmare. I shall soon awaken from it and find everything the same as it once was.*

The rug was rolled up again to be disposed of somewhere along the road to the next town, and the body was pulled to the wagon's edge.

"All right now, careful. That's it—we want to push it over the edge into the gully—there!"

A sickening thud followed and the rustle of grasses as the body went over the side and down into the gully.

"Quick! Away."

Karena climbed onto her seat, out of breath, looking back over her shoulder into the darkness as if expecting to see Leonovich's ghost pursuing.

Madame Yeva flicked the reins, and the horse pulled away onto the road. Karena, feeling dizzy, held on to the wagon seat while her mother snapped the reins to gain some distance between themselves and Leonovich's corpse.

By the time they were well on their way toward the next village, Karena felt a few drops of rain. Soon the drops were coming faster, spattering against their faces.

As they rode, the rain grew heavier, and the wind, sometimes in savage gusts, rocked the wagon, but the horse plodded bravely forward. Karena noted with growing concern that her mother was shaking from the cold rain and wind. Was she coming down with pneumonia?

"We'll need to stop at a rest house, Mother. Please, you're not well. In the morning, we'll buy our tickets for St. Petersburg."

Even before they reached the next village, Madame Yeva sought meager shelter under some thick trees to keep from the worst of the downpour.

Karena watched her mother. She hadn't felt well for a week, long before the nightmare they'd faced tonight.

"I'm tired is all. Don't worry so. I'll be all right. Your eye is swollen shut. That fiend—I'm not ashamed to say I'm glad he's dead. He cannot hurt anyone else."

The rain slackened, and Yeva snapped the reins. "Move along, boy. Food and rest await you in the town. I promise to sell you to a good master tomorrow before we board the train."

They were back on the road again, but not for long. As the clouds opened up, the women sought another interlude beneath the trees.

They huddled together with a blanket over their heads, but they were already soaked through. Karena felt her mother shivering. It would be a long ordeal on the train before arriving in St. Petersburg. And when they arrived, what?

We are like two lepers. We must keep our distance from those whose company we long for.

Perhaps they would find a small room in the peasant regions of St. Petersburg. Cold and badly bruised, Karena wondered miserably if matters could become worse.

She felt her mother's brow. "You're burning with fever."

"I'll…be better in…the morning."

Karena watched, silent and worried. She sensed her mother's deep depression and tried to cheer her, but all she could manage was a tired smile that for some reason caused her mother's eyes to well with tears.

Karena threw an arm around her. "I may look dreadful, but I'll recover. We'll be all right. As soon as we reach town, we'll get a bed to rest in, and then there will be a train to take us to our new life in St. Petersburg."

"May God help us, my daughter. Our new life, as you call it, offers little except trouble, with few, if any, to turn to for help."

Madame Yeva had come down with chills and was in the back of the wagon beneath what shelter Karena could piece together to try to shield her from the rainfall. Karena could have asked the family driver to bring them to the train station in the coach, except it would have involved him in their escape should it become known, or so the police would say, and put him and his family at risk. *How amazing,* she thought wearily, *that the seemingly personal decisions we make in life could end up affecting so many, as though there were no such thing as merely personal decisions.*

Karena drove the horse and wagon slower than she would have liked, for the rain was softening the road surface and exposing rocks in some places. If anything went wrong and an axle broke…

Karena feared her mother's throat might be injured, for as time wore on, she could merely whisper. Karena's own bruises ached and throbbed. She must drive the horse cautiously, for one of her eyes had swollen shut, and with both darkness and rain, it would be easy for her to tire and run off the road.

O God of Abraham, help us!

Karena sensed a bleak future while peering through the darkness over the winding road ahead. Henceforth, there would be a shadow cast over her: *murderess.* Could she ever fully justify herself and clear her name again?

TWENTY

The Winter Palace

St. Petersburg

As October dawned at the Imperial officers' barracks at the Winter Palace, Colonel Aleksandr Kronstadt arose to a snowstorm and an unexpected message from Countess Olga Shashenka, his stepmother.

Aleksandr, my son; it is imperative that I see you at once. I have requested of Czar Nicholas to favor me with your presence, and that of Gennady and Ivan, here at my residence in Tsarskoe Selo for a three-day leave. I shall be giving a ball here tonight, followed by a dinner party tomorrow evening. Madame Zofia and your Tatiana will be ending the festivities by hosting a skating party on Sunday, if weather permits.

Did you know that two of Tatiana's cousins from Kiev are now staying with the Roskov family here in Tsarskoe Selo?

I am looking forward to seeing you.

Your Matushka,

Olga

Alex pondered the words of his *matushka*, his "little mother." He stood half-dressed at the frosty window of the room he shared with his twin cousins Gennady and Ivan Sokolov, his companions since boyhood. The three of them had remained friends through childhood and had attended the same prestigious cadet school together, although Alex had always been the most serious and had not shared their penchant for pranks and occasional maliciousness. Ivan had been the worst, open to foolish dares by his fellow cadets because of his desire to prove himself boldest in their class. Alex had rescued Ivan from several debacles at school, including a blindfolded duel. He had matured somewhat since graduation four years ago and even hoped to marry the Countess Orlova's granddaughter, though Alex doubted Ivan would win her. Regrettably, he had turned to drinking, while Gennady was devoutly religious.

On the surface there was nothing unusual about the letter from Countess Shashenka, unless one knew his stepmother as well as he. Though wealthy and influential, she had not sought the role of a doyenne but had worked as a spy for the czar before she'd met and married Alex's father. Alex had not learned this until he'd been reassigned from his Imperial Cavalry regiment to the Okhrana. He'd been inclined to think that Tatiana's mother had been a well-meaning, but meddling, offender. Now he wondered.

His stepmother was not a proficient letter writer, nor was he, though they got on well. This was the first correspondence he'd received from her during the entire season she'd been on holiday in the Crimea. Alex hadn't expected to hear from her until the winter festivals began with a round of dinner balls, usually around Christmas.

None of this should have mattered until he considered that she had never met the Peshkovs of Kiev, nor would someone of her standing necessarily interact socially with a dissident Jew from Warsaw like Professor Menkin. He recalled that Menkin was involved with the cadets; his stepmother was wise not to tout this, though she shared the same political persuasion. Did it mean anything?

"We would be wiser to ride our horses to Tsarskoe Selo rather than chance the train," Gennady called to Alex, slipping into his military jacket. "A horse is not run by the government and is therefore loyal and dependable."

"Aha, now we have you! We should report Gennady's revolutionary comment to General Roskov," Ivan gloated, bleary eyed from celebrating his leave the night before. He reached for a bucket of melted snow and ducked his head into the water, surfacing a moment later with a shudder and a groan. "Do you wonder who I saw last night dancing wildly with the Gypsies?"

"The czarina?" said Gennady.

"Your tongue can be cut out for that! No, her *holy man,* Rasputin. He was drunker than anyone there."

"Drunker than you? No wonder you imagined seeing the godly starets there," snapped Gennady, crossing himself and casting Ivan a look of disdain. "You are always drunk. No wonder we are losing the war."

"We are not losing the war," growled Ivan. "You should be turned in to General Roskov for even suggesting we could lose."

Alex went on dressing while the words between the brothers ripped into heated debate. As Ivan persisted, Gennady grabbed him and attempted to force his head into the water bucket. His arms flailed wildly until Alex yanked the two apart and glowered at Gennady.

"Do you wish to drown him?"

"Yes."

When matters calmed again, Alex shouldered into his dark winter greatcoat and looked at his watch. He snatched up his military hat and leather gloves.

"Aren't you going to eat breakfast with us?" Gennady called.

"No."

"Can we stomach breakfast?" Ivan asked, drying his face and head with a towel, the skirmish with his twin already forgotten.

Gennady's expression saddened. "Just so. More rotten meat awaits us."

The train transport regularly bringing food and commodities into St. Petersburg from the farmlands of Kiev and the rest of the Ukraine was burdened to the utmost by military needs, so that provisions to the cities suffered. Now, with the first thick snowfall in St. Petersburg, Alex expected the trains would run late, if at all.

"If the bread shortage lasts very long, it will bring unrest among the working class," Gennady said. "The revolutionaries will be quick to take advantage of it."

Alex was thinking of the long bread lines. A survey undertaken by the Okhrana on the mood of the country offered a volatile scenario. The people's discontent over shortages of necessities could easily explode into open rebellion. Especially worrisome was the fact that for the first time in the experience of the security police, the anger of the populace was directed not only against the czar's ministers but also against the Imperial couple. The czarina was disliked and, because of her German origin, widely suspected of betraying Russian military secrets to the enemy. Military defeats at the front were also being used by the Socialists to undermine Czar Nicholas, claiming he and his generals were inept.

The dissatisfaction of the urban population was, for the present, mostly economic, but Alex had already written a report for General Roskov that warned it would take little provocation for the grievances to assume political form.

"Well, the call for more bread will be a political gift handed to the Bolsheviks on a jeweled platter," Gennady said.

"With the Romanov crown jewels?" Ivan quipped.

Alex turned swiftly, launching a verbal rebuke that caused Ivan to drop his head. To change the subject, he said, "I've heard Czar Nicholas may go to the front himself and command the army instead of the Grand Duke Nikolas Nikolaevich. I'd like to receive orders to join the grand duke's elite cavalry."

"The food would be better. Whatever it is they've been feeding us, they boil it so you can't taste it," Gennady said gravely. "I think it is rats." He looked over at Alex. "They skin them first. I once heard they use the tails and skins for soup."

"I feel sick," Ivan said, still sitting on the edge of his bunk. His head was in his hands, but he looked up. He had a pale yellow color round his cheeks.

Alex smiled pleasantly and folded his arms. "You'll be fine with a little decent food."

"No! All I want is coffee with a shot of vodka." Ivan groaned.

Alex looked down at him. "I'll have you court-martialed if you do."

"And with proper cause," Gennady snapped.

"Maybe that would be good," Ivan said, looking from one to the other with a challenging glare.

"And you should be shot for saying that," Gennady taunted with a serious face.

"With what will you shoot me?" Ivan sneered. "Ha! There are no rifles."

The army was not equipped for a long war; the shortage of guns, ammunition, boots, and uniforms for the conscripts was a growing scandal. The thought of millions of fine Russian soldiers dying for lack of supplies gripped Alex's heart with silent rage. He had heard how soldiers needed to wait for an armed fellow soldier to die before they could possess a rifle!

"I have a rifle," Gennady said, "but no bullets." He turned his head. "Alex?"

"I have bullets," Alex said too soberly, "and an American revolver."

Gennady looked at Alex curiously. "Where did you get an American revolver?"

"From Michael."

"He's become a religious fanatic," Ivan said.

Alex shrugged. "Maybe. Maybe not." He picked up his satchel.

"What kind of answer is that?" Ivan complained. " 'Maybe not'? Why wouldn't he be a fanatic, going to an unorthodox church? Such an idea!"

Recently, Alex had not given much thought to orthodoxy but to Imperial autocratic rule. The letters from Michael were affecting Alex's belief in the czar. Though he would not say so in uniform, the more he performed investigative work for the secret police, the less he liked it and the more he questioned the autocracy in the privacy of his own mind. Alex was beginning to wonder if Michael was trying to draw him away from the czar. Every month, he sent magazines and newspapers filled with stories on America's president, Woodrow Wilson, and what life and politics were like in the United States. Alex was fascinated with the concept of individuality. Michael also sent handwritten notes in Russian on the Bible study he'd been attending since May on a verse-by-verse study of the gospel of Matthew. Between Michael's exhaustive notes and diagrams, which were enough to put into book form, and Professor Menkin's half-finished manuscript on the Jewish Messiah, Alex found his fall evenings absorbed in research. He was in the process of concluding a report on Menkin's work for the secret police, but before he did, he wanted to visit the professor and discuss the findings. Alex was also curious about Karena. Menkin would be the one to talk to about her and Madame Yeva.

"Aren't you going to wait for me and Ivan?" Gennady called as Alex went to the door.

"No."

"You're not the only one going to the ball," Gennady said.

"Alex is jealous." Ivan grinned. "Tatiana likes to dance with me."

"Then you'd better stay sober or you'll fall on your face," Alex said.

He ducked out the door as Ivan picked up the bucket of snow water and threatened to drench him. His cousins hooted.

"A wager, Alex!" Ivan cried after him cheerfully. "I will lead off the first dance with the general's daughter!"

Gennady ran after him. "Wait! Aren't you supposed to escort that Hessian count in his carriage? He is leaving on the train for Moscow!"

Alex answered, "That was *your* order from Major-General Durnov."

"Mine!" Gennady looked at him with mouth open. "No, it was yours."

Alex pointed back toward their room. "No. Not mine. Go look at Durnov's order again. This time *read* it. You answered the door this morning. Captain Gusinsky handed you the order. You have an hour."

Gennady turned and ran back into the room, skidding on the slippery floor. Alex heard a groan, followed by Ivan's voice: "Are you hurt, Gennady?"

Shaking his head and smiling, Alex walked toward the barracks' stables.

Outside the barracks at the Winter Palace, snow drifted down, draping everything in white. For a haunting moment, the world looked pure, as though a white robe were atoning for creation's bondage to corruption.

Alex's notion that his newly acquired Arabian mare, a gift from his stepmother, would not like the snow and ice finalized his decision—he'd take the train to Tsarskoe Selo, "the Czar's Village," fifteen miles southwest of Petrograd. Since the czar's palace-residence was there, the officials would keep the railroad tracks clear and running smoothly.

He hailed a droshky, tossed his bag in, and climbed inside. The horse-drawn sleigh moved toward the railway station.

The wind whipped the snow against him, and he pulled his hat lower.

He pondered Olga's letter again. *"Did you know that two of Tatiana's cousins from Kiev are now staying with the Roskov family here in Tsarskoe Selo?"*

Alex thought of Karena Peshkova and her younger sister, Natalia.

The icy wind blew into his face sharply, like a slap of reality. *There is no reason why you should hope she is there. None at all.*

Everything he had planned was attainable through General Roskov's daughter, Tatiana. Further involvement with Karena could jeopardize his entire military career. He thought of the political reasons why he should avoid her. She was Jewish, and her mother came from a politically dangerous family in Finland and Warsaw. Only twenty miles from St. Petersburg, revolutionaries crossed the border into Finland to escape arrest and plot against the czar.

So then, stop wondering about her. So what if he found himself drawn toward her, what of it? He wanted to marry Tatiana. Thoughts of wishing to see Karena again were unwise.

Nevertheless, his orders to locate the Bolshevik leader, Lenski, required Alex to delve into Karena Peshkova's private life, which also kept her on his mind. He frowned. Even so, he would think of her with a businesslike indifference. The Okhrana, Major-General Durnov in particular, was convinced Karena Peshkova and Lenski were secret lovers, plotting together with Sergei and Ivanna against the czar's government officials. Alex would need to speak of this touchy issue with General Roskov. He would not have thought Karena the type to fall for Lenski.

A short time later, irritable and restless, Alex climbed out of the droshky, his boots crunching snow. Falling snow dusted his long greatcoat and blew in little swirls along the street. The storm had brought twilight at noon; even so, this was a mere harbinger of greater winter snows to come.

He paid the driver and climbed the high steps of the Petrograd station to await the train for Tsarskoe Selo.

People were coming and going, and the parkway was filling with coaches. Alex was preoccupied with unpleasant thoughts. He fussed irritably with his glove. He heard the hiss of the boiler on the rails and the rumble of the train. The whistle shrieked. The platform shook, and puffs of smoke and steam rose in the frigid air as the train came to a shuddering halt.

Alex snapped alert as an explosion split the air. After a timeless interval, there were screams, and then the urgent wail of an alarm erupted as people shouted and ran.

TWENTY-ONE

Assassination

K arena awakened from a fevered sleep with the whistle shrieking and the train slowing for its approach to another station stop. Her muscles were cramped, and she tried to stretch and could not. Her eyelids fluttered open, and she remembered; they'd been forced to ride third class, jammed into one of the filthy boxcars with so many peasants that she could neither move nor breathe comfortably. Madame Yeva, suffering from fever and nausea, had fainted, awakening in and out of a nightmarish sleep.

"Karena!"

"I'm here, Mother," she whispered in her ear. "Don't draw attention, don't say a word. There are so many people in here that no one notices us. We're packed into a tight, darkened corner, but we're all right. Don't be afraid."

Yeva's eyes closed again, and she appeared to sleep despite the noise becoming a part of their existence.

Karena's arm was growing numb from where her mother's head rested against her shoulder. They had been in this cramped position for hours, but try as she might, she could barely move. Neither could any of the peasants around her. Karena marveled at how they bore it all. She herself was in a weakened physical condition, and it was only worry over her mother's unexpected illness that maintained her determination.

Somehow, through the struggle, Karena had kept them both together even while undergoing harassment and insults by the Imperial train inspectors who had boarded at the second stop out of Kiev. The stop was a major interchange, and passengers needed to produce their identity papers. As soon as the inspectors learned that Madame Yeva and Karena were classified as Polish Jews, they were ordered from their third-class seats and put into this noisy boxcar. She and her mother looked so terrible after the rainstorm and from their injuries, the inspectors scorned them. *Thank God!*

Karena's skin tingled from lack of circulation, and she was sure fleas and lice had invaded her garments. She had a little water that she kept for her mother, and no permission was granted to get off at the various stops. They were told that the decent people of the towns and villages had no wish to mingle with Jews and dirty peasants. Yeva's illness kept her from arguing, and Karena continued to whisper that they must remain as unnoticed as they could. Horrendous crimes were known to take place in the boxcars, and the police did not trouble themselves over injustices to the Jews. Karena occasionally kept her hand near her coat pocket where she had hidden Papa Josef's Russian Nagant revolver.

The long hours rumbled by in semidarkness. She heard the groans of the packed peasants and Jews, heard from different corners of the boxcar the tubercular cough that she recognized. Her compassion reached beyond herself and Yeva to the wretched human beings jammed into the boxcar. Even so, she cringed when she heard their phlegm-filled coughing. She recalled Psalm 91:6: "Nor of the pestilence that walks in darkness." When the train began to slow, Karena wondered if she could still support herself and her mother.

After coming to a shuddering halt, the door of the boxcar was opened from the outside, and sharp voices demanded they get out and be on their way.

"Where are we now?" Madame Yeva murmured in a scratchy voice barely audible above the din.

"St. Petersburg. Here, Mother, lift your fur hood. It's snowing outside. Oh—*fresh* air! I shall never complain of the cold again."

"St. Petersburg!" Yeva's dazed eyes widened, and she shook with chills that came and subsided. She shook her head in protest. "We must not go to your Uncle Matvey. It will put him at risk, Karena. What about—"

Karena squeezed her hand, affirming a calmness she did not in the least feel. "We've no choice. You're too ill, and we're in desperate need of help."

"I'm—I will be all right again soon…"

"Uncle Matvey is expecting us, and you must see a doctor soon." She added reluctantly to strengthen her argument, "And we're out of money."

"Out of money…so soon… What about our savings?" she rasped.

Karena blandly informed her that it had been stolen. By whom, when, and where, Karena couldn't tell her. She suspected it had been taken by the Imperial inspectors, but even if she could prove it, who would care?

"We can't think about it now," Karena soothed, seeing Yeva's agitation. "There is nothing to be done about the injustice, Mother. We must leave it with God. I will find work. Believe me, it will grieve and upset Uncle Matvey if he learns that you were ill and that I didn't bring you to his apartment."

Someone must have fallen trying to step down from the boxcar because there came a woman's scream followed by shouting, and everyone began to push and shove.

Karena gasped for fresh air. She and her mother clung together in the rush to get out, then—a loud explosion.

238 LINDA LEE CHAIKIN

Alex was quickly out of the station and onto the steps. Below, on the concourse, a coach was smoking. Its doors had been blown off, and one of the horses was down. *Whose coach?*

Several policemen ran to the coach and reached inside. The situation could not have been worse. Alex's fears were confirmed: the target of the blast was Count Kalinsky, the official whom Gennady was responsible for escorting safely to the train.

Alex paused in the snow.

Several soldiers had joined the police. Alex thought of Gennady, who would be joining the elite guards back at the Winter Palace to assume the duty of guarding the count during his ride to the train. He would learn that the count had grown impatient and left early in his coach. Soon the news would follow about his assassination.

Gennady could be held accountable for dereliction of duty.

Passengers departing a train from Kiev added to the confusion. The revolutionaries who had thrown the dynamite were now lost in the throng.

Alex headed toward the coach, shouldering his way through the soldiers surrounding it.

What was that shattering blast? Karena waited until the boxcar was mostly empty, and then, with an arm around her mother, she led them slowly forward. Karena thought she had enough coins to hire a droshky.

"We shall soon have you in a warm bed, my matushka. With something hot to drink, you will be able to rest. Lean on me. We will walk slowly." Outside, there were banks of snow where workers had pushed it aside to keep the tracks clear. A haze hung low over all, like a drab mantle, but even so, it was appealing after two days of being crammed into the dark, foul boxcar. Karena climbed down and then reached back to help Yeva into the slush.

They were standing on the ground near the St. Petersburg station. This was not the arrival Karena had dreamed of. Dizzy and weak, she gritted her teeth as she guided her mother. A rush of cold wind and a sprinkle of snowflakes fell across her face. At least the flakes were fresh. They took a moment to breathe the clean air before walking. Ahead there was a slanted roof covering a raised wooden platform with benches, then the concourse and some steep steps leading into the station proper.

Something was wrong. Beside the normal rush of porters and attendants of the wealthier travelers, she saw several police guards on horseback and others on foot, all headed in one direction. Some soldiers clustered together with guns, pointing and shouting with stern faces.

Soldiers! Her heart began to pound. *Are they looking toward us?*

"Imperial guards," Karena whispered hoarsely to her mother. "They are searching for someone. Look, over there—in the concourse—there's a crowd. Something has happened—oh!—that coach, and a horse is down. Oh, how horrible! There is blood in the snow!" *The explosion!*

"Keep walking," Yeva said weakly. "They have no reason to suspect us."

The cold wind prodded them along. Karena's long, black skirt over leather boots rustled beneath the fur coat with its hood pulled down over her forehead to conceal her bruised face.

They could hear soldiers asking an older man questions. The man shouted as though deaf. "I was standing right over here when a young man runs into me and knocks me aside. Next, that coach comes around the corner, and when it pulls aside, he opens the door and tosses in fireworks. The explosion took me off my feet. There was a woman, too. Don't know where she went. They both ran. Who was blown up?"

An assassination. Karena wondered which official had been murdered.

She watched soldiers approach the damaged coach. One of them shot the injured horse in the head. The sight brought home the deadly consequences of a sin-tainted world. A newborn's first conscious response at birth was a wail, and innocent creatures suffered. It seemed an apt picture of the groaning creation still held in the grip of Satan's rebellion against God.

An armed Imperial officer ran toward the coach from the direction of the departing trains. He came nearer. Her breath caught in her throat.

It cannot be him. Not here, not now.

His hair was dark, and she remembered those grayish green eyes studying her when he had questioned her in Uncle Matvey's little office. It was Alex.

What if he learns about Leonovich? Could he already know? And now, this man murdered in the coach!

She watched as Alex turned his head, seeming to take in the area with a sweeping glance until his gaze connected firmly with hers. Her stomach flipped. Despite the danger, she experienced the same heated emotional assault she felt each time they met.

Colonel Kronstadt's alert gaze flashed to Madame Yeva, looked for someone else who might be with them, then swerved back to Karena again.

"It's Colonel Kronstadt," Karena hissed to her mother. "He's seen us."

Madame Yeva turned her head to look back.

"Come quickly, but don't run."

Karena tightened her hold on her mother's arm, moving her toward the milling crowd. Fear darted through her and must have brought strength to Madame Yeva, for her steps quickened.

Flee! Escape!

TWENTY-TWO

Lost in the Crowd

Surely it could not be *her*, but it was. Alex had recognized her when their eyes met. Her face seemed bruised. He frowned. What had happened? He intended to find out.

Shouldering his way through the crowd, Alex moved steadily in the direction of Miss Karena Peshkova and her mother, who were ahead in the throng. Was their presence a coincidence after the terrorist bombing of a czarist autocrat?

He could easily overtake them if he ran, but he held himself back. If he bolted after them now, the police would notice and blow their whistles. Anything could happen if the girl and her mother took off running and the police drew their weapons.

Alex made the cool decision to slow his steps. After all, he knew where to find her in St. Petersburg when he was ready. He was to make a call on Professor Menkin to ask further questions on Grinevich and return his manuscript. Alex was certain she and her mother were making their way to Professor Menkin's apartment now.

He continued following, but they were not in sight. He went to a raised platform farther ahead and peered into the throngs of people, many in the same kinds of fur coats and hats. Toward the square where droshkies waited, he saw two women boarding, the younger helping the older inside as though she were weak. He was certain it was the Peshkova women.

He hastened down the steps just as the droshky left the train station. He could have ordered the soldiers and police to stop its escape. As it rounded a corner, he saw a passenger turn and look back. It was Karena.

Alex stood, hands on hips, looking after her. In another minute they were out of sight.

It was reported that a woman was seen with the terrorist who hurled the dynamite that murdered Count Kalinsky.

Alex frowned as he stared after the droshky. *It could not have been Karena Peshkova.* So far, he had not reported the information he had on her to the Okhrana. If he reported seeing her at the Bolshevik meeting the night Grinevich was killed and that she had denied it, his own eyewitness account would bring her arrest. The czarist blade, however, was double edged, for if it was discovered that he had held back all he knew from his superior…

He walked back to the scene of the bombing. Why was he being lenient with her?

After spotting her here at the very moment of another attack on a czarist official, he rethought his silence. Was it possible she was a dedicated Bolshevik working with Lenski? After all, who was to say that a lovely charmer with blue eyes and fair, thick tresses could not feel hatred enough for the autocratic system of abuse to join radical terrorists like her brother's friend Lenski? The pogroms against Jews gave ample reason for such hatred. And Ilya—her fiancé, if indeed he was her future husband—had barely survived a pogrom in Warsaw that had taken his parents' lives. Karena knew all this. There were also, no doubt, tales from Grandmother Jilinsky's memories of persecution to influence her.

Alex was convinced her brother had been edging toward fanaticism against the czar and that it had only been his father's willingness to take his guilt in the Grinevich affair that returned Sergei to his senses and his university studies. Alex could see how Karena might have been influenced.

Also, Madame Yeva Peshkova had come from Finland from a revolutionary Jewish family. So why shouldn't her daughter, as well as her stepson, Sergei, nourish antigovernment ideas? Finland, a mere twenty miles from St. Petersburg, regularly sheltered men like Lenin. It was easy to slip across the border, engage in planning, and even secure bomb-making equipment. The border with Finland might be a wise place to look for Lenski, and he would need to look into how Sergei was doing at the university.

Even so, he could not see Karena Peshkova waylaying autocrats with dynamite in train stations. Before he cast the possibility aside as absurd, however, his sworn allegiance to the czar demanded that he find out.

He was still frowning when he walked back to the station.

He looked across the concourse. The destroyed black coach sat alone amid a scene of white, reminding him of the carcass of a dead crow. Beside it stood the newly arrived Major-General Durnov, his wide shoulders hunched forward beneath his oversized greatcoat. He appeared to be listening to an officer's report. Alex recognized the officer, his rival, Captain Yevgenyev.

So far, Durnov hadn't seen him. He preferred to keep it so, as he was off duty. He did not want to see the old bear yet and was just ready to turn away when Durnov lifted his head, surveyed the area like a sharp-eyed hawk, and saw him. *As luck would have it.* Alex gritted his teeth in frustration and walked to meet his superior.

"Good morning, Major-General Durnov," he said, coming up. They exchanged brisk salutes. "The revolutionaries are at work again, I see." Alex glanced across at the other soldiers out of earshot, and his gaze caught Captain Yevgenyev, whose square jaw set like a brick in mortar as he saluted.

Alex turned to Durnov, whose tufted brows and mustache were grayer than ever with stiff, white frost. His hard, wide face gave nothing away as he gestured a gloved hand at the burned-out coach now being hauled away.

"Most unfortunate, Colonel Kronstadt. Captain Yevgenyev says you were here. What do you make of it?"

Leave it to Yevgenyev to open his mouth and entangle him. "Yes, I heard the explosion, General. When I arrived, the police were already here with Captain Yevgenyev's squad and Count Kalinsky was dead."

"Yevgenyev reports there was a woman."

Alex kept an immobile face. "Can he identify her, sir?"

Durnov reached into his military jacket and pulled out a cigarette. He held it between his fingers while searching through his pockets for a match. Alex removed matches from inside his coat and struck one, protecting the flame from the snowy wind. Durnov leaned forward to accept the light for his cigarette. Alex studied his hard features.

"Captain Yevgenyev says you went after this woman," Durnov said.

Alex flipped the match into the snow. "Captain Yevgenyev is mistaken."

Alex dropped the matches back into his pocket. He looked over at Yevgenyev standing with Durnov's horsemen.

Durnov sucked on his cigarette. "You did not trail the woman?"

If Alex mentioned that he'd recognized Karena and her mother, Durnov would issue an order to locate, detain, and interrogate them with ruthless measures that were not used at Kiev. Karena's presence at the count's assassination would all but convict her in the minds of the Okhrana, especially if they laid the murder of the count at Lenski's feet. Durnov had gone easy on Sergei Peshkov only because he was a nephew to General Roskov's wife, Zofia, but Karena was not blood related.

Alex struggled with his emotions. He was a fool to risk his plans for a young woman he hardly knew. One slip would give Captain Yevgenyev ammunition to use against him. Even so, this was not a time for anyone with Jewish connections to be arrested and questioned by the ruthless secret police about terrorist assassinations; the czar had just recently agreed to strengthen existing laws against Russia's Jews.

There appeared no end to the anti-Semitism. In the past, Alex had thought little about it. Now, he found himself intrigued by the deep roots of its cause. Why so much hatred for the offspring of Abraham, Isaac, and Jacob?

Though Alex had expected and been mentally prepared for his superior's questioning, his next words took him by surprise.

"Captain Yevgenyev is jealous of you," Durnov said with a blunt voice. "There are too many officers with an eye for General Roskov's daughter. You are young. You do not realize the plots one man plans for another, even in the military."

Alex knew Durnov was wrong about the general's daughter, but he remained silent.

"I knew your father. We were friends, and that is why I warn you. If you do not watch your step, you will find yourself in much trouble. Not from me, you understand, but from others like Captain Yevgenyev. His father wants his son promoted and asks me often how his son is doing. Yevgenyev is under pressure to meet his father's expectations. Wanting to preserve my own standing, I will be inclined to please my superior where his son is concerned. Yevgenyev wants your position on my staff. He would like to see you sent to the front. So you see my problem."

Alex affected solemnity. If he could hand over his position in the Okhrana to rich and spoiled Karl Yevgenyev in exchange for his elite cavalry regiment, he would do so at the snap of a finger. But if he told that to Durnov, it would insult him. Alex was beginning to marvel at how much human pride complicated life.

"Thank you, Major-General Durnov. I will be on my guard," Alex said gravely, and added, "Before the explosion, my thoughts were on relaxing at a number of parties on my leave. When I heard the explosion and ran up, people were fleeing in every direction in confusion. I didn't see anyone—man or woman—whose actions inclined me to think they'd just thrown dynamite."

Durnov smoked his cigarette in silence, looking over to the place where the attack had occurred. The coach was gone now. They were removing the carcass of the dead horse. Fresh snow soon covered over the splotches of death, and the last remnants of the crowd dispersed, preoccupied with the war and lack of bread.

Alex was aware he'd just stepped over a line and put himself at risk to protect a young woman he should forget about.

"What are your thoughts about who is behind this, Colonel?" Durnov asked.

"A Bolshie."

"Not the Bund?" Durnov pressed, referring to an organization of Jewish revolutionaries considered extremists because they fought back for their rights to exist.

"Count Kalinsky was considered friendly toward the Jews. He didn't favor the new anti-Jewish laws. The Bund would have no cause to plan his death."

"Conspiracy works in strange ways."

"Exactly so, but they would need to be most strange, sir, if the Bund approved blowing up those who wish them no ill."

Durnov hunched his shoulders. After a silent moment he changed the subject. "Major Sokolov was ordered to see to the security of Count Kalinsky's departure by train, was he not?"

Now the storm cloud was coming.

"Exactly so, General."

"Captain Yevgenyev was also in that guard, and he insists Sokolov did not show this morning. If this is so, Colonel, it is a serious breach of duty."

Yevgenyev, again. He was a true "shadow man," the name given by the opposition to the czar's despised secret police.

"Major Sokolov was aware of his duty and was on his way to lead the guard to escort Count Kalinsky when I left the barracks," Alex said. "It appears to me that Count Kalinsky was impatient to depart and left the Winter Palace early. He chose on his own to not wait for the full guard to assemble."

Speaking his mind so bluntly and laying the responsibility on Count Kalinsky was risky. Even suggesting that Alex disagreed with his superior's judgment was dangerous, but he knew Gennady could be arrested for dereliction of duty and even put before a firing squad.

Durnov turned his head. His callous gray eyes studied Alex. This measuring was not new. Durnov had hinted he was suspicious of Alex's motives on more than one occasion. No harsh steps had been taken against him thus far. Alex believed it was because of Durnov's friendship with his father.

Durnov was silent, smoking his cigarette. After a final drag, he tossed it into the muddy slush. "I may agree with you, Colonel, but Major Sokolov will have to answer for this matter. The outcome will not be left to me. It will depend on the czar and his conclusions. I can do nothing but my duty in the matter."

Alex gave a short nod of his head as in a salute. "Just so, Major-General Durnov."

The train sounded its final whistle to board for Tsarskoe Selo. Alex turned and glanced back toward the station, then at Durnov. The general's hard mouth turned into a granite smile.

"You may go, Colonel Kronstadt. Enjoy your leave. If anything comes up of particular interest, I'll need to contact you there and ruin things."

He caught the slight emphasis in Durnov's words "of particular interest" and took this to infer there would be news.

Alex pretended he didn't notice, they exchanged casual salutes, then he turned and walked back to the boarding station to collect the bag he'd left with one of the young porters. He scowled, pondering.

The porter was craning his neck, looking in both directions. When he saw Alex, he rushed up with his bags.

"Your train for Tsarskoe Selo is departing, sir. This way, if you please, sir."

Alex boarded the train, thinking of the scene of needless bloodshed. *It's just the beginning. Russia stands on a precipice. Perhaps I am walking too close to the edge as well.*

TWENTY-THREE

Secrets

When Alex arrived at the mansion, he greeted his stepmother, Countess Olga Shashenka, with a perfunctory kiss on the hand and then on her pale cheek. Tall and thin, her smooth white hair was drawn away from her thin sculptured face into a chignon covered with a white netting of crocheted silk sprinkled with small pearls. She wore a smooth fringe of white hair cut across her forehead. There were diamonds at her ears, and a flower cluster made of pink pearls and diamonds set in gold was pinned at the shoulder of her draping, ivory satin dress with a long skirt.

"My dear Alex, how good to see you, and how dashing you are looking as a colonel."

She led him across the polished wood entryway toward the parlor. The ballroom to the right was busy with servants decorating for the ball to be held that night, and there was an anticipatory atmosphere and scurrying about with boxes of ribbon and tinsel.

He followed the countess into an opulent parlor decorated in plush ivory and magenta rugs and drapes. A massive divan along one wall and two chairs were done in satiny ivory brocade with rose and gold tassels.

An aromatic pinewood fire burned cleanly in the massive hearth while the snow twirled outside the windows. The draperies were drawn back, and the view was inspiring as always. He'd spent many long holidays here while growing to manhood. Large crystal lamps on polished wood tables sparkled like the jewels on the countess's wrist and throat.

The countess sat in a large upholstered chair of red with gold fringe. "I'm pleased you've been promoted. You grow more in appearance like your father each time I see you. No wonder you've got a name among the young women here. I shall need to fend them away, I see. Tatiana simply does not deserve you."

He lifted a brow. "A horse and saber and some excellent Cossacks to command would please me far better than prowling through police records at the Okhrana building. A very musty place." He placed an affectionate hand on her shoulder. "Come now, Mother, you know you could appeal to the czar, or even to your good friend Viktor, to deliver me from this fate worse than death!"

She placed her frail hand flashing elegantly with South African diamonds over his and patted with motherly concern. "Now, now…patience, Alex. Perhaps something can be done after all."

He leaned toward her. *"What?"* he enunciated wryly.

"Well, I do agree you're wasted in that bleak Okhrana. It's nothing like the intrigue and adventure you were involved in years ago. Durnov, for example. A near gangster, and hideously ill mannered…" She shook her head with regret. "You deserve better. I'm sure you've heard the rumors that Nicholas will personally lead the army at the front. What if I told you it was true? Would that interest you?"

He straightened, tilting his head.

Her eyes twinkled. "I thought so. It's possible a transfer to the czar's personal guard can be arranged soon. Viktor won't like it, of course. Neither will Tatiana—then again," and her voice was suggestive, "the poor girl is so taken up with her religious experience with the starets and his followers that she may be fully occupied."

He passed over the criticism of Tatiana, his thoughts upon the Grand Duke Nikolas Nikolaevich, commander in chief of the Russian forces.

"The grand duke is popular with the officers. Will Czar Nicholas actually remove him?" he asked.

"I have it on good authority that he's already made up his mind. The czarina and Rasputin had much to do with it."

Alex recalled General Viktor's words about Rasputin's placing under his pillow the names of individuals the czarina was considering for positions of authority, and then informing her the next day whether or not God approved.

"The starets is thickly involved in decisions affecting the Romanov family," the countess went on. "The czarina trusts him explicitly. As for Grand Duke Nikolas Nikolaevich, she worries he'll eclipse her husband's popularity with the officers. Czar Nicholas is jealous of his six-foot-six relative."

Konni brought in a silver tray with a small decanter of sherry, and Countess Olga handed Alex a cut-crystal glass.

He walked over to the bay window where the snow twirled tirelessly. He could see the wide boulevard that led to Alexander Palace, the abode of the Romanov family. The lights from other stately houses glittered in the snowy twilight.

"Alex, you're frowning. Is there something other than your promotion to the secret police that troubles you?"

"I was thinking of Gennady."

"Gennady?" she said, surprised.

"I didn't wish to ruin your evening, but you'll hear about it soon enough if General Viktor arrives." Alex told her of the assassination of Count Kalinsky and the trouble Gennady was in for failing to lead the guard that was to have escorted him. "He could face a firing squad," he concluded, staring moodily out the window.

"That's absolutely dreadful. Poor Gennady! I'll talk to Viktor. Something must be done. I'll go to the czarina if necessary."

He had thought she would feel strongly about this, as the twins were her blood kin. Although she showed frustration over Ivan's sudden drinking habit and perceived him to be failing to uphold the Sokolov name, she was very fond of both him and Gennady. In fact, she would have preferred General Viktor's daughter to marry Gennady rather than Alex. At the time, Alex had been irritated about it, for he'd thought Tatiana not merely beautiful, but intelligent. Matters had changed. The more leisure time he had to talk with her, the more disappointed he became over her inability to see beyond balls, dinner parties, beautiful clothes, and her like-minded friends. At the heart of their controversy was Rasputin. Tatiana grew more devoted to him with every passing day. At first this immature behavior had made him feel responsible for her, but his patience was wearing thin regarding her increasing devotion to the Siberian starets.

His disenchantment with Tatiana was not helping him keep Karena Peshkova off his mind. Had Karena and Madame Peshkova gone to Professor Menkin's apartment? He did not think they had much money. As he recalled the manor house at Kiev, it was pleasantly comfortable, but there'd not been evidence of wealth—just hard work and productivity in growing wheat. A rather pleasant existence, actually. He'd never thought much of balls and entertainments, though after the food at the military barracks, he could get enthused over three kinds of roasts and a dozen different cakes.

Alex tried the sherry. He frowned, afraid he was poor company for the countess, staring out the window and brooding as he was. He looked across the large room at her. She had placed a cigarette in a long gilded holder. Maybe she could help in his inquiries. Her years as a spy meant she understood the importance of information and made a point of collecting it. He walked to the table and picked up a matchbox.

"What do you know about Dr. Dmitri Zinnovy?" he asked. "I recall his visits to some of your dinner parties when I was growing up."

"Dmitri? He's a curious subject to bring up just now. As a matter of fact, he's been a friend for years, as has Katya."

He tried to read her response. "Odd, I don't recall Countess Katya ever keeping company with him at those dinner parties."

"No, she didn't. Poor dear. Unfortunately, she's been ill much of her life. She's completely bedridden now. Dmitri will be here at the ball tonight, by the way." She searched his eyes. "Why do you ask about him?"

He struck the match and held it to her cigarette. "He came to the rescue of Karena Peshkova the night Grinevich was killed by the Bolsheviks."

"Oh? Did he?"

"It seems an extreme risk for a doctor with such an elevated association with the czar. He has much to lose. And I can't see him doing it for a stranger, can you? "

He waited. She walked leisurely to one of the red wingback chairs near the fire and sat down. Alex toyed with the matchbox.

She looked into the pine embers for a long time before speaking.

"I'm not surprised he'd have concern for Karena Peshkova. Actually, I've thought he would have shown more through the years."

"Then, she is his daughter," he said unexpectedly.

She did not show surprise. "Yes. Dmitri was in love with Yeva when she was a medical student. He'd been under a false impression that Katya was on the verge of death. It was his colleague who diagnosed her with cancer. Fortunately for the countess, the diagnosis was false, and it ended Dmitri's plans. He refused to leave his wife to marry Yeva and asked her to be his mistress, but she refused. Then he found out through Yeva's close friend and roommate, Fayina Lenski, that she was to have his child. When they could not come to an agreement about the child, Yeva ran away to the poorer district of St. Petersburg. But he found her again through Fayina."

Countess Olga paused in her memory. Alex remained silent.

"He arranged her marriage to Josef Peshkov through friendly associates who knew Josef's wife had died and that he was left with a two-year-old boy, Sergei. As far as I know, Dmitri and Madame Peshkova have never spoken again, and Yeva's marriage with Josef was a normal one, and evidently a happy one until this affair over the Bolshevik meeting caused his arrest."

She looked up at him, her face reflecting gravity.

"Your explanation supplements my findings. I'd no choice but to delve into Madame Peshkova's life at the medical school. Dr. Zinnovy's record at the Okhrana made mention of a Miss Menkin, a second-year medical student at the time. You've put the flesh on the scant details for me."

"Alex, there's no need to bring any of this into the open, is there? It's been such a long time. Katya is seriously ill. This time the diagnosis is undeniable. She has a weak heart. She doesn't know a thing about Dmitri and Yeva."

Alex had no intention of exposing Dr. Zinnovy and disturbing his family. He was resolved, however, to speak with Dr. Zinnovy about Karena and her future.

"At least Madame Peshkova has Karena. A beautiful girl, I'm told, and quite intelligent," the countess said.

"She is, indeed."

She looked at him searchingly. "You've met Karena then? Oh, but of course you have, last summer with the Roskovs."

There was a pause. "Were you impressed with Karena Peshkova?" she asked.

Alex met her gaze. His mouth tipped ruefully.

"Ah," she said softly. "I see."

The silence settled into the room as softly as the snow fell outside the window. Alex sipped his sherry.

Countess Olga sighed. "Perhaps, then, it's even more important that you transfer to Nicholas's guard unit, far from St. Petersburg."

His gaze swerved to hers. He hardened his jaw. He started to speak, but her delicate, silvery brow shot up.

"Not because of Karena, dear—because of Viktor and Zofia. Viktor will be displeased, to say the least, if you don't marry Tatiana. I might as well get straight to the point. Tatiana is one of the reasons I wished to speak with you tonight before the guests arrive."

What was coming now? Rasputin and Tatiana! Was this why his step-mother had asked him here?

Alex walked to the window as the snow whirled and danced.

"If this has anything to do with her deception, Mother, I'd rather not discuss Rasputin."

"It hasn't a thing to do with that scoundrel. However, Viktor sent word a short time ago that he's coming over early before the ball to speak with you about him. Now, don't look at me like that, dear. I'd nothing whatsoever to do with his coming to see you. I do know he's exceedingly troubled over Rasputin and Tatiana, as he should be. Very understandable, don't you think? Even so, I shall let Viktor discuss all that with you."

He finished his sherry and deliberately remained mute. She came up and stood beside him at the window. "It's about the duel, Alex."

He set the glass down with a decisive snap. "I was hoping you hadn't heard."

"In St. Petersburg?" she scoffed. "In fact, I received a letter about Captain Yevgenyev while I was in the Crimea. It's the reason I returned early."

He regarded her curiously. "Who would write you about it?"

"Zofia."

Madame Zofia. She was no doubt worried over Tatiana's reputation.

"She's naturally concerned for your safety, but she's also worried over how the scandal will affect Tatiana. Alex, don't look so cynical. Of course, a woman like Zofia will be worried about such things. In fact, she can't sleep nights and is seeking sleeping medicines from Dmitri."

"I didn't know I was so loved."

"Don't be sarcastic, dear. Of course she cares about you, but a duel will be talked about for years. Anyway, I've been most upset about you. A duel over Tatiana! How could it have come to this?"

"Didn't Madame Zofia explain?"

"She gave me her rendition, naturally."

"Captain Yevgenyev is besotted with Tatiana. He was drunk and acted stupidly. He forced the insult until I accepted. There's little a man can do about it when his honor is trampled on before witnesses. It was set for August but delayed by his father on account of his own illness. Yevgenyev and I will eventually face one another. I'm sorry you heard about it."

"Something must be done. I blame Tatiana for this. She behaves quite foolishly when it comes to flirting with the officers. He should not have been invited to your holiday in Kazan. I can't understand Zofia's mind-set in allowing her daughter to act so unwisely."

"Tatiana does as she wishes. Madame Zofia hasn't the will to confront her daughter."

"So I feared," she said. "It's shameful."

"I'm not expecting more from her than I bargained for, Mother. Yes, bargained. It sounds as tawdry as it is." He tried to keep the scorn from his voice, but it seeped through. "We all know why this marriage was arranged. And Tatiana and I both agreed for purposes of our own. It's rather hypocritical of me now to expect sacrificial behavior on her part when love isn't motivating either of us."

A polite clearing of Konni's throat interrupted. His stepmother, now looking pale and tense, turned toward the door. "Yes, Konni?"

"General Viktor Roskov, Countess."

"Very well, send him in."

Countess Olga turned to Alex. He reached over and kissed her forehead. "Stop worrying," he said gently.

"You ask the impossible. I won't simply accept the inevitable, dear. You're the only son I have, and I'm not likely to shrug off a duel that must leave one of you seriously injured or dead." She walked to meet General Viktor, her hand held out to him, the diamonds flashing.

Alex was now in a riled mood. If he didn't expect more from his relationship with Tatiana than he'd just claimed, then he'd no right to be disappointed with her over Rasputin and Yevgenyev. Yet, despite the words he'd just spoken to the contrary, he was angry, perhaps even more so with himself.

Images of Karena flashed before him. Her desire to enter medical school showed valor. She had a noble purpose to pursue. He'd admired her at the manor when, despite the possibility of arrest, she'd been able to set aside her personal fears and rush off to deliver a peasant girl's baby.

He'd also been impressed with her desire to be involved with Professor Menkin's book that claimed Jesus was the Messiah. He pictured her at that small desk with open Bible and commentaries, painstakingly taking notes for her uncle. All of this had helped to define her in his mind, while Tatiana seemed a small-minded woman; beautiful, yes, but empty and lacking discernment. Tatiana earned his sympathy; Karena stirred him. *How can I speak of a duel to the death for soldierly honor and yet go through with this marriage?*

Inside the drawing room, Alex stood by the fireplace while General Roskov breathed out his exasperation. An Okhrana dossier on Rasputin sat on a table, and the general strode from the divan to the window and back again, hands interlocked behind his back.

The countess had left them alone to talk privately, and the general was speaking bluntly.

"I'm worried sick over Tatiana. I tell you, Alex, something must be done about Rasputin."

"I'll try to talk to her, sir. Where is she?"

"She's still at the residence with her Peshkov cousins. She expects you to come for her in the coach to attend the ball tonight."

Alex's interest sparked. "Her cousins, sir?"

"Yes, Natalia and Sergei. You've met Sergei under dire circumstances at Kiev." He frowned unhappily. "Poor Josef. I'm doing all I can to influence the czar to release him." He smacked a fist into his other palm. "I know he's not a revolutionary. Lenski's behind this entire debacle. If I could get my hands on that rebel, I'd hang him myself."

For a moment, when the general had mentioned Tatiana's cousins, Alex's thoughts rushed to include Karena. Did the general know Karena was Dr. Zinnovy's daughter? Evidently not. Nor had he mentioned Madame Peshkova's having arrived at the Roskov residence. He probably didn't know they were in Petrograd. Then he'd been right: they must have gone straight to Professor Menkin's.

"Then Madame Yeva Peshkova remains in Kiev, I suppose—she and her eldest daughter."

"Yes, they're due in a few weeks. It's terribly hard for Yeva to leave her home and land like this." Roskov gave a shake of his reddish gray head, tweaking his mustache. "That's another ugly problem in the family. I've appealed to the czar. So has the countess."

Alex was the one who'd first appealed to his mother to intervene on the confiscation of the wheat lands. There was no answer as yet, but the czar moved painfully slow. Autocracy was a clumsy bear. Alex heard from the

Okhrana that Rasputin was receiving an audience of petitioners in the parlor of his apartment, agreeing to bring certain appeals to the czar and czarina. In exchange for his efforts, the starets accepted cases of famous wines from certain wealthy petitioners. *By now his cellar should be well stocked.*

"Back to business," the general said, handing Alex the dossier.

The Okhrana, the general told him, was now spying on Rasputin at the request of the minister of the interior and the leader of the Duma. A large dossier on Rasputin's sins would be placed on the czar's desk soon, with the plea to send him back to Siberia.

"Perhaps you alone can convince Tatiana that Rasputin's powers are a sham," the general was saying. He pointed to the folder in Alex's hands. "Read this, and then talk some sense into your fiancée."

Alex clamped his jaw. *"Your fiancée."* He'd not yet given Tatiana an engagement ring, but the general was squeezing him into a box he couldn't get out of without serious consequences.

"Show Tatiana what we've learned about Rasputin," the general concluded, "then attend the meeting with her tonight. It will be held at Vyrubova's place. She intends to leave the ball early. Your report, added to the dossier, will slam the lid on Rasputin's coffin."

Alex had his doubts that anything would cause the czar to send Rasputin away. Every criticism heightened the czarina's hysteria. She believed the safety of her family and Russia depended on him.

"General, I've spoken to Tatiana before on the subject, and she becomes incensed. I'll do my best, sir. Maybe the proof in the dossier will at least plant some doubt. Once she begins to question him, logic should prevail. I've heard dreadful rumors about the czar and czarina attending Rasputin's séances, as well as meetings here at Tsarskoe Selo—meetings that border on fanaticism and immorality. Unfortunately, immorality plays a part in Rasputin's teaching. According to him, one must sin in the flesh to be free of its hold over the soul."

"Then the czar must be given proof of these matters, Alex. He must come to see that this scoundrel will bring us to ruin."

Alex restrained the hot words that stirred in his chest. General Viktor ceased his restless marching and came over to Alex, slapping a firm hand on his shoulder. His eyes reflected a fatherly affection.

"I could have confidence in no one more than you, Alex."

TWENTY-FOUR

Lifting the Mask

A lex left the countess's mansion with the Okhrana dossier under his arm and climbed inside the family coach.

Within a few minutes, the Roskov residence came into his view. Alex had visited here many times in the last year and a half. He entered through the wide doors and, as usual, asked for Miss Roskova.

"Miss Roskova is with her cousin, Mr. Peshkov, in the drawing room. Miss Peshkova is also expecting you, Colonel Kronstadt."

So, Sergei was showing himself within the Roskov social circle. It was bold of him. The Okhrana's "shadow people," as they were dubbed by those being spied upon, were watching him. He'd managed to slip away from the family manor in Kiev before Durnov could interrogate him, but he wouldn't escape again if they wanted him. Alex was tempted to let the major-general know he'd heard Sergei's inflamed rhetoric against the Imperial government, but to do so would be to expose Karena and Dr. Zinnovy as well. Alex had nothing against Sergei personally, nor was there anything to gain by harassing him now. Josef Peshkov had made his decision and was sticking to his confession. Alex imagined Sergei carried a crushing load of guilt—his father was even now at the Peter and Paul prison in Petrograd.

Alex dismissed the servant, saying he would announce himself, and made his way toward the drawing room.

The expansive rooms displayed a cohesive selection of Byzantine-style carpets and other furnishings of the old Eastern Empire. Wooden furniture and exposed beams were hand carved, oiled, and polished. Rich paintings, including one of the Romanov family, were prominently hung.

The drawing room doors stood open, and he heard challenging voices. Were the two cousins badgering each other?

Alex paused outside the wide doorway. Sergei stood, hands on hips, laughing at Tatiana. Alex could see at once that Sergei's humor held biting sarcasm.

"Rasputin?" Sergei said. "So he is our hope, is he? Heaven help the world of fools."

"How dare you laugh!" came Tatiana's clipped words.

"Why do I laugh?" Sergei took a turn around the room as if pondering. "All right, since you wonder, I'll tell you. To be honest, though, I doubt if you or your silly women friends can swallow the truth without choking. I laugh because women of the nobility who have everything but wisdom will turn to this peasant and sup with him. I laugh because when he tells you to lick sticky jam from his grubby fingers as an act of humility, you are stupid enough to do it. I laugh because you actually think this fool is from God—as if God would have someone half-drunk on vodka most the time. Oh, don't turn purple about it. Yes indeed, you will kiss his dirty hands, call him *Teacher* and *Shepherd*, and say he's good and wise and—worst of all—*holy*."

She gasped, stunned by his words. Sergei grinned. "Rasputin is an absurdity that women with an ounce of discernment could see through in a flash. But women such as you—educated, rich, and otherwise intelligent—have no discernment at all. They blindly and devotedly follow a fool, and that even includes the czarina! Dirty Rasputin cannot even help himself. He's drunk several times a week. Yet the women of nobility flock about him with their little elite band of disciples, claiming to be 'seekers of light.' 'Oh, Razzy! I adore you!' he mocked in a high-pitched voice. 'Razzy, Razzy, kiss me, my wise peasant teacher.'"

Tatiana's dark eyes flashed like a summer squall. Her palm connected with his cheek.

"You arrogant coward," she breathed, stepping toward him as he stepped back, still grinning wickedly, though his cheek was blushed.

"Kiss me, Razzy, kiss me," he goaded.

"Do you think I don't know how you allowed your father to be arrested and sent to the mines to protect your own skin?" Tatiana sneered.

Sergei's smile vanished. "You don't know what you're talking about."

"It is you and your vulgar Bolshevik friends who have no discernment. Count Kalinsky was assassinated this morning. It wouldn't surprise me if your best friend, Lenski, was involved. Oh, don't look surprised, as if you didn't know. Your little sweetheart Ivanna might have been with him hurling dynamite."

"Leave Ivanna out of this," came his warning voice.

Tatiana smiled now. "Ah yes, I do know. My father's in the Okhrana, my dear cousin, and I know oh so much."

"Snooping where you've no right, eh? It suits you perfectly. And what do you think you have discovered?"

"About Ivanna Lenski? Nothing, but about Karena? Oh, you'd be surprised. Tell me, little Bolshevik cousin, how old were you when your *sister* was born, eh?"

He frowned. "What's come over you? What are you talking about?"

"That pendant Yeva has, the one with all those treasured jewels, do you know where she got it?"

"Pendant?"

"The one from Dr. Zinnovy! And I'm going to get possession of it somehow and prove it. Countess Katya will know if it belongs to her set with one glance."

"You've gone mad. I don't know what you're yowling about. All it takes is the light shined on your Razzy, and you and the other females go nutty. The czarina is nutty too, if you ask me."

She stepped closer to Sergei and waved her jeweled finger under his nose. She pursued him across the room. "I know about the silly peasant girl, too, who died giving birth to your illegitimate daughter."

Bitter gall showed on Sergei's face now. His grin was gone, and there was nothing but hatred in his brown eyes. He flipped his dark hair back from his forehead.

"You reactionaries!" he scorned. "If Russia is destroyed, it won't be by revolutionaries like Lenski. It will happen because of people like you. You love your lies. The czar and czarina kiss the hands of a drunken peasant and call him their 'eyes and their ears.' While you, Tatiana, you and your rich and noble and stupid little friends fall at his dirty feet and believe he has the answers!" He gave his mirthless laugh again. "And you think Russia can remain strong? Lenin is right. The fruit on the tree is rotten! All we need to do is wait and shake it hard. Our culture will come tumbling down to be trampled underfoot!"

Sergei turned on his heels and stalked from the sitting room. He stopped short upon meeting Alex leaning in the doorway, dossier in hand.

Sergei gave him a measuring look as if he wondered whether he was going to have a fight on his hands. He narrowed his gaze. "Who are you?" he demanded.

Alex dipped his head in a small bow, a smirk on his lips. "Colonel Aleksandr Kronstadt, Okhrana."

Sergei paled, then rallied. "Now look here, Kronstadt. I don't want to take you on, but I will if you want it."

"The last time I wore my white dress uniform, I had wine thrown in my face," Alex said, bored. "Let's wait until I have dirty battle fatigues on, shall we?"

Sergei frowned and glared.

Alex arched a brow. "Or I could just arrest you this moment. You ran off from the Peshkov manor before Major-General Durnov could interrogate you about Grinevich. We're still looking for one of those who landed a few kicks to his ribs. Would you know anything about that sort of violence?"

Sergei licked his lips. "No, it wasn't me. I swear it wasn't."

Alex straightened, putting his height to his advantage. "You behaved like a fool tonight, mocking Tatiana the way you did. I might agree with most of what you said about Rasputin, but your goading was immature."

"I don't need your lectures where my cousin's concerned."

"You've a lot to learn, Sergei. I'm afraid your growing pains will be agonizing."

"Am I free to go or not?"

"You can go. But we'll be seeing a lot of each other, like it or not."

Sergei squinted at him. "What do you mean by that?"

"Where is Karena?"

He scanned Alex curiously. "In Kiev, with our mother. They're due here in a few weeks, though my mother wrote Natalia that they'd be staying with Uncle Matvey. Why do you ask about her?"

Tatiana stormed up. "Because Alex is falling for her, that's why."

Alex looked at her evenly. "You're terribly upset, Tatiana. Better sit down and calm yourself. We need to have a talk."

Sergei watched him with sudden interest, then flashed a smile and looked toward Tatiana. "So Karena's won him away, has she? Doesn't surprise me. She's twice the lady you are." He turned and marched out.

A terrible silence pervaded. Tatiana held her hands in fists at her sides.

"A Bolshevik. I knew it all along. You should arrest him and let poor Uncle Josef go."

"Please sit down, Tatiana. We need to discuss matters in a sane and sensible way. I don't want a yelling match like two children fighting."

She turned and flounced over to the divan and sank into it, folding her arms and glaring at him, eyes smoldering.

Alex closed the drawing-room doors and turned to face her. She bounced back up, stormed over to a cupboard, and drew out a bottle of burgundy. She was reaching for a glass when he walked up, caught her wrist, plucked the bottle from her hand, and put it back.

"I don't like women who need alcohol to face their mistakes."

She showed surprise and stared at him. She appeared to calm down, and after a moment of silence, she brushed past him to stand with her back toward him, folding her arms again.

"Well?" she challenged. "You heard everything I said about Karena and Dr. Zinnovy. Go ahead and rebuke me."

He walked over to her, took her arm, and turned her to face him. "You promised me in Kazan you'd leave this alone. Why are you stirring it up again?"

"You're infatuated with her. Admit it."

He searched her face. Anger flashed in her eyes, and he could see the pulse beating in her throat. "You're right. I am infatuated."

"You admit it!" she fumed.

"Yes. I'm sorry if this hurts you, but I'm not sorry my path has crossed with Karena's."

She sucked her breath in. Like an adder, her palm was ready to attack the second time that evening. He expected it and caught her hand, holding it.

"You're not ready for marriage, Tatiana. Like Sergei, you need mellowing. You're a firebrand ready to burn yourself out. You need time—and some hard lessons."

"And you're the expert. You have all the answers, all the mature responses."

"No, I've learned a hard lesson just recently. I'm thankful I recognized it before I allowed a mistake to happen that would ruin our lives. Marriage is a commitment established on love and values, not on career and inheritance. We're not meant for each other, Tatiana. It would end in tragedy sooner or later. We're not in love with each other, and you know it as well as I."

Her face reflected unexpected shock. "Oh, Alex, I do love you. You don't know what you're saying. You can't mean that you want to end our relationship."

"I don't think we've ever had a relationship. We've had a selfish agreement, and it's time to admit it. We're not engaged officially, so stop pretending we are."

"Wait till Father hears this," she warned. "You'll be ruined in the military. Is that what you want?"

He ignored the threat. "Your father sent me here to talk to you about Rasputin. Do you see this dossier? It contains accurate information on his habits and character. It will be turned over to Czar Nicholas by members of the Duma. You'd be wise to sit for twenty minutes while we go over this."

"I'll do no such thing. Snooping into someone's private life—"

"You don't appear troubled over snooping into Dr. Zinnovy's and Madame Peshkova's lives. You have no qualms about bringing misery to them or to Countess Zinnovy."

She walked away again, her back toward him. "I want to buy the pendant from Yeva. What's so dreadful about that?"

"Don't pretend. I heard what you told Sergei. You want to hurt Karena. You're jealous of her."

"She's come between us. Why shouldn't I resent her? She's ruined everything."

"She's ruined nothing. She's helped to reveal the truth about us. Will you read this Okhrana report, or won't you?"

"No. And Czarina Alexandra won't read those lies either. All of you are against him—merely because he's an uneducated peasant—and yet he shows all of you to be smaller than he. He has power to do good, and you wish to destroy him because of it."

"Then I'll read a few of the reports for you." He tossed the folder open. "Here is a copy of a letter from the czarina to Rasputin—"

"I won't listen!"

"Don't be so hypocritical. You're willing to shame others, including a great doctor. If this dossier were on Karena, you'd pay a high price to get your hands on it! Sit down!"

She did so.

He read from the Okhrana agent's report: " 'I followed Rasputin. Tonight Rasputin brought a prostitute to his flat; later in the day she was set free by the servant.'

"Twenty-sixth of May, 'Rasputin and a prostitute came home in Manus's (a financier) car in an inebriated condition. While saying good-bye, he kissed and fondled her passionately. Later he sent for the porter's wife to fetch the dressmaker Katia, but she was not at home.'

"Second of June. 'At one o'clock in the morning, Rasputin came home drunk in the company of Manus. Without going to his flat, he sent the porter's wife for the masseuse Outina, who lives in the same house, but she could not be found. Then he went to flat number 3 to see the dress-maker Katia. Here, he was apparently not allowed to enter, as he came back directly, and on the stairs he assaulted the porter's wife, asking for kisses. The woman managed to disengage herself and ring up his flat, whereupon Dounia, Rasputin's maid, led him away.'

"Twentieth of July. 'Rasputin paid another visit to Arapov. He left his host's house in a drunken condition and immediately repaired to the palm reader's wife. On his return home at five-forty in the afternoon, he once more set out in spite of Dounia's endeavors to prevent him. He rudely pushed her aside, telling her to "go to the devil," and, drunk as he was, splashed through the mud without picking his way. Later, he came out of his house and began questioning the agents about yesterday's happenings, sighing and wondering at having got so drunk, since, according to his own words, he had only three bottles of vodka.'"

He turned a page. "And this is a letter from the czarina to Rasputin when he'd been away from Petrograd. 'My beloved, unforgettable teacher, redeemer, and mentor! How tiresome it is without you! My soul is quiet and I relax only when you, my teacher, are sitting beside me. I kiss your hands and lean my head on your blessed shoulders. Oh, how light, how light do I feel then! I only wish one thing: to fall asleep, forever, on your shoulders and in your arms. What happiness to feel your presence near me. Where are you? Where have you gone? Oh, I am so sad, and my heart is longing. Will you soon be again close to me? Come quickly, I am waiting for you and I am tormenting myself for you. I am asking for your holy blessing, and I am kissing your blessed hands. I love you forever. Yours, M.'"

Alex looked at Tatiana and saw her shocked and sickened expression. "Shall I read more?" he asked quietly.

Tatiana stood and swept past him to the door. She looked back, her face white and strained, her dark eyes bright and feverish with emotion. "I hate you for what you've done, Alex."

"I'm sorry you do. A doctor who diagnoses a disease takes no pleasure in seeing his patient's grief upon learning the facts. But to ignore the disease will bring death. That letter from the czarina, with a few changes, might have been a prayer to the only one worthy of such devotion."

"I don't believe a word of that lying report. The Okhrana is persecuting Rasputin."

"Your father has ordered me to go with you tonight to Rasputin's meeting at Anna Vyrubova's place."

"You jest! Do you think I'd bring you there, knowing you're a spy? And you needn't worry about your commitment to me. Our engagement is broken. After tonight, I don't care to ever see you again."

He bowed in deference to her request.

"As far as Karena and Dr. Zinnovy are concerned," she continued, "I intend to learn the truth. If she's not related to me by blood, I want to know it."

She turned abruptly, opened the door, and walked out.

Alex flipped the dossier closed and walked toward the door. His emotions were mixed. He'd just unearthed another man's sins, and he didn't feel particularly pleased with himself for having dragged Rasputin into the bright light. Alex was fully aware that he, too, fell far short of God's perfect standards. His one consolation was the fact that Rasputin was standing in a position of holy authority, allowing the czarina and others to put their trust in him as someone righteous, someone who could carry them on his strong, wise shoulders in their weakness. Alex had learned from Michael's correspondence that there was but one holy Redeemer to whom every knee would bow.

In unmasking Rasputin to Tatiana, he'd turned on the light. She hated him for it.

What now troubled him more than her devotion to Rasputin was Tatiana's determination to learn the story about Dr. Zinnovy and Madame Yeva. She'd already promised him once that she would walk away from the matter of Zinnovy and the pendant. But even before he'd angered her about Rasputin and disappointed her about his growing feelings for Karena, she had baited Sergei with the secret knowledge she had vowed to forget. How could he trust her again?

Countess Olga Shashenka's mansion presented the sight of smartly uniformed Imperial officers and richly gowned women in a fairy-tale scene during the lightly snowing night.

Alex was late in attending the ball. He'd spent the last hour with Gennady, Ivan, and General Roskov, discussing the assassination of Count Kalinsky. Alex had also to inform him of the sober news of his daughter's bitter resentment.

"I read a few pages of the dossier to Tatiana, sir. I did my best to convince her of the hypocrisy of Rasputin's immorality and the danger his influence over the czarina presents to Russia. Her response was decidedly negative, and at the close of our discussion she informed me that she would not allow me to accompany her to Rasputin's meeting tonight."

The general frowned his discouragement and insisted he would smooth matters over.

"I think it best, sir, that I reconsider my relationship with your daughter."

The general looked too stunned to speak. Fortunately for Alex, Tatiana walked in with Madame Zofia and, ignoring Alex, called the general away to his guests.

Alex wondered again about Karena and her mother. He then noticed Dr. Dmitri Zinnovy, who'd just come from the library with the countess. Alex looked for Tatiana and saw her waltzing with Captain Karl Yevgenyev. He watched her float away in shimmering satin and pearls. For once, Alex felt relief at the sight. He turned away, walking the circumference of the ballroom until he came up beside Zinnovy.

"Good evening, Dr. Zinnovy."

"Colonel Kronstadt."

Alex recognized the wariness in his gaze. Zinnovy was probably wondering if he was about to question him on Karena's alibi.

"Doctor, I'd like to speak with you alone for a few minutes, if I may. It's rather urgent."

The wariness became veiled. He straightened his shoulders and gave a brief, polite nod of his head.

"Why, certainly. Will the library be sufficient?"

"Yes sir. Thank you.

"After you, sir," Alex said at the door. He reached over, opening it for him. Dr. Zinnovy entered, and Alex followed.

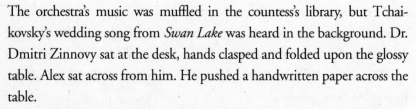

The orchestra's music was muffled in the countess's library, but Tchaikovsky's wedding song from *Swan Lake* was heard in the background. Dr. Dmitri Zinnovy sat at the desk, hands clasped and folded upon the glossy table. Alex sat across from him. He pushed a handwritten paper across the table.

"I copied this directly from a paper on file with the Okhrana. It details your visits to Yeva Menkin in years past."

Dr. Zinnovy read it and sighed.

"I have brought this to your attention, sir, to save time and argument. No man in public position who has money or power escapes being noticed by agents of the czar's secret police. You married Countess Katya Rezanova, and it is known that her father leaned toward government reforms. That is why they watched her—and you as well."

"Why do you bring this up now? If this has anything to do with the Bolshevik meeting back in August, I did happen to be in Kiev then, as my medical practice would have it, but it is known that I am strongly opposed to the Bolsheviks—not to mention their vile tactics. It was unfortunate I was in Kiev at the time."

"That depends on how you see it. You saved your daughter from arrest, and that was very fortunate."

Zinnovy met his gaze sharply.

"Karena is your daughter, sir. Is she not?"

"Karena should not be brought into this Bolshevik problem—"

"Dr. Zinnovy, I'd better declare myself. I've a personal claim in this. I'm falling in love with Karena Peshkova. I'm trying to protect her, and Madame Yeva. It's presently a serious concern. As soon as I can get transferred from the Okhrana to my old regiment, or to the czar's guard, I'll be done with dusty files of secrets. I've no interest in digging through dirty closets. We all have them. Some are not as dark and ugly as others, but we all have our trespasses against God and man. I believe, sir, this is a foundational truth of Christianity, that all have sinned."

Dr. Zinnovy removed his spectacles and placed a hand across his eyes.

"Let me go straight to the reason I've come to you, Doctor. There's a pendant that belongs to Madame Yeva—of great value. It has recently been recognized by someone as part of a set belonging to Countess Rezanova. If it's brought to the attention of your wife—well, you do see what I'm suggesting?"

He looked at him with a flash of realization. "The pendant!"

"Yes. I've a plan, sir. If you could buy back the pendant from a third party and return it secretly to the countess's set, would you cooperate? It would remove the pendant from exposure, and the possibility of embarrassing questions."

"I swear I'd forgotten all about it. Yes, of course. I would certainly cooperate to buy it back—discreetly, that is."

"I was hoping you would say that. I believe Madame Yeva is in difficult financial straits. You know about her husband's being sent to the Peter and Paul fortress. He's likely to get a harsh sentence when the case of Policeman Grinevich goes to trial. Without her husband, Madame Yeva lacks enough support to live and care for her two daughters until they marry. I'm sure she'd sell the pendant for a reasonable price. She's not the kind of woman who would extort, as you know. A reasonable price is all we would ask."

Dr. Zinnovy studied him for a long moment. "You're seriously interested in Karena?"

"Yes."

"I won't ask how this will affect your relationship with the Roskovs or your military career. But I'm sure it won't aid you in the least."

"I've already thought that through. I've made my decision. Even if Karena will have nothing to do with me, I'll not marry Miss Roskova."

He nodded. "A wise decision. Yes, of course, I'll buy the pendant at more than a fair price."

Alex snatched up the incriminating paper and laid it on the fiery coals in the fireplace. He turned to Dr. Zinnovy.

Dmitri stood and came around the table. "Thank you, Colonel Kronstadt."

Alex gave a small bow of his head. "Where shall I meet you?"

"At the medical college. I'm there each day from noon until seven."

"I'll contact you with the pendant as soon as I can arrange to meet with Madame Peshkova."

Alex bowed again, walked to the door, and departed.

Alex was standing in the archway that opened into the ballroom when Konni came up to him.

"Colonel Kronstadt, sir, Majors Sokolov are both looking for you. They are in the drawing room."

Gennady and Ivan were talking with Natalia Peshkova when Alex came in. Natalia saw him and quickly excused herself. Ivan turned his head with apparent interest to watch her leave the parlor.

"I like that young lady," Ivan commented.

"Very profound words," Gennady said gravely.

"Well, I do like her."

"You like them all."

"This one is different."

Alex cocked a brow at Ivan. "I happen to know that Natalia *is* different. So watch your behavior, my son," he stated with mock gravity.

"Just so, Papa."

"She's also happily engaged to a conscript named Boris, a veterinarian who is presently facing the Huns in Poland," Alex continued. "So if you like her, play the officer and gentleman, or she'll avoid you—permanently."

"She is also half-Jewish," Gennady said with a sober gaze. "You know what that will cost you if you should fall for her."

Alex stepped behind a masquerade of indifference.

After a moment of silence, Ivan looked at his glass and scowled. "It's empty."

"Good," Alex said.

Gennady rubbed the scowl between his brows, his dejection over the Count Kalinsky assassination showing. "Look, we've important things to discuss. What did Durnov say about me?"

Alex told him. Ivan devoutly assured his twin that he would take his place before the firing squad. "How will they tell us apart, I ask you?"

"Firing squad!" Gennady sank into a brocade chair and held his head between his hands. "All these things are against me."

There were no reassuring words that had not already been spoken, and the room lapsed into silence.

Alex walked to the window. Glowing lamps strung along the front pine trees emphasized the bleak silhouettes clawing in the breeze against the gray sky. His thoughts turned toward the pendant. He only assumed he could influence Karena's mother into selling the jewels back to Dr.

Zinnovy. He decided there was no time to lose on the matter—he'd leave for Petrograd first thing in the morning.

Then he heard a commotion in the entranceway.

"Sounds like trouble," Ivan said. "I'd know that gravelly voice in my nightmares."

Gennady turned quickly and stood.

Alex too looked toward the doorway where Konni appeared perturbed over Major-General Durnov's entering the house without waiting to be escorted and presented.

Durnov stood, his bulk behind the greatcoat blocking the way, reminding Alex of a sullen bear.

Alex suspected there was something more than Gennady's chance involvement in the Kalinsky assassination that morning to have brought Durnov here now.

Durnov then spotted Alex.

Alex heard a groan of despair from Gennady. "Here comes Major-General Death."

TWENTY-FIVE

A Reconciliation

A lex followed Major-General Durnov into a meeting behind closed doors with the hastily summoned General Roskov. As Alex drew the door closed, he caught sight of Gennady and Ivan near the refreshment table, appearing greatly relieved that Durnov hadn't detained Gennady for more questioning on the matter of Count Kalinsky.

Alex stood near a window with blue drapes, looking across the snow-clad park in the direction of the Romanov palace, where the lights were all aglow.

"What's this about?" General Roskov asked, scowling. Alex knew he didn't approve of interruptions during social events.

Durnov produced a scarred leather satchel from which he withdrew a police file he'd brought from St. Petersburg. The general snatched it and went behind the desk. Alex turned up the lamplight, keeping an immobile face, though his unease was growing.

"Well, sir, the Kiev gendarmes sent us this file on Policeman Grinevich's death," Durnov said.

"Grinevich?" Roskov raised his reddish gray head with a mutinous scowl. "That debacle took place in August!"

A twitch of Durnov's wide mouth unmasked his personal offense. "Debacle?"

Wait a minute, Alex thought, uneasy. *Durnov's no fool. A man of his military experience wouldn't dare show such boldness toward General Roskov.* Alex couldn't remember a time when Durnov had stood against his superior. Something was different about the major-general—about the way he spoke. He used all the right military manners, but there was a flavor of stubbornness about him. He had a cigarette between his fingers, but it went unlit. Usually Alex lit his cigarettes, as was expected, but in the presence of the general, he did not.

Alex glanced at General Roskov to see if he was noticing Durnov's insolence. The general's shoulders had stiffened.

"Yes, Major-General Durnov, a debacle! The wrong man pines away in the stinking Peter-Paul fortress—my wife's brother. We're in an endless process of trying to free him. While *you* and members of the Okhrana wile away the time trying to dig up proof to include my wife's nephew, Sergei Peshkov."

"General! Sir! That has never been my intention, nor is it now. It's not the Peshkovs, but the wife's side of the family—the Menkins."

Alex turned his head sharply.

"Menkins?" General Viktor looked incredulous. He leaned across the desktop toward Durnov. "It's Lenski I want arrested, Durnov," he gritted. "Lenski is behind it, working hand in glove with the Bolsheviks."

"Yes, General, just so! Petrov Lenski. And he's fully involved with Karena *Menkin,* as I shall call her. They are lovers."

Alex could have wrung Durnov's thick neck. But one fiery word of protest, and Durnov, who may already suspect him of an interest in Karena, would be onto him like a vulture. *Silence.*

"Karena?" General Viktor repeated, dumbfounded. "That is absurd. I know the girl. She's no more a murdering Bolshie than is my own daughter."

Durnov straightened his shoulders. "I risk myself, General, to respectfully disagree."

General Viktor growled, "Go on."

"The Menkins are Polish Jews, only connected to your esteemed Roskov family by the marriage of one Madame Yeva Menkin. The report on her family history in Poland and Finland points to much interaction with revolutionary groups." He gestured to Alex. "Colonel Kronstadt has delved into their Warsaw history. Is it not true, Colonel, that Professor Menkin spent two years in a work camp for revolutionary endeavors at Warsaw University?"

"Just so."

"His niece, Karena, is not Josef Peshkov's child."

So Durnov knew. But did he know about Dr. Zinnovy?

"I know that," General Viktor snapped, flipping closed the file Durnov had brought and dropping it with a smack on the desktop. "I've known for years, through Countess Shashenka, but that in no way links the girl with Grinevich's death, nor with the idea that she's involved with Lenski."

Durnov stood like a bull, shoulders back, his square neck looking wider. "General, I have been sent here by the supreme head of the Okhrana to inform you that Miss Menkin is working with Lenski. We believe Lenski's Bolsheviks were behind the bombing of Count Kalinsky's coach at the train station this morning in Petrograd."

Alex waited for the words of doom: *"And Karena Peshkova was there at that station."* But did Durnov know this, or was he fishing?

The general said, "Lenski's involvement in Kalinsky's death? Yes, that is likely. And it is Lenski we want arrested. But the Kalinsky bombing in no way connects Karena with Lenski. She and her mother are both in Kiev at the manor house, awaiting news on Josef's trial." Roskov held out his cigarette toward Durnov.

The match Durnov held between thumb and forefinger snapped in two. The general stared at it without moving.

Alex struck a second match and held the flame to the general's extended cigarette.

"You were there at Kiev when all this took place, Alex," General Roskov said with an irritated voice. "You investigated thoroughly. What are your conclusions on Karena and Lenski? Working together, do you think? Lovers?"

Aware of Durnov's watchful eyes, Alex looked for a moment at the burned-out match.

"As I wrote in my report to the Okhrana, General, I interrogated Miss Peshkova and Professor Menkin at the manor house back in August. I do not believe either of them is a Bolshevik revolutionary. Professor Menkin is a cadet in his political beliefs and a friend of the democratic historian Miliukov, but other than that, there was nothing to link him or his niece with the death of Grinevich. The professor's political days in Warsaw are over. He writes history now and critical works on religion. As for Miss Peshkova and Lenski, you would be the best witness, sir. Your family has, I believe, long stipulated that there was to be a marriage between Karena and the farmer Ilya Jilinsky, who is now, sir, fighting for Russia on the front lines."

Durnov's mouth spread back over his yellowing teeth. "And this morning, Colonel Kronstadt?"

Alex coolly met his cynical gaze. "This morning, sir?"

"You did not see Karena Peshkova?"

General Roskov looked sharply from Durnov to Alex. "This morning? That's impossible. She's in Kiev."

Durnov fixed Alex with the same cynical smile.

Had Durnov discovered she was in Petrograd? Alex affected calm. "As I reported to you this morning, sir, I heard the blast that killed Count Kalinsky and arrived on the scene a few minutes later to find the count dead. I did not see anyone who might have been involved in the assassination."

Durnov turned to Roskov. "There's more in this report, sir. Grinevich's assistant policeman at Kiev, a man named Leonovich, was discovered dead. Kiev is now linking the two deaths as to motive, done by the revolutionaries to avenge the death of Professor Chertkov and the arrest of Josef Peshkov."

Leonovich. Alex concealed his alarm. *Leonovich was the thug asking Karena questions about Grinevich in the kitchen at Matvey Menkin's bungalow.*

"Leonovich?" The general frowned, unable to recall the name to his memory, as he leafed through the papers.

"He was one of those involved in the investigation of Grinevich's death."

"And an enemy of Grinevich, sir," Alex added.

Durnov shot him a frown. "Why do you say so? I've heard nothing of it."

"A number of people mentioned a dislike between the two men. It's in my report, sir."

Durnov rubbed his jaw thoughtfully. "That's news to me." He turned to the general, who was still leafing through the information. "Leonovich was murdered—shot—and apparently struck on the back of the head as well. They found his body in a ravine beside the road to the village."

General Roskov dropped back into the leather chair and turned sideways to stare out the window, puffing the cigarette and holding a sheet of paper. "The report says Leonovich was first reported missing about a week ago."

"There's no telling whether he died from the bullet or the head injury, but it's more likely the bullet. A hunter and his dog came upon him at the bottom of a gully."

"The gun used?"

"Kiev found a 7.62-millimeter bullet, sir. They think it was likely from a model 1895 Nagant revolver."

282 LINDA LEE CHAIKIN

Dead about a week ago. About the time Karena and her mother had to have departed the manor to bring them to Petrograd. Did either Josef Peshkov or his son have a Nagant at the manor?

General Roskov slapped the report back down on the desk.

"Well, he's dead, like many better men on the front facing the Huns." He looked up with impatience at Durnov. "And what has Leonovich's death to do with anyone in my family, especially my niece Karena?"

"Leonovich was closely associated with Policeman Grinevich, sir," Durnov said with equal frustration, as though the general should understand without his explaining the reasons.

"I am fully aware, Durnov."

"The office at Kiev is convinced it was the Bolshies both times. The same Bolshies. And now, this morning, it was Count Kalinsky."

General Roskov shook his head. "No no. The count's bombing has no factual connection with Grinevich or Leonovich. The Kiev gendarmes were small fry, but Kalinsky was a powerful supporter of the Romanovs, therefore a target."

"You're right, General, but it's the work of the same group under Lenski. That's what I'm getting at, sir."

The same group. Durnov's effort put Alex on edge.

"Yes," Roskov said, "I can see Lenski being involved in the count's death and in Kiev, but for far different reasons."

"It's Lenski and his Bolshevik friends all over again, General. We think Lenski's in Petrograd. That he was at the train station this morning."

Alex was deep in thought over the gully where Leonovich's body was discovered. He remembered the roads around the village, as well as the direction Karena and her mother would have traveled to reach the train station.

Durnov took out a folded drawing from his coat pocket.

"With your permission, General. If you take a closer look at this map—I drew it myself." Durnov marked the region on the map around what, until recently, was the Peshkov wheat farm and manor house. Next he drew an *X* in the region of the road in question, evidently the area where Leonovich's body was discovered. Alex judged the distance between the manor and the gully to be about a mile.

"What does this prove?" Roskov snapped. "The village is small. Everyone living there is in close proximity to the gully!"

But Alex began to worry. Not because he thought Karena had anything to do with Leonovich's death, but because it *looked* as though they could have been involved, and that was all Durnov needed.

Was Durnov notifying the general to prepare his wife for another arrest in her family? Alex didn't think Durnov particularly worried about Madame Zofia, but he did worry about his own position. Despite Durnov's confrontation with the general a few minutes earlier, Durnov wouldn't want to move against a relative of Zofia. This would account for his assertion that the Menkins were *not* members of the *honorable* Peshkov or Roskov families.

"And they found Leonovich's body about here"—General Roskov tapped the map—"in a ravine?"

"Just so, General. About a mile from the Peshkov manor house."

Alex kept his gaze on the map. Durnov had shrewdly managed to link the manor occupants to where the body was discovered. He was either digging his own grave or slowly convincing the general.

"Why isn't Leonovich's death a simple robbery?" Roskov asked roughly. "Not every murder is the work of Bolsheviks."

"If a robbery, sir, there's the problem of why nothing was taken from Leonovich's pockets. Then again, sir, we should ask how Leonovich's body ended up in the ravine."

"What about Leonovich's horse?" Alex asked. "Was it found nearby?"

"Now that you mention it, no," Durnov said.

"Then that's a sign of robbers. They might have come upon him late at night on the road." General Roskov crushed the end of his cigarette in an ashtray and stood. "All right, Durnov. Well done."

"Sir?" Durnov wrinkled his brow.

"I'll have another look at the report tomorrow. At this stage, however, some of your conclusions appear to lack both evidence and credibility. In the meantime, I want Lenski found and arrested. No more excuses."

He lifted Durnov's report from the desk and placed it under his arm.

"What about Kiev, General?"

"Forget Kiev."

"I should like to go there and question Madame Peshkova and her daughter again. It may be they have seen Lenski."

"You're a bulldog, Durnov. Request denied."

Alex felt a surge of relief but knew Durnov too well to think the bulldog would give up until satisfied. Since Durnov had requested to return to Kiev, it must mean he did not suspect Karena and Madame Peshkova of staying at Professor Menkin's apartment.

Alex needed time, and he was running out of it. He would have preferred the general to authorize Durnov's journey to Kiev. It would have gotten rid of him for a few weeks and made it easier for Alex to quietly pay Professor Menkin a visit.

A light rap on the door interrupted. "See who it is, Alex," General Roskov said.

Alex went to open the door. An ensign stood at attention. He saluted, "Colonel, I have a message."

Alex stepped aside and gestured toward the general, standing before the window. When Alex shut the door, he turned.

"You have something to report, Ensign?"

The ensign gave a smart salute. "Yes, General. The countess, Madame

Shashenka, requests an immediate audience with Colonel Kronstadt in her private office. She waits there now, sir."

Alex took his leave and walked through the ballroom to speak with his stepmother. That she would send word to interrupt a meeting with the general and fetch him to her company was curious.

Alex entered Countess Olga's office. He shut the door, turned, and stopped abruptly. To one side of the room stood his rival and opponent, Captain Karl Yevgenyev, son of the count, standing erect, hands behind his back. Beside the countess stood Karl's father, Count Yevgenyev.

The countess came forward with a rustle of satin. "Alex, dear, I should like you to meet a friend of mine, Count Andrei Yevgenyev. Andrei, my son of whom I am most proud, Aleksandr."

Count Yevgenyev gave a precise bow with a little click of his polished heels.

The tense moment continued, despite the countess's attempt at niceties. At last, she sighed and tugged on the Belgian lace handkerchief in her hand. "Well, I see we need to get straight to the reason for our meeting like this." She turned to the count, obviously handing over the situation to him.

Count Yevgenyev looked at Alex, who returned a level gaze. "Colonel Kronstadt, my son made a grave and foolish error when he publicly insulted your honor in Kazan at the Roskov summerhouse."

Alex looked across the room at Karl and could almost have felt sympathy for him, had he not been so arrogant. There was a faint flush on his face, and he was staring at the toes of his polished boots.

"My son wishes to withdraw his challenge to your honor, to apologize, and to end the challenge to duel." He turned toward his son and gestured him forward. Captain Yevgenyev did so as straight shouldered and stiff as a wooden toy soldier in Tchaikovsky's *Nutcracker.* Yevgenyev bowed and removed a letter from inside his uniform. He presented it to Alex with another bow.

"My written apology, Colonel Kronstadt. It will be published in the newspapers, if you so request, for all to see. I was drunk that night. I retract my words questioning your integrity and honor."

Alex accepted the letter. He smiled. "Forget the newspapers."

Yevgenyev showed faint surprise. His gaze measured Alex with a spark of admiration.

Count Yevgenyev approached with a silver tray, a bottle of expensive wine from the countess, and a single glass. His solemn face might have been carved in marble.

Alex looked at the tray. "There's only one glass to toast the victory of Russia."

The count exchanged glances with his son. Countess Olga laughed in her tinkling voice and seemed delighted with Alex as she beckoned Konni forward with three more crystal glasses.

"Colonel Kronstadt," the count said with a brittle smile, "we thought surely you would wish to take a glass of wine and throw it in retribution in Karl's face. As you can see, he has on his dress uniform."

Except for the loud ticking of the grand clock on the mantle, there was silence.

Alex took the glass of burgundy Konni had poured, sniffed it, and smiled. "I've always been a frugal man, sir," he said to the count. "This wine is too good to waste on Karl's uniform. Not only that, the stain is most devilish to get out. You can ask Konni."

The stiff smiles eventually broke free on the faces of the count and his son, and there was a dry chuckle from Konni.

"To the victory of Imperial Russia!" Alex said, raising his glass.

The others responded in unison. "God save the czar!"

TWENTY-SIX

On the Run

T wo satchels, trunks, a medical box, and a book package were un-
loaded from the droshky and carted in a hand wagon by the apartment *dvornik,* where Uncle Matvey was staying, near Tverskoy Boulevard.
Karena could see the river Neva as well as the spiral of the Kazan Cathe-
dral on the Nevsky Prospekt. Across the bridge, guards rode majestic
horses at the Winter Palace. She vaguely wondered where Colonel Kronstadt was stationed.

She turned to Madame Yeva, who leaned against the seat, slumping
weakly inside her hooded fur coat. The snow flittered down softly. Karena
took hold of her mother and carefully helped her down to the snowy court.
Madame Yeva's body felt cold, and she started to shiver uncontrollably.

The L-shaped building, not a large one, faced a small, quiet square
with a security gate, bushes, and trees, some of which were pine, and the
others, summer shade trees, now skeletons in winter.

Karena worried that the last remnants of Yeva's strength were ebbing.
She tightened her arm around her mother's waist, urging her onward
through the apartment door into a dim hall. In the midst of a small,
square entry room, a stairway branched in two directions.

"Soon now," Karena encouraged.

They started up the stairs, but Madame Yeva crumpled, and Karena tried to brace her on the banister. Her mother slid down, her breath raspy, and closed her eyes.

Karena rushed up the stairs, turned left, and met the dvornik coming out of an apartment. Just behind came Uncle Matvey Menkin with a smile on his bearded face that departed with one look at Karena. She realized she must look dreadful.

"Karena!"

"Uncle Matvey," her voice broke with emotion. She half ran, half fell into his fatherly embrace.

"Karena, my child, what has happened to you? Have you been in an accident?" He looked around. "Where is Yeva?"

"She's on the stairs, very ill. I think it's pneumonia. Everything has gone wrong, Uncle. We must get her to bed."

"Go inside, Karena. The porter will help me bring her up."

Karena entered a lighted room with books, stacks of paper, and a familiar, comforting typewriter on a desk.

Madame Yeva was carried into the small second bedroom at the end of a narrow hallway, and Karena put her straight to bed. Her own head was throbbing. At last the world had ceased to sway. She drew the blankets up to her mother's chin. She was sure the clean sheets were welcomed, but waves of chills swept over her mother as her teeth chattered.

Karena turned as Uncle Matvey came to the doorway. He held an extra blanket and drew near the bed, looking at his sister. He added the blanket to the ones already on her. He stood watching her with such soberness that Yeva noticed him and tried to smile.

"Matvey," she rasped, "I'm...all right." Then her eyes closed as she drifted into sleep.

"What are those bruise marks on her throat? and on your face, Karena? What evils have befallen you?"

Karena fought the desire to weep. He had burdens enough and would have more with their arrival.

I must stay calm. Strength of soul and purpose must be cultivated.

"There's much I should tell you, Uncle. Give me a few minutes to get settled and make myself more presentable; then I'll come out to the kitchen. I'd give almost anything for a hot cup of tea or coffee." She tried to smile.

Uncle Matvey remained grave, apparently seeing through her brave attempt to hold together. He laid his palm on Madame Yeva's forehead. "She's very ill. She must have a doctor, some medicine. I'm going out, Karena. I'll find one—"

"Uncle—wait," Karena's voice came with urgency. "It's not wise."

"Not wise?" came his incredulous voice; then he hesitated. "What's happened? That bruise on your cheek—"

"I'll explain everything. I must first tell you about something else that took place at Kiev before we left."

His intense dark eyes studied her face. "Something else?"

"Yes, Uncle—" Her voice caught for a moment.

He paused and then nodded his head. "I'll wait for you in the kitchen. I'll put the coffeepot on."

He went out, closing the door quietly. Karena stood still for a moment, trying to adjust to the silence after all the noise of the boxcar travel. She went to the washstand and, with shaking hands, poured water from the pitcher to clean her face.

One look at herself in the mirror above the stand and she winced. She sank down on a chair and rested her head against the back, closing her eyes, trying to ready herself to tell Uncle Matvey about that horrible night. Her eyes flicked open as a certain masculine face emerged in her mind— a face with gray-green eyes that held her captive.

What if he came here?

Professor Matvey Menkin waited in his kitchen. When Karena joined him, he was much moved to see his favorite niece in such condition. *She has been through trauma. It is written in her eyes. First, I must calm her,* he thought. His voice was reassuring. "Come and sit at the table while I pour the coffee, Karena. I admit to missing Grandmother Jilinsky—although I am thankful she is safe with Natalia and Sergei at the Roskov house. There is not a better cook anywhere to be found. Here, try a few slices of this apple and cheese. They are very good together. The cheese is from Finland. A friend from there travels frequently across the border. When he does, he always brings my favorite cheese."

"It is delicious. We had nothing to eat or drink on the train but what we could bring with us."

He suspected far worse where the trains were concerned but thought it wise to minimize those worries for now. He noticed that Karena was tense. She was seldom this way, and he was more worried than he had been since the arrest of Josef. Harassment of Jews had escalated in the past weeks. He had written Yeva a few days ago asking that they not travel here alone. It was clear they had left Kiev before receiving his letter.

"How was the train?" he asked, deliberately calm. "I'm surprised you found seats."

"Oh, Uncle, it was horrible." She set her cup down with a nervous clatter.

He reached across the table and took her hand. "What happened?"

By the time she had told her story of hopeless roads, of being denied seats on the train, of conditions in the boxcar, she was calmer, as if sharing these things enabled her to accept them.

"And not only that, but just as we reached St. Petersburg Station, exhausted, with Mother growing more ill by the hour, we had the misfortune of arriving at the very moment a czarist official was assassinated. We had the double misfortune of running into Alex—Colonel Kronstadt—and what's more, he saw me. He may still be investigating."

Aleksandr Kronstadt. An intelligent young man who had treated him respectfully. Even now, the young colonel was still in possession of the important first draft of his manuscript, with all of his notes. Matvey had received a short correspondence from him last week telling him that he expected to return everything shortly.

Matvey frowned, reaching for his pipe. So there'd been yet another assassination. He doubted if Karena knew who'd been attacked and did not burden her with questions. That Colonel Kronstadt was there also complicated matters for Karena and Sergei. The colonel already suspected it was Sergei, not Josef, at the Kiev meeting that night. If anyone were involved with the revolutionaries at Kiev, it would more naturally be Sergei.

There was still no word on Josef's prison sentence. Matvey was growing more concerned for the outcome. Sergei had stopped by only yesterday, coming over from the Roskov house to visit him, pacing the floor over his father's future, and blaming himself. Time and again, he'd wanted to inform the police, but Matvey counseled him it would only make matters worse. No matter what Sergei did, the authorities would keep his father under arrest for concealing the truth. Matvey did his best to illuminate the evils of the communist/socialist/Marxist system of beliefs, pointing out that it attacked the core of human belief in a God to whom all must answer. Sergei listened but kept silent, and he'd not been antagonistic. There yet remained hope for the young man.

"We managed to escape Kronstadt," Karena was explaining. "I'd never have come here, Uncle, but with Mother as she is, I had no one else to turn to. She didn't feel comfortable going to the Roskovs."

Matvey looked up sharply over his old pipe. "*Escape?* Why did you feel you needed to escape Colonel Kronstadt?"

She fumbled with her cup and saucer.

Matvey watched her alertly. "He permitted you and Yeva to avoid further questioning by Major-General Durnov. If he'd been of a mind to do so, he could have hauled you both in to Petrograd. He let you walk away. He met you in Kazan, did he not?"

She nodded, staring into her cup.

"Is there an attraction between the two of you?"

She pushed a strand of hair behind her ear. She nodded. "More so on my part."

"I don't think so. Not after risking himself as he has to shield you."

She remained silent.

"Is there something more, Karena? about your escape, I mean?"

"It's Leonovich," she said with a burst of emotion. "He's dead."

Matvey listened in dismay as she explained the repulsive details. An appalling silence settled over the room. It was some time before he could gather his voice to speak.

"You should have sent me a wire at once, Karena. I could have come to meet you. Does anyone else know of this? General Roskov?"

"No one."

"You did well to come here. It will give us time to decide the best way to handle this. I must think." He got up from the chair and walked about the kitchen. Leonovich—he knew little about the man but remembered seeing him a few times during his visits in Kiev. An odious wretch, a prowler—

"I wanted to go to the police," Karena said, "but Mother didn't think it wise."

"After Grinevich? It's understandable."

"They wouldn't have believed me," Karena said, resting her forehead against her palm. "Not even the marks on Mother's throat would have convinced them. The marks are still there—you saw them—but they were even worse."

"I agree they would not have wanted to believe you. Still…" He shook his head, fearing the concealing of such facts. "Getting rid of Leonovich's body will only strengthen their suspicions of guilt. The facts must be given to someone who will listen to the truth. Kronstadt, perhaps."

Her head jerked up. "No, Uncle."

Matvey struck a match and absently lit his pipe. He could understand why she wished to avoid Kronstadt at the station; arriving on the heels of yet another political assassination could go badly for her. He let the matter pass for the present.

"We hope Leonovich's death will be blamed on a robbery along the road," Karena said. "The best thing would be if his body isn't discovered at all. We planned to contact you secretly and explain to the family. Natalia, of course, was the biggest worry in that regard, and Sergei."

"My dear, things don't work so simply in life. I think you know that. If the authorities wish to convict you both of murder, they will. We'll need to help one another, and by that I mean we Jews and those who befriend us. First, there is someone I must see. Please trust me in this."

"I trust your judgment, Uncle, but—you're not going to Colonel Kronstadt?"

Dismay covered her face, and he laid a steadying hand on her shoulder. "No, not yet."

"Not yet?"

"There's someone visiting in town, a lawyer friend from Finland. I've known him for several years. His knowledge is most valuable."

"We can trust him?"

"Yes, we can. Others have." He was thinking of those his friend had helped across the Finnish border into safety, yet he did not wish to alarm her now with the possibility that they must flee Russia. "After I've talked with him and others," he said gently, "we'll discuss matters." If escape were necessary, it would be wiser to move with as little disturbance as possible. Agents of Durnov may be watching the Roskov residence, and they may even have this apartment under surveillance. Yeva's illness made matters worse. It would be difficult for her to travel, especially across the border.

Matvey tried to conceal his fear from Karena. There was only one man in the Okhrana who might aid them. If Kronstadt did have a developing interest in her, he could be trusted.

Matvey made up his mind. He could only hide them for a short time. Karena was against contacting Kronstadt, but he must use his own judgment.

He thought of his Messianic studies. Many of his Jewish friends would be appalled to discover that he had become a believer in Jesus the Messiah. In his heart, he turned to his Savior and Redeemer for divine wisdom. *For their sakes,* he prayed, *may they, too, come to put their faith in Jesus, the Messiah.*

"We will make no further decisions just yet," he told Karena. "You need food and rest, just as Yeva does. While you see to that, I'll be going out. I need to make a few calls. I will return this evening. If I'm not back by supper, there are eggs and more cheese in the icebox and bread on the pantry shelf."

She followed him into the hall. He opened the bedroom door, and they stood looking at Madame Yeva. Matvey's anger was roused, as he understood the reason for the bruises on his sister's throat and the cuts and swelling on Karena. *Lord, I entrust this to you. There are so many trials in life that just can't be solved until your reign. Your kingdom come, your will be done, on earth as it is in heaven!*

Karena walked quickly to the bed. "Her brow is damp," she whispered to him. "She's flushed. Her breathing is heavy and troubled."

She came back out of the small bedroom and closed the door behind her. "Uncle, I don't think I should wait any longer to find a doctor."

He nodded. But now that he knew the truth, he was no longer comfortable with calling the doctor he'd first had in mind. The man might be trustworthy, but caution must prevail.

"She does need medical care," he said. "I thought so the moment I saw her. You've nothing, Karena, in her medical bag?"

"We brought little besides birthing supplies and some headache tonic. If I had mother's quinine tablets... But I've already looked, and she hasn't any. She either ran out or overlooked bringing them. But I am thinking of a woman she knows here in St. Petersburg. She knew her years ago at the medical college. She's a doctor now—Dr. Lenski."

The name jolted him. "Lenski's mother? It would be a mistake to bring her here. If the apartment is being watched, the Okhrana will move in the moment they recognize her."

"But they know where she is. She works freely out of the college—she and her daughter, Ivanna. If the Okhrana wanted to arrest them, they could have by now. Uncle, please. I'm sure it's safe. I will call on her myself. There are several matters I need to discuss with her."

"Then I'll leave the doctor business to you, and I'll make arrangements in town to see my lawyer friend. I should be back in time for supper." From a drawer he removed a spare key and handed it to her.

"Better get something to eat and rest an hour. Matters will work out, Karena. We need to believe that there are greater purposes at work in the world and in our lives than most people acknowledge. We ignore those purposes to our peril."

He saw a responsive flicker in her blue eyes and the beginning of a smile that tried to encourage him of her trust. He thought she might be close to believing in the Messiah. He patted her head, thinking of her as the little girl in braids he remembered from years ago.

"I wouldn't assume too quickly that Colonel Kronstadt should be feared."

Karena watched Uncle Matvey leave through the front door of the apartment. She stood for a moment, considering his suggestion, and then went into the kitchen to find food for her mother.

She found a piece of cooked lamb and set about to make a broth. While the meat simmered, she wet some hand towels, cooled them in the icebox for a few minutes, and with a small bowl of water, went to attend her mother's fever.

Her mother's eyes fluttered open. Karena watched her with concern. Yeva tried to reach for Karena's hand.

Karena leaned closer, laying the cool cloth on her forehead. "Mother, you're burning up with fever. A few days more like this, and you will waste away to nothing. There's no choice but to go for a doctor. I'm going to try to get Dr. Lenski to prescribe medication. Or perhaps even Dr. Zinnovy. I never told you this, but he was kind to me at Kiev and—"

Her mother's face turned rigid with protest. The reaction was so harsh that it surprised Karena.

"No," Yeva whispered in a croaky voice. Her head fell back against the damp pillow with exhaustion, and her breath rattled in her lungs. She felt her mother's fingers tighten on her hand.

"Dr. Zinnovy may not be able to come, Mother. But if he does, I am most confident he can be trusted now. He protected me from the police after Grinevich was attacked. He was there at the meeting too. I saw him."

Karena does not understand. She thinks I don't want Dmitri here because I fear he'll go to the police. Poor Karena, my poor little girl. She will never know he's her father, and I cannot tell her.

"I must do something or I'll lose you, Mother. I don't want to lose you—"

Don't want to lose you. Those words came journeying back from the past in the emotional voice of Dmitri. Yeva had not seen him in years, and she did not want to see him now. The old ember of resentment burst into raw fire again. She looked up into Karena's face, young yet wise beyond her years—wiser than she herself had been at that age when she'd met the handsome Dr. Dmitri Zinnovy. She closed her eyes again. She was tired—so very tired—as her mind turned and began walking backward in time to when she was pregnant with her child and his...

Yeva had fled the Imperial College of Medicine and Midwifery, devastated with her predicament and Dmitri's response to the news. With tears in her eyes and a heart squeezed with pain, she packed her bags in a rush. The door opened quickly, and footsteps sounded behind her. She whirled defensively. It was not Dmitri, but her colleague and friend, Fayina Lenski, in her second year of medical studies.

"Yeva, you cannot go away."

"But, Fayina, I must. You know the regulations." Any woman pregnant out of wedlock was dismissed. That was not the only reason she was leaving; she was running from Dmitri and his heartless betrayal. He had recommended an abortion.

"I know this hurts and shocks you, Yeva, but it is an answer that will safeguard us both," he had told her.

"Safeguard," she had cried as they met secretly and walked through the falling snow down Tverskoy Boulevard. It was ten o'clock at night, and the telega was parked a block behind where they'd gotten out to talk.

"Yes, we must safeguard your life and opportunity to go on with your medical studies, even as my position as head instructor must be guarded. I cannot leave the countess, divorce, and remarry. I've always said that."

Countess Katya Zinnovy of the great Rezanov family. Yeva realized she'd been a fool. Dmitri would never leave the countess, though he'd told Yeva he did not love Katya and that Katya had an incurable disease of the kidneys that would take her life within a year. Then, she and Dmitri would marry. There had been reasons to become Dmitri's mistress—all the wrong and selfish reasons that had seemed entirely logical and practical. She had compromised so much in the name of "love."

She turned from Dmitri and hurried back toward the telega.

In the medical dormitory, Fayina walked up beside her bunk. "Where will you go? What will you do, Yeva?"

"I cannot go home to Warsaw." There'd been a recent pogrom there, but she did not want to mention it. "There is an area of St. Petersburg where I can find an affordable room. I shall work among the poor peasant women. They will pay in food and commodities… I'll not destroy my baby, no matter what."

"You can stay with me. I have room. And if it's work you are worried about, I know a doctor who can use you in deliveries. He works with peasants, prostitutes, and Gypsies."

Yeva had been indebted to Fayina Lenski from that day forward. She'd moved to her inexpensive flat and was there only a week when Dr. Zinnovy unexpectedly arrived.

"Who told you I was here?"

"Fayina."

She felt betrayed, but Dmitri said he had elicited Yeva's whereabouts by threatening her medical studies.

"I am desperate. Forgive me, Yeva. Forgive me. No, wait. Please, let me talk."

And talk he did, pleading with her that, if she must keep their baby, she should marry to spare herself and the baby from shame. He knew the perfect man, desperate for an arranged marriage with a wise woman. He was a gentile, but one who looked upon the seed of Jacob with favor. He was a schoolmaster and a farmer, and his family had been favored by Czar Alexander I. His wife had died, and he had a small boy named Sergei. If she would accept this marriage to Josef Peshkov, whom he knew to be a kind and decent man, Dmitri would see to everything. He then produced a bag of silver coins to tide her over. He would make sure she had a dowry in order to enter the Peshkov family with respect. And when the child became a young adult, he would pay for the education.

Madame Yeva was staring up at Karena's lovely face, not seeing the bruises, but the past—her own struggle for love, meaning, and purpose in life. She had thought she had found it in Dr. Zinnovy, and for years afterward, she had grieved for him late at night while Josef slept beside her. Tears filled Yeva's eyes. Now it was Josef she missed, longed for, and had so many regrets about. Josef was not the handsome man Dmitri had been, but his character made him a giant among men. She missed him and worried about his health and whether he was getting enough food.

"Josef, Josef, if only you were here."

"Mother." Karena bent her head and rested it a moment on her bosom. Yeva smoothed the damp hair from Karena's neck as they cried together.

I do not regret having borne you, my dearest one. I thank God I did not get rid of you as they'd suggested—how precious you are.

❦

Karena raised her head. Her mother's eyes flickered open again, tried to focus, and then closed. "Not Zinnovy. Lenski…Dr. Fayina Lenski…at the college now…go there to her…" Yeva gave a shuddering breath that sent a dart of fear through Karena. She stood, clasping her slim fingers and gazing down at her mother.

She recalled her mother's alarm when she mentioned writing to Dr. Lenski about her admission to the medical school. It was a relief to see she knew she was in need of help, but why not Dr. Zinnovy?

Karena left the bedroom and looked back at her sleeping mother before closing the door. She stood there for a moment, thinking. She'd better understand what she was getting into. Dr. Lenski would ask about their bruises, as well as treat her mother's illness. She would want to know what they were doing here in St. Petersburg with Yeva's brother.

There would be no need to explain everything. Karena went to the kitchen and set the broth aside on the back of the stove.

She could explain their stay here with Uncle Matvey with little difficulty, but other questions could lead to problems, as he had warned.

She made up her mind. She had to trust her mother's old college roommate.

She slipped into her fur coat and went to Matvey's desk to write a note in case he returned before she did. As she was about to turn for the front door, her eyes caught sight of his Bible sitting open on his desk. While she pulled on her gloves, she leaned over and glanced at the page. Some of the words were underlined, and there were notes written along the margins. It was the book of the prophet Isaiah, chapter 53. "He *(God)* shall see the labor of His *(Messiah's)* soul, and be satisfied." In the margin Uncle had written: *"The* Suffering *Messiah: Jesus on the cross."* On a sheet of paper he'd written: *"This prophecy of the promised Messiah is fulfilled, as is most of chapter 53. The sin debt is fully paid. We now have redemption through our true Passover Lamb, the Lord Jesus Christ."*

Karena's tired mind responded in simple trust and faith. Her eyes moistened. *Yes, I believe it. Jesus is my Passover Lamb. God, forgive me for what happened to Leonovich.*

She left the apartment using her key. Her feet were still weary, her mind tired, and her earthly problems remained. But a peace calmed her troubled heart with an assurance that she now possessed peace with the Holy God.

TWENTY-SEVEN

A Door Opens

The first sight of the college Karena had dreamed of attending brought a smile of excitement. It was a four-story palace with a pale yellow, colonnaded front and rectangular windows trimmed in tones of pink and blue. The front of the building gazed out on what in the summer would be a grassy square surrounded by flowering shrubs and trees, but now the square was a carpet of white.

She glanced about in wonder. The topaz and gold-veined marble floors and walls were magnificent, lending dignity to those who studied and worked to serve the needs of the suffering.

In her research to learn how the palace had become a part of the medical school, she'd learned that Countess Irina Vasiliy, upon her death in 1907, had awarded the palace for the use of the college, years after Yeva and Fayina attended as students. The Lying-In Charity Hospital and midwife program, however, was a private enterprise begun by Dr. Zinnovy and now headed by Dr. Lenski.

She walked up the steps, entered a three-story rotunda, and climbed the great stairway to the second floor where the doctors' and administrative offices were located. Karena was shown to Dr. Fayina Lenski's comfortable office with a window that overlooked the Neva River. Karena's excitement died when her eyes fell upon the somber Peter and Paul prison fortress. *Papa's in there,* she thought, sickened. She was in earnest prayer for him when she heard voices, and a door opened. Karena turned away from the window.

Two women entered, one of them carrying a stethoscope and standing several inches taller than the younger, who had auburn hair and pleasantly attractive features. *That must be Ivanna,* Karena decided.

Her guess was correct. The young woman introduced herself as Ivanna and then turned to the older doctor. "This is Dr. Lenski."

Ivanna's face was stoic, as though she did not know who Karena was. But she had her name and must know she was Sergei's sister. Karena wondered how Ivanna had managed to escape Kiev. Did she know where her brother Petrov was hiding? Had the Okhrana interrogated her yet?

Dr. Lenski looked Karena over. "So you're Yeva's daughter. Yes, the resemblance is there. Dr. Zinnovy mentioned you are interested in medical studies." Fayina Lenski's curly auburn hair showed from beneath her cap.

Ivanna turned to her mother. "I'd better get back with the patient. Nice meeting you, Miss Peshkova," she said and left the room.

Karena found herself under scrutiny. "You should be putting salve on those bruises. Were you in an accident?"

Karena had rehearsed what she would say to the inevitable inquiry. "Yes, a minor fall is all. I shall be fine in a few weeks. I did not come for myself but for Madame Yeva Peshkova." Karena hurriedly explained that her mother was very ill and urgently needed help, and would Dr. Lenski be so kind as to come with Karena to the Sergievsky district where they were staying with her uncle?

"Yeva asked for me, did she?"

"She speaks highly of you, Dr. Lenski. Some of my earliest memories when following her around in her work as a nurse and midwife in Kiev are frequent mentions of your name. I'd fully expected—hoped—to attend the college this past September. Alas, I was turned down for—for overcrowding." *That was hardly the reason, but Dr. Lenski would probably know that.*

"Yes, overcrowding. An unfortunate situation. I keep hoping matters will improve. Unfortunately, I have nothing to do with admittance. I'd have helped you get in, if for no other reason than Yeva. Dr. Zinnovy wrote in his memo that your grades are excellent. Perhaps we will be able to do something."

Karena brightened, though she knew the lack of funds would thwart her even if an opening were found for her.

"What specialty did you plan to pursue?"

"Midwifery and nursing. The thought of becoming a medical doctor is hardly conceivable. I've been waiting for three years just to enter the midwife course. I've already helped with deliveries in Kiev. I delivered my first baby alone in August." She did not dare say who the baby's father was, since Ivanna was seeing Sergei. Did the doctor even know about her daughter and Sergei? or that Ivanna had accompanied Petrov to Kiev? Somehow she didn't think so. In any event, she would heartily disapprove.

Dr. Lenski nodded firmly. "Good, very good, indeed. I would have expected such from Yeva's daughter. Naturally, you can reapply for admission next year. We'll keep working at it. With Dr. Zinnovy on your side, your chances for admittance will be much improved."

"At present, I'm afraid finances have foiled me."

Dr. Lenski lifted her timepiece and considered. "Hmm. Well, this is my night in the charity ward. I have an hour before my watch, but that's not enough time to see Yeva. Perhaps I can have Ivanna fill in for me in the ward. Let me speak with her supervisor. I'll meet you out on the front steps. I have a coach. I'll send for it."

Karena thanked her, and they entered the corridor, walking briskly along. Karena was so exhausted she could hardly keep up with the doctor's long stride. Already she liked her. Her businesslike way and dedication to medicine inspired her.

"I would have Ivanna take you on a tour of the charity ward, as it's my program now, but I dare not bring you in there with Yeva ill. You do not look ill yourself"—she scrutinized Karena once more—"but we must be most cautious of germs."

"Of course, Doctor," Karena hastened. She had forgotten about that. Perhaps she should not have entered the building at all.

"With regard to the study of germs," Dr. Lenski said and sadly shook her head until her gray-red curls trembled, "it is *most* unfortunate that the status quo remains so strongly among those in leadership, except for Dr. Zinnovy. He's willing to listen to new ideas about cleanliness. Take the north wing for example. It's called the Anastasia, after the Romanov princess. The Anastasia is the charity ward where the peasant women of Petrograd receive care and help with deliveries by our midwives in training. Very seldom do our students need to call upon a doctor for help, though one is always on duty. The Anastasia ward has no beautiful heirlooms, no ancient carpets, draperies, paintings, or canopied beds left behind by the donor, the countess. The ward is all wood, with bare wooden floors—easy for the student midwives to scrub down. I've discovered there are fewer contagions in the charity ward than in the grand Elizabeth West Ward for the women of the nobility. Most enlightening, isn't it?"

"Yes, most interesting, Dr. Lenski. I've studied my mother's medical books and the biography of Florence Nightingale. She, too, was insistent on scrubbing everything with hot soapy water. It proved to save many lives."

Dr. Lenski smiled at her and nodded approvingly. "You will do very well here, Karena. We must get you enrolled."

Karena's heart sang.

"I'm quite sure the contagions thrive more because of dust catchers in the well-furnished Elizabeth Ward. What else could it be? Countess Vasiliy wished to leave many of her furnishings for the nobility, so we have many of the original tapestries, beds, and carpets. Do you know what happens to the women who birth and recover for a month in the Elizabeth Ward? We have a higher rate of puerperal infection. In addition, the official explanation for the different mortality rates in the two wings is that there are differences between noblewomen and peasants. The noblewomen are frailer, they argue, while the peasant women are a hard-wearing breed. Have you ever heard such a thing? Poppycock, as the British would say!"

Karena smiled. She remembered the two midwives in Egypt had made up a similar excuse about stronger and weaker constitutions when Pharaoh demanded to know why the Hebrew newborns were surviving after his order that all the boys should be thrown into the Nile. The midwives claimed that the Hebrew women were more robust than the Egyptian women and gave birth before the midwives could arrive to carry out Pharaoh's order.

"Your reasoning seems sound to me, Dr. Lenski. I recall my mother saying that the charity babies have less exposure to sickness. She told me that they remained with their mothers near the bed so that each mother could feed and care for her own child. But the Elizabeth Ward nobility mothers often wouldn't want to nurse their babies, which were kept in a central nursery."

"Yes, and with staff wet nurses suckling more than one infant at a time, we have outbreaks of all kinds that seem to get passed from one baby to another. In addition, Elizabeth mothers stay here for more than a month before going home, but Anastasia charity mothers are sent away as quickly as possible to provide empty beds. It is all clear, is it not? But just attempt to explain this to the staff doctors. They will not listen. Only Dr. Zinnovy listens and agrees. He's asked me to write a paper on the subject, sending my proofs and beliefs for possible college publication. Unfortunately, I've not the time. Perhaps one day soon I'll try."

Karena looked at her quickly. "I'm helping Professor Menkin with his research for a book to be published in New York."

Dr. Lenski looked at her intently. "Interesting. Perhaps we could get together on this project as soon as you are free. I will pay you well, of course. It might help toward your tuition."

"I would be thrilled to be involved in such a project, Doctor. Is Dr. Zinnovy the director of the midwife program as well?" Karena asked.

"No no. He was when Yeva was here." She looked at her again with a scrutiny that was frank and even sympathetic. "I must apply a new ointment on those bruises after I see Yeva. As I was saying, no, Dr. Zinnovy now teaches and practices at the Pavlov State Medical University. We are an independent school now, though at one time the schools were one."

At the end of the corridor, Karena took her leave of Dr. Lenski, thanking her, and went outdoors to wait on the steps. The snow was floating lightly down again as the afternoon wore on. But inside she felt warm. Except for the circumstances centered around the death of Leonovich, Karena's life was opening like a flower. She looked up at the gray sky and smiled. *Thank you, God. I want to know you. I've so much to learn about you and the Bible.*

A short time later, Dr. Lenski came out the front door in a rush, bundled in a heavy fur coat and carrying a dark medical satchel. "This way," she called, marching on. Karena hurried to catch up.

A private coach came around from the side of the west-wing parking area, and the driver helped them inside. Soon they were on their way through the white wonderland.

When they arrived at the apartment, Matvey had not yet returned. Karena hadn't expected him to be there yet, but she'd hoped to introduce them.

Karena went to the hall and opened the bedroom door. Madame Yeva stirred and turned her head on the pillow. The sound of her troubled breathing disturbed Karena. She walked up beside the bed.

"Mother, I've brought Dr. Lenski."

"Fayina?"

Dr. Lenski came up, setting her case down on the table. "Ah, Yeva, to see you again—but in such condition."

"Thank you for coming."

"Nonsense. You should have called me sooner," she scolded in a friendly tone. "How long have you been ill like this?"

"Not long…a few days…but feeling ill at the manor for weeks… all…"

Dr. Lenski took Yeva's temperature, counted her pulse while watching her timepiece, and listened to her heart and breathing through her stethoscope. She asked quick questions, looked in her eyes, ears, and throat, and pushed aside her gray-gold braids from her neck to notice with a sudden frown the bruise marks on her neck.

I had forgotten. Karena tensed. She glanced at Dr. Lenski's face to see her reaction, but her expression did not alter. Madame Yeva considered Dr. Fayina Lenski a longtime friend, but had she intended all along to tell her about Leonovich? If she trusted her, why the displeasure when Karena had wanted to write her after returning from Kazan?

Now what? Karena wondered, looking at her mother to see if she was aware the doctor had noticed the marks. Her mother looked too ill to be concerned. Surely Dr. Lenski would ask about them, even as she had asked about the marks and bruises on Karena's own face. A doctor would recognize they were finger marks on her mother's throat.

Dr. Lenski, however, asked no questions about the marks on her throat. A sign in itself she knew they were suspicious.

Perhaps thirty minutes later, after writing her diagnosis in a black book, Dr. Lenski placed it in her satchel and wrote some instructions for Karena on a sheet of paper. She also made Karena swallow some small square pills, then provided a bottle of medicine for Yeva, setting it on the bedside table by the pink-shaded lamp.

"Two teaspoons every four hours." She looked over at Karena. "She ought to be in the hospital, Karena."

"No, Fayina," Madame Yeva whispered.

"I'm her nurse," Karena said. "She could find no one more committed."

"I can't argue that. Give her a second and even a third pillow to keep her elevated. It may help her to breathe with a little more comfort."

Karena walked with Fayina into Uncle Matvey's living room, where she dispensed extra medications and ointments.

"Your help is invaluable, Dr. Lenski. I do not know how to thank or repay you. As soon as I get a job—"

Dr. Lenski waved a hand. She peered at her, arms folded across her middle while she leaned against the tall divan back, ankles crossed. "This *accident* that bruised your face, are you claiming that is also how Yeva received those bruises on her throat?"

Karena tried to sidestep the direct questioning that seemed typical of Dr. Lenski. "Much has happened recently. She has lost a husband and we have lost a father to the Peter and Paul prison. We have also lost our home where we all grew up from childhood, and the wheat lands have been confiscated by the czar. Our money was stolen somewhere on the train when we were forced to ride in the boxcar after paying perfectly good rubles for our seats. My sister's fiancé is on the front lines fighting the Germans— and now my mother is desperately ill with pleurisy."

"The times," Dr. Lenski said wearily, "are most trying. I might as well clear the air, Karena. I know about the Bolshevik meeting gone awry at Kiev—oh yes, I know about it. I should, since my own son Petrov was the speaker. He's being sought this very moment by the secret police. Yes, I know of these things. If I didn't have my work, I'd be driven to distraction. My consolation for losing my son to the revolutionaries is a belief that I am giving back to others through medicine."

Karena noticed for the first time how tired Dr. Lenski appeared. Karena's conscience was pricked for enumerating her woes in an attitude of complaint.

"You have Ivanna," Karena said, trying to comfort her.

"Yes, there is my Ivanna." Her small eyes twinkled with pride. "And I should say that I'm aware of Josef Peshkov's arrest and what his sacrificial confession has done to Yeva. That is not what I had in mind. I was speaking of those purplish bruise marks on her throat, and the bruises on your face. Yeva was choked; I recognize the prints of a man's thumb, a strong man. I suspect those marks on your face are from the same man's fist. What did you do—try to defend her and get struck?"

Karena looked at her for a long silent moment. She bit her lip and looked away from the doctor's sympathetic gaze. Karena tossed up her hands in a gesture of despair. Dr. Lenski knew. Karena realized it was unrealistic to think she and her mother could hide the physical signs from a doctor and not have them evoke questions.

"Do you want to tell me about it?" Dr. Lenski asked in a professional tone.

"I don't think I should involve you in something that can only bring trouble."

"I am Yeva's friend."

Karena shook her head and turned away tiredly. "I'd rather not, Dr. Lenski. I'd feel better if I let my mother explain when she is well enough. You understand, don't you, that I cannot take it upon myself now?"

"Yes, I suppose so. I think I can guess the facts anyway. Something happened in Kiev."

"The help I need now, Dr. Lenski, is in finding work as a midwife."

"I can see that, but you've no credentials to work at the hospital. It's unfortunate."

"I know that, but I've helped Madame Yeva since I was a child. I told you I delivered my first baby alone. What I didn't tell you was that it was breech."

Dr. Lenski looked alert. "How did you do?"

"The baby is alive and healthy."

She nodded, showing satisfaction. "And the mother?"

"She died of a hemorrhage, but it was not due to any error. Madame Yeva will tell you that."

She nodded. "I cannot give you work in the hospital, not even the charity ward."

"I realize that. Still…"

"But I've heard of women who could use your services."

"Yes?"

"Give me time to look into the matter. I may have Ivanna contact you in a few days, or I'll do so myself. I'll need to come and check on Yeva next week anyway."

Karena's mood immediately lightened. It was all she could dare hope for. "Thank you," she said.

Dr. Lenski straightened from leaning against the back of the divan and waved her gratitude away. "My Ivanna and your stepbrother Sergei are serious about their relationship. Sergei wants to marry her, but neither Ivanna nor I want that to happen until she gets her doctorate. She has two years before she graduates. The marriage is likely to happen one day. That will connect our families."

The front door to the apartment opened, and Uncle Matvey's voice called, "Is that you, Karena?"

With secret relief, Karena turned toward the hall. "Yes, Uncle Matvey, I've brought Yeva's friend from their medical days together, Dr. Lenski. The doctor was kind enough to come and treat her."

Uncle Matvey walked into the living room and paused in the doorway.

After perfunctory greetings, Dr. Lenski gathered up her fur coat and medical bag.

"If she worsens, send word to me at once. This is my home address." She wrote it down quickly and left it on the table beside the ointments and medications.

In the little hall, Karena held out her hand. "Again, thank you."

Dr. Lenski smiled. "I'll contact you soon about work. I suspect you'll want to work incognito here in Petrograd. "

"That would be appreciated," Karena said.

"I'll tell you this," Dr. Lenski said at the door. "The administration has decided to fund a few individuals, myself being one of them, to help certain women who have a higher mortality rate than any other group of peasant women in St. Petersburg. The women are prostitutes and have no place to go. They dwell on the streets. Many die while giving birth, and many babies freeze in the snow who should have been brought to the foundling house gate to be taken in. It is these women who need your skills." Dr. Lenski looked at her thoughtfully. "Ivanna needs an assistant. Does the idea of working with prostitutes trouble you?"

"One needn't agree with the decisions people make to show them mercy. If the day should come when I permit any woman to die in the cold and a newborn to freeze, I should renounce all desire for becoming a credentialed midwife."

"Good. I believe you have what is needed. I shall tell Administration that you'll be working under Ivanna."

"I shall be anxious to start, Dr. Lenski."

"Excellent."

Dr. Lenski turned as Uncle Matvey walked into the hall, putting his coat on again. "Let me walk you to your coach, Dr. Lenski."

"Not necessary at all, Mr. Menkin. I'm used to trudging about in the snow."

"I must insist. The snow is coming down heavier, Madame."

Dr. Lenski nodded and was out the door with Uncle Matvey without another glance back. Karena closed the door against the rising wind and smiled wearily to herself.

❧

She was in the kitchen, pouring hot tea into two glasses, when Uncle Matvey returned some fifteen minutes later, brushing snow from his shoulders and removing his hat. Karena felt in a lighter mood than she had been in for days. Her mother was in a warm, safe bed, medicine was available, and Karena had the promise of medical work.

"Here's some hot sweetened tea," she said. "It will warm you up."

He warmed his hands at the stove as he gratefully sipped. She noticed his grave manner. His mood had not changed even with the news that Yeva was expected to recover with medicine and rest. She sat down, watching him. "You returned earlier than I expected. Weren't you able to contact your lawyer friend from Finland?"

"We met and discussed matters. He's not optimistic where you and Yeva are concerned. These are troubling times in Russia. Our rights are few, and we have no friend in the czar. It's unfortunate, but reality must be faced. My friend is even more convinced than I. He advises that if Leonovich's death is not accepted as an accident or a road robbery, you and Yeva should flee from St. Petersburg to Finland."

Karena stared at him, speechless. *Leave Russia?* It was unthinkable. "You think Yeva and I would be convicted of murder in connection with Leonovich?"

He nodded, lifting his glass of amber tea. "Neither you nor Yeva has done anything worthy of punishment. Leonovich was the criminal. But we know, do we not, that here in Russia, such considerations will hardly matter to some in power?"

"But Finland—Uncle! I don't want to leave my country! I am loyal to the czar."

"If you are implicated in what will be called the murder of Policeman Leonovich, it won't matter, Karena. You must either run away or face long, torturous years in Siberia—or even death by hanging."

Karena sat down slowly on the chair. No, this couldn't be happening. They were innocent.

Uncle Matvey laid a hand on her shoulder and spoke gently. "This is very difficult, I understand. We need not plan yet. God willing, my dear, we won't need to follow through on an escape. But wisdom says we should take no chances. I think it best that I go ahead and make plans with my Finnish friend. Then, if it appears necessary, we will go to Finland to visit our distant relatives. And if matters do not deteriorate, then little is lost."

Karena stared at her glass of tea. *Finland...*

"After Leonovich's attack, was anything left that someone could find at the house or on the train?"

Karena looked down at her fingers curling around her glass of tea. "No, nothing." She put her hand to her forehead.

"Nothing of Leonovich's that would incriminate you and Yeva? Nothing at all to indicate he was there when he died? or connect the two of you with his visit that night?"

"No no—nothing, unless—but no."

"What is it, do you remember something?"

She shook her head, trying to remember the details. They seemed to be blurring, perhaps because she was so exhausted, or maybe because she wanted to forget. "No," she repeated, "nothing." *We got rid of the rug.*

Uncle Matvey walked over to his desk and stood for a moment looking down at his books and notes as if he did not see them.

"Dr. Lenski," he said after a thoughtful moment. "Is she aware that her son is a Bolshevik leader wanted by the secret police?"

"Yes. She said she disapproves of what her son is doing. But she's devoted to him and Ivanna. She mentioned how Sergei wishes to marry Ivanna."

"Does she approve of such a union?"

"I gathered that she would approve, once her daughter becomes a doctor. Surely there will be no wedding for some time, with the war and other problems. Sergei still has his schooling. Why do you ask, Uncle? Does this have to do with Leonovich and Kiev?"

"Perhaps not. I have an uneasy notion. One I hope I'm wrong about."

She watched him, troubled by his concerns. He looked at the various medications Dr. Lenski had left on the table.

"It may have been wiser had I gone to another doctor, a stranger to us."

Karena shook her head firmly. "Oh, Uncle, perhaps both of us are worrying too much. Dr. Lenski and Madame Yeva have been friends and medical colleagues since before Ivanna and I were born. She's even helping me find work as a midwife connected with the college's charity work."

"Yes, but regardless of her friendship, any connection with Petrov Lenski is precarious."

"The midwife work is with the college and hospital."

"That's helpful. But believe me, my dear, the Okhrana have their eyes on her as Petrov Lenski's mother."

Karena was silent. Did he think the secret police would have followed her from the medical college to his apartment? That would account for the gravity of his countenance when he arrived to find Dr. Lenski here. Or was there something more about Dr. Lenski that made Uncle Matvey so concerned?

Karena stood wearily. "I'll see if Mother is still asleep. I've made some broth for her."

"While you do that, I'll get supper warming. And Karena," he said and placed an arm around her shoulder, "it grieves me if I've brought new concerns to you. I want to see my niece happy, doing the medical work she is gifted by God to do. But God also expects us to walk circumspectly. We are in danger—as a people and as individuals. Our enemy is greater than we are. That is not a reason for despair, however, for in Messiah, we are accepted by God in the Beloved. Yet we still need to act with caution and not allow our hopes to overshadow our discernment."

She nodded and tried to smile. It wasn't until she reached her mother's bedroom door that she stopped to consider Uncle Matvey's words. *In Messiah, we are accepted by God in the Beloved!*

Karena pushed the door open. Her mother remained in a deep sleep.

TWENTY-EIGHT

The Charity Tent

The next day Karena went with Ivanna to the outskirts of St. Petersburg where Dr. Lenski and a few of her colleagues had set up a medical tent to treat the poorest of the peasants.

"We could have found a building in the city, especially in this weather, which is near the Gypsy area, but we wanted something we could pack up and move wherever it was needed. It took us nearly eight months to gain approval from the czar to open the tent hospital."

Karena was surprised. "To help Russia's poorest? Why should professional doctors need to wait so long?"

As they left the coach, carrying medical bags across the street through slushy snow to drier ground, Ivanna turned to Karena with arched brows.

"I'll tell you a little story Dr. Zinnovy told my mother, who was growing impatient over the delays. The widow of a respected general, upon her death, left money for four new beds for our old soldiers' ward. But before the hospital could have the endowment, the czar had to approve it. Innumerable requests such as these occur in all areas." She hesitated. "It's this kind of minute control by the autocracy that infuriates Sergei. So that's why we had to wait eight months just to set up our charity medical tent under a new name."

Karena was thinking of the Roskovs' appeal to the czar for a lighter sentence for Papa Josef and how long it was taking.

"Come, we'd better not sound too critical," Ivanna said casually. "You never know who may overhear and misjudge our loyalties to the Romanovs."

The large tent was erected in a vacant lot near nightclubs and gambling establishments. These were bleak and dirty dives with unkempt men sleeping in doorways and prostitutes walking the streets at night. She had known that most every town and village had its poor, their vodka dives, women who sold their bodies, and men who *owned* these women as chattel. It was an ugly side of life that Karena would have preferred not to see, but she had to if she was to show Christ's mercy.

She wondered how safe it was to be here. After the horrible experience with Leonovich, she was constantly looking over her shoulder, yet she could not discuss her fears with Ivanna.

Ivanna must have noticed she was tense. "It is reasonably safe here during daylight hours. At dark, we usually close. Your brother Sergei often comes for me at evening." She smiled. "He's the perfect bodyguard."

Karena, too, smiled. Yes, if only dear Sergei had been at the manor house a week ago. Leonovich would not have found her alone, and that dreadful business would not have happened.

Inside the tent, she helped Ivanna prepare equipment and medicines for nonemergency treatments.

"Do you mind working with these kinds of people? Many are alcoholics and prostitutes."

Karena looked over at her. "If I can help any of these women, it's worth the unpleasant environment. It's dark places like this where we can do the most good."

"You speak like a Christian. I thought you were Jewish."

"My mother is Jewish. We have attended St. Basil's in our village in Kiev, but I did not understand the Bible. Professor Menkin, my uncle, is making a most interesting study about the Old Testament prophecies of the Christ. He's writing a book showing that Jesus fulfilled what was written about the Messiah."

"Matvey? Sergei is very attached to his uncle. He speaks of him often."

Karena told her more about the work in progress, and Ivanna listened in silence.

"I've trusted in Christ for many years now," Ivanna said after a time. "It's Sergei who likes to argue about it. Sometimes I think he debates just because he's angry on the inside. Your uncle is a great influence on him, though. Someday Sergei will change."

Karena went on setting up her table, although receiving expectant mothers in such an environment seemed ludicrous. Even so, she was satisfied to be working with Ivanna. Ivanna appeared to be well on her way to becoming a doctor, and Sergei had best master his studies to become a lawyer if he expected to marry her.

"One of our other charities is working with the Gypsies," Ivanna said. "Every month we go there and set up the tent, usually for two weeks. The Gypsies have a camp by the river where they live in wagons. They do not run brothels, but many are thieves, some are fortune-tellers, and others are genuine dancers and singers who perform at nightclubs. They have a hypnotic form of music. Many of Petrograd's elite go to see the Gypsies sing, dance, and play the violin.

"The Gypsies, at first, refused to have anything to do with us," Ivanna continued. "They have their own customs and midwives. But they will respond once you have earned their trust, which is most difficult. They are a very tight society of people and do not look favorably on outsiders. Who can blame them? While it's true they are involved in much crime and people don't want them near their homes, they have been treated with as much bigotry as the Jews."

"Are they very superstitious?"

"Extremely so. No one outside their immediate family and clan is allowed inside their wagons. I doubt very much if you will ever deliver a Gypsy baby. Your talents will be used mostly among the peasant prostitutes walking the streets and hanging around the nightclubs.

"Mother said you delivered a baby on your own at Kiev," Ivanna continued. "Was she a peasant girl on the wheat farm? Whose child was it? The father, I mean. Do you know?"

Karena, startled, looked across the tent at Ivanna who was opening a side flap to let in more light and air, despite the snowy cold. Several small heating pots of burning coal were set about the floor, and some fresh air was necessary.

How could she tell her?

⚜

Alex arrived back in Petrograd early the next morning. He went straight to the Winter Palace and checked into his quarters, changed, and then slipped out a back entrance. He took a roundabout walk to Professor Menkin's flat. After climbing the stairs, he found the apartment number and knocked. After a few moments, a tall figure with keen eyes and a thatch of silver hair opened the door. A startled look crossed the professor's face, but Alex saw that he was not alarmed.

Alex held up his satchel. "I'm returning your manuscript, Professor."

A moment later, Alex was inside the apartment, as Menkin insisted they have coffee and discuss Alex's thoughts about his work.

Alex could see a back bedroom with the door closed. Were Karena and her mother there, or was he mistaken in thinking they'd seek refuge here?

Professor Menkin poured them each a cup. Alex sensed he wanted him there, that he had something to say and was wondering how to open the subject.

"What did you think of my manuscript, Colonel Kronstadt?"

"I have a cousin in America in a Bible seminary. He writes to me often. He would agree with you about Jesus being the Christ. He also believes the Bible teaches that, one day, the Jews will go back to Palestine in unbelief, but at some period in the future, perhaps through great tribulation, a remnant will recognize Jesus as their Messiah. Michael sent me the verse in Zechariah 13:6. I thought you'd be interested in it. I noticed you had other verses, but not that one."

Professor Menkin handed him his Bible, watching him intently. "Can you find the verse for me, Colonel?"

Alex did so, quickly noting the parenthetical words Matvey had written in the margin beside the text. He read: "And one will say to him *(Messiah),* 'What are these wounds between your arms?' Then he *(Messiah)* will answer, 'Those with which I was wounded in the house of my friends' *(Israel)*."

He handed the Bible back to him to read to himself.

The professor did so, taking his time, then looked up, a gleam in his eyes. "Just so," he said. He laid the Bible down. "I'm convinced I can trust you, Colonel. It's about my niece Karena Peshkova. Are you willing to listen?"

Alex looked at him evenly. "Miss Peshkova is the reason I'm here. I saw her and Madame Peshkova yesterday at the train station. I've reason to think they've come to you."

"They did."

"They're in great danger, Professor."

"I know that as well."

"Have they mentioned a policemen from Kiev named Leonovich?"

"I don't believe you understand what actually occurred on that night."

"Tell me everything. Hold nothing back."

When Professor Menkin finished the sordid tale, Alex had to restrain his anger.

"We may need to bring her and Yeva across the border into Finland," Matvey said in a low voice. "We've some distant relatives in Helsinki on our grandparents' side. I made contact with them two years ago and built a relationship with them. I think they'd receive Yeva and her daughter into a safe house until they could be resettled."

Alex's thoughts raced. He stood, moving about restlessly. "Yes, if it comes to that, we'll find a way. I'll arrange something. Would you be going with them?"

"I see no other way. Yeva is ill, and Karena will need help."

Alex considered. "It would be best not to bring Natalia yet, or notify Sergei."

"I agree."

"Later, perhaps, when matters are calmed down, they could join you in Finland. But first, there may be another way out of this danger for Karena and Madame Peshkova."

"What would that be?"

Alex told him about his meeting with Dr. Dmitri Zinnovy and what was involved. Matvey showed no dismay, convincing Alex he might have known.

"If anyone can influence the czar and czarina to absolve them of any guilt in Leonovich's death, it's Dr. Zinnovy. But the impact of such a request would not be as great unless he confesses to Czar Nicholas that Karena's his daughter. If Zinnovy will play the man in this, there may be a chance."

Professor Menkin bit the end of his pipe stem, and his foot tapped the floor. "Yes, yes, perhaps, but will Dr. Zinnovy make that step of confession for Karena and Yeva?"

"That's the question, isn't it? He will be risking his reputation before the man he most wishes to respect him, Czar Nicholas."

"It's worth the chance of discovering. When can you see him?"

"This morning, at the medical college." He looked toward the bedroom. "There's one other matter that's crucial before I see Zinnovy." He looked at Professor Menkin. "I've got to speak with Madame Peshkova for a few minutes."

The professor looked surprised and searched his face, but then nodded. "I'll do what I can. She was a little better this morning. I'll see if she's awake."

Alex paced while Menkin went in to his sister. Alex's mind was on Karena. Menkin had told him she was with Ivanna Lenski in the slum district, working at the charity medical tent. Thinking of how close Karena had come to becoming a victim of Leonovich's lust and violence infuriated him. *If only I'd been there!* Alex longed to hold her in his arms and protect her. He must see her and tell her so, soon.

When at last he was able to speak with Madame Peshkova, he came straight to the point.

"Madame, let us set aside all pretense for your sake and Karena's. I've spoken to Dr. Dmitri Zinnovy. He's willing to buy back the pendant if you'll sell it to him. It's important you do. The pendant was seen and recognized. The safest place for it now is with Zinnovy. If there's any question by the countess or anyone else, having it in his possession could safeguard your reputation and his, not to mention Karena's."

She stared at him wildly. But as he talked, she calmed, reason settling into her feverish gaze.

"That pendant has been a burden. If Dmitri wants it back, he may have it. I want nothing for it."

"You should receive its fair value, Madame. It is rightfully yours. He would not accept it unless he can buy it. It may be necessary for you to cross the border into Finland. If so, you will have means for your security and Karena's. If not, there's her tuition for the medical college."

She looked at him for a long, studious moment. "Colonel, how will this benefit you?"

"Your daughter, Madame. I have plans—if she permits and the war allows—to see a great deal of her in the future."

"I see. And what about Viktor and Zofia's daughter, Tatiana?"

His gaze did not falter. "We've both agreed to end the relationship."

She was quiet for a long moment.

"I trust Alex completely, Yeva," Professor Menkin spoke from the other side of the bed.

"Yes," she murmured. "I am also so inclined. Matvey, in my trunk, a small box, the pendant's inside. The key—here, under my mattress."

A few minutes later with the pendant in his satchel, Alex bent over Madame Peshkova's hand. She smiled.

"Thank you, Alex," she said weakly. "I feel very relieved." Her eyes smiled at him, and she tried to squeeze his hand.

Alex left Professor Menkin's apartment and took a droshky to the Imperial College.

TWENTY-NINE

Endings and Beginnings

Sergei Peshkov trudged along the snowy streets in a dark mood. He was carrying his pack, wondering what he was going to do now that he had earned Tatiana's and Aunt Zofia's indignation after taunting them about their devotion to Rasputin.

I should not have provoked Tatiana. At least Ivanna was no silly gosling. He had to see her.

He was walking along toward the Neva when he remembered—this was Saturday. She would not be at the medical college today, but at the other end of town, running the medical tent. He needed to talk to her. Afterward, he'd go to Uncle Matvey's apartment. Matvey was always patient, and his eyes would get a twinkle when Sergei got the best of him in an argument, usually about politics or religion. Sergei believed in God, but sometimes he behaved otherwise just to get Uncle Matvey in his most profound mood. Then they could talk for hours about the Old Testament and go through a pot of coffee.

Yes, Sergei liked to be around him. It was a comforting atmosphere, where he could take off his shoes and admit that he was miserable, feeling guilty about Papa Josef, and trapped. *How do I get free?* He had no choice but to get his degree in law, now that his father had taken his guilt. *I'd rather go to Boston and enroll in Harvard's journalism school. Ah, another impossible dream.*

Sergei reached Kyovsky Street and saw the tent. Ivanna was speaking to some bent old woman, giving her medicine. He was startled to see Karena come out and shake out an apron. What was she doing here in St. Petersburg? Why hadn't she contacted him and Natalia? *Is Mother here?*

He walked swiftly across the gray slush and called to her. "Karena!"

His sister turned in apparent surprise to hear his voice, but his joy in seeing her skidded to a halt when he caught sight of her face. *Those bruises and scars! Where had they come from?*

"You've been in an accident," he stated. "Where's Mother?"

There was relief in her smile over seeing him, yet caution in her eyes.

"Sergei, I'm so glad you're here. Mother's sick with pleurisy, but Dr. Lenski has been treating her."

"Is she at Matvey's then?"

"Yes, we both are. I'll be returning there at sundown."

"Good! I'll go with you. It will be old times for a while. I'll need to beg a space to sleep for a few days until my dorm opens at the university. I'm afraid I angered the Roskovs and had to move out."

"Oh, Sergei, no. What happened?"

"Nothing of permanent ruin." He smiled ruefully. "Just a wee argument about Tatiana's foolishness over Rasputin. I went too far."

"Sergei," she groaned.

"All right, I was wrong. But I refused to kiss his jam-spread hands to show allegiance."

"Refused to what? It sounds absurd."

"It is, but never mind, Sister. It will all pass over with time. Tatiana never stays mad for more than a week." He rubbed his cheek. "Even though she did give me a good wallop."

"Over Rasputin?" Her scowl of disapproval about Tatiana made him smile.

"Well, I was a rude. I deserved it. I'll apologize in a letter to her in a few days. She'll forgive me. She always does. But she's so bourgeois, so elitist. Rich, living outside reality, so 'Marie Antoinette,' if you know what I mean. 'Let the peasants eat cake' attitude. Dumb about what's going on inside Russia."

Karena shook her head ruefully. "I'm sure your analysis greatly impressed her."

"Tell me about your accident. Say—that left eye does not look too good, Sister. There are cuts around your mouth. Think they'll leave scars?"

She touched her lip with her finger, and he saw the look that came into her eyes—anger or fear. Suddenly, he sensed something evil, something that gripped him.

He took hold of her arm. "What is it? What's happened?"

Ivanna walked up. She had taken care of the old peasant woman and sent her away.

"Karena has a patient, Sergei. Come, I'd like something hot. That bar across the street is not too revolting this time of day, and they have decent coffee and sandwiches. Walk with me there?"

"You have only to ask, and the world is yours," he said lightly. "At least when it comes to my buying you a cup of coffee." He looked at his sister.

"I'll tell you everything later," Karena promised, then she turned and went into the tent to meet her first patient.

He turned to Ivanna, holding out his arm. "Come along, *Doctor* Lenski. By the way, I don't see the intern Fyodor Zinnovy anywhere about today. Does that mean you've discouraged his romantic intentions?"

She did not smile. "No, he doesn't come on until dusk."

When Alex arrived at the medical college, he found Dr. Zinnovy in his office bending over a stack of papers. The doctor looked up and saw him, his earnest gaze questioning Alex. *Were you successful?*

Alex opened his satchel and produced the pendant. Dr. Zinnovy took it over to a light and looked it over carefully. "Yes," he said simply.

Dr. Zinnovy produced a bag of gold coins. "There will be more if she needs it."

Alex packed the bag in his satchel and went straight for his goal.

"You've heard of the death of Policeman Leonovich. Durnov is out for Karena and Madame Peshkova. If he has his way, he'll soon have them arrested and in the Peter and Paul fortress with Josef. There's one thing that might make the difference for Karena. If you appeal to Czar Nicholas to have her absolved of any wrongdoing in his death—if you confess to him that Karena's your daughter—he might move with grace."

Dr. Zinnovy sank into his chair, stunned. "Karena and Yeva? charged with murder?"

Alex explained the truth as Professor Menkin had laid it out in the apartment. When he'd finished, Dr. Zinnovy rested his forehead on his hand.

"This is utterly despicable."

"The other option is for your daughter to leave Russia for Finland as soon as possible."

Dr. Zinnovy leaned back in the chair as if exhausted. "I doubt Nicholas will receive me now." He pushed himself up from the chair and walked slowly, with heavy feet, over to the window. "Something has happened over which I have no jurisdiction."

Alex waited, his tension growing. He could see his expectation for Karena's pardon crumbling before his eyes.

"I don't understand, sir. I do know we haven't much time. Durnov's determined. I'm going down to the Kyovsky district now. Karena's there with Dr. Lenski's daughter, working in the charity tent."

"Yes, Dr. Lenski told me."

"I'll be bringing her back to Professor Menkin's apartment. Careful plans need to be made for them to escape across the border."

Dr. Zinnovy turned to look at him across the plush office. His face was gray and his eyes, morose. "I spoke harshly of Rasputin, and my words have found their way to the czarina. She's turned against me. It's only a matter of time before I'm dismissed from the palace staff of physicians. Any request I may make to the czar is likely to be rejected."

Alex's last hope flickered. What was left now but escape to Finland?

He nodded to Dr. Zinnovy, who returned the gesture with misery in his eyes. As Alex opened the door to leave, he heard the doctor's quiet plea.

"Help them."

I will.

When Alex returned to the Winter Palace, he was met by an ensign.

"Colonel! There's a Bolshevik riot down by the bridge! You're to ride with the Cossacks, sir!"

Inside the tent, Karena could hear shouts from the street. Her last patient had departed minutes ago, so she hurried out of the tent to see what was responsible for the noise. People were rushing by; some were running.

"What is wrong?" Karena called to one of the passersby.

"The police. There's a bread riot farther up the street."

The police. She must not be stopped for questioning. She turned and ran back to the tent, grabbed her things, pushing them wildly into her satchel, and fled.

It had been snowing lightly for the last hour. She ran, walked, ducked here and there to avoid the crowds and the police, until some blocks later she saw a *lineika* going in her direction. She boarded, keeping her fur hood lowered over her forehead.

The lineika moved off through the falling snow. She clutched her medical satchel, looking over her shoulder.

Farther down the street she saw a crowd milling around, carrying red flags and shouting, "Down with the czar! End the war now! Down with the czar! End the war now!"

The driver pulled the lineika over and ordered everyone out, waving his arms in agitation. "I cannot get through. Go, go!"

"Oh please," Karena cried desperately. "I need to go farther down Tverskoy Boulevard to reach my flat."

"This is the women's march," he shouted. "Their demonstration for bread and peace has shut down the factories. You'll have to get out."

Ahead, there was shouting. Someone had climbed up on the nearest building and planted the red Bolshevik flag. The color red against the white snow brought tragedy to Karena's mind.

As she tried to go around the crowd, she looked toward the Neva River. The sight was dreadful to behold. The czar must have sent the Cossacks to end the demonstration. The feared guards on horseback were bearing down on the throng. Gunshots cracked through the cold afternoon air. People ran screaming from the gunshots, but where the bridge narrowed, they were being squeezed, unable to free themselves and escape. She saw some fall, and the crowd behind them pushed forward to flee the Cossacks.

The horses pressed close to break up the crowd, and more shots were fired. Karena saw several people down in the snow, wounded. Those behind her pushed and shoved to escape the throng coming from the bridge. There was a young woman ahead of her, trying to crawl in the snow toward the gutter and sidewalk. She'd been holding a breadbasket, and it seemed she had gotten caught in the whirlwind of destruction. She was garbed in a long black dress with a bloodied shawl and a battered gray headscarf tied beneath her chin. It was then Karena saw that she was expecting a child. She was reaching a hand for help toward the throng running by, but none stopped, so intent were they on escaping the Cossacks. Any minute now the terrified young woman would be trampled beneath a thousand pairs of running boots and clattering hooves.

Karena, in a cleft on the bridge where she'd been clinging to the rail, left her place of refuge and began running toward the pathetic figure, who was unable, in her weakened condition, to get to her feet.

Karena heard people running, the horses, the gunshots, and she feared at any second to feel a bullet rip through her and lay her low with several others. She reached the pregnant woman, whose fingers desperately clutched her wrist.

"Hurry, on the count of three, use your other hand and knees to push up. Go—one, two, three—"

Karena, never particularly strong, struggled to lift at the same time the woman gave her best effort. "I can't! I can't! God have mercy!"

"Stay calm! Look, they see us, the Cossacks—they're going around us. Look! That soldier on the horse is shouting at them to avoid us."

Karena stopped short. *Alex Kronstadt!*

Suddenly, they were surrounded by four Cossacks, guarding them, while Alex turned his black horse with ease and rode up and through the four Cossacks. He was down from the saddle in a moment and caught hold of her as though she belonged to him. There was a determined glow in his eyes.

"I've been looking all over for you! And believe me, I've more to say about how I feel than you're ready to hear. But you will listen because our time together is short. I'll start by saying Tatiana and I have mutually agreed to end any possible engagement."

Her eyes searched his, and even in the midst of havoc and death, she felt the same coming together of their hearts and desires. His dark hair showed wavy beneath his hat, and his black coat was blowing in the wind.

"I am innocent of all that is laid at my feet, Colonel."

"Stop it. *You know I'm Alex.* And before this is over, that's what you'll call me."

"But this poor woman is in desperate need, and she may be going into early labor."

"The last time, you got away from me by delivering a peasant's child. This time, Karena, the woman will go to the charity ward down the street, and I am bringing you to Professor Menkin's apartment. We have much to decide and little time."

He held her elbow firmly while he turned and commanded the Cossacks. At once, they obeyed his orders. How wonderful it felt to see someone with authority taking command. Soon the woman was to be carried to the hospital.

Meekly, she surrendered to his dictums as he picked up her medical bag and loaded it onto his saddle, then gestured her forward.

"Do you mind riding with me across the bridge?"

She shook her head no, now feeling a little shy at his attention, for he studied her with scrutiny. She must look terrible after working all day and getting caught in the riot. She saw his gaze take in her bruises, and she looked away quickly.

He held the stirrup as she mounted and then swung up behind her, taking the reins. As his arms closed around her, her heart thundered.

"I've already met with Professor Menkin," he told her as they rode across the bridge away from the ugly scene. "I've also spoken to your mother, Madame Yeva. She'll have something important to tell you when you see her."

She looked at him over her shoulder. Her gaze became lost in his.

"What needs to be decided?"

"You'll be leaving Petrograd for Finland."

She gasped. "Leave! I can't leave, and *won't*—"

"Matvey has decided you will. Your mother will agree as well. And so do I."

Karena wondered in utter amazement at the swift turn of events that had swept her up, carrying her away to unknown things that would alter her life. Is this what she wanted? Did she have anything to say about it?

Later that afternoon at the flat, Alex met with Uncle Matvey, and Karena heard them quietly discussing their options. Karena saw a small bag of gold coins and heard of plans to cross the border and of trusted men who would guard them.

When Matvey went into the bedroom to talk to Yeva about the decision, Alex came up to her and drew her aside. His gaze sought hers. His strong fingers clasped her forearms.

"Your uncle will explain everything. There's still a chance matters will turn out well for you and Madame Peshkova here in Petrograd, but only time will tell. Until then, Karena, your uncle wants you safe. And I want you safe. Safe, so I can find you again and tell you, show you, how I hope that one day we can plan a future together. I've felt something special about us from the moment I first saw you in that red hat."

"Oh...Alex—"

"And I don't want to lose you, Karena."

"I feel the same. I think you already know that."

"The times are against us. Each time we meet, something comes between us and tears us apart. For your safety you must go to Finland, and I have new orders to join the czar at the front."

Her heart sank. Again, separation. She reached out and took hold of him. He no longer belonged to Tatiana; he belonged to her. They must come together again—someday.

"The front?" she whispered.

"The czar is taking control of the army and is going to the front. I never liked working with the Okhrana. I put in a request to Czar Nicholas weeks ago to be transferred back to my old regiment in the Imperial Cavalry, but it seems that the winds of fortune, for good or ill, have also changed my future. I'll be going as a member of his guard. I want you to know that I'll be looking for an opportunity to speak with him about Schoolmaster Josef. The countess will also try to intervene with the czarina. I can't promise you a quick solution, but the door is open and there's hope. You can tell Madame Peshkova when she's stronger. Returning your wheat lands too, that remains a possibility."

"Oh, Alex, thank you... I want to spend time with you, but it appears as if that opportunity will be delayed again."

"Delayed," he said in a soft voice, "but not ended."

Karena, dazed by all that had happened, stood with her hand on his arm. She spoke her heart and heard herself saying with the same intensity, "I'll be waiting for you, regardless of when you return, Alex. I have no intention of leaving Russia permanently, not if I have anything to do with it. We can still meet again...in the future."

"I was hoping you would say that. Though I hardly know you, I have learned some truths about you. I have been thinking about you since Kazan."

Her heart raced. "I confess, I've thought about you, too. So many times."

"I don't know when I'll be back in Petrograd. But when I can, I will write to you. There's so much to say."

"Yes," she said simply, her heart excited and yet struggling with sorrow as well.

"It has been a bittersweet beginning, Karena. We'll make sure of the ending. Matvey has promised to stay in touch with my stepmother, the countess."

Bittersweet—yes, it was that. But she would dream of the day when she would see him again and he would stay—the day the rosebud would open into a full, red rose.

Thinking of all that had happened and was still to come, she couldn't restrain her tears. "There is hope," she whispered. "With God, there is always hope."

"Yes, what looks so dark and bleak may be the beginning of the sunrise, if not for Russia, then perhaps for us."

She looked down and saw his strong hand reaching for hers and raising it to his lips. She closed her eyes, relishing a new excitement she had not experienced before.

"Until tomorrow," he said. "Either in Finland or here in Russia, we'll meet again. When I ride out with Czar Nicholas, I'll be thinking of you."

She tightened her fingers around his. He hesitated, and then suddenly drew her toward him. She came willingly. He paused. Then their lips met, and his love was burned into her heart, becoming a promise as wondrous and sweet as anything she'd known before.

"Somewhere and somehow, by God's fair favor, we'll keep our promise, Karena."

"Until then," she whispered.

In a moment, he was gone. Karena was left with the warmth of his promise burning on her lips and in her heart. Whatever the winds of revolution and war brought their way, she would remember his words of hope in God's care.

She hurried to the window and looked below at the falling snow and the strangers passing by. She saw Alex—the snow beginning to sprinkle his dark greatcoat, the wind tugging at the hem—leaving. He turned and looked up as if knowing she would be there. He raised his hand, and she touched her fingertips to the window pane. "Good-bye, Alex," she whispered. "I love you."

Eventually, she became aware that Uncle Matvey had come up beside her, laying a hand on her shoulder and telling her Yeva wished to speak with her alone—about a secret. Karena smiled at him, putting her hand over his, and lingered at the window for a moment longer.

Tomorrow stretched ahead into the future. The road would wind on to spring's flowers and summer's bountiful harvest. Would she ever return to the manor house in Kiev? She closed her eyes and imagined the winds blowing through the wheat fields. She could see the large harvest moon in the indigo sky, smell the ripened grain, and see the smiling faces of those she loved.

The manor would be returned. Ilya would come home to a new life, find a girl, and fall in love. Boris, too, would come home, and happy voices would sing at Natalia's marriage. Aunt Marta would make her special wedding cake. Grandmother Jilinsky would return to her little bungalow. Papa Josef would take them to the opera again. And Sergei and Ivanna would embrace their families.

She closed her eyes in a humble petition to God. Would her losses be returned? She wanted to believe they would.

And now, as well, there would be *her* Alex.

ABOUT THE AUTHOR

LINDA LEE CHAIKIN has written more than thirty books. She has been a finalist for the prestigious Christy Award, and two of her novels have been awarded the Silver Angel Award for excellence. She is a graduate of Multnomah School of the Bible in Portland, Oregon.

Linda lives with her husband of thirty-four years in Northern California, where her favorite recreations are reading and taking vacations where the wind blows through lonely deserts and ghost towns.

Please stop by Linda's Web site at visit www.lindachaikinbooks.com.

More rich tales
of romance and danger
by Linda Lee Chaikin.

To learn more about WaterBrook Press and view
our catalog of products, log on to our Web site:
www.waterbrookpress.com